CHILDREN OF THE DROUGHT BOOK THREE

DREAMS
OF THE EATEN

ARIANNE 'TEX' THOMPSON

D1052012

SOLARIS

For Jonathan Rafferty
"There and Back Again"
Thank you for going the distance with me.

And for Sandy Thompson
A kindlier wizard there never was.

DREAMS OF THE EATEN

'This author can really write. If you loved
Stephen King's *Dark Tower* series – or even if you're
a hardened Cormac McCarthy fan – you will find
this book right inside your wheelhouse. Living, witty
dialogue, and a familiar-yet-strange world inhabited
by vivid characters. I loved it. And I don't say that
about a book very often.'

Paul Kearney, author of *The Ten Thousand*

First published 2017 by Solaris
an imprint of Rebellion Publishing Ltd,
Riverside House, Osney Mead,
Oxford, OX2 0ES, UK

www.solarisbooks.com

ISBN: 978 1 78108 488 5

10 9 8 7 6 5 4 3 2 1

A CIP catalogue record for this book is available
from the British Library.

Designed & typeset by Rebellion Publishing

Printed in Denmark

CONTENTS

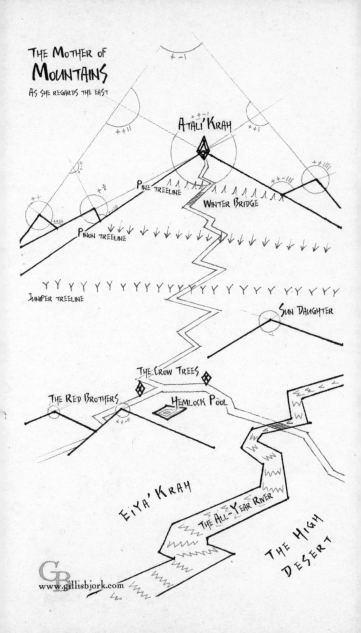

THE STORY SO FAR

IF IT WEREN'T for the smell, one could mistake the coffin for a shipping crate.

It's compact, almost a cube, made of plywood too scarce to be called cheap. Inside, the body of Dulei Marhuk has been tied into a fetal position, his gruesomely-ventilated forehead leaking onto his updrawn knees. He's been waiting there for over a week now, restless and rotting.

But even in death, he is a prince, a son of the crow god, Grandfather Marhuk – and he must be taken home to the mountain city of Atali'Krah to receive his final rites. Escorting him is his young, childlike uncle, Weisei, and Weisei's irascible guardian, Vuchak. They've brought an educated slave, Hakai, to serve as a minder and translator along the way – because the final member of the funeral party is their prisoner, Appaloosa Elim: the man whose blind, unthinking bullet ended Dulei's life.

Losing Dulei has been hard enough. Getting him home may be impossible. Parched, sickened, and robbed of their supplies, the funeral party has barely survived the trek across the drought-stricken wasteland. With the last of their strength, they made it to the All-Year River, the border that marks the beginning of Marhuk's domain, and relative safety – only to be ambushed from the water by a cohort of fishmen intent on kidnapping Elim.

They wouldn't have hurt him, of course. They wouldn't have hurt anyone. They had heard he was a powerful wizard, the son of the Dog Lady, and could call animals with his magic. Such a man would have made a fine gift for their prince, Jeté, to present to his intended bride. But the fishmen had scarcely stolen their prize before he was stolen from them in turn – by a monstrous great she-beast who tore through the cohort with a murderous fury.

Día could have told them something about that. The young grave bride had been lost in the desert for days, guided by the strange, cheerful mother-dog who never left her side. As Día wandered in heat-sick madness, she began to hear canine thoughts, and feel maternal longings – but she didn't realize the truth until it was too late. After following Elim's scent for days, the dog found the place where his blood had soaked into the parched earth – and transformed on the spot. The mother dog became U'ru, the Dog Lady, the ruined goddess who once drove her own people to extinction in the hunt for her missing child, and who has now become a monster of revenge.

Leaving a trail of thoughtless slaughter in her wake, she has ripped through the fishmen's ranks, left Día to drown in the river, and disappeared into the foothills with Yashu-Diiwa – Elim – her beloved baby, her special puppy, the child who was stolen from her twenty years ago... and who now flees in terror at the sight of his mother's beastly face.

That is mostly Shea's fault. Or Water Dog, as she used

to be called. Or Champagne, as she was before. She's had more names, more lives, than even she can keep track of – not bad for an amphibious old trickster. But her well-meaning plan to save the Dog Lady by stealing her child all those years ago backfired horrifically, and her penance now is a nasty one: do whatever it takes to get Elim to accept the truth, and acknowledge the Dog Lady as his mother. A little dose of hemlock seemed sure to do the trick: force his animal divinity to surface and save his life, and even he wouldn't be able to deny his nature. But magic comes from identity, from continuity and belonging – and for as long as he can remember, Elim has belonged to the Calvert family. This time, Shea's plan worked all too well: the boy lies unconscious, his animal divinity displayed for all to see. But there's no dog in his face, and no place for the Dog Lady in his heart: Elim the horseman is now more horse than man.

Now a sodden, gray day dawns on the wreckage of everyone's best-laid plans. Hakai and Día have been stolen or drowned. Vuchak and Weisei struggle just to keep themselves alive as half a cohort of grieving fishmen plot revenge. Shea is alone and universally reviled, with no company but the malformed boy at her feet, and the eerie, mourning cries echoing from the mountain foothills.

And Dulei's coffin is missing. The crow god's slain child is nowhere to be found.

But the remains of another unfortunate young man have recently been sighted. A lone figure is still walking west, still searching for Elim, still calling itself Sil Halfwick in defiance of logic, probability and all the gathering flies...

11

PROLOGUE

AH CHE, A child of six winters, played in the fields of the Maia, and was happy.

CHAPTER ONE
FACES IN THE WATER

THE PRINCE, JETÉ, squatted in the muddy shallows of the All-Year River, and grasped his prey by the neck. His free hand pressed between the human man's shoulders, pinning him down; his webbed feet splayed out for balance, keeping his leviathan bulk upright. For a long, peaceful moment, there was no sound but the purling of the current around their bodies. Then the prince thrust out his arm, and shoved the man's head underwater.

The man, Hakai, awoke in a kicking, thrashing panic.

The prince considered his victim for the length of a cold-blooded blink. Underneath his six hundred pounds of mildew-green flesh and amphibian muscle, the man's struggles were nothing but the frantic, feeble windings of an earthworm in a puddle. Presently, the prince consented to take hold of the man's hair, and pull his head from the water.

The man gasped and coughed, water streaming from his nose. His sodden clothes clung to him, as did the black cloth he kept tied over his eyes. He shivered in the cold, but did not speak.

The prince did not speak either. He had a voice to do that for him.

The voice, Fuseau, stood waist-deep in the river, facing the man and the prince. Human-sized, bald save for the gill-plumes at the back of its head, it watched the proceedings with no flicker of emotion in its black eyes or blue-white skin. At a glance from the prince, it spoke in Marín, the most common of the human languages. "You, earthling – tell us that you understand."

The man said nothing at first. His hands felt at the rocks and mud, and the water rushing past his chin. When he finally found his own voice, it emerged as a fearful quiver. "I understand."

"Good. Then tell us why you are still alive." The voice spoke the words out loud, and made hand-signs to translate them for the prince.

The man gritted his teeth and arched his back, straining to lessen the pain of the prince's hold on his hair. "I am alive because... because I spotted your ambush, and gave Vu – and gave the a'Krah enough warning to arm themselves and start shooting when you rushed up out of the water. And, and they must have done a good job, too, because otherwise you'd be sitting on them instead of me. So I think I must be the only one you caught, and either you're going to torture me as punishment for however many of you they managed to kill, or else you need me for something."

The voice signed this too. Around it, more bald heads peeped up from the river like so many amphibious prairie-dogs, their gill-plumes lifting with interest as they watched their sibling's hands. None dared to emerge past the nose.

The prince, Jeté, answered with a low, rumbling *fffrrooooaak*.

The voice took this as leave to continue. "Very good. Now tell us about the monster."

The man frowned behind his blindfold. "What monster?"

The blue-white flesh of the voice darkened in vexation. "The monster who – you know what monster!"

The mountains around them might have known something about the monster too, but they watched unmoved: silent, slumped and sullen. The cold autumn wind cut between them, under a sky the color of a dead fish, and the only voice that volunteered anything was the mindless chatter of the river current.

About half a mile downstream, silver minnows had begun to nibble at the body of the princess.

The man tucked his arms under his chest and shivered harder. "I'm sorry, but I don't."

The prince let go of the man's hair, and allowed him to resume drowning. He kept his own royal personage still and serene: his globular eyes unblinking, his river-colored flesh unchanging – a model of composure for his submerged audience.

The faces in the water watched in reverent silence.

The man could not resist the huge, webbed hand that kept his chest pinned to the bottom, or hold his head far enough out of the water to breathe. But he could make a sign language of his own, and use his hands to draw wild, desperate promises in the air.

The prince, Jeté, consented to hear them.

"Tell me what it looks like," the man gasped when he was pulled again from the water. "The monster – do you mean Elim, the two-colored man?"

The voice resumed signing. "No," it said. "That is the wizard. The monster stole the wizard. It is a horrible earth-creature, big and haired, that four-legs-runs, and makes howls, and –" Its grammar began to suffer as it struggled to simultaneously speak and sign the nature of an animal for which it had no name.

"Like a wolf?"

"Yes, a wolf," the voice repeated, "if a wolf can grow big enough to carry you in its mouth."

It couldn't. But then again, a frog couldn't grow large enough to hold him down and play at drowning him, and yet here they were. "It might be a god, or the child of a god," the man said. "I don't know, but I'll – let me help you look for it."

The prince wished to make a reply. But he needed both hands to sign an answer to his voice: the one that held the man's face out of the water, and the one that kept his body pinned to the ground.

So the man was plunged face-first back into the river – just as that terrible weight lifted from his back. In an instant, he pushed himself up out of the frigid water, heaving huge, shocked breaths. But he did not dare move out from under the prince's shadow as the silent conversation played out over his head.

"'We will not look. You will not help.'" The voice, Fuseau, read its prince's gestures aloud. "'You will tell us where the monster is, and hope that we believe you.'"

"Will you believe me if I tell you it's over there?" The man pointed at a rumpled pile of rock to the southwest, and then at the slumping mountain to its left. "What about over there – is that better? Or will you believe me when I tell you that I don't know where it is?"

This insolence went unpunished as the prince and his voice considered the indicated places.

"You knew where we were," the voice said at last.

The man looked down at the eddies between his hands, water dripping from his nose and chin. "I know where some things are," he said. "Earth, stones, metals, wood, living plants, dead ones if they're close enough..."

As the voice's hands translated, the faces in the water glanced at each other, unable to spot any of the named items on themselves or their neighbors.

"Knives, for example, or rakes, shovels, nets..." the voice thought aloud. "Or bullets."

"Yes," the man agreed. "Especially a bullet being carried in the body of a moving creature."

The prince looked from the man between his legs to the gestures of his voice. His skin flickered in a quick, violent spectrum of emotions; his throat-pocket pulsed. "'Then you know where to find Champagne.'"

There was a keenness to the voice's translation, an intensity which suggested that this missing Champagne might have some relationship with the monster.

The man chose his words carefully. "I did," he said, "until I pulled the bullet out of her. You recall the blood in the water."

The faces in the water seemed to recall that all too easily, and traded dark looks between themselves.

"The wizard, then," the voice replied. "He had a gun of wood and metal, and plant-clothing, and the net we caught him in was made of agave fibers. Tell us where to find him."

The man turned his head. He might have been thinking. He might have been listening. For a long time, there was no sound but the wind and the chattering of his teeth.

"... I'm s-sorry," he said at last. "He must be at least a mile away, but I don't know the direction."

The voice, Fuseau, did not begin to reply until the prince had finished signing.

"'You don't know what the monster is, or where it came from. You don't know where to find it, or the wizard, or Champagne. You don't seem to know anything at all.'"

The man, Hakai, flinched at the touch of the prince's hands on his neck.

"'We, in turn, don't know of any reason why you should continue living.'"

The prince's hands drifted up, their cold, wet palms closing around the man's temples, their long, sticky fingers lacing together under his throat. It would be a messy way to crack an egg.

"'You may make a suggestion.'"

THE BATH WOULD have been delightful, if it weren't for the damned fishmen.

It should have been a wondrous indulgence, as this was the one treat Vuchak reserved especially for himself. There should have been hot stones and steam, a bowl of fresh yucca lather and another one of warm water for rinsing. He should have been able to massage his scalp at his leisure, pleasantly recalling the way his grandmother's hands had once done it for him, and make beautiful curtains of his glossy black hair as he poured the rinse-water just so, and afterward sit tweezing his chin-hairs and thinking loose, warm thoughts until he was as fresh and dry and perfect as an hours-old spring duckling.

Instead, he was here: naked and shivering under a sullen gray sky, doing his utmost to ignore the foot-biting sharp stones and the testicle-shriveling chill in the water as he braved the river just long enough to wash the blood from his arms and the grease from his hair. And all the while, he kept an anxious eye on the current.

They had stolen Dulei, and Hakai, and probably Ylem too.

They would almost certainly come back to finish the job.

They didn't need to surface to breathe.

Which meant that any water too deep or too murky to show its bottom was a hiding-place for them, and the soft chattering of its flow more than loud enough to cover an ambush. And with no way to discover their wants, Vuchak was left with just his own: to finish cleaning himself and get back to camp before even one more awful thing could spring out of hiding and throttle him.

"Excuse me, please..."

Vuchak nearly jumped out of his skin.

She was walking upstream along the bank, dressed in white and carrying a folded black garment and so dark herself that Vuchak might have mistaken her for a fellow a'Krah – but no, of course not. She was speaking Marín, for one thing, and wearing her hair in fearsome waist-length dreadlocks, and a moment's longer looking showed him exactly what she was: not a'Krah, not native at all, but one of the Fire Tribe – Afriti, as they called themselves.

But what was this one doing in a'Krah territory?

She kept coming, her eyes averted. *"I'm sorry to*

disturb you," she said. "*Please, can you tell me where I am?*"

Vuchak glanced between the woman and the water. They were allies, the free Afriti and the freshwater fishmen – and one would make a perfectly convenient distraction for the other.

Damn it.

He waded ashore, snatching up his spear and wet clothes as he did, and retreated until he was far enough up on weedy bank to watch the woman and the river simultaneously. They had the advantage this time: his bow was broken now, and they knew it. At the first sign of an attack, he would have no choice but to run for camp, and hope that Weisei could revive the horse in time to make their escape. "*Who sent you?*"

She was smart, then, or at least smart enough not to come any closer... though she could have had the courtesy to look him in the eye. "*I don't – nobody. I'm alone.*"

So she was stupid, then, or at least stupid enough to think he'd believe that. "*Don't lie to me,*" he said. "*You're not carrying any supplies, no weapons or waterskins or even any shoes, which means that either you've left them with your friends, or hidden them somewhere to fool me into giving you some of mine. I won't do it. Tell your friends that I want MY friends returned to me, alive and unhurt,*" well, except for Dulei, obviously, "*because if I have to go looking for them, I'm going to –*"

"*I don't have any friends!*" she cried, in a voice startlingly near to tears. "*I'm lost. I live in Island Town, and I got lost, and I'm trying to go home.*"

At the mention of Island Town, Vuchak wiped his eyes and looked again.

Yes – yes, actually, this was the same woman. The grave woman, the one who lived in the Burnt Quarter and buried the bodies of unlucky foreigners. A little spot of gold glinted at her neck: that was the holy sign she wore, and there in her arms was the black robe he always saw her in, and those were a firm promise that she was who she claimed to be.

Vuchak slicked back a soapy strand of hair. *"What's your name?"*

She met his gaze for half a second, but obviously didn't recognize him. He didn't expect her to – they'd never spoken – but that was no reason for her to so rudely hold her gaze away from his face. *"Día. I serve the First Man of Island Town."*

That was true. But she also served a more powerful master, one whose hand Vuchak could see clearly now. The grave woman stood there in her white smock – the color of death, their holy color – with her hair falling like a nest of black matted snakes from her head, and the golden glint at her throat making her loyalties perfectly clear: she was a citizen of Island Town, yes – but first and before anything, she was a servant of the Starving God.

"Please," she said, as if reading his hesitation, *"I can help look for your friends, if you would – if I could just have something to eat."* But still she kept her eyes away from him, as if he were a dog, a menial to receive her words as the garbage pit would receive her waste.

Well, she might be a witch, but Vuchak wasn't going to be spoken to like a thrall. *"Look at me when you ask me favors!"* he snapped.

She seized his anger and lobbed it straight back at him. *"Put your clothes on and I will!"*

Vuchak looked from her stubbornly-turned face down to his undecorated body. Why would he do an idiotic thing like that? His clothes were still wet from washing, he still had the deer's gut-stink under his fingernails, and soap was still dripping down his back. And why should she care anyway?

For a moment, he thought she feared what his immodesty might tempt him to do – even though she was strikingly ugly, even though anyone could see that his penis wanted nothing more than to continue hiding from the cold. Then he realized the awful truth. She was one of the Eaten, after all, a servant of the Starving God – the great devourer of wealth, of land, of people, who instilled in his followers a desperate, insatiable appetite for bodies and souls alike. She wasn't afraid of his lust. She was battling *hers*.

Vuchak recoiled. Of all the vile, filthy...

"*Go away,*" he said. Better yet: "*Go that way.*" He lifted his chin to the northeast, and took care to see that she followed the gesture. "*Walk until you see the smoke, and follow it until you find a man at the fire. You can explain your business and beg for his charity, but don't let me find you taking advantage of him, or I will make your god sorry he ever sent you here.*"

She did look at him then, her thick brows and full lips compressed in perplexity. "*... Thank you,*" she said at last. "*I'm sorry to have disturbed you.*" And she went walking away.

Vuchak watched her until she was nearly out of sight. This was the safest course, he told himself: if there was even the slightest chance that the grave-woman was working with the fishmen, he had to question her – somewhere out of their sight and hearing.

So the smoke from the fire would draw her to their camp. The traps he'd set around it would keep her there. And though Vuchak's teeth itched at the thought of letting this infidel stranger anywhere near his sick, soft-hearted *marka*, Weisei was still a holy son of Marhuk: she wouldn't be able to bewitch him or steal his soul, and he had no interest in women. Besides, he had already met her back in Island Town, back when the two of them had worked together to...

Vuchak stopped still, chilled by a thought that had nothing to do with the cool mountain air.

She and Weisei had prepared Halfwick's body, after the hanging.

The very same Halfwick who had been wandering around yesterday, as clueless and ghastly-looking as one of the unburied dead.

So that wicked power had not only worked foul magic on Halfwick, but also sent this she-snake after him – and she'd already crossed the river. The Starving God had already infiltrated Marhuk's domain... and there was no telling what he meant to devour next.

Vuchak resumed his washing with renewed urgency, trusting the traps to hold her until he got there. If her god was as all-knowing and all-powerful as his followers claimed, it might not work – but if he wasn't, Vuchak would be pleased to give the Starving God something to choke on.

WELL, THAT COULD have gone better.

Día had no idea what that strange, irritable fellow had been thinking of – but if he was as honest as he was peculiar, she would be grateful for him.

Truly, she was already grateful for him. It had been an awful thing to wake up beside the river, soggy and freezing and alone. More terrible still to realize that she had nothing, literally nothing to her name but her smock and her robe and her knife, and no idea how to use any of those to feed herself. She was so far from home now, the plants strangers to her and the animals keeping their distance. And as for the dog...

Sobbing, the voice whispered in her head. *Snarling. Biting.*

Día shook her head, unable to dispel the echo of that faint, foreign grief, and plunged on through the shrubs. The rusty grasses nipped and tickled at her shins; clouds of crickets blossomed around her bare feet, their panic punctuated by the occasional crispy squish of those she crushed thoughtlessly underfoot. Día had no time for disgust or remorse: after uncounted days spent lost and hallucinating in the desert, she was nothing now but a wisp, a strand torn and dangling from the thin, tenuous web of human civilization.

She should not have taken such a tone with that other strand back there, naked and angry as he was. Modesty was a virtue, but so was discretion. So was patience. So was –

– *food.*

Día smelled it first: the most heavenly, savory scent. Then she saw the promised sign: a shimmering column of smoke. Then she broke into a run.

But not a run, she chastised herself, not unless she meant to be shot for an intruder. A walk – a very, very purposeful walk – even as the air promised her roasting meat and hot fat, even as her stomach threatened to cave in on itself. *Please pardon my intrusion,* she mentally rehearsed, plowing heedlessly through rabbitbrush and sedge, *but your very-kind companion at the river said that perhaps you would allow me to earn a share of your meal.* Her heel sank into a granular softness that might have been an ants' nest; she hurried on. *I would be glad to help you look for your friends, or to explain my business to your satisfaction, or to sit quietly and say nothing at all.* The sodden black cassock over her arm caught on a mesquite branch; she tore it from the thorny wooden fingers without changing her course or her fixation on that tantalizing little camp on the hill, *and you have my most potent promise that I will keep my attention on whatever part of you politeness demands, taking absolutely no notice of your clothing or lack thereof –*

That thought ended in tandem with her next step: in sudden, searing sharp pain. Día jerked her foot up with a half-strangled gasp – bringing a six-inch cactus arm with it.

"*Vichi?*" From the campfire up ahead, a blanket-wrapped figure stood up. He was tall, with black hair spilling down his back, and so beautiful that Día might have mistaken him for a her if she hadn't been told otherwise.

The needles in her flesh were enough to rip the prepared words from Día's throat like the cry of a woman in childbed. "Please pardon my –"

"Don't move!"

They spoke at the same time, and stopped at the same time, and as he rushed toward her, Día gathered her wits enough to look down and understand his frantic gesturing – even if she couldn't fathom what sadistic trickster would break off dozens of cactus branches and hide them in the dirt.

Then again, thinking back to her encounter at the river, maybe she could.

It hurt like the very devil, too. Struggling to balance herself on just the toes of her wounded foot, Día glanced down and winced. Some kind of cholla, with spines as thin and abundant as razor-fine cat-hair.

"Fire child? Is that you?"

Día glanced up at the strange name. She had been called that once by someone-or-other, a lifetime ago in Island Town.

"Weisei!" It started as a question, and finished as a declaration of perfect astonishment – just before he closed the last of the distance between them.

Weisei cupped his hands behind her neck and drew her forward until their foreheads touched. "By every god, what are you doing out here?" he said, looking her up and down with an expression knee-deep in shock and alarm. "How did you – no, nevermind. Come here, come right here and let me have your arm – we'll have three legs to get us to the fire just there, and then see to your poor lady foot." He hissed in surprise as she laid her arm across his shoulder. "*Tsa!* And your dress is all wet, and your hair! What's been done to you? Wait, hold on – don't step there..."

He went on like that as he helped her hobble towards the fire, demanding answers and then cutting himself off before she could begin to give them. It was endearing and faintly odd – but the camp before them was strange beyond imagining.

There was a stone-lined fire pit, and a grate set over it to roast the meat – so much meat! – but that was where Día's understanding of woodcraft ended. Three gnarled branches made a huge tripod over the fire, and halfway up its length, resembling nothing so much as a thick, haphazard flesh-web stretched wide above the fire, was the most improbable array of rope and buckled leather, every inch of it drooping with strips of raw meat. Little offal-filled pans perched precariously here and there, like pie-tins set out under a leaky roof, while a kettle sat half-buried in the ashes. The small bloodied carcass off to the left suggested that a deer had contributed the meat... and the huge, still-intact one on the right implied that the drying rack had been rigged from the harness of a dead horse.

Día stared at the shapely half-ton black corpse, working hard to assure herself that no living animal would lie like that. Then she belatedly drew her attention back to Weisei, who had apparently reached the end of his verbal chain reaction.

"... what in the World That Is happened to you?"

She could have asked him the same. He was still tall and handsome and as dark as she was, with the same high cheeks and large eyes and prominent eagle nose she remembered. But if he had been thin when she'd met him back in town, he was positively gaunt now, with dark hollows under his eyes and collarbones protruding like the inside of a chicken's ribs. Día could feel frail skin sliding over his thin shoulders, even through his clothes. He strained under a fraction of her weight.

And selfish as she was, that was not even her first question. "I'll be glad to tell you everything, all of it, if I could just – if you would be so kind as to let me eat with you." Her voice thickened uncontrollably as she said it, not from the prickling fire lancing her foot, but because even acknowledging the possibility of a 'no' frightened her to tears.

But the answer assured her of what she should have already known: God was good, and Weisei was kind. "Of course, of course – oh, and you're so cold! Come here, come right over here and lay your dress by the fire. We don't have any hot tea – it's tallow in the kettle – but there's a warm space for sitting just here, and by the time Vichi comes back, the food will be ready and we'll all eat together, and I promise we won't let you leave until your foot is mended and your stomach has had everything she wants."

As he talked, he helped her to that strange rickety flesh-tent of theirs, lay her cassock at the downwind edge of it, and brought her to sit on the opposite side. It took a bit of ducking and scooting to get her back to the fire without disturbing the meat hanging above her head, and a moment more to find her self-control amidst that enchanting, intoxicating food-smell. She was a civilized person, she told the ravenous want inside her, and a guest besides: she would eat what she was served and when, and entertain nothing but gratitude in the meantime.

She was grateful for his hospitality. She was grateful for the sharpened clamshell he produced, and for the exquisite gentleness with which he tweezed out each one of those thin, vicious cactus spines. And when he was done, he offered his hand to help her stand again, to satisfy himself that he'd gotten them all and that she could walk well again, and when THAT was done, there was nothing left to prevent her from satisfying his curiosity.

But she couldn't bring herself to let go of Weisei's hand – and he didn't ask her to. He sat with her under the meat-heavy makeshift tripod, sharing a kindly silence, letting her drink in the warmth of his palm and the feel of his fingers and the reassuring closeness of her chestnut skin to his mahogany, and did not press her for anything.

And that was a feast in itself.

Here at last was someone who was not a mereau or an animal or a corpse – not an amphibious foster-parent or a dangerous furry god-creature or a body needing to be cleaned or buried or pulled from a festering pond. He was alive. He was human. And here, with pieces of the unliving and the inhuman literally hanging over their heads, the space they occupied together made a warm, living oasis – a comforting human microcosm taking shelter under death and all the empty heavens.

AND THAT WAS how he found them. Just sitting there holding hands, backs to the fire, silent and still as the meat burned on the grill behind them.

"I told you to watch it!" Vuchak snapped, momentarily more aggrieved at the neglect of the meal than the possibility that the woman actually had managed to bewitch Weisei.

They startled at his voice, jostling the tripod overhead – and then steadying it by Weisei's quick intervention. "I WAS watching it! I just..." He looked Vuchak up and down. "... why are you wearing wet clothes?"

Vuchak shot a glance at the woman, and went to rescue the food.

She blanched and looked down, and Weisei took that as his cue to switch to Marín and make the introductions. "*Anyway,*" he said, "*this is... oh, forgive me...*"

Well, it wasn't really burnt, anyway – just a bit on the

well-fired side. "Día," Vuchak supplied as he turned the meat, his irritation abating. "And yes, we'll feed her, but don't tell her our business – yet," he added, on seeing Weisei open his mouth to protest.

And as the woman sat there confused and anxious amidst ambient dinner-smells and a language she couldn't understand, Vuchak made himself the source of all remedies. "*I'm sorry for being rude to you earlier,*" he said, and managed to mean it. He had thought about this on the walk back: she was strange and untrustworthy, but that was all the more reason for the two of them to be gracious. For one thing, it would dispose her to speak openly, and for another, this was Marhuk's land, and Vuchak and Weisei were his people: if their god had deliberately invited hers into his domain, then they had better be good hosts.

"*Not at all,*" she assured him – and if she resented him for not warning her about the cactus traps, it was nowhere on her face. "*The fault was mine. Thank you for your kindness, Vichi.*"

Vuchak stared death at Weisei, who had just enough sense to hide his face in chagrin. That infantile nickname should have died on the day that Vuchak became a man – and yet Weisei kept it alive like an incontinent housepet, too full of childish sentimentality to let go of the embarrassing old thing.

The woman saw that she had made a mistake, and began to stammer an apology. So Vuchak smoothly took the pan with the deer-brain from where it had been kept warm above the fire, and held it out to her with a nice smile.

"*You might find 'Vuchak' easier to pronounce – and you're very welcome. I'm afraid we don't have any intestine to offer you,*" he said, and declined to mention that this was because he'd stolen the deer carcass from a pack of coyotes, who had eaten the best of it already. "*Would you like the brain instead?*"

She wouldn't, of course – the Eaten never did. But now she was too busy avoiding new rudeness to worry any more about the old one, which Vuchak would count as first-rate hospitality on his part. And she did a surprisingly good job of keeping her face straight as she demurred. "*I wouldn't like to deprive you of the best fruits of your labor,*" she said. "*Please, keep what you intended for yourself, and I'll be content with whatever is to spare.*"

So she did have some manners after all. Vuchak passed the brain to Weisei, who knew better than to complain about receiving such a treat, and speared the most handsome of the steaks with a kindling-stick for their guest's better pleasure. When she took it, he could see her struggling with the ravening, unholy hunger inside her – fighting to keep herself from wolfing it down on the spot.

But still she didn't succumb. "*Thank you very much,*" she said, careful to look him in the eye as she said it. "*Do you give grace before a meal?*"

Not with you around, he thought. "*A little later,*" he said as he served himself and took a seat. "*The food is yours to enjoy.*"

And enjoy it she did. It was a fascinating, sickening thing to watch her eat: Vuchak could see that she was desperate for it, but she wasn't like the half-man, Ylem, who devoured his slops with the reckless joy of a starving hog. She did not allow herself to gulp her food, or stain her mouth or face, and she kept half an eye on Weisei all the while – watching, Vuchak belatedly realized, to take a bite only when he did, as if in this way she could disguise herself as a wholesome person.

Vuchak had no love for the Starving God, or for the people who served him. But he did appreciate cleverness, and discretion, and respect, and this woman here – Día, as she was – had at least a passing facility with all three.

So he served her a second steak, and then a third, and by the time she had found the top of her stomach – by every god, she could eat! – Vuchak was full and his clothes were nearly dry, and he could think useful thoughts again. He could consider not just the next necessary thing, but its children and grandchildren.

And as the father and provider for all those whining, screaming needs, Vuchak was the very definition of parenthood: well fucked.

He HAD to find Dulei and Hakai and Ylem – that before anything else. Two of them might still be alive, though every passing hour diminished their chances. And retrieving Dulei's body was no less urgent: the longer the fishmen had him, the greater the likelihood that they would break open his coffin and discover the value of their rotting hostage. One glance at his holy black-feathered cloak would tell them that this was a son of Marhuk – a prize worth an exorbitant ransom, and one that Vuchak and Weisei absolutely could not return home without.

And yet they could not take even one more step. At this time yesterday, Weisei had been on the very brink of death: he was ruined, emaciated, utterly spent... and though he would never, ever admit it, Vuchak was not far behind. He'd given everything he had to carry his dying prince to water, to fight off the fishmen, to hunt down food – well, scavenge it, anyway – and build the camp and lay out traps and do every single other necessary thing just to keep them fed and defended – just to keep their last, tiny guttering hope alive. Vuchak had no help and no plan and no energy left to think of one, much less execute it.

What he did have was a strange woman named Día, and an urgent need to make her useful somehow – to make her tell them something that would lead them to their missing men.

"– *so much indebted to your kindness,*" she was saying. "*Please tell me how I can be helpful to you.*"

"*You don't owe us anything!*" Weisei predictably replied. "*Right now we're looking for –*"

"*– a better understanding,*" Vuchak finished with a pointed look. What had he just said about not revealing their business? "*Tell us: how did you get so lost?*"

Día set down her barren stick and looked into the fading fire. The gray sky was already darkening towards night. "*Well,*" she said, "*I have to start by telling you something that you might find difficult to believe. Weisei, your friend Halfwick is – he's actually still alive.*"

"*Oh, I know!*" Weisei burst out, nearly spilling the last of the liver. "*Isn't it awful? We saw him just yesterday, and he looks absolutely –*"

"*Weisei!*" Vuchak snapped. "*What did I just –*"

"*He's here?*" Día interrupted. "*Where?*"

Well, there was no getting around it now. "*Our paths crossed briefly,*" Vuchak conceded, "*on the other side of the river. And we'll be glad to tell you about it, but first we would like to hear the rest of what you have to say – respectfully, and without interrupting you.*"

Weisei returned Vuchak's glower, and drew his blanket more closely around him.

It was obvious that Día wanted to ask more about Halfwick, and that she understood that her hosts had other motives. She drew her dried black garment into her lap, and brushed the dirt from it as she spoke. *"Well, you will... you might imagine my surprise. And he insisted that he had to catch up with his partner, Elim, the one who..."* She trailed off, her gaze flicking between the two of them, and the moment she spoke Ylem's name, Vuchak could have finished the thought for her: *the one who killed Dulei.*

"... the one who shot the prince of the a'Krah. So I helped to smuggle Halfwick out of Island Town, and please understand: I would not for the world have let him steal Elim away from his just punishment. I was only escorting him out so that he could find his partner and share in it. But Halfwick, he – he took advantage of my trust," and Vuchak heard some of that anger creep back into her voice, *"and stole the horse I'd borrowed, and left me stranded alone in the desert, and I can't... and the heat isn't good for me. I got lost in visions, hallucinations, and there was a dog – just a small and ordinary dog, when I first met her, but the longer she stayed with me, the more I began to think peculiar thoughts, and to feel peculiar things."* Día drew her knees up, pressing the garment to her chest, and as she stared into the fire, she might have been hallucinating all over again.

"And she spoke to me, in my head. She wanted me to follow her west. Then she asked me to pull a corpse from a lake. One night, she made me start – I started a fire, a huge, awful fire that ate up half the desert, for reasons I can't even remember."

Vuchak met Weisei's glance in an instant. Here was the source of their salvation, then – the miraculous arsonist who had thrown up a wall of fire between them and the *marrouak* hell-bent on their deaths. Ylem had behaved as though their reprieve had come from the Starving God, but only now did Vuchak believe it.

Día frowned. "*I don't understand what happened after that. She found something – some sign – and she changed. She grew and grew, and she was ANGRY. I realized that she was not the child of an earthly god, as I'd first thought, but a god herself. And I was her, and she was me, and we – we tore down to the river, bounded right into it, and I'm frightened to say so, but I think we might have killed someone.*"

"Who?" Weisei asked, but Vuchak already knew. He had seen the huge she-creature with the dark figure clinging to her back – he might have mistaken her for the Grandfather of Wolves at the time – and how she had taken the queen of the fishmen down with a single throat-rending bite. If the fish-queen had survived, Vuchak would be surprised indeed.

After all, the Dog Lady had once wrecked an alliance, made an enemy of Marhuk himself, and led her own people to their deaths trying to find her missing son. If she was awake again after all these years, what wouldn't she do?

"*I don't know,*" Día confessed. "*We tasted blood, and tore at flesh. We were furious, because someone was stealing our – was stealing her child.*"

The fish-queen had been carrying Ylem away in a net.

"*That's probably not very helpful. I'm sorry. I feel like I don't know anything anymore.*" Día wiped her face, which was ample time for Vuchak and Weisei to share a glance, and an understanding: if she realized what she'd done, it would add tremendously to her guilt... and if the fishmen had caught even a glimpse of her during the battle last night, they would be ready to kill her on sight.

More to the point, this Día was not going to solve any of their problems: she had come with too many of her own. *Damn it.*

"*And she's gone now?*" Weisei asked.

"*Yes,*" Día said, "*though I don't know where. We were separated in the water, and she – you know, she left me. After all that, she took her child and left me.*" Her voice hardened as she said it, the dwindling fire throwing shadows across the soft contours of her face.

It was difficult to find a reply.

"*In our language, we have a saying,*" Vuchak ventured. "*We say, 'don't make her responsible for us', which is our way of acknowledging the things that we cannot understand.*" He did not glance at Weisei until after he had finished speaking, but by the look on his thin face, he had gotten the message: this woman here was being used by powers beyond her understanding, and it would be both dangerous and cruel to add to the knowledge that could be torn from her mind and used against them.

After all, if Día found out that they were looking for the body of Dulei, a holy son of Marhuk, she would realize that they were the funeral party that she and Halfwick had tried to find – and that Ylem had been with them.

And if Día, and by extension the Dog Lady, found out that Vuchak and Weisei had been taking Ylem to his very-probable execution – had stolen him for far longer and more sinister a purpose than the fishmen – it would be as good as inviting the fish-queen's fate on themselves.

And if she found out that she had just eaten dinner with another son of Marhuk – another holy hostage ripe for the taking...

The daylight was now nothing more than an orange-red glow on the western horizon. Weisei scooted a little farther back from the firelight, drawing his blanket more closely around himself. Without the silver he had worn in Island Town, he was already changing with the onset of night: already his skin was just that little bit darker, the whites of his eyes just that little bit thinner as their black centers spread outwards. Even without wearing his black-feather cloak, he would soon be unmistakable as anything but the crow god's son.

And that would be unfortunate for everyone.

"*Do YOU understand it, though?*" Día asked. "*Did any of that make the least bit of sense?*"

"*Oh, yes,*" Weisei hurried to assure her. "*It can be a frightening thing, to feel a holy spirit moving you in an unknown direction. But you must have been very pious and diligent, to have come so far, so faithfully, and it sounds like you've assisted her in accomplishing a great thing – in finding her missing child. What could be more wonderful than that?*"

Well, that was overstating it: if the son of the Dog Lady had killed a son of Grandfather Marhuk, then what happened next was going to be anything but wonderful. In that moment, the decision was out of Vuchak's hands: they could not retrieve Ylem. One of Marhuk's children was already dead because of him, and Vuchak had no right to risk a second one.

"*– and besides,*" the second one was saying, "*you said to me before, how you preferred to make your mistakes by doing too much, too generously, than to worry yourself into doing too little. Didn't we agree then that our ways were different, but still born from kindness? Is your reason so big, and the world so small, that no kindness can exist outside your understanding, and no gratitude can be expressed beyond your hearing? Truly, isn't it –*"

Weisei stopped, hearing the roughening rasp in his voice, and hurriedly stood. He was changing fast. "*And, and speaking of kindness, I had better go and make the offerings, before the blood congeals.*" He picked up the pans of deer-blood from where they had sat warming above the fire, made the sign of a benevolent god, and went away into the dark.

Which left Día and Vuchak alone together.

She remained silent, as if considering what Weisei had said. He kept silent too, fighting the weary ache in his bones, striving to anticipate whatever questions she might find next, and conjure suitable lies to answer them. More work. More last-ditch cleverness, hiding and scheming and covering their tracks – not nobly, not to achieve something for the honor and betterment of the a'Krah, but in the manner of a wounded animal fighting to survive the next hour, and the next one, and the one after that.

Finally, when the fire was nothing but glowing embers, she pulled on her garment and found her voice. "*I know that there is more going on than you can tell me about,*" she said at last, "*and questions I shouldn't ask. If I can have just one, though –*"

Vuchak stopped poking the coals, and readied himself for the inevitable.

"– *will he be all right?*" She nodded at Weisei's empty place.

And that was one question Vuchak was glad to answer. "*Yes,*" he said. "*He was sick, but he's getting better now.*" And if she were anyone but herself, he would have told her how they'd run out of water crossing the desert, and how Weisei had been sickened to the brink of death by the spiritual pollution seeping out from that tainted oasis – and how the children of the gods could eat more than any three ordinary people combined, when it came time to replenish their strength.

As it was, though, Día could not be allowed to know who Weisei was, because the Dog Lady could not be allowed to gain any leverage in her looming feud with Marhuk. She would be perfectly willing to steal Marhuk's child in order to secure forgiveness for her own – and if hers were killed, she would be the first to trade blood for blood.

It was easy enough to spare Día those thoughts, though – and she looked pleased in innocence. "*I'm very glad to hear that,*" she said. "*And your friends? What can I do to help you find them?*"

Very little – though Vuchak found himself savoring the question. It was a rare pleasure to be asked about his needs, even by someone so ill-equipped to satisfy them.

Well, he couldn't tell her about Ylem or Dulei, but that didn't mean he couldn't tell her anything. He had to make her useful, no matter how limited her use might be. "*There is one friend we are especially worried about,*" he said. "*His name is Hakai, and perhaps you've seen him in Island Town: he's lighter than we are, plainly dressed, with a blindfold over his eyes, and graying hair tied behind his neck. We would be grateful if you would sleep here with us tonight, and help us look for him tomorrow. The sun is unfriendly to our eyes, and you might be able to see him before we do."*

Actually, Vuchak was less concerned about seeing in daylight than in keeping someone on watch here at the camp: the fishmen could be anywhere, and at the moment, Weisei was good for nothing but eating and sleeping.

"I'll do my best," Día pledged, her voice full of earnestness and warmth. *"I'm so much in your debt, and very glad to have made your acquaintance."*

That was pleasing to hear. But she made that peculiar holy sign of theirs as she said it – the four-pointed crossing motion over her chest – and the image stuck in Vuchak's mind long after she had surrendered to sleep.

It was a reminder, as if the universe thought he needed one, that he could not afford to make a tempting mistake. That she was not an a'Krah woman in need of his protection, no matter how much the selfish unshareable part of his mind might wish otherwise. That she was not trustworthy, even if she was trusting. That she was not his enemy – but she could not be a friend.

Vuchak thought his thoughts alone in the dark, repeating them until they stuck in his mind, and then plaited his hair tightly enough to keep them there.

THE MAN, HAKAI, stopped walking.

He stayed where he was, standing still and quiet in the dark, with no sound but the singing of the crickets and the lapping of the river.

Less than a quarter of a mile to the west, hidden behind a hill, a circle of stones sat sheltering the grave of a fire. Above it, a pyramid of branches spoke of its use for cooking. Around it, gathered and still, three bodies pressed the grass flat. One wore a small piece of gold.

The man reached down and pulled on the rope tied around his ankle. Its other end was invisible in the water.

The voice, Fuseau, emerged up to the neck.

The man, Hakai, turned his blindfolded face to the west. "They're here."

CHAPTER TWO
THE MISSING AND THE DEAD

IN THE DREAM, *Día was seven years old, and the church was burning.*

She huddled in the sacristy, fingers jammed in her ears, as the fire roared outside. The door cracked and swelled, the wet rags stuffed underneath steaming from the heat, but the holy water was all gone now, and the fire had long since eaten the screams on the other side of the wall. God's house was burning, and Día was about to burn with it.

So she drew up her knees and tucked her head and clasped her hands behind her neck, rocking herself in the heat and the darkness. And she prayed.

Divine Master, author of light, architect of glory
Hold us in your likeness
Keep us in your mercy
Now, today, and for all –

A key turned in the lock. The door opened, flooding the room with gray light and cold air. Día looked up, astonished, as Miss du Chenne fixed her with a disapproving gaze.

"Young lady, I am profoundly disappointed."

The schoolmistress reached in and pulled Día out by the wrist, her hard, clammy grip and brushing musty skirts a promise of what would happen next. What had she been thinking, hiding in the coal shed?

"Please don't tell my father," Día begged. Mesquite thorns tore at her dress, and clouds of crickets bloomed and squished under her bare feet on the way to the schoolhouse.

Miss du Chenne picked up the switch from behind her desk, and snorted in derision. "I wouldn't worry about that – he's been dead for dog's years."

From where she had obediently bent over the desk, Día pushed herself up in protest. "No he's not!"

But Miss du Chenne only smiled that awful little smile, the one she used whenever a student had embarrassed himself in answering a question, and prodded one of Día's sagging breasts with the switch. It swung like the pendulum of a grandfather clock. "Do we need to practice telling the time?"

Día looked down in horror at her nude, withered body. Arthritic hands. Wrinkled flesh. Dreadlocks gray with age, dragging almost to the floor. Of course her father was gone – he'd died of old age – and she'd wasted her life hiding from her lessons. She'd wasted everything.

Día bent over the desk, her eyes filling with tears. "No," she whimpered. "I didn't mean to."

But Miss du Chenne just tsk-tsked and circled around behind her. "Such an ungrateful child." She drew back the switch.

Día started upright. "I am not!" She was grateful – always, always grateful. She loved God, who had saved her from the fire, and her father, who had put her in the sacristy to protect her from it, and Fours, her dear papá, who had taken her out again afterwards, when everything was smoke and ruins –

– yes, that was right: her father hadn't died of old age. He had perished when the church burned. He had LOVED her.

Día turned around, every fresh recollection fermenting into anger. "You've been lying to me."

Miss du Chenne's smug expression faltered. She backed up a step. "Why, I would never –"

But Día remembered the truth, now. She was old by human standards, yes, but she wasn't frail. She was FIERCE. She stalked forward, her flesh filling out fat and strong, her black cassock turning brown and furry, and her hands clenching in rage. "You did," she said. "You stole him. You TRICKED me!"

Miss du Chenne blanched – an inhuman blue-white flickering of her skin – and backed up further. "No, no – of course not, no," she stammered. "It was for your own good – I did it all for you –" She stumbled over the stove. Her wig fell to the floor. She dropped the switch and shielded herself with one arm, cowering. "I saved him!"

"YOU RUINED HIM!" And with a sharp, fang-baring snarl, Día lunged forward, and tore out her throat.

DÍA BOLTED AWAKE.

She sat up, overwhelmed by nausea, and smothered her first waking gasp.

From the other side of the camp, Weisei froze. He was sitting with a half-eaten steak in his hands, and stopped at the sight of her. "Fi– Día? What's wrong?"

Killing, whispered the voice in her head. *Grieving*.

She glanced from point to point, anchoring herself in the cold camp and the hard ground and the gray predawn light, and did not speak until she had mastery of her stomach. "A dream," she said, though the word was weak and bleached of conviction. She could still taste blood. "Just a bad dream."

At least she hadn't woken Weisei: he was dressed in the same knee-length yellow shirt and moccasins she'd seen yesterday, finished with a handsome black-feather cloak at his shoulders, and looked as alert as if he'd been up for hours. Then again, he was a'Krah, so maybe he had. In Island Town, they kept the Moon Quarter running from dusk to dawn – though heaven only knew what there was to do out here. "Did I disturb you?" she ventured.

Weisei smiled, and set down his breakfast. "Certainly not. My Vi – Vuchak won't sleep unless someone stays up to keep watch." He tipped his head to the blanket-wrapped figure at his left. Vuchak lay on his side, his face turned away, but Día could see the rhythm of his breathing. She didn't remember him braiding his hair.

"Why don't you keep me company for a little while? My mouth has been wishing for another chance to talk to you."

Día had no illusions about who was doing a favor for whom, but she didn't need to be asked twice. She arranged herself to sit cross-legged, drawing the borrowed blanket around herself, and shivered as her cold sweat turned colder still. "I'd be glad to," she said. "What would you like to talk about?"

Weisei tipped his head from side to side. "Well, I wanted to apologize for leaving so suddenly – you know, when we were doing that sad work together in Island Town. And more than that, I want... oh, pardon me, please – would you like to eat with me?"

Día had had quite enough flesh for one day. But apparently she was the only one: there must have been ten pounds left on the grill when she went to bed, and half looked to have vanished in the night. "No, thank you – but please, don't deprive yourself on my account."

Weisei flashed her a sheepish smile. "You're kind to indulge me. I have a baby's appetite these days." Then he turned serious. "Anyway, what I was going to say was... that is, if the question doesn't upset you, I want to ask: how did it happen with Afvik?"

It took Día a moment to recognize the name – and when she did, his hesitation became instantly understandable. He was asking about the Eadan boy, Sil Halfwick. "It doesn't upset me," she said, though she couldn't meet his gaze. It had been a holy moment, a sacrament gone terribly wrong.

"It happened the morning after you went," she explained. "He was clean, wrapped in the winding sheet, and there was only one thing left to do before I buried him. I leaned over to give him his last breath" – and she would never, ever forget the way those cold lips had abruptly opened under hers – "and then all of a sudden he... he gave it back to me." Día shook her head, still scarcely able to believe it herself. "And you may imagine how I startled, and how he sat up from the altar slab, and how angry he was to discover himself in such a... an unfortunate state, but I swear – I can sincerely promise that I did only what was prescribed, and only with the most faithful intent." Only then could she look back up at Weisei, hoping for his understanding.

If he had any, he was holding it in reserve. "And there was nothing peculiar about him before that moment? Nothing strange or stinking?"

Día was not sure how literally she was meant to take that last word, *apestoso*. Perhaps the a'Krah equivalent had a different connotation. "No," she assured him. "Well, almost. You remember how cold he was when we washed him? He stayed that way, all through the night and into the morning. It seemed odd, but he was – he's a Northman, the first one I've met, and I thought it might be a death-sign common to his race. Like the way mereaux dry out." She mentally extricated herself from those cold limbs all over again, and returned her attention to the wholesome, living present. "Does that remind you of anything? Have you ever heard of such a case?"

That might have been too forward: just because Weisei was a'Krah didn't mean he had any supernatural insight... though that black-feathered cloak at his shoulders was a potent reminder of Marhuk – Grandfather Crow, the earthly god of the a'Krah – and his reputation as a mediator of life and death.

Weisei finished a bite, and shook his head. "I haven't. I was going to ask you the same thing. But I've been thinking about it since we met him again yesterday, and I wonder if he might have gotten a bit... stuck, somehow."

"Stuck?" Día echoed.

Weisei made a peculiar hand sign, though not the same one she'd seen yesterday. "Well, you know how vulnerable things are during their in-between times. When travelers aren't at home or safely arrived, and pregnant women aren't maidens or mothers, and right now, when the world isn't day or night."

Yes, Día thought, *though it certainly is beautiful.* The sky had cleared sometime during the night, and the eastern horizon was warming to a pale, orange-tinted pink. It was a lovely, fragile time of day, when timid creatures risked their lives to venture out for food and drink, and people were apt to pass away in their sleep.

"And I think of Afvik, and how he died on the island between two lands, at the time between day and night, when he was between the age of a boy and a man, and how he might be a little bit, eh... stuck, you know?" Weisei finished the last of his cold meal, wiped his hands, and then turned them one over the other. "Like an infant turned the wrong way around, who can't see anything but the womb he's always lived in, and doesn't know how to finish being born – who might not even realize that he NEEDS to be born."

Día thought again of the purpled flesh on Halfwick's back – pooled blood-marks so plain to her incredulous eye, and yet perfectly invisible to him. And she had seen enough animal carcasses to imagine what a few days in the desert heat would do to a human body. "And you believe he needs to be 'born' sooner rather than later," she said.

Weisei nodded, and his eyes were dark and serious. "Very soon. And I would have invited him to come with us yesterday, you know, so we could ask Grandfather to help him, but we couldn't..." He jerked his chin up, at the still black shape lying nearby. "The horse couldn't take more than the two of us, and Vichi doesn't want to think of anything else until we find my – find Hakai, that is, and we're already so far away from our plans, and it's just..." He pressed his palms to his eyes, and then pushed his fingers through his hair until they met behind his head. "Everything is a little bit ruined right now. And so I was hoping that you had come to help make things right. I was hoping that the Starving God had sent you to help Afvik finish his life."

If they were going to have any kind of lasting association, Día would have to find a moment to ask Weisei not to use that term. He was 'God', nothing else.

This was not that moment.

This moment was for considering what he had said, and wondering again what she might have been brought here to accomplish... because after everything she'd done, after every mystery and horror and blind, brutal miracle, Día absolutely had to believe there was a reason for it. She closed her eyes. The smell of smoke and the taste of blood lingered in her senses, clinging to a growing suspicion that the dream had not been entirely hers.

Lost puppy, came the whisper from the west. *Ruined puppy.*

"I do want to help," she said at last. "And that's what I meant to do, when I brought him out of Island Town. But ever since he left me, I've been drawn in this other direction." Her hands clenched around the edges of the blanket in her lap. "What do you know about the Dog Lady?"

She had been one of the earthly gods – Día knew that much – but an earthly god was an avatar, the spirit of its people... and her people, the Ara-Naure, had long since been killed or dispersed.

Weisei squinted at the name, as if reminded of an especially nasty wound. "Ah, well..." He tipped his head, and picked up a nearby stick to poke at the coals. "Her name is not used kindly among the a'Krah."

"Because she accepted settlers?" Día knew that had been a point of contention, a generation ago: the native peoples who shared their land with white and mixed Eadans were often attacked by those who suspected them of fostering foreign diseases.

"Because she stole our future." Weisei's voice was hard and serious; he tucked his hand sideways under his chin. "In the years before I was born, the wars were going badly. Our allies were falling or deserting us: the Pohapi had been Eaten, the Irsah were fleeing their homelands, leaving a trail of diseased bodies in their wake, and the siege of Merin-Ka had given our enemies a powerful hold to the south. In his wisdom, Grandfather understood that the a'Krah needed to craft a new, more powerful alliance – to stop putting our trust in weaker peoples, and find our equal in strength and numbers."

"The Azahi?" Día guessed. Of the four Great Nations, three were left: the a'Krah in the west, the Azahi in the south, and to the north –

"The Lovoka," Weisei said. "We had never been friends, and the locust-swarms driving them south had tempted them to replenish their supplies by raiding our towns, and replace their lost people by stealing ours." He sighed. "But we could only afford one enemy, and nothing would have made the Eaten happier than to watch the crows and wolves consume each other."

Eaten, of course, was a bitter twist on *Eaden* – so close in sound as to be almost indistinguishable. In Marín, however, the translation was harsh and unmistakable: the settlers east of the border were *Devorados,* the hungry children of a 'starving' god. It was an ugly name, one that Día was certain Weisei would not have used if he were thinking of her as one of them. So she sat still, feeling oddly like an infiltrator or spy, and went on listening to his uncensored thoughts.

"So before we could have an alliance, we needed peace between us – and for that, we needed a peacemaker. Have you heard of the Moon Singers?"

Día shook her head, anxious not to draw attention to her ignorance.

Weisei took it in stride. "You might know them by a different name. They are four siblings: Grandfather Coyote, the Maiden Fox, Father Wolf, and the youngest is the Dog Lady. Father Wolf is not a gentle god, but he has a great love for his little sister – and so the Lovoka always took care to leave the Ara-Naure in peace, and pleased both gods by feeding stray or hungry dogs."

Día could see where this was going... and she already knew it wasn't going to end well. "You-all used her as a go-between."

Weisei bobbed his head. "It was easy enough to make an agreement with the Ara-Naure. They were so small, no more than a thousand, and by that time the Eaten had taken their holy land – Island Town, you know, and some of the lands to the west. It was not difficult to help them understand that by bringing together the a'Krah and the Lovoka, they would be helping us to reclaim their sacred places, and make a more peaceful world for everyone. So the children of the Dog Lady prepared a place, and the sons of Father Wolf and daughters of Grandfather Crow filled it, and all drank to finish the agreement: from then on, we would be united as one."

"You weren't," Día said. It wasn't a question.

"We would have been!" Weisei insisted. Then, with a hasty glance at Vuchak's still-sleeping form, he lowered his voice again. "But they couldn't agree. The Dog Lady insisted that peace could only be found by peaceful means, and Father Wolf would not be satisfied until every one of the Eaten had been killed or driven back east of the First River." Weisei sighed. "So the Lovoka went on killing the Eaten, and the Eaten – the peaceful ones, anyway – fled to the army-fortresses or took shelter with any native people who would have them... and thanked their hosts by infecting them with the diseases they had brought. And so the Lovoka took to burning plague-villages, too: any white or two-colored person, any sick person of any color, was to be killed on sight. One band of the Lovoka even turned to apostasy, attacking the Ara-Naure to 'cleanse' them of the tainted people they sheltered."

And you let them. Día didn't dare say it out loud. But she had heard exactly what Vuchak thought of her and her 'Starving' God, and could hear even more in what Weisei left unspoken: through it all, the a'Krah had held their noses and accepted that much slaughter as the cost of doing business.

"But the thing you have to understand is that it was *working*." Weisei's thin features hardened with uncharacteristic pride. "We didn't just stop losing our lands – we started taking them back. For the first time, we had the upper hand. For the first time, the Eaten were afraid of us."

Weisei stopped there, staring into the coals. Their embers highlighted the blue-black sheen of his curtain of hair, and he seemed to see in them another world – a different present.

"And then..." Día prompted.

He didn't look up. "By that time, the Dog Lady was openly defying Father Wolf. The Ara-Naure were a spot, a fleck next to the power of the Lovoka – but they were a holy, untouchable fleck, and they knew it. They had been welcoming Eaten refugees, had even been – forgive me for saying it, *coupling* with them. The Dog Lady herself had..."

Weisei stopped. He put one hand over his mouth, and then the other.

"What?" Día asked. "What is it?"

Weisei's hands went to the sides of his face, as if some huge, terrible idea were about to hatch out of his skull. He reached over as if to shake Vuchak awake, hesitated, and stood. "Excuse me, please – just for a minute." And he began to pace.

Día had gotten this sort of treatment before, in Island Town: they had been washing Halfwick's body together, and as soon as she'd asked who was responsible for his death, Weisei had been thunderstruck with some personal revelation – and bolted on the spot.

There wasn't much danger of that now, but she was getting tired of tripping over these vast gaps in her understanding... and beginning to suspect that these two a'Krah were deliberately digging them deeper. "Weisei," she said, nodding at Vuchak, "what doesn't he want me to know?"

He took her meaning at once: his gaze flicked to his companion, then back to her. "Please don't ask me that," he pleaded, wringing his hands with a genuinely apologetic expression. "Just, ah – wait there for a moment, will you? I just have a small debt to pay, and then I promise we'll finish the story."

And what could one say to that?

So Día sat and waited, growing pleasantly warmer with the rising sun even as her thoughts cooled and congealed like so much leftover grease on the grill. She had been so *thirsty* for this, yesterday – so gratified to find other living people, and Island Town neighbors besides which, and in Weisei, a kindly acquaintance who was at least half a friend. But today, it was as if the world was conspiring to remind her that she wasn't really one of them: she might enjoy their hospitality, but she certainly didn't have their trust.

So she would just have to get along by reason, intuition, and guesswork.

It stood to reason that Vuchak and Weisei had been chosen to take home the body of Dulei Marhuk. Back in Island Town, the master of the a'Krah had promised Elim that he would be escorted by the dead boy's uncle and manservant. And while neither of these two young men looked anything like her imagining of an uncle, she could not think of any more likely explanation for why two Island Town a'Krah would suddenly be transplanted all the way out here... wherever 'here' was.

Día's intuition suggested that something had gone terribly wrong: besides Weisei's 'a little bit ruined' remark, this was not a well-supplied camp. It had been cobbled together from rocks and sticks and pieces of dead things, up to and including that hair-raising horse-carcass over there. Whatever their original mission had been, she was now dining with stragglers – survivors.

And judging by Vuchak's strident demands to have her friends return his, she could guess that they had been attacked. That might explain Dulei's absence, and Elim's, and that of their other 'friend' – Hakai, if she'd heard right.

But by the time Weisei returned, Día was no closer to understanding why any of that needed to be a secret.

"I'm sorry," he said again, once he was within softer speaking-distance, and sat down beside her, hardly an arm's length away. "I don't mean to hold you at a distance, and I know you mean well. If I were alone and responsible for myself, it wouldn't take me even five minutes to tell you everything. But he's so much cleverer than I am, and he thinks of things that I don't have any idea about, and I can't..."

Weisei looked across the fire-pit at the slight, soft breathing-rhythm of Vuchak's turned back. To Día, he looked still and ordinary: a youthful, masculine frame wrapped in a stained old blanket, two freshly-braided pigtails draping over the ground, and a battered pair of moccasin-boots sticking out from the bottom: all hallmarks of a weary man best not disturbed. But there in Weisei's eyes was such a groundswell of feeling, such a peculiar admixture of pride and guilt and overwhelming tenderness, that he only kept it from leaking down his face by swallowing it down to thicken his voice instead. "... and he works so hard for me."

Día had seen that expression before. It was the way that Fours, her *papá*, used to look at her when he thought she was asleep.

She did not want to think about how he looked now, after she'd been missing for who-knew-how-many days.

Missing, the voice echoed in her mind. *Lost. Missing. Sad.*

Be quiet, she thought. *Just shut up.*

"Anyway." Weisei heaved a huge breath and found his place again. "She had a baby – the Dog Lady, that is. She had a baby with one of the Eaten men, just because she knew it would infuriate Father Wolf. One day, it went missing. And that's when everything fell apart."

A prickle crawled up Día's spine – some crucial connection just waiting to be made – but she had no chance to think on it: Weisei had had time to consider his tale, and now seemed determined to get straight on through it. "An a'Krah war-party had left them just the night before, on their way to help break the siege of Cloud Town. The Ara-Naure believed we had stolen the child and its nursemaid on behalf of the Winter Wolves – the heretic Lovoka who had been attacking them – perhaps with the blessing of Father Wolf himself."

"Surely they didn't –" Día began.

"They did," Weisei said. "The Ara-Naure ambushed us in the middle of the day, during our sleep, killing half our number in the first assault. When they didn't find the missing child, they took the survivors as hostages, and let one go to give the word: every sunrise, an a'Krah would be killed and the body buried upside-down in the ground, and this would continue until the infant was returned." Weisei closed his eyes. "They didn't realize that one of their captives was a daughter of Marhuk."

Día said nothing. She was not going to like whatever came next.

"She never revealed herself. She was courageous and clever to the end. She couldn't tell what the Dog Lady might do to another god's child, but she knew that if the alliance were going to have any chance, whatever happened to her had to be forgivable by ignorance. Her faith in Marhuk's rationality never wavered."

That was a difficult reversal to follow: it was strange to think of taking comfort in the fact that one's parent was cold enough to accept a child's execution in the name of the greater good. "But she might have saved herself," Día said.

Weisei made a see-sawing gesture. "Or she might have been tortured, or made to confess secrets to spare the lives of her fellow a'Krah. We can't know. All she knew was that the Dog Lady had become so demented, so poisoned by her love for this one infant, that she would kill to find him."

Well. If Día needed any proof that her understanding of virtue was not shared by the a'Krah, there it was. She did not need any proof that the Dog Lady was capable of murder. "I take it her plan didn't work," she said at last.

Weisei shook his head. "It might have. Marhuk wished for a peaceful resolution. But the a'Krah who came to bargain for the hostages were led by another of his daughters – a fierce young woman, equally courageous, but perhaps not so clever. When she learned that she had come too late, and that her sister was among the slain... oh, it was terrible. She sang her grieving-song, and the free a'Krah sang with her, and those imprisoned heard and added their voices too. And their anger and sadness drifted through the air and soaked into the ground until her dead kinsmen clawed through the earth and climbed out of their unholy graves, and then..."

Weisei glanced at Día, and whatever he saw in her face seemed to suggest that he did not need to recount all the bloody particulars. "By the end of the night, she – we had killed nearly fifty of the Ara-Naure, and two of the Dog Lady's children. And when the sun came up, all the still-living gods knew what we had done: we had freed the living and avenged the dead, but there was no more hope for friendship. Father Wolf saw what we had done to his sister's people, and paid us in kind. Our allies rose to our defense, and smashed everything that was left of the Ara-Naure. And by the time everyone had lost their appetite for killing, half of the high desert people were dead or Eaten."

Weisei sighed and stared morosely at the coals. "I don't hate them, you know – the Eaten, I mean. But I think about what it must be like for them. One god. One language. No marks or gifts or god-children to separate one from another. Everybody all alike, always agreeing. It must be so EASY."

Día suspected that he was considerably mistaken about some of that. But it had been twelve years since her father had put her in the sacristy – twelve years since she was truly 'alike' with anyone – and she did not pretend to understand anything about life on the other side of the border.

And she was apparently just as ignorant of the goings-on on this side, too. Día rubbed her aching eyes, overwhelmed by the need to get home, and beset by the sick, sodden fear that she might never see it again. She felt the grief that didn't belong to her, and the hesitation that did.

"Weisei," she said at last, "what would you say if I told you that I can still hear her, in my head? That I might not... that the Dog Lady might not be finished with me?"

For a moment, the young man of the a'Krah looked at her with an expression verging on envy. Then he tipped his head, left and right, and went back to watching Vuchak sleep. "I would tell you that it's often considered a great honor to be called by one of the gods... even though we may not understand the reasons for it. Do you think she has a purpose in mind for you?"

Día shook her head. "I'm not sure she even remembers

me. But she's in so much pain, and it doesn't seem right to leave her like that."

Weisei did not answer, and she could see the struggle in his face: the natural compassion of this newer generation soured by the blood feuds of the last one.

Día tried a different tack. "What's over there?" She pointed west by northwest at the nearest of the mountains, and if she'd had a gun in her hand, she could have shot the source of the foreign presence in her mind – that was how precisely her intuition guided her.

"Eh?" Weisei looked up, roused from different thoughts, and followed her gesture. "Nothing very much – a few little springs, a couple of good shelters if you're traveling in winter, and if you circle about a mile around to the south, you will find the cart-road up to Atali'Krah, where Grandfather Marhuk lives." He nodded up at the mountain's eroded peak, though Día couldn't see anything exceptional about the rumpled gray-white rock. Weisei glanced nervously back at Vuchak. "Ah, maybe I wasn't supposed to tell you that."

Día did not contradict him: she was far too surprised to speak. So this was the land of the a'Krah – and she was practically loitering on Marhuk's doorstep.

And she wasn't the only one.

"She shouldn't be here," Día realized. She hadn't thought it could get any worse, but after what Weisei had said, things now seemed poised on a fatal precipice: the Dog Lady was awake, violent, crazed with grief – and right at the feet of Grandfather Crow, whose people she had murdered in a mistaken act of vengeance, and who had destroyed her own people in turn. "What if she kills someone? What if he attacks her?"

It took Weisei a moment to catch up to her reasoning.

His gaze darted between her and the root of the mountain she'd asked him about; he made the connection with a nervous squeak. "She's there? You're sure?"

From the other side of the camp, Vuchak rolled over. "*Hihn?*" he mumbled. "*Hihn netsigwa?*"

Weisei touched his throat in alarm. "*Gai, Vichi,*" he replied in a soothing voice. "*Aga'vish koche.*"

And he sat there in anxious silence, hand over his mouth, waiting as his partner's breathing slackened again.

That was more than enough time for Día to understand what had to be done. "Weisei," she said at last, in a voice barely above a whisper, "I think it's time for me to go."

His large eyes widened, and in that moment, she was endlessly grateful for the concern that shone through them. "Now? Yourself? Please, if we've offended you with our secrets-keeping –"

Reassuring him might be her last easy task. Still, the more she thought of it, the more inevitable her decision seemed. She glanced between Vuchak and Weisei, as out of place as ever. How could she stay here, a stranger imposing herself between two kinsmen? How could she ignore the friend – and whatever she was now, Mother Dog HAD been a friend – who had comforted and guarded and nursed her through mad days and lonely nights?

"No, not at all," Día replied. "But you two have to find your friend, and I – I really should do what I can for mine." Her gaze rested on Vuchak, searching for the right sentiment. "She worked hard for me, too."

Weisei didn't answer, but steepled his hands on either side of his nose. Finally, he pressed his hands to his knees and rose to his feet. "Then that's how it will be," he said.

And just as Día began to wonder what that meant, he set about plucking strips of half-dried jerky from the wooden frame. "Now, does your dress have hand-mouths? Yes? Good: take these for later, and this to eat first, before it spoils." Día found herself stuffing her left pocket full of jerky, and weighing down the right with a flank steak the size of a dinner-plate. "Be sure to eat plants as you can, or it will take you a week to pay your debts. The mesquite beans and cactus-pears here are just as they are in Island Town, and if you see any red berries growing from four-leaved green stems, take all you can, but eat them only a little at a time, or your stomach will be angry with you. Don't touch silver-nettles at this time of year, unless you're making an offering to the Deer Woman, and be sure to bury anything you leave behind – that's how Grandfather will know you as a respectful guest."

In that moment, puttering and fussing over her and rattling off the most strict and sensible instructions, Weisei was so much like her doting *papá* that Día was hard-pressed to keep her heart in check. She tried to push her feelings aside, and think carefully about what else she might need to know. "And if I meet other people here? How will they know me?"

Weisei wiped his hands on the hem of his shirt and then bowed, his outstretched wrists turned upwards. His forearms were sickeningly thin. "Make your elbows touch and put your arms out like this, as if you were offering your veins. This is how you show deference. And if you can remember the words, say '*kalei ne ei'ha*', which means, 'please see me kindly'."

Día hadn't thought of that, but yes, of course – these weren't the borderlands, and there was no guarantee that any of the local a'Krah would know Marín. Her resolve faltered as her perspective widened, reducing her to an irritating foreign speck in the eye of an unfriendly god. Had she strayed so far from home, and did she really propose to go traipsing about here on her own? Was she truly foolish enough to abandon the first living people she'd met in the hundred lonely miles between here and Island Town?

Weisei must have seen the hesitation in her face. His expression softened, and he reached out to smooth the collar of her cassock. His slender fingers felt like delicate birds' feet at her shoulders, and he smelled exquisitely, handsomely human. "Don't be frightened, fire child. We are the dearest children of still-living gods, and their love never leaves us."

She smiled at that, though it was hard to feel terribly brave just then. "It's not my god I'm worried about."

He brightened at the little joke, and cannily tapped the side of his nose. "Well, I don't know how it is with yours, but remember that our gods have no tongues: they speak in your heart, and can only be heard by those who strive to listen. As long as you remember yourself, she can't have any power over you."

Now there was a real comfort: she could handle everything else, as long as she could keep from being overwhelmed by that strange, alien mind. Día dipped her head, grateful beyond expression. "Thank you, Weisei – for everything. I'm sorry I haven't been more helpful to you, but I'll do my best for her, and for Halfwick if I can, and I..."

How to say it? What wouldn't be too forward?

"... and no matter what happens next, I'm very sincerely glad to be your friend."

For an instant, Weisei's smile lit up his face – and just as quickly disappeared into a powerful full-body embrace. Día could not have been more pleased to return it. "Go bravely," he said, his breath warming her ear, "and goodness will always find you."

He couldn't have known how tempted she was to disappoint him just then – to abandon her intentions and stay right there with him and Vuchak, safe and sheltered between two splendid young men. When she couldn't smother the force of her affections, she finally tore herself away by transferring them instead – by taking what she'd received from Weisei and carrying it from the a'Krah camp, west by northwest, to the place where it was most sorely needed.

I'm coming, Mother Dog, she thought, the new day warm on her back. *Wait for me – I'm coming to help.*

Día's courage was tiny, a leaf in a churning river. But it stayed afloat, pushed by the wind and warmed by the sun as she headed for the anguished presence lurking in the foothills.

CHAPTER THREE
ONE OF MANY

"– AND THAT'S WHY I told her to go."

Vuchak waited for his *marka* to finish speaking before he resumed pounding out the jerky. "Of course you did."

Apparently this was not good enough. "You don't believe me," Weisei said, his voice equal parts accusation and hurt.

"I do," Vuchak assured him, punctuating it with another meat-rending strike from the stone in his hand. It was miserable work without real tools. "I believe that she said each of those things to you, and that you answered her with sincerity."

Weisei was foolish, but he was no fool: he had no trouble hearing what Vuchak had left unsaid. "You think she was lying to me."

Vuchak put down the pounding-stone and sat back on his heels. Everything was a soured blessing today, as vexing as a warm bed and a full bladder. The day was bright and clear, but had shone no light on Hakai or Dulei. The jerky was dry, but didn't want to turn to powder no matter how much he pounded on it.

The grave-woman had pledged loyalty and help, but had taken what she wanted and then vanished like the faithless vagrant snake-daughter that she was, and Vuchak had no-one but himself to blame for that. He should never have believed her.

Still, he wasn't going to let his anger spill over to Weisei. She'd taken their food and their trust, but he wouldn't let her have their peace. He'd worked too hard for it. "I think it's clear that neither of us knows enough about her to say what is or isn't true," Vuchak said as diplomatically as he could. "And I think we need to take care of our own business before we waste any more time on hers. Are you sure you can handle the horse today?"

"YES, Vichi!" The answer was fast and exasperated. "How many more times do your ears need to hear it?"

Well, his ears would have an easier time if his eyes didn't keep contradicting them. Vuchak wiped his brow and glanced up from where he knelt under his *marka*'s thin, shrinking shadow. From this angle, with his disheveled black-feather cloak pulled close around him and his nose protruding from his gaunt face and his bony toes splayed out in the grass, Weisei looked like a tarred and starving heron. He'd done hardly anything but eat and sleep since they scraped the campsite together, which was as it should be... but that was only a day's rest, and those hollows under his eyes confessed that he needed at least a week. By every god, Vuchak was exhausted just thinking of everything that still had to be done, and he wasn't the one about to animate a half-ton of horseflesh.

Well, all the more reason to hurry up and put that ungainly carcass to good use: the sooner they found Hakai, the sooner they could put him to work, and the sooner they recovered Dulei's body, the sooner they could go home. Vuchak dusted his hands, tied the *yuye* over his eyes to shield them from the worst of the sun's light, and pushed himself up to his feet, viciously tempted to forsake everything and go back to sleep. "Then we might as well get started."

So Weisei put on his shoes and Vuchak picked up his blanket, and together they went to the horse, who was just then beginning to mother its first generation of flies. The rot-smell, still relatively mild, reminded them of the passing time: they would not have more than two or three days before the carcass decayed past usefulness. Vuchak threw the blanket over the horse's back, glad that the circle of chalk had kept the ants out of that sun-bleached black coat, while Weisei put his hand to the gunshot wound above its eyes.

Then he began to sing. This was not the grieving song, of course, as an animal could not be mourned in the same way as a person. Instead, the deep, delicate melody that bloomed from Weisei's throat was the remembering song – a tuneful, wordless encouragement for the body to leave off returning to the earth, and recall its living functions.

That had been easier at this time yesterday, when the horse had only been a day removed from the living world. Now the death-amnesia had blurred more of its memories, making it hard to remember a time before stillness and decomposition. Vuchak, no son of Marhuk himself, did not understand exactly how it worked, but he knew that somewhere in Weisei's song was a reminder of grazing, of rolling in the dust, of banishing flies with skin-twitching, tail-swishing diligence, and always, always watching for signs of danger.

An ear flicked. Weisei kept his eyes closed, but he slowly lifted his hand, bringing the horse's head up as if that blood-crusted black face were bound to him by magnetic attraction. Then one forehoof braced itself in the dust, as stiff and clumsy as that of a day-old foal. Then the other. And then –

A distant cry rang out.

Vuchak startled, but saw nothing. "Weisei, stop."

Brows drawn with effort, Weisei was just then inspiring the horse to push itself up by its forelegs. There again, almost smothered under his song, was the faint sound of someone's fear.

Vuchak patted urgently at his *marka*'s arm. "Weisei, stop!"

That was enough to break his concentration. The horse collapsed with a rancid *whud*. "Vichi, what –"

The cry came again, and this time there was no mistaking it: that was a man's muffled scream – and it was coming from the river.

Vuchak's weariness evaporated in a second. He snatched up his spear and bolted, seized by the single-minded need to...

... fall right into a fishman's trap?

No, no – what kind of idiot was he? If someone was in trouble in the river, then it was almost certainly because someone else had arranged for it to happen.

Vuchak dropped and crawled forward on his stomach, making a man-sized worm-track in the dirt as he inched through dry nettles and angry patches of blister-root, eating up distance even as he excreted time. Then – finally! – the ground rolled away before him, and from the little rise, he glimpsed the nearest bend of the All-Year River.

The sun-blunting black mesh over his eyes muddied the details, but he would have to have worn ten *yuye* to miss the scene in front of him: there was the fast-flowing gray stripe of the river, and there was the unnatural disturbance in the current, and THERE – gagged, bound, and thrashing in a panic – was the reason for it.

Hakai! Vuchak nearly said it aloud. They'd tied him face-down to some driftwood or piece of furniture, binding his hands around it and tying a sack over his head to stop his eyes and mouth... all but daring Vuchak to come and take him.

It was a trap. It could only be a trap. Vuchak's gaze scoured the shorelines, the current, the horizon, but even on a full-moon night, he did not trust himself to spot a fishman. Their camouflage was second to none – a fatal fact just waiting for him to venture into that water.

Vuchak glanced back at his *marka*, still holding frozen to the spot, his wide eyes pleading for instruction.

He was Weisei's *atodak,* sworn to guard his life before all others.

He would not leave his frail prince alone out here.

He couldn't risk it for a slave.

Another muffled cry echoed off the hills. Vuchak had just time to catch a glimpse of Hakai as he kicked, rolled – and went under.

Vuchak dropped his spear. "Weisei, take the horse and get out of here!"

Duty went forgotten as he pulled the knife from his boot. Reason deserted him as he tore down the hill. And if his life was shortly to end as he plunged into the viciously cold current, at least Vuchak would die as he had lived: doing something poorly-considered, mostly useless, and embarrassingly preventable.

* * *

THAT WAS HIM. Porté drew themself further up out of the water, careful to stay river-colored and invisible as they watched the earthling man dive into the current.

That was him – the terrible death-eyed archer from the House of the Crow, whose arrows had ended all happiness.

But as the man threw himself into the water to rescue his drowning kinsman, the part of Porté that longed to pull him down to his death grew strangely silent.

The archer didn't understand what he had done. He couldn't. He knew only that he had shot some 'fish-men' two nights ago. How could he understand that the body he'd left crumpled in the mud had been little Flamant-Rose, the smallest and brightest of the Many? How could he know that his arrow had killed a brilliant young geologist – a shy, delighted smile – a look of manic triumph whenever they managed to steal a rice-cake from their bigger siblings at the dinner-fight – an endless, boundless wonder at every turn of this grand expedition?

He couldn't. He just couldn't. Porté could grab the man and wrestle him down to the bottom of the river, pin him down and watch as the bubbles escaped his mouth and the light left his eyes, and he would understand only that he had been murdered by the same unfathomable monsters who had attacked him before.

It wasn't supposed to be like this. Porté wished they knew enough earth-words to say so. *Nobody was supposed to get hurt.*

But the man wouldn't understand them, and Fuseau wouldn't hear them, and Prince Jeté wouldn't listen to them. Nobody had room for those feelings anymore.

Someone's elbow jabbed Porté in the ribs, prompting a painful twinge from that half-healed arrow wound. They looked over to see Tournant's angry black eyes – the only part that couldn't camouflage – beckoning Porté to put themself out of sight.

Porté obediently sank back down into the shallows, treading water with the rest of the Many as they all watched the earthling man take the bait.

No, there were no words in any language that could make him understand what he'd done. But if Porté had had the means, they would have apologized for what was going to happen next.

VUCHAK SHOULD HAVE been dead by now. He should have been stabbed, strangled, drowned four times over. In throwing himself into the river, he had offered his life – but no invisible webbed hand had reached up to take it.

Maybe they were busy with Hakai instead. As Vuchak closed in on him, adding his strength to the river's to catch up with the drifting, spinning human wreckage caught in its flow, Hakai's head emerged just long enough for a sodden gasp of air through the linen sack – and then he was down again, trapped in a deadly embrace with the flotsam pressed to his bare chest.

So maybe the World That Is didn't actually want to kill Vuchak. Maybe it just wanted to watch him abandon his *marka* and his duty, and come back with nothing but a waterlogged corpse to show for it. Historically, Vuchak had gratified the universe's latent sadism with active humiliation as much as passive misery.

That thought lent him new strength as he plowed through the water, all power and no grace, preparing to feed his knife rope instead of flesh. He was fifty yards away, then twenty, then ten, and then –

– and then the heinous, familiar stench hit him full in the face, and he belatedly recognized the contours of that boxy coffin.

Dulei! By every still-living god – they'd tied Hakai to Dulei, and now he could rescue both together!

Or rather: they'd tied Hakai to Dulei, and now he was going to have to figure out how to rescue both together.

There was no cutting Hakai loose – the coffin would be long gone by the time Vuchak made it to shore and back. Still, towing two grown men, one actively panicking and the other a literal dead weight, was going to take everything Vuchak had left.

Time to start giving. With a deep breath and a quick prayer, Vuchak set the knife between his teeth and lunged forward. He grabbed Hakai's left arm and pulled to flip him back to the air-breathing world –

– and was rewarded with a blind kick to the gut. "STOP!" Vuchak hissed between clenched teeth, glad that he didn't have time to meditate on how easily a boot to the knife in his mouth would widen his smile.

But Hakai either didn't hear or couldn't understand him. He answered with a choking gasp and a renewed struggle: the damned fishmen had tied the sack – his shirt – over his whole head, and his every intaken breath sucked in more water from the sodden gray cloth. The poor bastard probably thought he was still drowning, and with no easy way to get that gag out of his mouth, or to talk around the blade in his own, Vuchak was just going to have to haul him back kicking and screaming.

Well, it would make a pleasant change from doing it to Weisei. *Be calm*, Vuchak willed him as he took hold of the rope lashing the *ihi'ghiva*'s arm to the coffin's side and started the hard swim back to shore. *Breathe slowly. Lie quiet and still.*

Hakai did not do any of those things. Soon, Vuchak didn't care. The river only understood one direction, and as he fought to cut sideways through its current, Vuchak began to fear that he'd badly overestimated himself – that this might take more strength than he had left to give.

Before he'd made it even halfway there, his legs ached, his lungs burned, and his spirit faltered. *One more*, he told himself, and managed another feeble kick. *One more*, though that one was even weaker than the last. *One more*, but his eyes told his legs how they were being lied to: the ten yards between him and dry land might as well have been ten oceans, and his courage sank as doubts poured in from a thousand cowardly crevices.

After all, he was *a'Pue* – born under no star, possessed of no luck. What made him think he would be allowed to succeed here, now, after a lifetime of failure? In just the last week alone, he'd already made a mess of Halfwick's death... brought shame to the Island Town a'Krah... lost Pipat's affections, gotten Weisei robbed and nearly killed when he'd fallen asleep on watch, defied Grandfather Marhuk himself and ignorantly ruined whatever great miracle he'd intended at Yaga Chini, and that wasn't even counting all the terrible things that had followed after.

Vuchak's teeth parted as he heaved for breath; the knife slipped from his mouth. He caught it by the hilt before it became an offering to the All-Year River, and leaned forward to resume his shoreward swim.

Nothing happened.

When they left Island Town, he had been all youth

and health. But he'd spent so much of it on that arduous march through the desert, wrung himself out so hard and thoroughly just to make it here to the river, and now he could no more swim to land than fly up and put out the sun. Now the trap became apparent: he would drown here after all, by no hand but his own. Hakai would drown with him, doomed by his service to a well-intentioned weakling...

... well, wait a minute.

Vuchak looked behind him. Hakai was still tied to the coffin, but it was no longer a morbid embrace: now he was using it like a child learning to swim with a plank of wood, letting it support him as he kicked – not a panicked thrashing anymore, but a soft, thudding, productive rhythm in the water.

He wanted to live. Vuchak ought to help.

He *deserved* to live. Vuchak *had* to help.

And as it turned out, Vuchak still had a little more left to give.

BY THE TIME he dragged himself ashore, the world was rich with miracles. Vuchak let the knife drop from his mouth into the grass, gasping gratefully as he crawled over the sedge, pausing at each step to haul Hakai and Dulei another eight inches behind him. When he felt the coffin firmly beached at last, he collapsed onto his side and lay there, endlessly delighted by stillness and firmness and the euphoric rush of air into his lungs. Hakai seemed content to do likewise, his knees resting slack in the weeds as he remained prostrated over Dulei's box. Even the death-stench was a welcome comfort – how pleasant it was to breathe!

It was so pleasant, in fact, that for long, bottomless moments, Vuchak forgot who he was. Consumed with the joy of having rescued Hakai, and recovered Dulei – of having done a vital thing deliberately and with unqualified success – he let whole minutes slip by before remembering the order of his life: if he had succeeded at one thing, he was already failing at something else. But what?

Weisei. The realization hit him like a fishman's slap. If they had allowed him to rescue these two, it was because they wanted him distracted while they ambushed his *marka.*

Vuchak staggered up to his feet. There wasn't a second to lose. "Hakai, get ready to run," he said, picking up his knife and bending to cut the rope. "We have to..."

Vuchak paused in spite of his fear. He had never seen the *ihi'ghiva* in any state of undress – but now, as he contemplated the honey-colored flesh of Huitsak's shirtless slave, it was impossible not to notice the strange, spotty pits under Hakai's nearer arm.

Surely not. *Surely* not.

With fingers shaking from exhaustion and cold, Vuchak sawed through the rope, took Hakai by the wrist, flipped him over to lie on his back – and took a horrified step backwards.

"Don't touch her," Vuchak's father said, keeping firm hold of his hand as they walked past the dead woman, her mouth hanging open and her chest a scarred, pitted wasteland. "Don't even look at her."

Vuchak had obeyed then. Even at four, he had understood that the diseases of the Eaten spread through every sense: by touching, by smelling, even by seeing the afflicted, you invited the sickness into yourself.

So it was more than a bit foolish to stand here now, a grown man past twenty, gaping at that flabby wall of white, puckered divots, meditating on the pox-ravaged flesh of the very same slave he had just...

... or was it? What proof did he have that this was Hakai? As the mutilated man on the ground curled up to cover himself, Vuchak reached down to yank away the shirt wound around his head.

It was and it wasn't. That was Hakai's gray-streaked black hair, all right, and his soft, fortyish features, and that was almost certainly his *yuye* that they'd gagged him with, but his eyes...

Vuchak had never seen his eyes before. He wasn't supposed to. Hakai was an *ihi'ghiva* – a sacred scribe. He could not be bought or sold or beaten, could not be deprived of his possessions or forced into any service that ran contrary to the interests of Aso'ta Marhuk, the one true master of all *ihi'ghiva'a*. He was untouchable, incorruptible, and to symbolize his removal from worldly temptations, he wore the *yuye*, not just in sunlight, but always.

But now the black cloth was trapped between his teeth, and there was nothing between the world and his eyes. Soft brown eyes, worried eyes, middle-aged eyes just beginning to show Marhuk's marks at their corners...

... eyes that did not squint in the harsh daylight, or find any purchase in their surroundings.

Vuchak tore off his own *yuye*, not trusting what he saw beyond the fine black mesh, but there was no mistaking it: that was Hakai, and he was blind.

And he was even now calmly reaching up to get the blindfold out of his mouth, to pick out the knot around his left wrist, to unfold his shirt and slip it on as if nothing had happened – as if he were a clean, wholesome person.

"Sir, I understand –"

"Shut up." Vuchak buried his fear like a cat covering its waste, careful not to leave anything that might smell of weakness. *Weisei*. He had to think of his *marka*, not this infectious plague-blinded slave. He had to decide whether to go slowly, burdened by Dulei's weight, or make a run for it, and chance leaving him behind. He had to guess how far downstream the river had carried them, and how long it would take to make up the distance. He had to think of everything, anything besides those horrible puckered scars.

"If I could just –"

Vuchak turned on him in an instant. "I said SHUT UP. I don't have time to think about you or talk to you – I don't have one more minute to spend on you. I left Weisei behind, gibbering idiot that I am, and now I'm who-knows-how-far away with you, poxy liar that you are, and by the time we..."

Hakai pointed.

It was a crass, obscene gesture, making a vulgar weapon of one's finger. Yes, there were rare moments when an uplifted chin just wouldn't do... but for Hakai to do it unprompted and in full view of his superior was as brazen and shocking as a maiden's fart.

As a result, it took Vuchak a long beat to recover his wits enough to wonder what Hakai was pointing *at*.

He turned, squinting in the sunlight, but his beleaguered eyes found nothing of interest in the rumpled red-gray landscape. He was facing upstream, to the north, with the Mother of Mountains a little to the left, her soft, weathered crags majestically silhouetted against the blue bowl of the sky. The trees and grasses nearby all sang a green song of gratitude for their nearness to the life-giving water of the All-Year River, while the shrubs and cacti on the hills weathered the drought with rust-colored stoicism. That was as it should be. This was the Eiya'Krah, the ancient home of the a'Krah people, gifted to them on the fourth day of the World That Is, loved and honored every day for the thousands of years since – and it was beautiful.

Beautiful, and yet utterly unhelpful.

Vuchak glanced again at Hakai's crude finger, and back out at the place it seemed to be aiming at – and just there, as if by magic, a tiny figure appeared over the nearest hill. It grew quickly, too large and too fast to be a person on foot. As Vuchak replaced his *yuye* and shielded his eyes, he was delighted to see the dark, unmistakable shape of a man on horseback – well, almost a man – coming for them at a gallop.

Vuchak squelched the temptation to call out and make a spectacle of himself, lest he break his *marka*'s concentration. Instead, he reveled in the stomach-slackening relief of knowing that Weisei was well and within sight – that everyone who had been made a part of Vuchak's responsibility at the beginning of this godforsaken expedition had now returned to it alive, or at least no more dead than before.

Well, except for Ylem... but that was more than the wrung-out twitching of Vuchak's muscles could contemplate. "You can stop now," he said, his voice as drained as the rest of him.

Hakai put his arm down and resumed reassembling himself. He said nothing, as Vuchak had ordered, but now the silence between them had a stiffness to it, and

Vuchak had no idea what to fill it with. A week ago, his old, automatic anger would have burst forth with furious zeal, blaming Hakai for lying by omission, for endangering everyone by disguising himself as a sighted person, for drinking and eating and sleeping and breathing alongside wholesome, unblemished people without ever once disclosing the pestilential ghosts he had bottled up inside him.

But the greater part of Vuchak's anger had burned up in the fire, and the rest had washed out in the water, and there was nothing left now but wet, ashen rationality: Hakai had done everything anyone had asked of him, as well or better than expected, and any fault in his service or danger in his person existed only as an unsubstantiated what-if. He hadn't made anyone sick. He hadn't failed in his duty. He'd even spotted Weisei, by whatever divine gifts he used to supplant his eyes – which reminded Vuchak that he still had no idea what god or nation had authored this strange, inscrutable servant.

"Vichi, I'm here! I'm –" Weisei, now within shouting distance, had apparently just then spotted the two of them. He waved and called out – and left off the remembering song. The horse collapsed as if it had been shot, its hard gallop disintegrating into a dust-churning wreck of tangled limbs, hurling its rider headlong into the brush.

Vuchak bolted forward. "Weisei!"

But the gods loved children and fools, and Weisei was something of both: he rolled forward as gracefully as a summer clown, and bounded back up to his feet. "Vichi! I'm sorry; please don't be angry – I didn't mean to..." He was coming forward, walking off a limp and talking all the while, and soon that effusive fountain of speech would be at Vuchak's ear, and this peculiar moment with Hakai would be over.

Vuchak turned back to the *ihi'ghiva*, disturbed at how easily and completely he had already composed himself: shirt tucked, *yuye* tied, hair neatly bound at the base of his neck, without a strand out of place. If he hadn't been soaking wet, Hakai could have sat down right there and commenced taking dictation.

So Vuchak felt no guilt at all in dictating. "We aren't going to speak of this again," he said. "We're going to wait for Weisei, and then carry Dulei back to camp together, and as long as we're in public, we're going to conduct ourselves exactly as we did before."

"Yes, sir." Hakai was invisible and impervious again behind his blindfold, his vulnerabilities vanished as if Vuchak had only imagined them.

"I'm not finished. When we get back to camp, YOU are going to tell me exactly what you've done, and what was done to you, since you left our service. And when we get to Atali'Krah, I'm going to tell Aso'ta Marhuk exactly what you are, and then we'll see how much you're worth to him."

There was a flicker of something behind that black cloth – a hint of an expression, a twitch of Hakai's lip, and Vuchak could all but hear the unspoken rejoinder: *what makes you think he doesn't already know?*

But all Hakai said was "Yes, sir."

That would have to do. With this much understood, Vuchak retrieved his knife, resheathed it in his moccasin-boot, and then turned with squelching footsteps to discover what this improbable turn of good luck was going to cost them.

NOW THERE WAS nothing to do but wait – and only one sensible place to do it.

So Porté swam down and down, following the acrid grief-taste in the water, until they sensed the grim, familiar shapes in the murky wash: two small cairns of stones at the bottom of the river, flanking a third one as long as both of the others combined. Pirouet, Flamant-Rose, and Princess Ondine. A lone figure swam lopsided circles around the three graves, around and around like a maimed fish in a bowl.

It – they – brightened aggressively as soon as they sensed Porté's approach. *Relax, même,* Porté signed as soon as they were close enough. *It's just me.*

Bombé's posture loosened, but their colors softened not at all. *What happened?* their hands demanded, every gesture sharp with anxiety. *Did it work?*

It did, Porté assured them. *It will.*

It had to.

Bombé stared at them for a long moment – long enough to start drifting downstream, and for the rope tied around their waist to pull taut. The other end kept them tethered to the big stone in the middle of this makeshift graveyard. *Then why are you here?*

Porté struggled to give an answer – but Bombé didn't wait to receive it. They carried right on as they had before: swimming and swimming in pointless, crippled circles, their tail and one good leg struggling to compensate for the one the archer's arrow had hamstrung into uselessness.

There was no need to be so rude. There was no point in swimming to keep the nibbler-fish away, either. The greedy, covetous fingers of the Amateur – abetted by the deadly, murderous aim of that archer – had already stolen the lives of their siblings and their dear princess. Now their bodies were returning to the greater order of creation, to the cycle of water and life that had no beginning or ending but the sea... and when the current carried their essence all the way down into the blackest part of the ocean's abyss, into the primordial volcanic heat of the Artisan's deepwater forge, she would reshape their old souls into new bodies, so that someday they would live again in the House of Losange.

Porté did not say any of that. Instead, they swam down and set about replacing the smaller stones that the current was slowly tugging downstream, filling in the little gaps in their siblings' stone blankets that might tempt the fish to taste them. Maybe the dead were past caring, but it mattered to Bombé. For now, that was enough.

Porté snuck a glance at their distraught sibling as they swam their pointless, manic circles over the largest and longest of the three graves. More than anyone, Bombé had delighted in playing with Princess Ondine – in tying fanciful streamers to her gill-plumes, and building turtle-houses and mud-mazes with her, and camouflaging just poorly enough that she could find them in games of hide-and-seek. More than anyone but Prince Jeté himself, Bombé thirsted to have her death answered – to see that the dog-monster who had torn out her throat was found and slaughtered.

And that was why the archer had to be let go. They would deal with him later – Prince Jeté had promised that. Now and before anything else, the princess's life had to be paid for.

Porté paused as their hand closed around something strange – a jagged, glittering rock, unlike anything else in the river-bed. Where had they seen this before?

Look what I found! The memory of Flamant-Rose's voice was as fresh as yesterday. *It's mostly quartz, but look at this chalcopyrite crystal here – a four-way twinning!* Porté turned the rock over and over, scrutinizing it in the green freshwater haze in a vain attempt to find the part that had occasioned such excitement. There were little brassy gold-looking bits studded in among the quartz, but which was the special one? At the time, they had barely been listening.

Why hadn't they listened? What else could have been more important?

Porté dug their long toes into the sediment, struggling to stay anchored as the current pushed them relentlessly back – towards the sea, towards death, towards the place where they should be going and Flamant-Rose had already gone. The Amateur had taken an incomparable prize that night: in a handful of minutes, he had stolen a vivacious young princess, a brilliant budding geologist, and poor homesick Pirouet, too. He had chiseled out all the golden parts of the stone, and left the dross. After all, what need did he have for Porté – a lump of common quartz; a worthless, mindless hulk; a stevedore with no more talent or ambition than to move things from somewhere to somewhere else? What good were they to anyone now?

Porté's webbed fingers closed around the stone as they camouflaged and curled over, seeping grief from every pore. In that moment, the temptation to let go was overwhelming – to loosen their toes and let the current carry them away – to follow Pirouet and Flamant-Rose and Princess Ondine out to sea and beg the Artisan to reforge them all together – to let them be born again in the same house, the same cohort – to be perfectly matched once more, as so many eggs in one innocent, immaculate roe.

The sudden presence from behind caught Porté by surprise. In the space of a moment, Bombé slipped their arms around Porté's broad chest, copying their colors and folding themself over the big stevedore like a second identical skin – and then bit them in the neck.

Porté relaxed into the pain, waves of love and gratitude washing through them as their sibling's teeth drew blood. *This one is mine,* Bombé's bite said to the Amateur. *They're precious and special and now I've spoiled them, so you won't.*

It was good to feel important. It was good to remember that Porté had left home with eleven identical siblings, and nine were still here – still alike with them, still together with them, still wanting and needing them, perhaps now more than ever.

Porté turned their head, relishing the protective embrace as their sibling sucked the wound, and touched their teeth to Bombé's nose. It was not a love-bite, but a sharp-edged *thank you.*

There was no more circle-swimming after that, and no more grief-taste either. With Bombé's tether and Porté's toes, they held their place in the current, and shared their sameness in silence thereafter.

"AND THEN WHAT?" Vuchak's voice sounded harsh in his own ears.

"And then they let me go." Hakai's patience seemed to crystallize even as Vuchak's dissolved.

He would not give up. "And then what?"

Hands clasped behind his back, Hakai nodded in Vuchak's direction. "And then I was rescued by your very-reverend self."

Vuchak spat. "*Horseshit!*"

"Vichi!" Weisei scolded him from across the tripod of drying meat, his face half-obscured as he crouched by the circle of stones and worked at rekindling the fire. "Go to the horse if you want to swear at someone – I won't have you saying such things to our Hakai."

But that wasn't all. That couldn't be all. Vuchak held his tongue and forced his fists to unclench. He would apologize – but not to a servant. "I'm sorry, *marka*. It's just – I can't understand how that could be true. I can't understand why they would take hostages from us and then simply return them, with no message, no demands, no vengeance of any kind." And though he didn't say it, the evidence echoed loudly in Vuchak's mind: *Because I know I killed at least one of them.*

Neither of the others had seen that part. Weisei had been unconscious, on the brink of death, and Hakai had been knocked down and stolen at the very beginning of the fight. But Vuchak still remembered drawing back the bow, taking aim at a living, reasoning creature, and unleashing each steel-pointed arrow to seek a new home – in a chest, a throat, a heart, a head. He still remembered that meaty *whunk*, and the almost-human cry of pain that followed, as one of his arrows sank to the fletching into a fishman's eye. How could there be any forgiveness after that?

"Well," Weisei said with a dismissive wave, "they

wouldn't dare to offend Grandfather Marhuk at his own doorstep. Now strip down and hang up your clothes, both of you, before you freeze."

Vuchak and Hakai exchanged a blindfolded glance. They had trudged all the way back to camp in shivering silence, carrying Dulei's coffin between them, mindful not to distract Weisei again as he revived the horse and led it back at a walk. All the while, Vuchak had watched the sodden, shifting folds of Hakai's gray shirt, and thought of the private horror that lay beneath it. And now that they were here, and conversation was inevitable...

... well, Vuchak had said that he wouldn't reveal anything about Hakai. He'd never promised to make excuses for him.

"Thank you, sir," Hakai said smoothly, "but I don't have the gift of your dark skin, and the sun is unkind to mine. I would prefer to remain as I am."

At another time, Vuchak might have enjoyed watching Weisei offer a blanket and Hakai craft an excuse not to take it. But Hakai was clearly well-practiced at hiding what he wanted to keep unseen – and Vuchak couldn't afford to let him bury the truth about the fishmen. "So you've explained how they questioned you, and how you told them everything you know – but you haven't explained why it took you two days to do it."

There – let him try to talk his way out of that one.

A light breeze cut through their damp clothes. Hakai shuddered, and began to pace. "It didn't. It took them two days to believe me."

Moved in spite of himself, Vuchak sucked his teeth. That carried some grim implications.

Which weren't lost on Weisei, either: he stopped feeding the fire and bounded up to his feet, overcome with dismay. "How awful! Vichi, isn't that awful? Hakai, what did they do to you? Wait, no – you don't have to tell me. Come here, come sit right here and warm yourself, and I'll get you something to eat. You can have anything you want, as long as it's venison."

"Thank you, sir," Hakai said again, "but I wouldn't be so rude to the meal as to spoil it with conversation. We should satisfy your *atodak* first."

Vuchak bristled, hot words boiling up from his throat at this naked challenge – as if *he* were the impediment here! "You –"

No, no – this wasn't right. Vuchak pressed the heels of his hands to his eyes, too tired to think straight. Hakai was a liar, but he wasn't a traitor. He'd been the one to spot the fishmen's ambush that night. If he were working for them, all he would have had to do was stay silent, and let Vuchak and the others walk into the trap. If Hakai was hiding anything, he was doing it to save his own pitted hide... and Vuchak hadn't helped that by threatening him. He had to get around that somehow, move past all this petty sniping and figure out the fishmen's next move.

"... you better us with your diligence," Vuchak said at last, and forced himself to mean it. "Now I would have you better my understanding. Did they say anything to you about what they intended? What were they going to do after they released you?"

Hakai tipped his head, as if pleased to receive this much civility. "I believe they're going upstream to look for the monster. They could not seem to consider anything else until it was destroyed."

Weisei snorted. "Well, they're not going to find her there!"

For a moment, Hakai paused his slow, circular

ambling around their pitiful camp, his tone just a little too interested. "Oh?"

But Weisei was full of satisfaction at having gotten the fire going, and took no notice at all. "Yes," he said as he set about swapping out the jerky-strips between the upper and lower tiers. "And she's not a monster at all. She's U'ru, the Dog Lady, and she –"

Vuchak couldn't think quickly enough to justify it, but something in him wanted to keep the grave-woman and everything she'd brought with her out of the discussion. "You don't know that," he said. "We don't know anything about her. Now, Hakai, why did you –"

"Begging your pardon, sir," Hakai said, in a tone that begged nothing at all, "but if our prince has received a vision, I'd like to hear it."

Vuchak said nothing, momentarily speechless with surprise. Had this impertinent menial just interrupted him?

Weisei suffered no such hesitation. "Oh, it wasn't a vision at all – it was Día! She's a servant of the Starving God, the one who lives in the burned church in Island Town, and she's also the one who used her fire to save us from the *marrouak* those nights ago, and she –"

"– promised her service and then left us –" Vuchak broke in.

"– to go and help the Dog Lady, as I told her she should!" Weisei finished.

"Or so she says." Vuchak should have been kinder to his *marka*. It would have been easier without itchy wet clothes crawling up his crevices.

"Do you want to find out?" Weisei retorted, gesturing rudely at the roots of the Mother of Mountains. "Shall we go to the trailhead and see for ourselves?"

"No!" Vuchak snapped, propriety dissolving like snowflakes in mud. "Do you know why? Because now we have Hakai, and you, Dulei" – this with a deferential nod to the coffin – "and Ylem and the Dog Lady are Marhuk's problem now. They can camp out at his doorstep from now until the end of the World That Is, if he will tolerate them: our job is to take ourselves home with no more delay."

It was absurd, really, to think how badly their plan had crumbled. Huitsak had sent them from Island Town with instructions to make Ylem a peace-offering to the fishmen, and give Halfwick's head to Dulei's grieving mother. Now Ylem was gone, the fishmen had become mortal enemies, and Halfwick's head was still attached to his festering unnatural body – and the less said about that little mix-up, the better.

Weisei had no good answer to that. "Well, you can't just... I don't... Hakai, you are making my eyes dizzy! Won't you at least sit down and have a smoke?"

Hakai stopped. For a moment, he didn't say anything. "... later, sir – perhaps a little later." His voice was peculiar, weighted by a strange, unfathomable strain. Had he lost his pipe, or drowned the herbs? Why not just say so?

But Hakai consented to sit, cross-legged and straight-backed at the edge of the little fire, and to place his hands on his knees with perfect composure. "Still, I would be equally comforted, if I could ask you one question."

Weisei sat down too, his face drawn with concern. "Anything. I'll answer you honestly, and my *atodak* will be silent."

Vuchak hardly needed prompting. He folded his arms.

"I don't fear the fishmen," Hakai said. "I believe what they told me. But what if the Dog Lady decides to punish us for taking her son? How will we protect ourselves?"

"Oh, Hakai!" Weisei said, overflowing with the same light-hearted compassion one would use for a child's sincerely-confessed fear of toenail-gobblers. "You don't need to worry about that. Marhuk won't let anything happen to his own people, on his own land, and..." A belated realization crept across Weisei's face. "... well, and of course we'll keep you safe, too. Look, you see," and he jerked his chin up at the matched pair of hills behind his left shoulder. "We know from Día that the Dog Lady is camped between the Red Brothers, so if she comes at us from that direction, she'll have to cross all these wide-open fields, and certainly we'll be able to see her coming. If that happens, I can wake the horse and take you to safety while Vuchak and Dulei placate her in Marhuk's name. Does that satisfy you?"

Hakai bowed his head in gratitude. "Completely, sir. Thank you for explaining it to me."

Weisei glanced up at Vuchak. "And you, Vichi – do you have any sound reason to object to our camping here for the remainder of the day?"

Vuchak did – he was sure of it. Something wasn't right here. Even if the fishmen wanted to destroy the Dog Lady first, they had no reason to return Hakai and Dulei. Why give them back? What were they going to get out of this?

But he was too tired to think, to argue, to contemplate even one more last-ditch skin-saving maneuver. He had nothing left.

So Vuchak surrendered. "No, *marka*. Your will is mine."

Weisei rose, satisfied and somehow more commanding, as if he knew Vuchak could no longer hold the reins himself. "Good! Now both of you are going to dry off and rest yourselves, and I don't want to hear one more word between you until sunset. We'll camp here today and start again tonight. Are these words clear to you?"

"Yes, sir," they replied in unison – and Vuchak couldn't speak for Hakai, but his own pledge was sincerely meant. He'd spent everything he had, but it had been worth it: to rescue Hakai and Dulei, yes, but also to enjoy this rare opportunity to subordinate himself to a superior presence, and be what he always should have been – an unquestioning avatar of loyalty and service.

And having finally reclaimed his rightful place, Vuchak was glad to peel off the sodden remains of the day, and follow his last order straight to bed.

THE MAN, HAKAI, did not sleep. He sat in place, straight-backed and cross-legged on the ground, and waited.

But it was impossible to stay still as he shivered.

The prince, Weisei, regarded him fretfully. "Please, Hakai – won't you have anything?"

The knight, Vuchak, was long since asleep.

The man dipped his head in deference, and repeated his reply. "Later, sir – a little later. I'd like to keep watch for now."

The prince held silent then, as if he might order him to do otherwise. Finally, he folded himself in his blanket and reclined to rest on one arm. "Well, all right, then... but see that you care for yourself. We're very glad to have you back with us, and we don't want anything else to happen to you."

The man made the *ashet*, holding out his upturned wrists in the traditional gesture of fealty. The prince contented himself with that, and lay down to sleep.

For a short while, there was nothing but the wind in the hills, and the distant lap of the river, and the cold, constant light of the sun. The man, Hakai, weathered it all with stoic indifference.

But it was impossible to stay silent.

"Sir... you know I didn't mean to be taken. You know I would never choose to leave you."

The prince, Weisei, answered in a voice smeared with weariness. "Hakai, of course we do. Both of us. Vuchak's just anxious, that's all. He'll be more reasonable when he's rested – you'll see."

The man nodded. Nothing more was said. Soon, the prince had followed his knight into the land of exhaustion and dreams, and only the man was left to guard them.

He sat watch as the sun dried his clothes, and an unwholesome sweat dampened them again. He held fast as his shivering stopped, and an uncontrollable tremor replaced it. He kept the promise he'd made, even as he was afflicted by the one that had been extracted from him.

In the end, it was impossible to stay.

So the man, Hakai, stood and walked down to the river, where the voice, Fuseau, waited to receive him.

PORTÉ WAS AWAKENED by a disturbance in the water. They opened their eyes to a kin-shaped figure swimming downwards, whitening for attention.

By the time they were close enough to sign, there was

no mistaking them: that was Entrechat, the swiftest and second-brightest of the Many... brightest, now.

They stayed just long enough to deliver their message, their gestures uncharacteristically constrained. *The earthling came back*, they said. *Prince Jeté is calling for us.* Entrechat spared a glance for Bombé, but did not need to add the obvious: their crippled sibling could not keep up, and would have to be left behind.

Porté would not argue the point – but nor would they leave so quickly. *I'll be right behind you*, they promised. And as Entrechat swam off, Porté tried to think of an appropriate goodbye. *Don't worry* –

But Bombé wasn't listening. They were diving down to the smallest of the three graves, rooting through the delicate layer of stones with a strange, profane urgency.

What on earth...?

It was no use signing – Bombé wouldn't see it. Porté dove down afterwards, intending to bodily accost their sibling. But even as they reached out, Bombé pulled something up from the cairn and thrust it into their sibling's grasping hand.

Porté didn't even have time to flinch. They floated there, staring stupidly at the thing in their hands, until the current began to pull them downstream.

This was Flamant-Rose's bag of treasures – the little sack they'd used to keep all the most interesting rocks they'd found on the trip. The one they'd emptied and filled over and over again, struggling to find some arrangement that would let them fit in just one more stone without spilling.

By and by, Porté noticed its sibling's gestures.

– must have fallen out. But I think most of them are still there. You should take it with you.

The tie-strap and draw-strings waved in the water, still fed through the slits in the mouth of the bag. Flamant-Rose had worn it as a belt... but it would never, ever fit Porté.

They watched dumbly as Bombé took the bag away. They floated useless in the current as their wounded sibling tied the straps. And they did not object as the belt was fashioned into a crude necklace, and the bag became an oversized amulet, and the weight of all those little stones drifted down to hang with firm finality around Porté's neck.

When they finally glanced up, Bombé's black gaze was waiting to meet them.

Thank you, Porté said, their colors softening with a sentiment too immense for words.

Bombé's colors remained dull and fixed. *Get it done.*

Too late, Porté understood. The bag of stones was not a gesture of love. It was a mortal obligation, a guarantee that they would not falter or fail in their duty – a promise that Porté would do in Flamant-Rose's name what Bombé would have done for Princess Ondine... no matter how grim or sinister the task.

And who could say no to that?

I will, Porté replied, though the sign came out small and sloppy, and swam up before their sibling could question their resolve. They glanced back, just once, to see Bombé finish replacing the cairn-stones over Flamant-Rose's body and resume swimming in relentless, tethered circles.

It was hard to know what to think about that... and not for the first time, Porté was powerfully glad not to be asked to think.

At any rate, it wasn't hard to find the others: a

churning cluster of legs and tails distorted the glittering light from above, casting scissoring freshwater shadows as the Many watched something of interest in the air-breathing world. Porté surfaced into the blinding sunlight, their inner eyelids clearing to show them a repeat of the scenario they'd witnessed yesterday: there was Prince Jeté, squatting majestic and serene at the shoreline, and Fuseau translating for the blindfolded earthling before him.

Porté was impressed in spite of themself. They knew the earthling had been blackmailed somehow – Jeté would never have let him go without first ensuring his return – but they'd missed out on the gossip while paying respects with Bombé. What invisible string had pulled him back here?

Well, whatever it was, it was all but choking him: this time, the human man was just standing there, dry and dignified – but if anything, he seemed more distraught now than before.

Please, you promised to give it back to me, Fuseau's hands translated.

Prince Jeté bared his gum-ridges in a sneer, revealing a small canister clasped between them. *And you promised to lead us to the monster,* he replied. *We will return your dirty treat when she is dead.*

As Fuseau rendered the signs into foreign words, Jeté turned his head and spat the canister at the Many. Plié caught it, and passed it to Demi-Plié as quickly as if it might explode. Porté squinted, brimming with curiosity. What could it be?

The man was talking again, his voice fear-sodden and stammering. *Yes, but I need it to keep helping you. I'll be ill without it.*

The answer was swift and pitiless. *Then you had better satisfy us quickly. We won't –*

Porté registered a rough poke in the arm. "Here, take it," Tournant whispered, and passed them the canister.

Porté stared at the innocuous little tin. It was round and plain, probably watertight, with years of accumulated dents and scratches marring the black-and-yellow print on the lid. It wouldn't have been legible even if Porté knew the language. "What? Why me?"

Tournant jerked their head to the half-empty bag hanging at Porté's chest. "Because you're the one with somewhere to put it!"

Well, there wasn't much arguing with that. Porté shut up to do as they were told... but not before sneaking a peek at the contents. It was light, but not empty, and didn't rattle when shaken. Something was in there, but what?

Kicking harder to put their head and shoulders well out of the water, they closed their webbed fingers over the tin and carefully pried it open. There was something brown and mounded inside, like dried grass clippings – but the first whiff told Porté everything they needed to know.

They shut the tin hurriedly, before anyone caught them snooping, and watched the earth-man's pleas with a sinking heart. Poor fool... no wonder he'd come back.

– *between two hills,* the man was saying, *which the People of the Crow call the Red Brothers. It's the entrance to the southern path up the mountain, which is called the M-A-I...*

The translation slowed as Fuseau began to spell a strange word, and the sharp, sweet aroma from the little tin lingered in Porté's mind.

Back home, *tarré* was one of half a dozen spices kept stocked in the larder. One couldn't imagine mackerel-cabbage or mussel stew without it. But only the master-chef was allowed to add the *tarré*, because it had to be kept locked up. For mereaux, it was a pleasant, savory seasoning – but for earthlings, it was a ruinously addictive drug. In the House of Losange, any human fosterlings caught with it had to be cast out at once: they would inevitably spread their addiction to others, and if an overdose didn't kill them, the withdrawal probably would.

– and I'll be glad to show you the way, if you would graciously allow me one pipeful, just a pinch –

Porté couldn't bear to watch the translation any more. They shouldn't have cared at all – not after a tragedy of such magnitude, and not when half of it was the result of this earth-man's collusion with the traitor Champagne. And yet somehow, watching this poor warm-blooded worm beg for his life's last pleasure was all that much more pitiable: sadness after sadness, and waste following waste.

Porté treaded water, holding themself upright and visible in case Prince Jeté would change his mind and want to give the earthling some relief after all. But no mercy was given, and when the audience was over, Porté was glad to tuck the terrible little tin away in the bag, pull the drawstrings taut, and follow its siblings underwater, where they didn't have to hear any human voice, or abet the torment of any living thing.

Soon. It would all be over with soon.

Maybe it could even be over now. Maybe there was some other way, some other price that wouldn't demand death and more death. After all, weren't the House of the Crow rich and powerful, and wasn't this mostly their fault anyway? Couldn't they be made to give up one of their own royal children to replace Princess Ondine – a human ward to come and live with the House of Losange? After all, that was how the Emboucheaux handled things between themselves. And of course it wouldn't do to question the prince directly, but perhaps if Porté could get a private word with Fuseau –

Porté halted as they realized that nobody was going to the river-bottom – that the cohort had not been dismissed. Prince Jeté had turned and crawled into the water, but stopped in the shallows, when he was barely submerged. This wasn't usual. Something else was happening.

Porté dug their toes into the rocky sediment, holding themselves in place within easy noticing-distance of their greatest sibling, and waited for his instruction.

Jeté's metamorphosis had darkened him handsomely. But now he paled to his old, juvenile coloring – white down his front, a soft blue-green over his back and sides, as he had been when he himself was one of the Many. This was a captain taking off his coat, a commander dismounting to address his troops as a level-footed equal, and as his heavy haunches settled and the water cleared, Jeté's vast amber eyes regarded the cohort with fraternal affection.

Myselves, he addressed them, *I have failed you.*

Some of the cohort whitened in surprise and protest, but none ventured to interrupt their prince's graceful gestures.

I have failed you. The fault which has brought us to this unforgivable sadness is mine. And I am sorry that the burden of correcting it must fall equally between us.

Jeté closed his eyes, a blink as slow and old as a grandmother-river. *You know that I did not seek to carry our house's name. Just so, I know that you did not choose this task. There is no shame in acknowledging our fears, our doubts, our regrets. In the end, we have only to do what is asked of us, in love and bravery. Our Mother asks for nothing more.*

Porté knew he was telling the truth. Placid, steadfast Jeté had never wanted to become one of the Few. Tournant had always been the ambitious one. But Mother had selected Jeté, and they – he, now – had undergone the painful change with as much stoic dignity as anyone could have wanted. Now he was asking the rest of his siblings to follow his example.

But what they were about to do...

We cannot bring back our dear Ondine, Jeté continued, the water sharpening with his grief-taste as he made the two-handed undulating wave that was her name-sign. *But even as her life was the last given to our house, we pledge that her death will be the first paid for. Promise me this, myselves. Promise it with me.*

The cohort repeated the sign, copying Jeté's colors as they did. *Promise.*

But Porté's doubts only grew louder. The monster had slaughtered Ondine in five effortless seconds. In the time it needed to spring on her, and bring them both crashing down into the water, it had already torn out her throat. Who could stand against a thing like that?

But there was something else in the water now – an odd, intoxicating flavor mixed in with the taste of Jeté's grief. Porté flexed their toes in the sediment, fidgety and strangely impatient.

And we promise this not because we hold Ondine

more dearly than our Pirouet, our Flamant-Rose, but because they have trusted us to carry their share of the burden – to act in love and bravery on their behalf. Believe that they go with us, myselves. Believe with me.

Believe, the cohort signed back, this time in almost perfect unison. The taste grew stronger, making Porté's gill-plumes prickle and ripple with desire. In that moment, they could have carried *any* burden, swum to the sea and back and thrashed any treacherous earth-person who got in the way – oh, if only there was someone to beat!

They didn't believe, though. They didn't believe that their slain siblings would have wanted this.

We will destroy the monster who has taken our dear princess. We will destroy the traitor Champagne. And when they are dead, we will take the man who shot our Pirouet, our Flamant-Rose, and you will decide his fate. Fight for them, myselves, in love and bravery. Fight with me.

Fight, Porté signed back, stiffening with the barely-suppressed urge to do exactly that – and too late, they realized what was in the water.

Jeté had been one of the Many, yes. Now he belonged to the Few – the rare mereaux whom Artisan had gifted with sex, with gender... with power. Female and male, she'd made them – mothers and consorts, tailed and tailless, nurturing and commanding, in love and in war.

Now love was dead, and there was only war.

Porté had heard stories of princes in battle – how they used their war-voice on land to terrify the enemy, and seeped rage into the water to inspire their cohorts. *One taste*, the old-timers would say, *and you aren't Many anymore.*

We have been Many, Jeté was signing, his colors darkening again. *Now we must be One. One from Many. Many to One.*

The cohort was darkening too, swelling and mottling to a sinister crimson-black. *One from Many*, they repeated. *Many to One.*

No, Porté tried to say, even as the rage gripped their body and clouded their mind. *This isn't love or bravery. They wouldn't want this. Flamant-Rose wouldn't want us to do this.* The weight of the stones hung heavy around their neck, the cords of muscle underneath straining against the urge to wreck something. With a titanic effort, Porté tore their gaze away from the prince to seek agreement from their siblings, to see whether anyone else understood that too...

... but the others were already gone. Already their eyes were going hard and fixed, and the thousand tiny tells that distinguished one from the next were fading away. Rambunctious Plié and Demi-Plié, eager Entrechat and fair-minded Fuseau, and even rude, rough Tournant... all were melting down into a single many-bodied extension of their prince's will. All alike. All the same.

Stop, wait, Porté's ebbing mind urged. *One from Many,* their hands said.

They looked back to Jeté, pleading with him through their eyes as their heart raced and their muscles clenched. *This isn't right. This isn't us.* They were Porté, they fought to remind themselves, one of Many – a stevedore, a helper, a good sibling, a bad-joke-teller, a strong and gentle mover of things... *Please don't do this. Please, please don't make me do this.*

Then Jeté's vast amber gaze met them, and an eddy in the current jostled the bag of stones into a brief and fatal weightlessness, and Porté could not recall any reason why they ought to resist. They'd wanted this. They always had.

They had wished to be alike with their siblings, as matched and perfect as eggs in a roe – and now they were. They had wished to be useful, valuable – and now they would be. They would make the man and the monster and the traitor Champagne matched and perfect with Ondine and Pirouet and Flamant-Rose. Two small bodies and one large one. All alike. All the same.

So they drank in the rich, thickening rage until nothing else was left – until Porté, one of Many, finally became One.

CHAPTER FOUR
THE GLASS KEY

THE EARTHLY GODS had no tongues – that was what Weisei had said. They could speak only through the hearts of those who sought to listen.

So as Día walked higher and farther into the high desert sunlight, she listened... but not too much.

Puppy, the voice echoed, for perhaps the ten thousandth time. *Big puppy. Strange puppy. Sad.*

Día was not about to answer back. She let the voice pull her toward it, mindful to hold her own thoughts high and apart, as if she were carrying a bowl of corn porridge with a lunging dog circling around her.

That was the easy part. It was harder to know what path to take: the Dog Lady could not have been more than a few miles away, as the crow flew – but Día was no crow, not even an a'Krah, and finding her way through the strange, alien foothills of Marhuk's domain was a slow and laborious task. Weisei's directions were as well-meant as they were impractical: the tree he had cited must have been cut down or blown to flinders by lightning, and the fresh wildcat droppings dissuaded her from trying the footpath she found, and even a lifetime of going barefoot had not made her soles tough enough for the razor-edged scree that littered the nearer slope of the great red hill. By the time Día finished backtracking and picked her way around to the other side, half the afternoon was gone, and she was footsore and famished.

So she sat in a shady hollow and ate from the cold venison steak, squelching the temptation to loiter in the dry bluestem: she would not like to find herself still out here alone when night fell.

Then again, did she really want to see what the Dog Lady would become at sunset?

Loves-Me. He-Loves-Me.

The waxy deer-grease lingered on her tongue as she brushed herself off to resume her meticulous course – an unpleasant reminder of the soap Miss du Chenne had been so fond of applying to the mouths of impertinent children. Día could not have said why she had appeared in that strange nightmare, though she was as unwelcome there as anywhere else: Miss du Chenne had been a bad teacher and an even worse foster-mother, and Día would not forgive her for running off and leaving poor Fours to try and parent a human child alone.

Child. Human child. Earth child. Mine. Mine. Mine.

Día stopped with one foot on an out-jutting rock. That was too close for coincidence. Could the Dog Lady hear her? Was she listening, even now? Or was Día beginning to lose her reason again? It was a warmer day than yesterday, but nothing like the heat of Island Town's river valley.

The wind picked up, a strong gust pushing Día forward, and she couldn't resist glancing up at the afternoon sun. God had made human beings with earth and fire – that was what the Verses said. Mereaux were born of earth and water. And above them were the angels: bodiless beings of air and fire, spirits of divine inspiration. Día did not dare stare at the sun looking for a telltale shimmer in the air – that was how her mother had been caught, all those years ago – but she quickened her pace, willingly pushed along by the wind at her back, and her thoughts picked up in tandem.

A child – a half-human child. The Dog Lady's child. The whole cause of that bloody disaster in Weisei's story, the reason the Dog Lady had apparently dragged Día through half the entire loveless desert, the source of her strange, awful transformation that night after the fire, as she tore someone apart looking for him...

... or having already found him?

Lost puppy. Stolen puppy. Mine.

Día remembered clinging to that huge, furry back as she – they – plunged into the water. She remembered tearing apart a living, thrashing body. And she remembered that last, desperate echo in her own mind, pleading for rescue as the great lady's jaws closed around some other drowning soul, pulling him from the water even as she abandoned Día to the mercy of the current. The Dog Lady wasn't looking for her baby anymore. She had already found him.

So then why such sadness? Had she been mistaken? Had he died?

Día's foot slipped, sending loose stones spilling down the little rise as she hurried on. Her thoughts flashed to the a'Krah's missing manservant, but Vuchak had described him with gray hair. Not him. Not their slain prince, either – that was Marhuk's child.

No, the Dog Lady had been lying with settlers, Weisei

said. Eadans. White people. And the only white person she'd seen out here had stolen the horse right out from underneath her and vanished.

Half white, she belatedly realized. The Dog Lady's child must have been half white.

Now see here, she'd said to the Halfwick boy, in the hour before his betrayal. *I've brought his horse, his shirt, and his dog –*

He'd cut her off there. *He doesn't have a dog.*

But maybe the dog had had him.

Surely not, though. Surely, surely not. Yes, Elim was mixed, and yes, he was of a plausible age – but he didn't have any marks, and he was too big to belong to anyone but the Washchaw, and besides which, he already had a family back home across the border. Even if he weren't technically theirs –

MINE. The voice in her head hit her like a gunshot. *MINE!*

Día instinctively dropped, flattening herself to the ground and clapping her hands to her ears.

Not yours, she thought back. *Not you!*

But she still felt it – someone else's anger bubbling up in her chest – someone else's grief rending her mind. *God is my one master,* she countered. *I will for nothing want. He holds me fast. I shall not waver. He lifts me up. I shall not fall.*

She went on like that, repeating the words until they were nothing but meaningless sounds – until the wild, foreign thing inside her finally went quiet.

When she finally opened her eyes and uncovered her ears, the sun was still shining, but the wind had died away. The angel of inspiration, if there had been one, was gone.

And in its place was just a voice – an ordinary mortal voice, speaking in Ardish and echoing faintly off the hills.

"... THAT for your stupid useless hide! As if I've got nothing better to do..."

Día picked herself up by inches, absently brushing the first exploratory ants from the shoulder of her cassock as she climbed up the little rise and peered over.

There was Elim, lying beside a little pool – but not the Elim she had known. This one was monstrous, massive, well past seven feet tall. His nearer hand had swollen and hardened to something twice its natural size, like a vast mottled gauntlet, and his farther foot was gone, replaced by a huge hard-walled hoof, and all over him, from his bare chest to his naked left eye, his every spot and patch glistened with a coat of fine brown hair.

And there beside him, almost as an afterthought, was Miss du Chenne.

"– ROTTEN, UNGRATEFUL CHILD – I should have drowned you when I had the chance! And after everything I've done for you –"

A stone tumbled down the slope. Someone was there. Shea shut her mouth and camouflaged in an instant, blanching to a rocky dappled gray... but there was no hiding the boy.

She squinted, her ruined eyes just able to discern a dark shape peering over the southern lip of this pocket-sized little valley – an a'Krah?

"Miss du Chenne?"

No, not an a'Krah. A familiar voice, and a name she hadn't heard in years – used by someone who absolutely should not, should NOT be here.

"Día?" Shea dropped her camouflage and stood, closing the distance as fast as her foreshortened feet would take her. Yes, that was her – black face, black hair, black robe, black everything – standing there as dumb and incredulously as a child watching a road accident. God, what a sight!

"What is this?" Día asked weakly, her gaze riveted on the boy. "What –"

Shea didn't let her finish: she accosted her just above the elbows and shook her, her grip damp and kitten-weak. "What are you doing here?" she demanded. "You stupid, stupid girl – you're going to get yourself killed!"

Día's gaze lingered on the boy – Yashu-Diiwa, or 'Elim', as she probably knew him – and only belatedly looked down to register Shea's presence.

Then, of course, Día remembered herself. She jerked out of Shea's grasp and stared down at her, all incense and indignation. "I am not your pupil or your property," she said, "and I'll thank you not to touch me again."

Ugh. Insolent child. "Well, thank heavens for small favors," Shea snapped. "Any pupil of mine would have more sense than to wander about in the middle of the godforsaken wilderness."

They glared at each other for a moment, Shea trying hard not to look as wizened and pitiful as she felt. There was Día, who'd once been small and timid enough to pick up and carry, now looming tall and grown and fearless over her... and there was Shea, who'd once had her every instruction instantly and unquestioningly obeyed, now bald and nude and stripped of every human artifice. Easy enough to keep a classroom in line in those hard shoes, that god-awful corset, that pitiless itchy wig... but now there was nothing to hide her amputated toes, her tailless backside, her withered gill-plumes and scarred, squinting eyes. This impertinent girl had gone and turned herself into a grown woman while Shea wasn't looking, and there was no turning her back again.

How extremely tedious.

But there was still something girlish in her, or else some other reason for her hesitation. "Well," Día said presently. "Be that as it may..." Her gaze flicked again to Yashu-Diiwa's huge, useless bulk, and even Shea's poor vision could see curiosity burning through her.

That would do for a start. "You want to know about him? Answer me first: how did you get here? What did you think you were doing?" Día didn't look terribly worse for the wear – Shea could see that much – but her cassock was weathered and stained, and her prayer beads were gone, and if she had any supplies at all, they weren't on her person. "Tell me you didn't come all the way out here by yourself, and without even a pair of shoes. Tell me you aren't that stupid."

"I don't have to tell you anything," Día retorted, hands disappearing inside her pockets. "If you can't even –"

"Then tell it to Fours," Shea broke in. "Or better yet, give me the message, since you've apparently taken it into your empty god-bothering head to die out here!"

Día recoiled, stiff as a board, and some trick of the wind made her dreadlocks move like a nest of waist-length black snakes. "Since when did you ever care about Fours?"

Shea stared at her for a moment, breathless with astonishment. Then she slapped her.

And Día slapped her right back.

But she was a woman now, a full-grown earth-person, and she didn't know her own strength. Frail and unprepared, with no proper toes for balance, Shea toppled back to land with spine-jarring, ass-lacerating indignity on the sharp stones behind her. She camouflaged automatically, pain radiating up through her hips as she broke out in a predator-deterring, pointless bitter sweat.

Then, of course, Día was all shame and remorse. "Oh – I'm sorry, Miss du Chenne, I didn't mean –"

"Go to hell," Shea snarled as she righted herself, "and take him with you!"

To hell with her, and him too. To hell with all of them. She clambered over the rocks on hands and knees until she got to the little placid pool at the edge of the mountain's root, and slipped into it like a hatchling turtle going out to sea. The whole blighted world could go take a good fuck to itself – see if she cared!

THAT WAS BAD. That was a terrible, stupid, awful thing to do. Día held still as Miss du Chenne crawled away and disappeared into the little pond, fighting the urge to call out again. There went her best chance of... well, of anything, and Día had all but spit in her eye.

Why did that woman have to make everything so endlessly difficult? Día curled her fists inside her pockets. Forget compassion and empathy – if she could just be *civil* for a moment...!

Well, let her sit and stew. That pond was far too small to keep a mereau breathing: it wouldn't be even five minutes before Miss du Chenne would have to surface again, and then they'd see what her little sulking spell had done for her attitude.

Ugh. And now Día was starting to sound like her. This was all wrong.

She sat down beside Elim, mindful not to touch him, and leaned forward to pull her hair across her face. This was usually the part where she would take out her prayer beads, but they were all gone – lost or smashed or thrown away in a fit of blasphemy – and now she had nothing to comfort herself but herself. She breathed deep, relaxing into the faint, familiar smell of smoke and oil, and gathered the ends of her dreadlocks – the parts her father had backcombed and waxed himself. It had been twelve years since she'd felt his touch, but six inches of her remembered it still.

So she sat there, head down, elbows resting on her butterflied knees, holding the tips of her hair in two horizontal fists – holding her father's hands as she sought to center herself between them.

She had come this far. She had followed a dog and an angel and the directions of a holy man of the a'Krah to get here. She was right where she was supposed to be, even if she didn't yet know what to do. That was all right. She would put away anger, and guilt, and fear. She would be still and quiet. She would listen.

She let down her guard, readying herself to receive more of the Dog Lady's anxious cries. But in the still, arid afternoon, there was nothing but the sound of Elim's breathing – deep, even, and almost supernaturally slow.

Día did not look up. It would be rude to stare more than she already had, and dangerous to touch him.

But it might be all right to have a soft word.

"I'm sorry," she said to the rumpled black fabric in her lap. "I wish I had helped you down when I had the chance. I wish I had asked better questions. I wish..." *I wish none of this had happened.*

But that seemed a petty, shortsighted thing to say when the Dog Lady was newly awakened and Elim had been transformed and Halfwick was stuck in the crevice between life and death – when so many unknowable celestial gears seemed to be turning on this one time and place. "I wish I understood."

"Well," said that ageless, sexless alto, "that we might be able to arrange."

Día dropped her hair and straightened. Miss du Chenne was crouching – squatting, really – at the edge of the pool, her skin its natural blue-white color and her expression unreadable.

If this was her chance at a fresh start, Día would take it. "I'd be tremendously grateful for that," she said.

The old mereau eyed her. "Does 'grateful' include 'mannerly'?"

"Yes ma'am," Día said, and stood up to curtsey. It was a funny thing to do in a cassock. "I don't have an apple, and you don't have a desk, but I'm sure we can make do." And she stepped forward to put a handful of Weisei's jerky strips on a flat rock halfway between the two of them.

For a moment, Miss du Chenne darkened in suspicion, as if she were being patronized or humored. Then she squinted at the rock. "What foolishness is this? What are you..."

Día watched her old teacher crawl out to satisfy herself, and felt an irrational pang of remorse. She had been so fierce, so frightening back then – all spine and stride and iron-tight bun. It was hard to reconcile that memory with the wet, half-blind creature now ravenously stuffing herself with dried meat.

"Now that's more like it," Miss du Chenne said around her first mouthful. "Your *papá* must have taught you some respect after all. Now you sit right there and mind the lesson, because I don't intend to repeat myself – and when I'm finished, I will be the one asking questions. Is that clear?"

"Yes ma'am," Día said again, and folded her hem to sit in an uncharacteristically ladylike style, knees and ankles together and hands in her lap. It wasn't the most comfortable posture, and the rocky ground didn't make for a particularly fine seat – but if this was the price of enlightenment, she might yet call it a bargain.

"Now then," Shea said, when her errant student had composed herself. "Once upon a time, there was a beautiful princess... and not technically a princess, but an immortal queen, the youngest of all the earthly gods. And she wasn't exactly beautiful, either. I suppose you might call her classically handsome." Actually, she was downright homely – too much dog in her face, even in human form. Nevermind. Shea splayed her toe-stumps out over the rocks and went on.

"And her name was U'ru, the Dog Lady, and her people were the Ara-Naure. Her domain was healing, and earthly pleasures, and the love that grew between human beings and all the tame creatures of the world. She lived with her people in the Etascado river valley, in and around the place we call Island Town, and they were all very happy together. The end."

"No, it isn't." Día's voice was calm and unapologetic.

Shea decided to let this bit of juvenile contrarianism slide, and paused to help herself to more of the jerky. "Yes, it was," she said. "The rest is all tedium – history and misery, names and dates. Nothing worthwhile in any of that. What do you care who did what, and who killed who? They're all dead now anyway."

That was not true, of course. But every time the story was told, people summarized and selected, and a little more of it got lost. Shea might be the only one left alive who knew or cared that Osho-Dacha, her favorite of all U'ru's many children, had been a wild-minded boy of eight – that she had taught him how to fish, that he had stained his face with blackberries every chance he got and once made her a wig of cottonwood fluff. Soon, all that would matter was that he had been trampled to death when the Winter Wolves came – his body lying in the street just one more grisly tragedy. And then he would not even have a name anymore – he would be one of forty-five, or of fifty-eight, or whatever number some cloistered page-molester decided had died in that one of a thousand unnamed, unimportant little clashes. He would be a statistic, which would then become a footnote, which would then be shelved and forgotten. And why should Shea abet that? Why should she be complicit in that damned summary, in that genocide by abridgement, just to satisfy this squirming larva here?

But the larva had her own ideas. "He's not dead," she said, and it took Shea a moment to realize that she was talking about Yashu-Diiwa over there. "And the Dog Lady isn't either."

"Oh?" Shea said, and could not repress a teeth-baring sneer. "And pray tell, what do you know about the Dog Lady?"

Día looked away, and while Shea would never believe the girl capable of lying to her, she might very well be deciding how much of the truth to tell. "Well, I know that she misses her child. And I know that she did some terrible things while she was trying to find him. And that she had him in order to defy the people who didn't want her sheltering the –"

"No," Shea said, instantly revolted by the idea. "No, no, no." Who had been filling her head with such nonsense? Obviously Shea was going to have to clean out these garbage half-truths and start over. "Listen," she said. "What did I just tell you about her?"

Día frowned. "That her people were the Ara-Naure... that her home was the Etascado river valley... that her domain was healing and pleasure and the love of tame creatures –"

"Yes, exactly," Shea cut her off: how had she ever had the patience for this? "And how does one tame wild animals? No, don't waste my time – I'll tell you. You start with the most timid ones first. You feed them. You teach them to trust you."

"The refugees," Día said, incredulous. "She was trying to tame the white settlers, so they wouldn't keep stealing land."

"Yes, exactly," Shea said. "Now don't interrupt me. So you tame the timid ones first, and send some of them back out to coax more of the wild ones in – but they aren't really tame, of course. No matter what you do with them, they're still wild creatures at heart. If you really want to be able to trust them –"

Día put a hand over her mouth. "– you start breeding your own."

Shea gave her the eye, but only for propriety's sake – the girl always had been a quick study. "What did I say about interrupting me? Anyway, she made a grand pronouncement about it – that the Ara-Naure would bring forth a child of two worlds, one who would unite them. You know, something grand to stir up the people and buy more time from her allies. And then she got down to business."

And God, what a business it had been. Shea could still recall that rich laugh of hers, that flushed, panting, delighted face, the way she'd accost and all but drag some milk-faced man right through the middle of the camp, romping and rolling with him through every hour of the day and night, dog and woman and dog-faced woman, until he inevitably collapsed in a sweat-streaked human heap, perfectly content to die there.

"Did she love him?" Día asked – adorably assuming that there had been only one 'him'.

"Of course she did!" Shea snorted. "She loved everyone. Everything. She was drunk on it, sick with it, just – just stupidly besotted with the whole world."

And if Día wanted proof that U'ru had been criminally undiscriminating in her affections, she was staring right at it. The Dog Lady, great glorious foolish innocent that she was, had even loved Shea.

Needless to say, it had been a fatal mistake.

There was a thing in Shea's chest, like an heirloom glass, long ago packed for moving and accidentally smashed in transit. She'd been so careful, wrapped it so well beforehand that the little package still held its proper shape... but every now again she could feel it jostle, the broken pieces inside shifting and grinding, threatening to rip right through the taped paper. She would be all right, if she could just keep it still. She would be all right, if she could just pretend that the thing inside her was still whole.

"... Miss du Chenne?"

She opened one eye and glared at Día, irrationally irritated by that hoary old spinster-name. "What are you mewling about now?"

"The baby," Día repeated. "What happened to U'ru's baby?"

"For god's sake, what does it look like?" Shea snapped, flinging her arm out at Yashu-Diiwa's vast, insensible weight.

Día followed her gaze, damnably calm and rational. "It looks like he's a horse," she said. "But I don't see how that could –"

"Oh, don't you?" Shea replied with acid contempt. "Don't you know, with your pretty little necklace and your fire-starting feet and your ridiculous silly hair? Don't you know, with your dear doting *papá*?" And then in Marín, since Fours would never teach her Fraichais: *"Don't you know better than anyone?"*

Día fixed her with an icy stare. "If you have a point to make, you're doing a terrible job of it."

And if Shea had any hair of her own, she would have torn it out. "Girl," she said, with the last bottom-scraping dregs of patience and civility, "you are a human being. You are not merely the product of a sexual act. You are as much a reflection of the people who raised you as the ones who birthed you – and so is he."

Día glanced back over at the boy, and Shea did likewise. This time, she saw past his monstrosity, taking in his stained pants and his cowlicked brown hair and that horseshoe-C brand at his arm, which had once given her so much hope. *They treated him like property*, it had promised her. *They left him empty.*

"His 'folks,'" Día said, almost idly. "The people he was selling the horses for. He was so anxious to get back to them. They must love him."

"They RUINED him!" Shea cried, though it amounted to the same thing. "They took a filet mignon and fed it to their pigs – cut down a thousand-year tree to make room for their sty – found a priceless book and tore it up for the latrine! They took all that she'd given him, all his power and divinity and potential, and – and made him THIS...!"

"How?"

Shea stopped, caught off guard. "How what?"

Día raised her eyebrows, her voice too slow to be casual. "How did they find him? How were they allowed to raise him in the first place?"

She couldn't suspect the truth of course – she couldn't have the least idea about any of it – and yet Shea's guilty heart skipped. She gestured to the brand on his arm. "Obviously they bought him! What makes you think I know?"

Día rose to her feet, her expression hardening. "Well, teacher, you seem to know a tremendous amount about everything else – about her, and what she was like, and what she was planning and why. And you're as far from home as I am, just-so-happening to have camped out within kicking-distance of the child she's spent twenty-odd years hunting for. So I couldn't help but wonder –"

"– if it's my fault?" Shea interrupted, rising with equal indignity but not even half the grace. "Is that it?"

Día folded her arms. "If you ran out on her like you ran out on us."

Shea stood rooted to the spot, darkening to a livid blue-black. "Why, you atrocious little shit –"

A psychic scream knifed through her mind, so sharp and sudden that Shea camouflaged in an instant. That was U'ru. Something was wrong.

"What's happening?" Día cried, hands over her ears in a futile effort to ward off a noise that had completely bypassed her hearing.

Dumbstruck as she was, it took Shea a moment to understand that. "You can hear her too?"

Before Día could answer, another scream ripped through Shea's mind, and spread out from there. Suddenly she was tasting fresh dirt, smelling foul water – and all but deafened by a multi-throated amphibious war cry.

Oh, shit.

"Where is she?" Día cried, shaking her head as if to clear it. "How do we get to her?"

"You're not going anywhere," Shea snapped, loping over to the western slope as fast as her wounded lung and foreshortened feet could take her. "You stay and watch him, and I'll –"

A cavernous, rumbling *FRRRROOOOOOOOAAAK* crashed through Shea's mind – and also reverberated off the western hills.

Just like that, Día took off running.

Just like that, she had bounded effortlessly over the ledge and disappeared down the farther slope.

Just like that, Shea was left in the dust.

"God DAMMIT." Swearing in three languages, Shea hurried after her, with no more thought to spare for the boy: if U'ru's last child were slain, it would destroy her

– but if Prince Jeté's cohort caught her now, trapped in mortal form during the daylight hours, they would kill her. And if Fours ever found out that Shea had let his errant foster-daughter get herself killed likewise – by every god, Shea would never hear the end of it.

So she hopped and hustled and skidded along: too old to keep up, too cynical to hold any hope, and too bloody-minded to let the world go to hell without her.

WHERE ARE YOU? Día steeled herself for the answer even as she asked the question.

The reply was an avalanche. *Cave. Hiding-cave. Dirt-sticks-water-dark-yell-snap-bite –*

Wait. Día cut her off for her own sanity. *Wait – don't drown me – I'm coming.* It was a poor formulation, one only half expressed in words: Día was running at breakneck speed, bounding between rocks and sliding down sheets of foot-biting gravel, and she absolutely could not afford any confusion of her senses.

Even so, there was no telling which of them was responsible for the terror swelling in Día's heart, save to know that it belonged to someone in immediate fear for her life. As she raced the little mountain creek downstream, drowning out everyone's thoughts with a constant, wordless prayer not to put a foot wrong, Día imagined the hand of the Almighty closing around her, as it had back at Yaga Chini: His palm at her back, His fingers folding over her shoulders, His grip gentle and firm and unyielding. She did not stop to imagine what would be waiting for her, or what she would do when she found out. She did not speculate on what would happen if she failed. Instead, the small part of her not busy negotiating between her feet and the ground gathered up the fear that belonged to her, and the fear that didn't, and offered them both to a higher power.

"STOP!" The word was out of her mouth before she even knew what she was doing – before she saw anything more than a crimson-black swarm massing at the foot of the hill.

There was a peculiar echo to her voice, the sound coming through the Dog Lady's ears as much as through Día's own skull-bones, and maybe the prince of the mereaux heard it too: he turned his leviathan bulk in Día's direction, and froze everyone on the spot with a single sonorous *HRUM*.

That included Día. She stopped, helpless not to stare – at him, at his glistening muscular mass, at his pulsating throat-pocket and cold amber eyes, at the way the others gathered around him like so many tadpoles hiding in the shadow of a century toad.

And now that she had the attention of this primordial titan, Día had very little idea what to do with it. "Thank you," she said for starters. *Where are you?*

She felt the answer like a heat-beacon: there was a little rocky overhang not twenty feet to Día's right, a cave with a mouth like a tight-lipped grimace, so narrow that Día would have had to lie down and flatten herself to get inside. No wonder the mereaux hadn't gotten to the Dog Lady yet – but she was truly trapped.

Come out, Día thought at her, and edged closer to it. *Come to me.* "I'm sorry," she said aloud. "I came to tell you that I'm sorry – WE'RE sorry."

The mereaux stared at her, their blood-feud colors fading not at all, and Día noticed that their weapons weren't spears and tridents, as she'd first thought, but rakes and hoes – garden tools repurposed for war. Where on earth had they all come from?

Their prince settled back onto his vast thighs, and made a sign with his hands – something that looked like a bird in flight.

Día glanced up, half-expecting to see crows flying overhead. *It's me*, she belatedly realized, and looked back down at her hands – the ones whose color had so nicely complemented Weisei's. *They think I'm a'Krah.*

That might be useful, especially if they understood that they were guests in Marhuk's domain. And she didn't need to live the lie very long – just long enough for Miss du Chenne to catch up and sort this out... somehow.

So Día put her wrists out in the gesture of supplication Weisei had showed her, and tried to remember the words that went with them. *"Kalei ne ei'ha,"* she said, even as that foreign canine second-mind flattened and pressed and rolled itself between a dirty floor and a rocky ceiling. "Please see me kindly."

But what the mereaux saw was the person – the being – who was currently inching her way out from under the lip of the overhang, and the first glimpse of her was enough to incense the prince all over again.

"HRRRRK!" At his first enraged bellow, the other mereaux surged forward, garden-weapons raised for a brutal, messy kill.

Día leapt forward to put herself between them and the cave, holding her arms out and sending a great burst of fire through the soles of her feet. It didn't catch – there was nothing very much to burn – but the smoke and stench and sheer pyrotechnic surprise was enough to halt the attackers again.

"I'm sorry," she repeated, in Ardish this time, wishing

to high heaven that Fours had taught her Fraichais or that Miss du Chenne would hurry up. "*We're sorry. We're very sorry. Please don't hurt us.*" Día ransacked her memory for the collection of Fraichais words she knew had to be in there, struggling to wring something relevant out of all the hours she'd spent poring over the works of Glaçure and Fondre – but for all their groundbreaking investigation into the nature of energy transfer and matter conservation, none of their research had yielded anything as useful as an apology.

Sorry? The questioning voice bloomed in her mind. Día looked over, astonished to see a human woman standing beside her.

From a distance, Día would have seen just a plain native woman: dark eyes, russet skin, and a plump matronly figure wrapped in a brown fur robe. But here, not even an arm's length away, there was no mistaking her for an ordinary person. From her baby-soft bare feet to the dead leaves stuck through her disheveled black hair to her long, deep-nosed face – a feminine copy of Elim's – the Dog Lady was exactly what she appeared to be: an ageless, frightened spirit in human form, staring at Día with fathomless confusion. *Why sorry?*

She must not have understood, or maybe she didn't remember. *You – you and I, we hurt someone,* Día thought, reviving her memory of that sudden, arresting blood-lust, that snarling plunge into the water, the thoughtless, heedless rage with which they had closed their jaws over living flesh and shaken it like a dog snapping a hare's neck. The Dog Lady probably didn't know any more than Día who that had been, or what had become of them afterwards, but they surely were some relation to this angry mob here. *We have to tell them we're s –*

NO. The answer was so loud and hateful that Día flinched. For a moment everything in her was outrage – outrage at the water-babies who had netted and dragged her stolen puppy away, outrage at the water-daughter who was even then carrying him away across the river, outrage and blind murderous fury for everyone and everything between her and him –

"STOP!" Día cried aloud, earning a blink from the prince of the mereaux, and resisted the urge to turn and berate the mute mother-goddess beside her. *You don't have any idea what you've done – you don't even realize what you've gotten us into –*

"He can't understand you," came a faint voice from far in the back of the amphibious mob. There was someone there, a human man, almost invisible in his dirty earth-colored clothing. "And they won't listen. He's done something to them." He was a gray-haired native, plain and average except for the black cloth over his eyes and a sickly sheen over his brown skin. This had to be the a'Krah's missing manservant – what was his name?

The mereaux prince turned, rumbling a warning at this impertinent interruption, but Día had to try her luck. "What do I do?" she called back. *Help me,* she begged U'ru. *Help me get us out of this.*

She spared only a glance for the Dog Lady, whose long features reflected a slowly-dawning concern – as if she were only then realizing that what happened now mattered to people outside herself. *Sorry,* she said, though it was impossible to tell whether anyone but Día could hear it – or what she was apologizing for. *Help.*

"One of them is a translator," the man called back. "If you can get its attention –"

He was cut off by a wet snarl from the prince. *Call her here*, Día thought, with as strong an image of Miss du Chenne as she could conjure. *Tell her to hurry.*

"Which one?" she called, as much to wrest the prince's attention away from the man as anything else.

It worked all too well. The frustrated prince flushed blood-red and sucked in a breath for the battle-cry that would end the unauthorized parley and unleash his cohort...

... and Día, in a moment of divinely-inspired panic, touched her thumb and fingertips together and then sent them from her lips.

I love you. It was the only freshwater sign she knew. Fours, in wisdom and paranoia, had refused to teach her any other signs, knowing that the least suspicion of her being in league with the hated 'fishmen' would ruin her. But her *papá* was also a lonely soul, a forgotten spy thirty years removed from his own home and kin, and the love-sign he shared with his secondhand daughter was his one act of defiance – a secret, silent familial code.

The prince's throat-pocket deflated, his colors fading in confusion. He sat back again, replying with a long string of signs whose meaning Día couldn't begin to guess. She repeated the love-sign again, making eye-contact with each of the mereaux in turn – a glass key trying one iron lock after another. Which one was the translator?

Coming, U'ru thought, and for a moment Día's webbed toe-stumps were limping along on the same painfully sharp stones she had kicked up not five minutes ago. *Water-Dog coming.*

"Which one?" Día asked again, without a glance to spare for the manservant. The mereaux were almost ruthlessly uniform to her eyes, naked and indistinguishable save for their weapons.

"I don't know," the man called back, his voice taut with controlled fear. "I'm – I can't tell them apart."

Well, he'd probably have more luck if he took off that blindfold of his, but there was no time to quibble. Día's roving gaze fell on a big mereau near the back, holding a net and wearing a weighted bag around its neck. What did that signify? *I love you*, she repeated, her brown eyes fixating on the mereau's black ones, her fingertips moving from her lips towards theirs specifically. It was literally a feeding-gesture, Fours had told her once, the act of giving food from one's own mouth, and she mimed chewing just in case that might make it more real. *I love you. I feed you. I love you.*

The big mereau blinked. Their colors wavered, that ruthless, thoughtless crimson-black lightening towards a beautiful cobalt blue, and Día dared to hope that she had chosen right – that this was their translator. *I love you*, the mereau repeated, the net still tangled in their fingers, the glaze slowly fading from their eyes.

Día could have jumped for joy. "Help me," she said, as slowly and clearly as her trembling voice could manage. "Help me talk to him. We're here to apologize – we didn't mean to hurt you. Can you tell him that? Will you help us?"

Please, she thought as hard as she could, petitioning God and the Dog Lady and all the mereaux massed before her, praying to anyone who would listen that this might still be saved – that somewhere in this grievous angry jumble of signing and thought-sharing and hopelessly crude mouth-languages, a spark of understanding might still catch. *Please, please help us.*

But the big mereau's brow furrowed in confusion or sadness, and when they spoke, it was in a fearful whisper. "*J'ne comprends pas.*"

That was all it took. The prince whipped around to hunt for the traitor in his ranks. The big mereau panicked, instantly camouflaging to match their kin. And when the prince didn't find the guilty party, it took him no time at all to rear back, pick up a child-sized piece of jagged granite, and hurl it at his enemies.

Día dodged. U'ru did not. It hit her full in the chest, slamming her back into the rocky overhang with a sickening wet yelp.

"Run!" the blindfolded man called, pointing away up a trail between the twin hills.

Día staggered, dizzied by U'ru's pain – but there was no time to lose. The prince's bellowing war-cry spearheaded the charge: in an instant, the whole crimson-black cohort came boiling up the slope, bearing down with blades and edges.

The rock had crushed U'ru's foot. She clutched her robe to her chest and stared at the onrushing horde, breathless with shock. With one superhuman shove, Día rolled the stone away, grabbed U'ru's hand, and tore off running.

There was no telling where the trail went – but it wasn't going to get them there fast enough. Día tried to conjure that divine swiftness she had felt the night of the fire, when she was nothing but surety and alacrity and cinder-kindling grace. But her surety had come from the mother dog at her side, and the dog was now a helpless woman, and the woman was limping on a broken foot, gasping with broken ribs, threatening with every agonized uphill step to collapse in the dust.

Come on, Día thought, irrationally doubling down on her own breathing to compensate. *Come on come on come on –*

A thrown rake narrowly missed, clattering to the ground inches away. The net didn't. The latticed ropes slapped over Día and U'ru, bringing them down in a tangled heap of pain and confusion. Día writhed and turned, fighting to free her knife, fantasizing about cutting their way out, stepping on the dry fibers and setting them alight before she hurled the whole burning mass right back at her attackers –

– but as her fur-clad companion froze in terror and the red-streaked raging horde closed in, Día's last prayer was that it would all be over quickly.

THE MAN, HAKAI, did not join in the frenzied blood-rush. He staggered a few steps behind them, slow and sick and safely forgotten, until he stood at the base of the vast craggy hill overlooking the west side of the trail.

Then he planted his feet and bowed his head.

The cohort rushed up the trail.

He began to breathe faster, his fingers picking nervously at nothing.

The two women fell, ensnared by the flying net.

He turned his sweat-stained face to the sky, his small earthy figure weak and trembling.

The cohort swarmed forward for the kill, their prince croaking encouragement as he trundled along behind, their dark bodies all but swallowed by the shadow of the mountain's foot.

Then the man, Hakai, said a word to the hill.

And the hill collapsed.

CHAPTER FIVE
MEAT

AH CHE, A CHILD of *seven winters, peered out from behind his mother at the strangers standing in the street.*

They were peculiar people, tall and badly-dressed, with mixed faces and heavy, ugly boots. They were supposed to become Maia – that was what his father had said – but Ah Che didn't see how. The strangers didn't know any real words, or any manners, either. They didn't know anything. Just that morning, their older child – Ah Che couldn't tell whether it was a boy or a girl or both – had tried to climb down into the kiva, where only men could go.

Mama must have seen him staring at the other children: she looked down at him and clicked. "Go on," she said, nodding out to where Ah Set had already gone to greet the younger child, to see whether they would understand the circle game. "Be friendly. Teach them how to play."

Ah Che clutched his hoop and stick tighter. It was unthinkable not to share – he knew that – and yet his feet didn't want to move. He had none of his brother's bravery. "What if they break it?"

Mama shifted the baby in her arms and smiled. "Then you'll teach them how to make a new one."

"– FAITHLESS, EYELESS, POXY *son of a milk-drinking Eaten whore!*"

Vuchak finished with another bone-jarring strike of the stone in his hand. His wrath had all but powdered the jerky on the flat rock below... for all the good that did.

Weisei stood a few paces off, arms folded in disgust. "Are you done yet?"

"No." Vuchak switched hands and put a fresh meat-strip on the stone, willing it to become Hakai's insufferable face. "*He's a tribeless, traitorous, godforsaking bastard – a shit-picking goat-fucker – a rat I should have left to drown!*"

He had to stop then, as much to catch his breath as to craft a suitable Marín expression for 'mangy-balled childless masturbator'. Even if ei'Krah had words to do it justice, Vuchak wouldn't use them here.

But that gave the aching weariness in his bones enough time to seep back out into the rest of him, and his free-soul enough time to remind him of how deeply unproductive this was, and by the time Vuchak had enough wind to resume his venison-vengeance, he'd lost his appetite for it. He sat back and glowered at the stones. "I never trusted him anyway."

Weisei rolled his eyes. "We're wasting time."

Wasn't that the truth. Hakai had turned traitor, which meant that they couldn't afford to stay here and wait for him to lead the fishmen back to their camp. They had to move. That meant packing up, and THAT meant breaking down the makeshift drying rack... figuring out how to turn it into a travois for Dulei... mixing the pemmican... cleaning and stowing the dishes... finding some way to pack the remains of the deer, since half their bags had burned up in the fire. It was an ant-hill of a list – individually simple, collectively impossible – and just thinking about it all was enough to make Vuchak nauseous. He rubbed his face. He could count his sleep-hours on the fingers of one hand, and with no wholesome source for energy, he had nothing to draw from but anger.

"Whose fault is that?" he snapped, striving to re-kindle the dwindling fire inside him.

"Yours." Weisei might have been deliberately feeding Vuchak's efforts, or simply running out of patience.

Regardless, Vuchak would take it. "Mine?" he retorted. "Am I the one who abandoned the people who saved my miserable skin? Am I the one who walked off in the middle of the day, after making you grand elaborate promises about staying? Am I the one who betrayed us?"

"You don't know that," Weisei replied. "We don't know what they did to him, or why –"

It was a wretched thing, running on anger – an endless cycle as self-sustaining and counterproductive as licking one's lips in a blizzard.

Still, it did work. Vuchak found the strength to haul himself up to his feet, rising to the argument. "We know there are only one set of footsteps leading down to the river," he interrupted, "and that no shoeless people could come inside our camp-circle without getting a footful of cactus-hairs. So the only way that belly-crawling eggsucker could have –"

The ground shook. It was faint, just a tremor – but that was enough. Vuchak held still and waited to see whether it would happen again. "Weisei, did you feel –"

"Vichi, look!"

Vuchak followed his *marka*'s upturned chin to the north, where a flock of crows had just taken flight. One of the Red Brothers was collapsing.

He stood there, dumbstruck, watching the western slope of the hill disintegrate like a pile of dry beans. It wasn't a rockslide, not anything that started from the top. Rather, it was as if someone had scooped away part of the hill's foot, leaving everything above it to slide down like so much corn flour.

Vuchak and Weisei stared, watching a giant dust cloud waft languidly up into the air. Silence stretched out between them.

"... I think we should take the eastern trail," Weisei said at last.

Vuchak could not have agreed more. Whatever had just happened on the southern side of the mountain was entirely beyond their feeble power. Marhuk would have to sort that one out himself.

Vuchak made the sign of an unfathomable god, and wearily turned his attention to the packing. "Let's get started."

By THE TIME the terror in Shea's mind finally ebbed, she was ready to lie down and let the heart attack claim her. U'ru's contagious panic – so like what she'd felt thirty years ago, when the Winter Wolves had first trampled and burned their way through the Ara-Naure camp – had Shea running and skidding and scrambling over sharp rocks and treacherous gaps until she was gasping like a hooked trout.

Then, as now, Shea was too late to do anything... but maybe this time she wasn't needed. She halted as the earth shook, rooted to the spot by a fear all her own – and then felt U'ru's panic lift and dissipate in tandem with the dust cloud rising before her. She was alive, albeit in pain, and Día was safe.

Thank the gods for that, Shea thought.

The answer was quick and cold: *Not the gods. Not you. Black puppy.*

So U'ru was still angry with her, then.

Her name is Día, Shea thought, dropping into an exhausted squat. *Come back.*

There was a moment of hesitation, some kind of impediment to going back the way they'd come, but it was swiftly blotted out by suspicion. *Did you find my son?*

Shea was panting too hard to sigh. She had the boy, yes... but not one who would acknowledge U'ru as his mother. Not one she would recognize as her son.

Don't come to me without him. Don't speak to me again.

Then the lingering presence in Shea's mind withdrew, leaving just the cavernous echoes of her own ugly thoughts. She slumped forward, head between her knees, and waited to catch her breath.

The boy would wake soon. He would have to: that whopping monstrous body of his was healing, burning through his reserves at a fantastic rate. He was already leaner today than he had been yesterday. Soon he'd have to wake up and eat – and god only knew what Shea had to feed him. God only knew how she was going to feed herself.

She ought to work on that. She ought to have some food on hand to bribe him with, some way to make him sit still and *listen* this time.

Well, she had no chance of catching anything here on land, and there was nothing growing in enough quantity to satisfy a gut like his. She might not be too far from the river, though, and if she got there before dark, she could...

Shea lifted her head, astonished at how easily she'd forgotten to wonder about the other mereaux – and appalled to realize she'd already found them.

The dust was clearing, helped by a light western breeze. The sun was sinking behind the remains of a half-crumbled red hill whose lengthening shadow stretched out over a hundred tons of outspilled earth. And here and there amidst the rubble were bodies.

Shea blanched – a slow, stupefied camouflage as she faded into the landscape. She held perfectly still for a long minute, frightened more by the possibility that the rockslide had killed them all than the danger that it hadn't. The House of Losange would want her dead – she knew that – but as her ruined eyes raked the scene before her, hunting in vain for any slight movement, the least little sound of someone stirring, it seemed increasingly likely that none of them had been left alive.

And apparently the children of Marhuk were coming to the same conclusion: even as Shea watched, a crow fluttered down to alight on a half-buried corpse.

"Hey!" she snapped, breaking camouflage and limping forward with righteous indignation. "Who do you think you are? Go away! Shoo! Go eat your own – these aren't yours!"

The crow flew off, leaving Shea alone with the body.

It was unrecognizable, caked from head to toe in coarse

red earth, which was already turning to mud as the death-seep began. Left alone, it would lose half its water in the next few hours, which would make it far easier to excavate... but when had Shea ever done anything the easy way?

She sighed, glancing up at the late afternoon sky. Yes, she really ought to head back and see to the boy... but maybe she'd done enough fussing about him for one lifetime. Maybe the humans and their benighted gods could get along without her for a few hours. Maybe it was time to be a mereau again – just for a little while.

So Shea bent down, ignoring the cantankerous ache in her back, and set her scarred, webless fingers to digging up some company.

IN THE DREAM, *Elim was four years old and squatting in front of the wash-bucket as he starved.*

Behind him, the grace was already starting. "Come, good Master, be our guest. By your bounty, we are blessed."

He scrubbed harder, biting his tongue as he attacked his right hand again with the nail-brush – even though he'd already scoured it to bleeding, even though he already knew it wasn't going to work.

"For this bread, your will be done..."

The aroma of beans and bacon made a pain in his stomach to rival the one in his hand. He glanced back over his shoulder, hoping against hope that Ma'am might relent, but she had her head bowed and her eyes closed. The other children did likewise, their legs swinging under the table in anticipation of the meal.

Elim plunged his hand into the bucket, tears springing to his eyes as the soapy water stung his raw flesh, praying as hard as he ever had this time would be different – that this time he had scrubbed all the way down past the dirty part, past the bleeding part, to the clean white part that he was sure had to be in him somewhere.

"... we thank you, Master, every one."

But when he pulled his hand up, the only white part was the soap running down his wrist. Everything else was bastard brown and raw, runny red... just like it always was.

And the clatter of cutlery started up behind him, just like it always did, and Ma'am conducted the supper without him, just like she always had, and as Elim leaned forward to cry, as he only did when he was sure he could do it quietly enough to keep out of a switching, the drops ran down his face, salting the pink-tinged soap-water in the bucket as they disappeared.

ELIM GROANED, HOVERING somewhere between two nightmares. Something urged him to keep tacking towards the old one, the twenty-years-finished one, the one he'd long since mastered and outgrown.

But the new one had a hold of his body, and parts of it were waking up without him, each one adding its peculiar complaint until their combined clamor forced him up out of sleep like a crowbar ripping a rotted stump out of the ground.

Too late, Elim understood his mistake. Too late, he wished to have the old nightmare back again. Here in the waking world, the dog-monster had witched him somehow, and then the treacherous lying fishman had tricked him somehow, and now he was... he was...

... he was *starving*, that was what.

Elim sat up, doubling over on a full bladder and a ruinously empty stomach. The world clashed and blurred and shifted around him – something was god-awfully wrong with his eyes – but there was no sign of the monster OR the fishman. There didn't look to be anybody anywhere.

So he spent his next minutes negotiating between the ordinary and the indescribably strange. It was odd to stand up to relieve that old familiar crick in his back, and find himself a foot taller than when he'd laid down. It was unsettling to unbutton his fall-fronts for a good hearty piss and have to manage it with just his left hand, as certainly he wasn't letting his witch-twisted right one anywhere near his Goodman Thomas. And it was peculiar, just powerfully, overwhelmingly peculiar, to walk a half-dozen paces to the little pond for a drink, and feel himself clopping along on one bare foot and one big hoof.

It was a damn good one, though. Unshod, of course, but clean as a whistle. Straight, solid walls. Tight, white line. Firm frog – so strange to actually feel the pressure of his own thumb! Soft sole, too soft for this hard ground, but considering he'd literally never walked on it before...

Elim stopped as he realized what he was doing – sitting there hunched over the abomination on the end of his own leg, investigating it as idly as if he were peeling dead skin off his feet. He put a hand to the hairier side of his face, marveling first at his own lightheaded stupidity, and then at the sudden clarity in his vision. The blurry greenish-yellow-grey dropped away as soon as he covered his left eye, leaving just the world as it ought to be: green plants, reddish-brown dirt and stones, blue afternoon sky warming to orange in announcement of suppertime.

Supper. A pang of dread and hunger shot through him. Soon it would be night, and he had no gun and no shelter and no idea when the monster would be back for him, and he absolutely *had* to eat.

So Elim leaned over the pond and drank as much as his stomach could hold, the cold water outlining every inch of his puckered guts on its way down. That would do for a start.

Then he clambered up out of the little valley and followed the creek down through the foothills – because it ran to the river, and the river was where he'd left Bootjack and Way-Say and Hawkeye, and they were Sundowners but at least they were human, and God almighty, he would throw his lot back in with them in a barn-burning minute if it meant escaping the monster and the fishman and whatever other devil-spawned hellraisers lived out here.

So he kept his human hand clapped over his horsey eye and his other arm wrapped over his stomach, and did his utmost to ignore the ravening thing inside him. He'd never felt such an unholy hunger. It was like an unending punch in the gut, like a heart attack twelve inches too low, and fear did nothing to fill it up or drown it out as he stumbled along trying to calculate how long it would take to starve to death, and whether and how you felt it coming.

He hadn't wondered about that since... why, not since he was five years old, not since he'd been small enough to hunch over a wash-bucket, scrubbing and scouring and already knowing that he wouldn't get a seat at the table with the other children, because you had to have clean hands to eat at the table, and Elim's hands were never, ever clean. He curled his right one into a head-sized hard fist, imagining what Ma'am would think of it now.

But it didn't matter, did it? It hadn't mattered for twenty years. He was twenty years bought, twenty years saved, twenty years fed and taught and wanted. All he had to do was put himself back in his rightful place. All he had to do was go home.

At some point, his monstrous fist unclenched and moved up to clutch the pale, scarred horseshoe 'C' over his left arm – and thank God it was still there. The dog-monster must have hexed away his burns and wounds and bruises while he was asleep, but she couldn't erase Calvert's brand.

So Elim held it tight as he worked to whittle wash-bucket starvation back into plain old hard-work hunger, the kind he felt after he'd come in from the barn, pulled off his hat, washed his face and hands – just once, just like anybody would – and sat down to supper. He remembered the table and the linens and the parts of Boss and Lady Jane's wedding crockery that were still fit for use, because Lady Jane didn't believe in saving anything for best – or rather, didn't believe that a workaday meal with her family was anything but best. He remembered fresh garden greens and ripe summer strawberries, creamy white milk and the hot corn-bread he liked to pour it over. He remembered clasping his hands for the grace.

And by the time Elim had finished recollecting all that, his two bare feet were stumbling in tandem over the rocks, and his two human eyes agreed perfectly on the color and clarity of the world, and he was himself again.

Or rather to say: he was himself again, standing in front of the monster's cave, and staring at the fishman's rock-smashed remains.

"A LITTLE FARTHER," Día coaxed again, with an entreating tug of U'ru's hand. "Let's go just a little bit farther."

The doubt flowering in Día's mind was mirrored by the hesitation in the Dog Lady's dark eyes. She wasn't badly wounded anymore – Día couldn't see her ribs under that coat of hers, but her foot had taken less than an hour to heal – and yet she seemed to dread going further up the trail.

Stay, she answered, and made to sit down. *Wait here.*

Día worked hard not to sound as impatient as she felt. "Yes," she said, "but we don't know who still might be trying to hurt us, and it's very important that we find Miss du Chenne." And it was going to be dark soon, and Día absolutely did not want to spend the night on Marhuk's mountain.

The Dog Lady's thoughts turned cold at the mention of Miss du Chenne, and some small, petty thing in Día fed itself with the knowledge that she wasn't the only one with a less-than-pleasant opinion of the old schoolmistress.

Bad, U'ru thought with a glance up at the mountain's nearest ridges. Crows were gathering in the branches of the piñon trees. *Not welcome.*

"Yes," Día said again, struggling to measure her temper along with her words, "and that's why we have to keep going. The other trail will meet us right up there, you see," and pointed to the little crossroads about a hundred yards up and to the east, "and then we can use it to get back down again, and that way we won't stay to trespass where we aren't wanted."

The Dog Lady didn't follow her gesture. She clutched her robe with her free hand, like a child making an anxious wad of its pinafore, and her gaze wandered back out to the foothills below and behind them. *Puppy. Lost puppy.*

Día had had just about enough of 'puppy'. She was cold and footsore and thirsty, had been lectured and berated and slandered, nearly gotten herself killed and possibly abetted the deaths of a dozen others – she still didn't understand how that had happened – and for what? For this ageless, witless, tyrannical toddler here? For 'puppy'?

"Soon," she said, striving to remember that it wasn't the Dog Lady who'd abandoned Día outside Island Town – not the Dog Lady who'd made her wander in the heat. That was all Halfwick's doing.

But it *was* the Dog Lady, or at least the mother dog, who had stayed with Día through days of blistering madness and nights of shivering fear, who had guarded her and nursed her and kept her alive and safe through every trial. Now she needed the favor returned, like a frail parent reaching out to steady themselves on the arm of a grown child.

And Día would not fail her. "We'll take the other trail back down to the place where he's sleeping. I know where it is." She did not let herself picture Elim's current state, but focused her thoughts on the stone valley with the little green-ringed pool, and how safe and nice it was, and how well she would be able to take them there, if only U'ru would trust her to lead.

And she did, or at least her feet kept moving.

So Día kept thinking of confidence and certainty, and talked to reinforce it as she led U'ru – as she led her friend up the darkening mountain slope, keeping her voice strong to smother the disconcerting cawing of the crows. "It won't take us nearly as long to get down as it did to get up here, and I still have a little something we can eat if you're hungry, and as soon as we –"

Día registered the sudden tightening of U'ru's grip, half a second before a feathered missile crashed into the back of her head. Its claws tangled in her dreadlocks as it flapped and twisted, but Día didn't even have time to reach up for it before another one slammed shrieking into her face, and then another, and another, and suddenly the world was a cacophony of scratching talons and beating wings and *caah-caah-caah*.

Día screamed and bent to shield her eyes, her feet instinctively scorching the dirt and leaving her coughing, choking on acrid earth-smoke as she stumbled blindly backwards –

– and then a hand took a solid hold of her arm and pulled her back from the edge. She was led stumbling down the trail, down and further down until finally – mercifully! – the crows broke off their assault. The scratching and pecking stopped, and the cawing died away soon after. Soon the last stragglers had flown off, and there was nobody left but U'ru and Día, together and safe... somewhat.

"WHAT WAS THAT FOR?" Día shrieked at the sky, shouting to squelch the overpowering urge to cry. "We didn't – we weren't hurting anyone!"

Bad, U'ru thought again, and Día belatedly noticed that they'd gotten her too: her long black hair was even more of a tangled mess, her plump face marred by fresh red scratches. *Not welcome.*

But in spite of her injuries, her thoughts were calm and rational, which left Día's at liberty to be neither. "I don't care!" she cried. "He didn't care when the mereaux were lining up to kill us – he didn't care when half that hill dropped on them – he didn't care when you or I or Miss du Chenne were running helter-skelter anywhere else today – so why in heaven's name does he want to pick a fight now?"

U'ru's eyes wandered up to the ridge above them, the crow-laden trees silhouetted in the red light of sunset. But her mind went to a much deeper place, and though Día didn't catch more than a flicker of a feeling – of violence and grief and remorse – it was enough to remind her of Weisei's story, and the grim, matter-of-fact set to his voice.

Every sunrise, an a'Krah would be killed and the body buried upside-down in the ground, and this would continue until the infant was returned.

Día put a hand to her mouth, scarcely noticing as it came away smeared with blood. "You... you've made enemies of *everyone*." All the a'Krah she had killed... the mereaux she had somehow *gotten* killed... and Miss du Chenne, probably the only person within fifty miles that didn't actively hate her, was *persona non grata*. Who was left? Who was going to help them now?

Día stared at the thin streak of blood on her fingers, chilled to her core at its implications. Marhuk had made no distinction between the two of them, and any mereaux left alive wouldn't either. Día had already had her chance, and she had chosen to leave Vuchak and Weisei behind, to throw her lot in with this –

this *creature*, this guileless doe-eyed monster, who didn't understand anything but love and babies and slaughter. As far as the world out here was concerned, Día belonged to her now, and there was no going back.

She couldn't tell how much of that U'ru understood. There was some dim confusion from her, a faint, reciprocal anguish echoing from Día's own thoughts. But she perked up at the idea of belonging, of permanence, and reached out to enfold her troubled puppy in warmth and reassurance: she was part of the tribe now, the newest member of a vast, deathless family, and her love-mother would always be there to care for her.

Día, who could neither resist nor be comforted, felt herself pulled down to a seat. She sat there on the cold ground, her back against a stone and her front facing a wall of furry brown certainty, and looked up in a dull-eyed daze. "What now? What are we supposed to do now?"

Maternal pleasantness bloomed in her mind, accompanied by a lip-popping *pip-pip-pip* that Día could only guess was a hush-noise for someone without a tongue. It was the first sound she'd heard from U'ru's own mouth. *Stay*, she repeated. *Wait here.*

So the Dog Lady's newest disciple sat and stayed, nestled amidst the mountain's cold and darkening crags as her hair was petted and her wounds kissed, and did not think any more about anything.

THAT WASN'T CHAMPAGNE. Elim stared at the wet corpse until he was sure of it. Not at its head – not at what the rock had left of its head – but at its long, webbed toes and wide, flat tail. This was *a* fishman, but not *the* fishman – not the tailless, toeless old hellbender who had gone spouting off about dog-mothers and gratitude and then duped him into eating hemlock. There was no telling where that snake-bellied swindler had run off to, except that maybe, hopefully, it had taken the monster with it.

Or maybe the two of them were still here. It had been as dark as the Sibyl's shit-pit last time Elim passed this way, but he was middling sure that that big spilled hill hadn't been there before... and judging by the stray limbs protruding here and there, there were probably a whole passel of people whom it had taken by surprise.

Elim shivered in the cool mountain air. He needed his gun, that was what – and then he needed to light a shuck out of here.

So after a thorough inspection of the cave's narrow mouth, he lay down and wormed his way inside. It was just a little pocket in the rock, hardly enough for two people to lie down in – but sure enough, there was his gun and his poncho and the moccasin-shoes Way-Say had made for him. Even the net the fishmen had used to haul him away.

Perfect. And more perfect still, the crows had already descended on the bodies.

Elim quashed a pang of anxiety as he dragged himself around to lie on his stomach and sighted through the low opening in the rock. He knew this was the crow god's land, and that he might not take kindly to visitors picking off his black-feathered friends. At any other time, that might have been enough to put Elim off the idea: he'd already shot the old croaker's son – or maybe grandson – and didn't need any more help making enemies.

But there was nothing else to hand, and no promise of another opportunity, and at the end of the day, Elim didn't belong to the crow god, or to the fishmen, or to any monstrous furry mothers who might or might not be some blood relation of his. He belonged to Boss and Lady Jane, and he was going to do what it took to go home.

So he lay flat on his stomach, with his rifle at his shoulder and his elbows level on the ground. He sighted down the barrel with his right eye, and waited in stillness until the crows descended again on that rock-smashed body outside. They were huge, too, bigger than any Elim had ever seen. But their beady eyes and black flapping wings and hideous croaking *caah-caah-caah* promised him that these were animals in the truest sense of the word, living and lawful according to God's covenant, and Elim felt no remorse as he steadied his aim and pulled the trigger.

Nothing happened.

Well, hold on: if it wasn't loaded, then why was it already cocked and set? Elim cracked the barrel to check –

– and was nearly blinded by the belated hangfire CRACK as the rifle discharged into the ground, blasting dirt into his eyes and sending a wild ricochet into the rock overhead.

"GoddammitsonofaBITCH," he swore, dropping the gun and clutching his face, thanking God's infinite mercy that the ricochet hadn't ended with a bullet in his skull. What kind of idiot just grabbed his gun and fired? What kind of neckless, nutless deep-fried pie-biter snatched up a rifle that had been *dropped in the river* and scratched his trigger-finger without so much as a cursory once-over?

A stupid one, that was what. Elim sniffed and wiped his face on his arm, massaging his eyes 'til they'd washed out the worst of the dirt. Then he picked up the rifle to do what he should have done the first time... somehow.

Then the grim realization hit him. Nevermind what he was going to clean it with – what the dickens was he going to load it with?

Elim set it down and felt over the ground, twisting and turning to search over every last musty corner, but the little bag of bullets was nowhere to be found. Hadn't Bootjack given it to him before they got to the river? Hadn't he had it before?

He writhed and shifted in the tiny crawlspace, shaking out the poncho, emptying out his shoes, pressing the back of his head flat up against the inches-low ceiling to try and feel a telltale lump underneath him. But regardless of whether the fishman had stolen it or Elim had dropped it or it was sitting at the bottom of the river, he was left in the same dire fix: alone and starving, with nothing but the clothes on his back and an empty, useless gun.

Elim lay there in the barren dirt, stunned to utter stillness.

Boss had taught him how to shoot, and fish, and clean what he killed. He hadn't taught him how to feed himself with nothing but his own bare hands. He had no hook or line, nothing to make a snare with, not so much as a pocket-knife to his name. He had *nothing*, not even the know-how to figure out which of all those alien weeds wouldn't leave him retching himself blind again – or worse.

Elim's eye caught again on the fishman's corpse, the clamor of the gunshot having evicted the crows. An evil genius took root in his mind.

If he didn't have the means to kill something, he might just have to make do with what was already dead.

No, no – that was a person – not a human, but a person, or had been – and he didn't have to consult the Verses to know what God would think of that. He would go find his Sundowners, that was what. He would just get up and go find them, just like he'd planned.

So Elim flattened and pushed and eased himself out from the little cave, and then reached back in to extricate his supplies. He put on his moccasin-shoes and his poncho and took up the net too, just in case he might could use it to catch something in the river.

And then he went. Around the wet limbs sticking out from under the landslide, through the steep shadows of the mountain's foot, towards the river and the oncoming night.

Even though he wouldn't be able to see for beans in the dark.

Even though the frog-monster and the dog-monster were still out there somewhere, and who knew what else besides.

Even though Bootjack and Way-Say and Hawkeye were already dead, for all he knew – even though he'd watched them being swarmed over by murderous fishmen – and the only thing dumber than staying here was going out to crash and stumble around in the dark, unarmed and ignorant and advertising himself to every evil thing that lived in these hills, or happened to be passing through.

Elim stopped, not twenty paces from where he'd started. What the hell was he thinking?

His gut erupted with another stricken gurgle. He smothered it with his free hand, as if to silence it before it gave them both away. It was a strange thing to put his hand to his stomach and feel nothing but skin and muscle and the sag of his pants. The little paunch he'd left home with was all gone – all Lady Jane's biscuit-and-buttermilk breakfasts vanished as if he'd never tasted them – and he had nothing, *was* nothing, but fear and indecision an urgent, animal need.

He had to go – go find help, go feed himself.

He couldn't go. It would be dark soon.

He had to stay – at least for tonight.

Elim glanced back at the fishman's fleshy wet carcass.

He couldn't stay. It would be dark soon. He would be as good as blind soon. And then that body would be nothing but fresh, unclaimed meat. Then there wouldn't be anything left to stop him.

Come, good Master, be our guest. By your bounty, we are blessed.

Elim dropped the net and shivered, dizzy with hunger, paralyzed by dread. He shouldn't be here. He shouldn't be looking where he was looking, shouldn't be thinking what he was thinking. He should... he had to...

... he had to go home, that was what. He had to go home, or Boss and Lady Jane would spend the rest of their lives wondering why he hadn't.

Elim took a step back toward the cave – back toward the carcass. He squinted just-so, blurring its open-mouthed stare into an amorphous, anonymous mask of meat.

He had to go home.

He didn't have to tell anyone what he'd done to get there.

All he had to do was eat.

For this bread, your will be done...

"Elim? Elim, can you hear me?"

He looked up, his heart seizing on the spot. That was Sil's voice!

... which meant that it was the fishman, Champagne, fishing for him again. Because of course it was. Because Sil was a week dead and a hundred miles east of here, with his head bagged up in a sack.

Well, good enough: Elim would give the fishman a hard sock in the jaw on Sil's behalf, and a solid kick to the teeth for that little stunt with the hemlock, and once he had it down on the ground, he could help himself to whatever victuals it had brought along for the trip. That would do nicely.

"Yeah, sure," Elim called back. "Come and get me, short-stack."

"Elim! Elim, is that you?"

The running footsteps coming up at him, combined with that rotten adolescent squeak of surprise, made a mockery of his lost hopes. "Damn it, fishman," Elim snarled as he started forward, "I am gonna knock you into a cocked hat if you don't – Sil?"

He knew that black hat cresting over the hill. He knew the white face bobbing up under it. He knew them in an instant – and in an instant more he was running to meet them, and in an instant more Elim had grabbed Sil bodily up off the ground in a rib-cracking bear hug.

It was true. God was good, and it was true.

"I thought I was gonna have to take you home in a box," Elim mumbled, his voice molasses-thick as he pressed Sil's slight frame closer in, firm and real and –

– *ripe*. "Phew, buddy – you'd stink a dog off a gut-wagon!" And that wasn't a good honest body-odor smell, either. That was...well, it was more like the odor of a body.

Sil squirmed and pushed away. "Ugh, put me down – I'm not well."

"No kidding," Elim said, helpless not to stare. Sil looked *horrible* – sickly and bloated and fishbelly-white, almost green around the edges, with bloody pinspots in one eye and a festering blue-green bruise around his neck where the noose had gotten him... *almost* gotten him, Elim corrected himself. "What the hell happened to you? How did you get all the way out here? And do you have anything to eat? Please God, Sil, tell me you do."

Sil stared up at him, confusion souring to amazement. "Food? Is that it? I hike all the way out here through the devil-knows-what to find you and all you want is a slop-out?" His voice sounded like rusty water through a gunked-up pump, and his breath was *heinous*.

Elim shook his head, as desperate to dispel the smell as he was to be understood. "No, no, it ain't – I ain't kidding, Sil. I'm dead serious. I gotta eat, or I'm just – I just don't even know what. Please..."

Sil's astonishment softened just slightly at the cracks in Elim's voice; he nodded at the rifle in Elim's hand. "Well, my god, it's not that bloody difficult – just heft your gun and shoot something!"

"No, I can't," Elim stammered, struggling to come to grips with the idea that Sil had brought no food and no tools and didn't know the first thing about outdoorsmanship – that he wasn't going to be any help at all. "I ain't got any bullets left – I blew my only one."

Sil's brows furrowed. "What, honestly? Then what's that in your pocket?"

Elim followed his gesture down to the bulge at his right hip.

He fished out the little cloth bag and stared at it, feeling the roll and clink of the cartridges inside.

Then he put his hand over his eyes as the world dissolved into a wet blur.

"... Elim? Elim, what the devil's the matter with you?"

But he could only stand there, head down and shoulders heaving at the thought of what he'd done – what he'd come within a six hellbound paces of doing – and all his explanation came out as a hoarse, helpless creaky sob.

"Oh, Elim, I'm sorry... really, I'm sorry I got you into this mess. It'll be all right – you're just hungry and over-anxious, that's all. Come on, put yourself together and we'll set to it. You can shoot something and I'll fix a fire, and you'll feel much better after your supper, won't you?"

Elim drew in a deep, raggedy breath and wiped his face. "Yeah. Yeah, sure we will."

Sil's voice sounded like a clogged gutter, but it managed some cheer. "That's what I mean. Come on, let's get out of here."

Then a cold, clammy hand curled up under his arm, and led him away.

For days now, Sil had thought of nothing but Elim – of getting him out of that mess in Sixes, first of all, and then of finding him out here, doing whatever it took to catch up to him and set him free.

He'd expected him to be in rough shape, of course. He'd expected the a'Krah to use him like a rented mule. He just hadn't expected... well, *this*.

And yet here he was, sitting by a greasy, smoky brush-fire, watching Elim use Sil's little pocket-knife to mutilate a dead rabbit: sawing off the limbs, peeling back the fur, and eating the flesh raw.

"'m sorry," Elim mumbled, once he'd gotten down to the guts.

"It's fine," Sil said, briefly meeting the rabbit's glassy-eyed stare. Hopefully it would keep Elim busy long enough for the grouse to finish roasting. "You were hungry."

"No – I mean, yeah, but what I meant was about all of this." Elim laid down the carcass and wiped his mouth. It left a bloody streak on his arm. "I didn't mean for you to have to come out all this way looking for me. I wouldn't of let them take me if I thought for a second that you were still there. But they said you were dead, honest – they swore it up and down, and they had a head in a sack and showed it to me, and honest to God, Sil, I thought it was you..."

"Really, it's all right," Sil said, anxious for Elim not to go to pieces a second time. "I could fill a book with what I wish I'd done differently, but it's not important. We're here now, and we're going home."

"Yeah." Elim's gaze drifted down to the bird on the spit, as if struggling to read something in its glistening skin. "Yeah, sure we will. But I gotta tell you..." Elim glanced up, his expression profoundly pained. "I mean, about Actor. I'm so awful sorry, Sil – I had to..."

"I know," Sil cut him off at the mention of the horse. "I saw him on my way here. Don't worry about it – Will's going to know you did everything you could."

Best not to tell Elim what Weisei had done with the body afterwards.

Actually, Sil had some confessing of his own to do. He'd been rehearsing it for hours now. *I'm so sorry,* he would say. *I took Molly to come and get you, but I was careless and stupid and I lost her. She ran away and I couldn't get her back, and it's all my fault. I know how much she meant to you. I'm awfully, awfully sorry.* That was it. That was what he would say.

But it was impossible to concentrate with the smoke in his eyes and that damned fly pestering him, and the words kept getting caught in his throat. "I, ah... I don't suppose you've seen Molly?"

Elim shrugged and looked away.

Damn it. "Here, mind that before you burn it," Sil said, and shifted the subject. "So how did you get free anyhow?"

Elim gave the spit a halfhearted turn. "Ran away."

"Well, it must have been a good trick – Vuchak said the fishmen had you. What happened?"

Elim returned to his grisly meal. "Don't know."

Sil rolled his eyes and moved closer to the fire. "Riveting story, that."

He regretted it at once. Still, it was impossible not to be frustrated. There was Elim, clean and fit and fine – better than fine, even: he'd lost that little bit of a gut and taken on a lean, subtly muscular look, and all without a scratch or a burn left on him. But despite this tremendous stroke of luck, Sil began to think that he wasn't going to be able to bring Calvert's groom back in the same state as he'd taken him away – that no matter what happened now, this Elim was no longer *that* Elim, and Sil had no more power to undo that than to un-cook that spitted bird.

"Here," Elim said, ripping a wing off and passing it

over. "Start on that – I think the outers are just about done."

Well, maybe eating like a human would help Elim remember how to act like one. Sil decided to humor him and took a bite. The hot grease didn't bother his fingers, but the taste was unpleasantly stringy, almost rancid, and he wasn't the least bit hungry. In fact, he was uncomfortably full. He hadn't eaten in days, but he hadn't been able to ease himself, either.

So he pulled his shirt out to hide his swollen stomach, tore off little crispy morsels of skin to chew on, and watched Elim rip into the remainder with as much mannerless urgency as if he hadn't already wolfed down a whole rabbit for his starters.

"Good, isn't it?" Sil said presently, mostly to give himself a break from pretending to eat.

Elim eyed him over the fire. "Wouldn't know it to look at you. You better hustle up and eat that – I ain't having it from Nillie for bringing you back looking like chopped chickenshit."

A week ago, that would have been all right. A week ago, this had been the normal order of business: Elim stuffing his guts at the county fair and henpicking Sil to hurry and eat his greens.

But an awful lot had happened in the past week, with an emphasis on 'awful', and Sil was in no mood to hear it. He chucked the wing at Elim, who plucked it almost casually from the air. "Surprised you didn't catch that with your teeth. Stuff your guts and let me be – I'm in no mood for it."

But Elim actually left off eating and stared at Sil with that insufferable worried-dog expression of his. "Sorry, Slim – you know I didn't mean it. But you just look so... are you sure you're gonna be all right going home?"

No. Not at all. "Of course. I'm just tired – I've hardly slept since you left. Finish your supper so we can go to bed. We'll both feel better in the morning."

Elim looked deeply skeptical. "All right, well... I'm settin' this aside for your breakfast, and we're not leaving 'til you eat it."

Sil was tempted to snort in disdain as he watched Elim rip a leg off his greasy treasure and set it aside – as if Sil would ever have eaten that at any hour of the morning, sick or not! But he said nothing contrary, and passed the time agreeably until they lay down for the night.

Except that Sil couldn't fall asleep.

He wanted to, was every bit as frantic for it as Elim had been for supper. He desperately needed to pay off whatever miracle of shock and borrowed time had let him walk the desert for days without food or water or rest, was fully prepared to sleep for three days and be ill for a week afterwards.

But still nothing happened.

No bill was presented for the extraordinary endurance he'd somehow bargained for. No second shoe dropped. He rolled over and back again in a vain attempt to find some comfortable position on the ground, got up and lay back down again after one final, futile attempt to ease that awful bloat in his stomach, closed his eyes and opened them again as he alternated between the world's darkness and his own.

So Sil, left with no means of settling his debt, lay awake through the night, shooing flies as the fire died.

* * *

THE LADY, U'RU, did not change at sunset. She sat still and patient and almost-perfectly human until her companion was deep asleep – until the pilgrim, Día, lay with her head in the lady's brown furry lap.

Then she changed a little, just enough to lean over and lay a crown of kisses in an arc over the girl's forehead – just enough to keep her thoughts peaceful and dreaming.

Then she changed a little more. The fur of her robe tightened, clinging and spreading as the body beneath it stretched and grew – as the moonlight threw her shifting shadow clear down to the dry valley floor – as the starlight caught in the black of her eyes, and turned them golden bright.

Then the lady, U'ru, picked up her newest puppy and went walking down the mountainside.

IN THE DREAM, Elim was fourteen years old and lying with Eula Lightly when he heard the creaking of the old barn door. But he was so captivated by flesh and heat and sweaty gingham sweetness that he scarcely noticed when she stiffened and twisted astride him, did not begin to understand until the long shadow spilled over them from above.

She slid off him, shrank fearfully into the straw beside him, but Elim had no such luxury. He had to rise to meet the shadow, to stand up with his hat and shirt in hand and bits of straw clinging guiltily to his cowlicked hair and go, walking straight out the door and through the yard and left onto the dirt lane, with no promise of what lay before him but an absolute certainty about who was following behind.

It stopped at the property line, but Elim kept right on going, down the lane and right at the gate and straight up to the white-washed house, to knock, to wait, to realize a little too late that he hadn't actually put his shirt back on – to pull off his hat as the door was opened and look Elver Lightly square in the eye and say the hardest words of his short life.

"Mister Lightly, I am so awfully sorry for the outrage I have done to your daughter."

ELIM WOKE WITHOUT stirring, the dream still vivid in his mind.

It faded with his first fresh whiff of that godawful smell, and his first glimpse of Sil, still sitting across from the dead embers in the pre-dawn grayness, and his first sharp pang of disappointment. The night hadn't improved him. He looked worse than ever – more gross and sick and haggard than Elim had ever seen him.

"You twitch like a dog in your sleep." Sil's voice was even rougher than it had been yesterday.

Elim groaned and sat up. "And you sound like you just choked on your own teeth – and how come you ain't even pretending to sleep, sickly?"

Sil glowered at him with one blue and one bloodied eye, both made heavier by the dark smudges, like purple-black bruises, malingering above his sunken white cheeks. "I'm not tired. And if you're rested enough to carp at me about it, I'll take that as leave to get moving."

Elim sighed, the emptying of his lungs making more room for worry in his stomach. At least today it was a human stomach. "Yeah, sure. Let me inspect the crops and then we can go – and see you eat your breakfast while I'm at it."

Sil's gaze tracked Elim's pointed nod to the cold grouse-meat lying by the ashes. "You're daft if you think I'm eating that."

Of course. Because if Sil actually ate a proper meal or got a decent rest, he might actually get better, and they couldn't have that.

But Elim bit his tongue and trudged out for his morning constitutional, relieved at least for his own sake. It had been a short night on rough ground, but he already felt so much better for having had a meal and a drink and a rest all on the same day, for finally having a reprieve from his body's constant *screaming* for something-or-other. As wholesome and human as he felt right now, it was easy to imagine that all of what came before had just been a bad dream... except that Sil was a waking nightmare.

He needed a doctor. He couldn't possibly last all the way home. Hell, Elim wouldn't even have wagered on his being able to walk *now*, and who knew how long that would hold true? What the dickens was Elim supposed to say if he set out preparing to answer Will Halfwick for the death of his horse, and showed up having to answer for his little brother too?

He couldn't do it. It just couldn't be allowed now – not after he'd gone so far expecting to do that very thing, and having just now, just yesterday been granted this miraculous reprieve.

He would, though. He would, if it came to that.

Elim paused, hugging his knees and staring with unfocused eyes at the gray light in the east.

Boss had walked behind him that day, to see that he

did the right thing. He'd left Elim to go the last of the distance himself, but he'd stayed there at the edge of that white-washed fence to watch – and it was a good thing he had, because otherwise there would have been nobody to stand between Elim and Elver Lightly's shotgun.

Elim looked over his shoulder at the mountain, its rumpled outline silhouetted against the fading stars. He had walked quite a far ways by himself now, and done it with every intention of confessing himself honestly – of taking Do-Lay's body home, as he'd promised he would, and answering for the crow boy's death. But there was nobody to watch out for him now, nobody to intercede on his behalf. Not even if his honesty cost him his life.

And if that happened, how was Sil going to get home? Him, now, in the state he was in? He might as well be executed at Elim's side.

And somebody had to get home. That was what Elim had asked Día to relay for him, all those days ago in Sixes. *One way or another, one of us has to get home.*

So when he finally walked back to their cold, reeking camp, and Sil opened his mouth to make some sharp remark, Elim cut him clean off. "Can't go back."

Sil shut his mouth, appalled into silence.

Unfortunately, that was about as far as Elim had gotten in his speech-making deliberations. "Which is – what I mean to say is, I been thinking about it and I can't – I think we have to finish this here, to have our reckoning for it, I mean, before we can –"

"Elim," Sil said, with a blistering heat on his bloodless lips, "what the devil is the MATTER with you?"

Elim could have answered that on the spot. *You look*

like death and smell like hell, and I can't hardly get within ten paces of you without wanting to sick up my insides. But that was unkind, and Sil couldn't help it, and Elim knew that he was imagining it worse than it was: that after a week of hauling Do-Lay's rotting box and then all that mess with the fishman's corpse and the drowned people and Ax – God, he could still see the hole where that poor horse had been eating himself – the lingering death-stench in Elim's nose had him imagining it other places too.

So he took a deep breath – through the mouth – and steadied his aim. "I'm cursed, Sil. I think we both are. And I don't expect it's gonna get any better for either of us until we finish what's started, and go own up for killing D – for killing that boy."

Sil rose to his feet, plainly astonished, and for a moment Elim was dumb enough to imagine that that meant he was really thinking about it – that he might actually see reason.

But then, Elim never had been the brightest brass knob.

"I don't believe you," Sil said in a hoarse whisper. "I came all this way – I was HANGED trying to get you out of this mess – and you're telling me you want to go right on forward as if I'd not bothered with any of it? As if none of that matters?"

"No!" Elim said, stung to the core. "I'm so glad you came – I need you, Sil – I can't do it by myself, I just –"

"Good," Sil said. "Then I'll see you shortly." And he turned east and set off walking.

But the neat turn of his heel reminded Elim of the neat turn of his horse, of the way Sil had up and absconded on that last morning at the fair – of the arrogant, casual blackmail that had dragged them into all this mess in the first place – and Elim's jaw clenched at the presumption of it all.

"No," he said, "you won't. I'm going to go finish what I started, with or without you. And if you get home before me, you can tell Boss that I went where you didn't care to go, and you weren't any master of mine to make me do otherwise."

Sil stopped and turned, incredulity growing in his ghastly mismatched eyes. "Why, you audacious son of a bitch. You really mean to do it."

Elim folded his arms over his poncho. "I do. And I sorely wish you'd join me, even though it ain't your debt to settle."

Sil locked eyes with him for a moment. Then something broke inside him. "For God's sake, LOOK at me, Elim – do I look like I have that kind of time?"

Elim flinched, taken aback by the strangled terror in Sil's voice... but when your horse got spooky, you had to stay calm. "No," he said. "You look about to die, Sil, and that's exactly why I want you with me. Use your brains: it'll take us days to walk back to Sixes, and days more if you go bad and I have to carry you, and you and I both know you ain't going to last that long." Elim nodded up at the mountain. "We know there are people up there, and they're a hell of a lot more likely to know what's wrong with you than I do, and you don't – and it's not you they're holding a grudge on." He looked back at Sil, and weighted his voice to sink. "Come on, Slim. Let's do it right this time."

Sil didn't answer straightaway. He put a puffy white hand to his face and closed his eyes, like a man sapped by days and nights of the most exhausting pain. "... I don't want to die, Elim. Honestly, that's all I can think of right now."

Me too. "I know, buddy. Trust me, I'm familiar." But there was no more time for selfishness or doubt, and Elim kept his mind firmly fixed on his partner. "Let's go get you fixed up."

Sil stood there a little more, as if gathering his nerve. Finally he sighed, took off his jacket, and reached down to pick up the remainder of the grouse. By the time Elim caught up with things, he was looking at a cheaply-tailored carry-sack for their rations, which Sil defended with a sharp up-and-sideways-stare. "Don't look at me like that," he said on his way past. "I'm not having you whine at me about how you're oh-so-hungry again in half an hour's time. Honestly, Elim, it's like I can't take you anywhere..."

Well, that was probably about right. Duly chastised, Elim fell into step next to Sil – upwind of him, specifically – as they headed back to the crow mountain's sprawling foot, and whatever might wait for them at its peak. No, there was no safeguarding shadow walking behind Elim this time – but he was powerfully glad for the plain and irritable one beside him.

CHAPTER SIX
UNBURIED ALIVE

AH CHE, A CHILD of eight winters, lay dying.

It had been ten days since Ah Set lay down, and did not get up. Three days since the baby stopped crying. Now it was Ah Che's turn to cry – harsh, gulping screams that only served to inflame the blisters in his throat.

The world was being swallowed, one vital piece at a time. First to go was the outdoors: it shrank to a strip of light under the door-curtain, too bright and painful to look at. Then it was gone. Then the indoors, the pots and clothes and white earthen walls eaten away in a fever dream. Then Mama.

She lived in the dream-world now – the one place that had not yet been eaten – and doted on him as lovingly as she ever had. But the body she'd left was ripening, and her dream-self could not bring him water.

So Ah Che thrashed and cried and sucked on his sweat-drenched blanket as reality contracted around him – as the world worked to un-birth him. He would go gladly, he promised Mama, if she would just pull him in, as she'd once pushed him out. He would go bravely, *if she would just help him out of his stiff-necked and shivering self. He would –*

Something jostled the ground – a clunky, rhythmic intrusion. Faintly familiar. Coming closer. Ah Che fell silent as the world expanded to include the sound of heavy, ugly boots.

WHEN DÍA WOKE, she opened her eyes to the dull-eyed stare of a dead squirrel.

Or more accurately, to its head and the better part of its spine, and to the fresh raw meat-smell clinging to both, and in the time it took Día to flinch and sit up, she'd solved the mystery: she was back at the little stone valley again, and there was Miss du Chenne again, busy hacking apart a lizard with a knife – Día's knife, she realized with a hand to her side – and the mound of bloody skin and bones that had greeted her eyes' first opening looked to be the remainders of the old mereau's grisly breakfast. "What... what is this?"

Miss du Chenne glanced up. Not for the first time, Día wished she would either clothe herself or leave off that obscene squat. "I was going to ask you the same thing," she said. "What sort of hour do you call this, young lady?"

Día blinked. It was daytime, well on towards noon. She had survived the night, been removed from the mountain, and the Dog Lady was nowhere in sight. For that matter, neither was Elim. It was chilly there in the shadows, and Día had apparently been sleeping on the bare ground, and yet she felt wonderfully rested, just as she had back when...

Día sat up straighter and clutched her stomach,

interrogating her palate for any telltale milky aftertaste. "Please tell me she didn't..."

Miss du Chenne snorted. "Nurse you? No, and you can thank me for that: I told her that you would prefer to eat with your teeth. Better get to it." She pointed to a peculiar pile at Día's feet.

There was the body of a horned frog and a blue-gray bird, a cluster of berries and a hare whose fur had been mangled by rough teeth and slobber, three dirt-streaked leathery eggs, a big pinecone, some kind of grass snake... Día stared at the morbid cornucopia, recalling U'ru's loving, smothering, uncomprehending delight at having initiated Día into the family – one whose matriarch was near-universally reviled as a murderer.

And there to prove it was a thoughtful little collection of deaths for her breakfast.

Día hunched forward and rubbed her face. She cupped her hands around her forehead, keeping her gaze fixed on the soft, familiar black-fabric folds in her lap. "Miss du Chenne," she said, "I'm sorry for being so rude to you yesterday. I didn't mean to be thoughtless or careless. I didn't mean to leave home at all. I just" – no, she couldn't even begin to explain about the Halfwick boy – "I got caught out in the sun, and then I got lost, for I don't even know how many days now, and I've been so frightened, and the Dog Lady – she was just a friendly mother dog, and I was so glad for her company, and I thought – by the time I realized that she wasn't..." Día's voice thickened with disappointment: she'd spent all this time thinking of the dog as a gift from God, as a holy companion given especially to her, and now...

She swallowed. "I would very much like to go home."

At first, there wasn't any answer. When Día looked

up, Miss du Chenne had set down the knife and was staring off at something only she could see. "You weren't wrong, you know," she said at last. "About her, I mean. She used to be so splendid – so alive, all glory and grandeur. You would have loved her."

Día would have to take her word on that. "Do you think she can be that again?"

Miss du Chenne's black eyes lost their fog of nostalgia. They sharpened to the present, and their calculating attention slid over to Día. "Can you do what I tell you to?"

She would have preferred explanation before promises. "Yes."

Miss du Chenne nodded. "Have you finished being headstrong and hysterical?"

Día bristled at the question. Then she reminded herself that she was talking to her first, best chance of fixing all this, of getting home with body and soul intact. "Yes."

Miss du Chenne arched a hairless eyebrow. "And will you put aside your childish piety and petty sensibilities, making allowance for the fact that I'm a cantankerous shrew with no tact or patience, and that she's a grief-stricken child who doesn't understand what she's done?"

Día strongly suspected that one of those things was well within Miss du Chenne's power to affect. *Honor thy father and mother*, she thought to herself. *Tolerate thy selfish old not-even-a-mother just long enough to get home to thy poor long-suffering father.* "Yes."

The old schoolteacher might have read her thoughts, or at least her face. She returned a withering look. "We'll see about that." But she picked up a lizard-leg and grimaced as her sharp teeth tore its tough, scaly flesh. "Now eat," she said, gesticulating with the bloody knife – which was to say, *Día's* knife – at the mini-massacre by her feet. "You can have the fruit if you're squeamish, but at least handle the meat so that she smells it on you when she gets back. She's decided you're her new puppy, and you're going to act like it."

Well, Día was certainly spoiled for choice. Those red berries looked like the ones Weisei had told her about. That might do for a start.

Then she glanced back at Miss du Chenne, who sat there expectantly, just waiting for her to admit her timidity and take the berries, or challenge her and ask for the knife back. Waiting to see whether they were going back to the old schoolroom hierarchy, or the new, pointless antagonism.

Día picked up an egg, tore open the leathery shell with her teeth, and squeezed its contents into her mouth in one runny burst. She kept her gaze fixed and her face straight as she chewed, working hard not to give Miss du Chenne the satisfaction of watching her gag at the squishy, stringy texture. Whatever-it-was had already made a respectable start on growing a spinal column.

Then she swallowed, wiped her mouth on her forearm, and cast the eggshell into the pile of remainders. "What's the plan?"

SIL STILL DIDN'T much like the idea. Even if the two of them managed to find their way to the crow city without guidance or supplies, even if the a'Krah didn't haul off and execute Elim on the spot, even if they knew some real medicine... why on earth would they share it? Sil had no money and no connections and his only bargaining chip was this two-colored rube here – the one he absolutely could not scheme or swap or barter with.

But it wasn't as if Sil had any better ideas.

So he followed along as Elim led them back to the mountain's foot, back the way they'd come yesterday. He kept his pace up and his temper down. He walked well downwind while Elim polished off the rest of the grouse along the way. And when Calvert's mule stopped at the creek, Sil didn't protest the delay.

Still, it was a hard thing to watch. As Elim knelt to drink and wash, Sil privately burned with envy: at the big man's huge, hardy appetite – at his hay-hauler's physique and farmboy's tan – at the perfect ease with which he moved, equally ignorant of his body and clothes. He was effortlessly more than Sil had ever been, and now, as Sil struggled to avoid seeing or touching or thinking about any part of his own unbearable person, a vain, frightened despair welled up inside him, like so much putrid mucus pooling in his lungs.

Maybe it wasn't too late. Maybe when he got back home, if he spent more time outdoors... took some regular exercise, the way Nillie was always nagging him to... made himself eat properly for a change, before he finished his growth. Yes. That was infinitely easier to imagine than the string of miracles he would need just to make it back to Hell's Acre, and Sil hung his hopes there like a castaway clinging to a driftwood plank: he would just muddle through this next bit, and when he was home and finally on the mend, he'd make a fresh start of everything.

"Here, get you some." Elim straightened and jerked his head at the creek.

Sil didn't want any. By every god, he didn't want to try stuffing anything else into his swollen stomach.

He also didn't want to hear more of Elim's hennish fussing.

So he bent and pretended to drink, watching the slimy stones at the water's bottom in preference to the ghastly reflection rippling on the surface. But the towering shape behind his god-awful face, the one matched by the shrinking shadow on the ground...

Sil glanced back at Elim, simultaneously familiar and strange. He was more native now than he had been. And it wasn't just the alien geometry woven into his wool poncho, not just the moccasins on his feet and the contrast they made with his worn brown trousers and old Federate rifle. The cold-water wash had turned his hair black and straight, bringing out that indigenous crease in the corner of his eyes until he looked like a trapper or a scout, like the kind of guide you'd hire at a trading post somewhere on the edge of the wild, like... well, like someone who belonged out here.

Elim caught him staring, and turned the spotted side of his face away. "What?"

Not for the first time, Sil remembered leaving Elim tied up and roasting in the afternoon sun, and coming back to find him passed out and grotesquely changed, his spots and patches all covered in fine brown hair. He'd known right then that there was something else living in Calvert's groom – and Sil meant to see that it stayed buried. "Let's go."

So they went back to the place where they'd first met: to the little narrow-mouthed cave and the field of rubble just beyond it. Sil had seen the side of that hill collapse yesterday – from a fair distance, thankfully –

and while there was no telling how stable the remainder might be, there was also very obviously a trail buried under all that earth, the only one either of them had seen. If they could just make it over the heap, they'd be well on their way.

It was a disturbing climb. There were strange muddy pockets in the earth – dead fishmen, Sil realized after he accidentally exposed a wizened wet arm – and at least one such pocket had been broken into, leaving an empty grave-like crater and drag marks where the body inside had been hauled away. Sil didn't care to guess what sort of creature might have done that. He didn't ask Elim what had happened here, and Elim didn't offer him a hand up. They moved separately and in silence, the air between them filling with things unsaid.

"Hello?"

Sil glanced up, to where Elim had just crested the top of the landslide.

The big mule called out again, his voice echoing faintly off the hollow hillside. "You okay? Hey, can you hear me?"

Well, if whoever-it-was didn't, someone else certainly would. Sil paused in testing his next foothold. "Elim, don't –"

"Holy God – wait, hold still!" Elim bolted ahead, disappearing from view – and dislodging a pile of broken stones. Sil had just time to look up before the largest came cracking down on the top of his head. He shrank forward, pressing into the heap as dirt and rocks rained down.

When the dust cleared, Sil wasn't dead and he hadn't fallen – no thanks to that blundering clod.

"Hang in there, buddy – wait right there!"

Sil glanced up, but Elim's voice wasn't meant for him. Of course not. It was fading away down the far side, as bold and thoughtless as a bawling calf. Sil resisted the urge to put a hand to his head – if it didn't hurt, then there was no need to go feeling it – and set about extricating himself from Elim's clumsiness.

By the time Sil made it to the top, Elim was already down at the bottom – and he wasn't alone. There was someone else there, lying prone, feebly moving, and absolutely caked in red earth.

Elim looked up from where he'd crouched at the man's side. "Sil, come quick! That way – move that way, so you don't spill on him."

Oh, by all means – just imagine what a mess that might make. But Sil bit his tongue and started down, his ire dwindling in the face of curiosity and growing concern. The stranger could be a boon or a huge liability – one Sil and Elim absolutely could not afford.

And he was in terrible shape. As the slope leveled out and Sil passed the last of the rocky ruin, he realized what should have been obvious from first glance: whoever that fellow was, he'd been buried alive.

He might have been native, to judge by his moccasins, but otherwise there was no telling: aside from a few dark patches where he'd bled through the dirt, the man underneath all that earth could have been any color. His long hair was a tangled mess, most of it pulled out of a pigtail at the back of his neck, and his clothes were plain and ordinary, and aside from the blindfold tied over his eyes, his most striking feature was the sickening angle at which his right leg dragged, smashed through the mid-thigh as completely as if he'd grown a secondary sideways knee.

Sil stood to one side and resisted the urge to wipe his mouth. A liability, then – a god-awful liability.

"Hawkeye – come on, buddy, talk to me." Elim took him by the shoulders, but couldn't turn him onto his back without making an agony of the man's leg – and the man seemed to want nothing to do with it.

He pushed forward on his stomach, reaching for a gap, a hole in the rubble – not one he'd crawled out of, Sil belatedly realized, but one he'd been digging into. "*Help me get him out,*" the man said in parched, hoarse Marín. "*I need him.*"

There was no telling what 'him' might be – a person or an object, any masculine thing. Regardless, 'he' was well buried, and had been for over a day now.

"We're here to help," Elim promised, perhaps having understood the first bit of that, and tried again to dissuade him from digging. "Sil, what's he saying?"

Sil looked down at the quandary at his feet. Elim knew the fellow, so he was probably one of the a'Krah party. He was trying to dig out someone else. And as much as Sil hated to think Vuchak or Weisei might be under there, the cold fact was that anyone still buried was dead – and they had neither the time nor the tools to go finding that out firsthand. Sil had to – *they* had to keep moving.

Sil shook his head. "He's delirious," he said. "Maybe we'd do better to leave him here while we..."

One look from Elim withered that idea on the vine.

"Well then what do you propose?" Sil snapped. "He can't walk, and we haven't anything for his leg – you can't even carry him with a break like that."

Elim cast around defiantly, as if he could make a splint and bandages appear by sheer force of righteousness.

Then he spotted his rifle.

Damn it. Sil watched in stifled silence as Elim reached across to the man's far shoulder and flipped him – a quick, ruthless motion that yielded up a shriek of pain.

"Sorry, buddy – you're gonna hate me worse in a second. Sil, hold him down."

"Don't," the man begged in Ardish this time, struggling like an upended tortoise on a flat rock. "Stop, please wait – I have to get it out – I need my –"

Sil's squeamishness vanished in a second, replaced by an urgent need to shut him up before he put any more humanitarian ideas in Elim's head. He dropped down to a mean crouch, his knees jamming the man's shoulders into the ground – just as Elim gave his shattered leg a hard, bone-setting yank.

The scream echoed off the mountains. When it died, there was nothing to replace it – just a wet patch on the man's trousers, and a blanket of galled calm.

Elim had gone pale under his spots, but he didn't relent. He slipped the rifle under the man's leg, bridging the fracture with the widest part of the stock, and motioned to Sil. "Gimme his blindfold."

There was no movement, no objection as Sil gingerly pulled it off the man's face, revealing a swath of clean, honey-colored skin – and white, half-open eyes rolled back in his head.

Well, that was probably for the best. Sil watched as Elim tore the fine black cloth lengthwise, tying one strip above the break and the other below. He offered neither help nor objection as Elim worked out the logistics, finally settling on a squatting posture that would let him washpin the poor bastard around his shoulders like a hundred-and-thirty-pound human ox-collar.

And then they went on, Elim stooped and leading, Sil idle and following. Every now and again, he glanced from the dead weight on Elim's back to the mountain's peak high above, fixating on the task ahead until he'd managed to forget whatever they'd left entombed behind them.

BUT EVEN THOUGH Shea was the soul of courtesy just then, even though she explained the plan as thorough and plainly as anyone could want, she got nothing for her efforts but Día's strained, wordless hesitation.

"What?" Shea demanded at last. "You can't manage that much?" It was the simplest thing in the world: Día only needed to have a civil conversation with Yashu-Diiwa – one earth-person to another. She could persuade him to leave off his irrational hysteria and understand that U'ru and Shea had come to save him from the a'Krah. Then the whole lot of them could pack off back to Island Town together. The trip would take days – plenty of time for U'ru to make her own start on winning his trust. What was so hard about that?

Día's mind was somewhere else. Her expression didn't even flicker. "No, it's not that," she said. "But I don't think it will work. Elim isn't... he doesn't like me very much." This, with the lap-knotted hands and guilty downcast eyes one would expect to accompany a confession of some abortive schoolyard romance. At any other time, Shea would have laughed aloud.

Today, however, she needed Día's cooperation. More than that, she needed her enthusiasm: U'ru would pick up on any unvoiced misgivings, and who knew what she would do with them? "Nonsense," Shea said. "Of course he does: I saw you talking with him only last week."

Día looked up. "Saw us? Where?"

Well, Shea hadn't meant to advertise it, but nevermind: "Just south of Island Town, when you were picking your little flowers – right after he and that other fool nearly ran over you."

Día rose straight to her feet. "You were spying on me!"

Shea couldn't match her height, but she was more than capable of answering rudeness. She swung up out of her long-legged squat and tossed the masticated lizard-carcass aside. "I was watching out for you, and a good thing, too – those corn-pone clowns could have killed you! And just look at this mess you've gotten yourself into, wandering out here like a sleepwalking moon-calf: if I'd been watching you then, you'd be home right now!"

Shea couldn't see well enough to make out Día's expression. But there was a little well of silence, like a poked hole filling up with groundwater, and when Día spoke again, her voice was nothing like what it had been before.

"If you're so wise and righteous, why does everyone hate you?"

That stung. It wasn't true, of course. There were plenty of people who didn't... why, she could name at least...

Well, for one thing, Faro didn't hate her – he was content to use her. And there was that bounty hunter a few days ago, though technically Shea had been using him. And besides which... well, and besides which, what did she have to prove to anyone anyway?

Shea snorted, and tacked into the wind. "Depends who you ask. You hate me for leaving you, while your dear *papá* resents me for spending all these years chasing after that useless mongrel boy. The boy, meanwhile, detests me for rubbing his nose in his heritage – which may have involved some less-than-sporting use of the local flora – while his mother despises me for stealing him away in the first place. Take your pick."

This time, the quiet was as short and sharp as a whipcrack. "You WHAT?" Día's voice could have cut paper. "Are you telling me you're the one who... all this is because of YOU?"

"Of course not!" Shea snapped. "I'M not the one who decided to start torching houses and trampling children in the street! I'M not the one who thought it would be a good idea to lead my cohort on some damned silly suicide mission! I'M not the one who –"

Water Dog, be quiet!

U'ru was coming back. That was probably for the best, as it wouldn't be prudent to say the last part aloud: *I'm not the one who threw away my whole nation for the sake of one missing child.*

She appeared at the lip of the little stone valley: a plain brown dog with one more hapless furry thing in her mouth. On seeing Día awake, she hurried down to deposit the dead prairie dog in the pile of provisions, and then wound happy, wagging circles around her newest puppy's feet.

It was a clever strategy. Bound to just one form during the daylight hours, U'ru had this time chosen the one best-suited for finding prey – and not coincidentally, the one most likely to encourage Día's affections.

U'ru did not share whatever she said to the girl, but Día

knew how to play her part as Shea had instructed: she smiled and clasped her hands before her favorite furry friend. "Good morning, Mother Dog – I'm very glad to see you again. Shall we go out again today?"

It was all part of the plan, and yet Shea folded her arms, irrationally embittered by U'ru's fawning delight. What had Día ever done for the Dog Lady? For any of the Ara-Naure? When had she ever nursemaided a rambunctious litter of half-grown heirs, or translated for a milk-faced stranger, or washed the bedding after one of those wild three-day trysts? Really, who did she think she was?

"Thank you very much for my breakfast," Día was saying. "I couldn't finish it all, but I'll look forward to having more later. Miss du Chenne was just going to return my knife, and then I'll be ready to go."

That scheming trollop. Shea bared her teeth in a false smile, Día returning a flat-edged version of same as she strode forward to collect her due. "Thank you, teacher," she said as she sheathed the knife.

And that was how it was. Día had done nothing and was loved; Shea had done everything and was hated. And nobody batted an eye at this gross perversion of order as the three of them headed out in single file: the mother, the maiden, and... well, Shea wasn't *that* old.

Ingratitude – had there ever been such rank, naked ingratitude?

GRATITUDE. DÍA KEPT her mind clear and her thoughts fixed on gratitude: for food, for love – even frightening, smothering, horribly misguided love – and for this fresh chance at getting home before Fours despaired of ever seeing her again.

Really, U'ru's part of the plan was even worse than Miss du Chenne's: the great lady meant to use her newest puppy to show her older one that he had nothing to fear from her – to teach Elim to love her by example.

Día could think of several reasons why that wasn't going to work.

Still, she didn't let herself dwell on any of them. She had no better ideas, for one thing, and for another, Elim had apparently started on his way back to Island Town – and that was a haywagon Día desperately needed to catch.

Even if their last meeting had been an exceptionally bad one.

Even if she'd had to tell him that his partner was dead.

Even if he hadn't spoken to her since.

Día didn't imagine that he would be especially glad to see her, or inclined to trust anything she said, but Miss du Chenne was right about one thing: he would be far less hostile to Día than to the mereau who'd tricked and poisoned him, or to the 'monster' who'd transformed him. That had to count for something.

So she followed U'ru's curly brown tail, carefully picking her steps even as her mind filled with secondhand thoughts of eagerness and surety. *Smells*, her guide assured her along the way. *Puppy man skin-smells. Feet. Fire.* And it was as if Día herself had picked up the scent last night, followed it all the way out to the foothills, and watched her sleeping child beside his dwindling speck of a campfire, a huge maternal shadow in the dark.

There had been other smells too, though: blood and feathers and gunpowder, smoke, burning rabbitbrush, something freshly dead and something else too – something old and rotten and unbearably foul. Día swallowed at the borrowed memory. *What was that?* she asked.

U'ru's answer was the vague shape of a man – a smelly, rancid man, all bloat and blisters – but she couldn't have been less interested in the particulars. What child didn't love finding little dead things to play with? What did it matter, when the real thrill was watching them cavort and parade with their rotting novelties?

Día had no good answer for that – and no time to find one, either. U'ru suddenly stopped and lifted her ears, her senses perplexed: she had been following the trail from last night, but now there was a new one – a fresh one.

Día looked up at this half-familiar place: there was the little narrow-mouthed cave where she'd found U'ru, and the scorch-marks on the ground in front of it, and beside and beyond it, huge, ugly, and unmissable, was the landslide that had saved her.

And somewhere inside her, the sprouting kernel of someone else's fear.

"Mother Dog?" The old name was as dumb and automatic as Día's concern. "What's wrong?"

The dog – the Dog Lady – dropped her tail and whined. She put her nose back to the ground and hurried forward, following the fresh invisible second-trail up the slope, to the slumped pile of earth and then up its nearer side, faster than Día could keep up. U'ru bolted up the side, making it all of twelve feet before tumbling down in a pile of stones, but that impeded her not at all: in an instant she was back at it, choosing her path more carefully but with no less urgency, halfway to the top before Día had even found her first set of handholds. "Wait!" she called up.

The hand on her shoulder was soft and damp and

wordless. One glance at Miss du Chenne's expression sufficed: Día waited with her there at the base of the hill, still and strangely anxious. Why would Elim have returned to the mountain? He wasn't bound to the a'Krah or the mereaux or U'ru – couldn't he do whatever he felt like?

No! U'ru had reached the top of the heap – and in the midst of her darkening thoughts, her answer hit like a lightning bolt. *Mine!* She barked, a plaintive cry that ricocheted off the mountain's face, and then she tore forward and disappeared.

"Well, isn't that splendid." With an ages-old sigh, Miss du Chenne dropped their provisions and slumped down to a bandy-legged squat.

It took Día a longer time to untangle her mind from U'ru's. When she was confident that she was herself – childless, stationary, and calm – she looked around again, casting about for something useful to do.

That might take some imagination. It was a cloudless day, bright and cold, with precious little to call attention to the quiet, barren geography around her.

For one thing, there were no crows, perhaps because there was nothing much for them to eat. Día turned and studied the rubble, failing to find even one mereau body. But there was one small area that spilled out much farther than the rest, as if it had been dug into separately, after the fact. And at its bottom was a wide, grooved pattern in the dirt, as if something person-sized had been dragged away. There were three such trails, in fact: a second one coming from a big rock in front of the cave and another from a rusty-looking spot on the ground just beyond. All three converged about twenty feet away – heading east towards the river.

Día looked down to ask about that, but then thought better of it. There was Miss du Chenne, hunkered down in the dwindling shade of that huge earthen tomb, her eyes closed and her head tipped back in some private moment of weariness or disgust. It was hard to tell with her – hard to imagine anything coming out of Día's mouth that she would find pleasant.

But it was easy enough to observe the old mereau's wizened, shrunken gill-plumes – a sure sign that she'd been too long out of the water – and the scabby little cuts and bruises around the scarred stumps of her toes… and the dirt caked under her fingernails.

I'm not the one who thought it would be a good idea to lead my cohort on some damned silly suicide mission.

That was what she'd said – one enigma in a heap of others. Día hoped it wasn't literally meant – that those mereaux weren't actually Miss du Chenne's relations, and that they hadn't meant to die here. Not for the first time, she wished Fours hadn't always kept her in the dark.

Día badly wanted to ask about it. She wanted to find out once and for all if her suspicions were true: if she and U'ru really had killed one of the mereaux, if that was why the rest had to go to war with digging-tools and garden-rakes, if Miss du Chenne had known them or seen this coming.

But Día couldn't seem to talk to her without ending up in some awful spat, and any answer she did get was liable to be unhelpful or dishonest or both, and they already had enough to worry about with U'ru. There was no sense in opening up another old wound – or rubbing salt into a fresh one.

So Día stood there, hands clasped, and tried to craft a question that the hearer might actually want to answer. "Miss du Chenne," she said at last, "can I help you with them?"

The old schoolteacher opened one eye, its inner eyelid only half retracting.

"With them, I mean," Día said, nodding towards the earth-heap, and anyone who might still be buried in it. "While we wait."

She blinked, her gaze tracking Día's gesture. Then her colors warmed to a brief, beautiful amalgamation of orange and pink – a whole sunset of unspoken feeling. "I always said you were a promising child." And then, before Día could recall even a single time she'd ever said that, Miss du Chenne patted her foot. "Now you sit here: let's just have a little rest, and then we'll get to it."

Well, that was something, wasn't it? Día sat down, closed her eyes, and breathed deep from the clear mountain air. She privately resolved to savor this rare moment of tranquility, and to avoid imagining whatever fresh hell would end it.

EVEN SO, IT was over far too soon. Día was roused by sadness – by huge, bowel-churning waves of distress. She staggered up to her feet, struggling to recall what she was so upset about. Something was wrong. Someone was missing.

And by the time she realized that that queasy cold feeling didn't belong to her at all, U'ru was back, sending pebbles skittering down the hillside as she hustled down the slope, her fur dirty and bloodied and her tail tucked.

Gone. She announced herself with a plaintive whine. *Not welcome.*

So Elim's scent had led her up the same trail they'd walked yesterday, past the place where the crows waited, and U'ru could go no further.

Going. U'ru made an anxious circle around Día's legs. *Going. Going.*

Struggling to find the boundaries of her own mind, Día had no answer but her own confusion: what good would it do to go back up there?

"Absolutely not!"

Both U'ru and Día stopped. Miss du Chenne had risen to her feet, staring down at the one even as she gestured over at the other. "You can't send her up there after him – I don't care how near he is!"

U'ru growled, and Día's mind filled with wordless, angry certainty. The crows had only attacked her yesterday because she was escorting an unwelcome god: by herself, Día was a plain human, scarcely distinguishable from those that lived on the mountain, and Marhuk would take no notice of her.

"Nevermind that," Miss du Chenne snapped. "Look at her! She has nothing – no hat, no coat, not even a pair of shoes, and she doesn't know the first thing about this mountain or any other. She's got no business being HERE, nevermind up there, and I won't –"

U'ru bared her teeth, unleashing an onslaught of ideas. Día running up the trail – Día finding Elim and leading him back down again – Día and Elim back within the hour, safe and secure.

"You can't possibly guarantee that," Miss du Chenne said. "For all you know, the a'Krah already have him."

U'ru radiated confusion; her hackles lost their edge.

Why would the children of Marhuk take her son?

Miss du Chenne did not reply in words, but she must have communicated something. Día received U'ru's growing comprehension in vague, primitive images. A spotted puppy, alone in a strange place. A crow, startled into flight. A leap, a bite, a black-feathered body on the ground. A long shadow spilling over both of them. Tail-tucking. Understanding. Fear.

A reciprocal-understanding burst out from the Dog Lady then, like steam erupting from water slopped over a molten stone. Another time. Another dead crow. Another terrible, indelible mistake.

Día swallowed, nauseated by a crippling, bone-deep dread. She had ordered the death of Marhuk's daughter – had killed some of the others herself – and now her own son had followed her down the same fatal path. There was a faint flicker of something from Miss du Chenne – some mention of confession, some possibility of understanding – but it died like a candle-flame under glass, extinguished by U'ru's heavy, leaden certainty. There was no chance for forgiveness, no hope for mercy. If Marhuk's talons closed over her child, he would die.

Día closed her eyes, fighting not to be sick on the spot. Her shaking hand found the tips of her dreadlocks, holding fast to her father's handiwork to distance herself from that terrible grief-in-waiting. She was not a mother, she reminded herself. That was not her child. This was not her life.

But that was her friend: head bowed, ears back, and shoulders hunched in anticipation of an unsurvivable blow.

Día let out a breath. Miss du Chenne wouldn't allow it. Fours would tell her to go straight home. So would the Azahi, though he'd phrase it more practically: she didn't have the knowledge or the resources to do this responsibly, safely, or perhaps at all.

But when she reached past the clamorous voices of the living, to the one she had to be still and quiet and empty to hear... then it was easier to know the right thing, and to accept what might happen if she tried.

Día opened her eyes. "I'll go."

Strangely enough, there was no reaction from U'ru. The dog sat staring at Día with perplexed golden eyes, as if mystified by what she saw.

Miss du Chenne suffered no such difficulty. "Absolutely not!" she repeated. "You don't have any – you can't just up and – do you know what Fours is going to do to me if something happens to you?"

Día's first, decidedly unkind thought was that Miss du Chenne had never demonstrated any such regard for Fours' feelings or Día's welfare, busy as 'Shea' was enjoying her new life in that house of ill repute.

But there must have been some spirit of fire in the sky overhead, some angel of inspiration nudging her to think of the name that her teacher had abandoned, and to wonder if *du Chenne* might have been originally rendered as *du Chienne* – literally 'of the dog' – and to realize, years after the fact, that this business here was far, far older than Día could have imagined.

She looked down into the old mereau's fathomless black eyes, wondering how many lifetimes she had quietly accreted, each layer of living sediment passively burying the one below. "I know," Día said, pushing hard against the limits of her ignorance. "But you said... earlier this morning, you said that Fours resented you for spending so much time on this – on her, on looking for her son. And if that's true – if you left him and me for the sake of, of her and him..."

Día tried to reconcile that and hit a wall. No, it wasn't all right, and she wouldn't pretend otherwise. You couldn't just abandon people who were counting on you for the sake of someone else's unfinished business.

Even though that was exactly what Día was proposing to do now. She rubbed her face, struggling to draw some distinction, articulate some even half-reasonable rebuttal that would justify this present decision without validating that past one. What Miss du Chenne had done wasn't right, but it was done. And two wrongs didn't make a right – but squaring a negative did make a positive.

Día dropped her hands. "... well, it had better not be for nothing. Yes, that's what I mean: you spent yourself all on them, and I don't have to forgive you for that, but I'm not going to let it go to waste. Maybe we can't fix it, but it's my turn to try."

Miss du Chenne's hairless brow furrowed. Her river-colored skin shifted, the pale blue and stark white blending to a much more familiar shade – to the ordinary Eadan peach-color that she had been back when Día's dark hand was small enough to disappear in that wet, bony grip. "You know I can't go with you," she said. "If anything happens, I won't be able to come get you."

Día didn't have to ask why. She was grown now, tall enough to look down and see Miss du Chenne's withered gill-plumes, and the frail slump of her shoulders, and to understand that the old mereau could no more climb a mountain than Día could swim to the bottom of the sea.

Still, it was comforting to hear the unspoken sentiment folded inside that. "I know," Día said. "I'll do my best to stay safe."

U'ru's ears lifted. *Going?*

Miss du Chenne's expression hardened. She stood straighter, as if drawn up by invisible corset-strings. "Well, if you're going to do it, you'd better do it right. Now listen here, young lady: when you find that boy, you bring him straight here. Do whatever it takes, do you understand? As far as we know, he's the last of U'ru's line, and if he dies..."

Día glanced down at the Dog Lady, who only last week had been an almost-ordinary dog, and needed no further explanation. The earthly gods lived only as long as their people – which meant that U'ru's life, or at least her mind, was hanging by a single two-colored thread. "I understand."

Miss du Chenne nodded. "Good. And if the a'Krah have him, then... then tell them that his name is Yashu-Diiwa, son of U'ru the Dog Lady – youngest of the Moon Singers, eternal mother of the Ara-Naure – and she expects... and she would appreciate an opportunity to bargain for his life."

Día repeated it twice to herself, and didn't reply until she could do it with confidence. "I will."

Down. Come down.

Día saw herself kneeling – in heaven's name, she was never going to get used to speaking in ideas – and drew up her hem to make it so.

She planted her knees in the dry earth and received the Dog Lady's wet blessing: a crown of kisses, meticulously licked in an arc all along Día's hairline. There was love in them, warmth and strength and gratitude, and something else, too.

Sorry.

Día looked up into those mysterious golden eyes, the

ones that had watched over her through more days and nights than she could ever have survived alone. But she found no clarification there, no picture-thought to accompany the feeling. There was no telling whether U'ru meant to express regret to Día for what she was about to attempt, or to the a'Krah for what U'ru herself had already done, or whether the queen simply wished to endow her knight-errant with the right to apologize on her behalf – to make amends for wrongs that her own damaged mind could not even grasp, let alone correct.

Well, whatever the intention, it would suffice. "Don't worry, Mother Dog. We've come this far, haven't we? We'll be all right." And Día broadened that thought, that *we*, to include everyone she knew: herself and U'ru and Miss du Chenne, Elim and that godforsaken Halfwick, Vuchak and Weisei and anyone else she could find or meet – anyone living or incompletely dead out here on this old, cold mountain. She would help and solicit help in return, and keep faith throughout.

But after she'd traded embraces and said her goodbyes, Día was left to start up the precarious ruined road with no company but herself and the Almighty – and to trust that that would be enough.

SHEA WATCHED HER go, her thoughts sinking even as Día climbed.

She shouldn't have allowed it. She should have made her take the rest of the fruit. She should have bitten her during that last awkward hug, given her a love-flaw to keep her safe from the Amateur's roving eye. It was superstitious nonsense, but she should have done it anyway. Fours would have.

Be safe, puppy, came the thought from beside her. *Come back soon.*

Shea stared dully up at the lip of the landslide, blinking to clear the dust as Día crested the top. It had been a hard thing to keep from correcting her – to let the girl go on with her innocence intact. Yes, there was U'ru and the boy and that had been part of it... but the cold, ugly truth was that Shea didn't want to be anyone's mother. She never had. She wasn't made to parent earth-people and their sad, strange little families. It was all right to help out with the younger cohort, wiping sticky faces and separating squabblers and keeping the smallest ones from making a mess. That was what she'd done for U'ru, what she'd done for Mother Melisant before that. But to be a *mother*, the architect of a family, half of some helpless creature's entire world... who could ever bear it?

Thank you.

Much easier to let Día go on believing her own homemade explanation. Easier to maintain a generous silence than to tell the truth: *I don't want you and I never did, and if I'd had my way, Fours never would have taken you up in the first place.* Shea sighed, watching the black blur disappear over the hill. Well, she'd give herself some credit: whatever her other sins, she'd never said that out loud.

Water-Dog?

Shea glanced down at U'ru, a parent who was now half a child herself, and idly wondered when they'd gotten back on speaking terms again. "I'm sorry, Mother – what were you saying?"

The dog sat attentive and still. *Thank you.*

Shea stared at her. "God, whatever for?"

It was a terrible tone to take, and yet the rude contrarianism of the past twenty minutes had apparently succeeded where all her prior pleading failed: U'ru was calm and sensible, her tail swishing just that tiny bit. *You let her go.*

No, I didn't, Shea could have said. *She was never mine to 'let' do anything.* But she had known U'ru a long time – long enough to have learned how to keep her thoughts to herself. Regardless, Día was out of her reach now, and Shea had other concerns.

"That was her own choice," Shea said, and began running her hands over the less rocky parts of the earth-heap next to her, searching for any telltale damp spots. There had been twelve in the cohort, and so far, Shea had found only three. "I know she made it gladly."

Just as she'd hoped, all that patting and feeling about elicited a bloom of curiosity. *What are you doing?*

Shea smiled in spite of everything. "Well, while we're waiting, I thought we might play a game to pass the time. It's one I've just now invented – a delightful combination of find-the-smell, dig-the-hole, and fetch-and-carry..."

As luck would have it, U'ru turned out to be a stellar player. She still didn't care much for the House of Losange – not their stealing of her son, and certainly not their recent attempts to kill her – but pitied them enough to help dig them out and drag them to the river. Shea kept her mind on the work, and tried to ignore the guilty little voice in the back of her mind: if the cohort hadn't met her, if she hadn't sold them on the idea of 'wizard-hunting' for that damned boy, they would be off clearing a dam somewhere on the Calentito River, alive and oblivious a hundred miles away.

Well, and if that vast fool Jeté hadn't kidnapped, manhandled, and threatened to kill her, they might have still gotten their silt-shoveling happily-ever-after. Too late now. They were dead and so was he – god, Shea didn't even want to think about what it would take to haul his ungainly carcass out from this muddy midden – and now they were nothing but a mess to be cleaned up and disposed of.

But Shea and U'ru did their grim penance all that afternoon, and the work was good for both of them. It was only later in the day, when they finally climbed to the top of the landslide, that Shea noticed the strange crater near the slope of the hill.

She splayed out her stubby toes, treading carefully on the loose ground, until she was so close that even her poor eyes couldn't be mistaken. There was a pit there, a hole as big and conspicuous as if someone had taken a spoon to a wheel of soft cheese... as if something huge had crawled out of its own grave.

CHAPTER SEVEN
THE MOST ODIOUS OF SINS

AH CHE, A CHILD *of nine winters, lay still and waited.*

It was a hard thing to do. The cot was coarse and itchy, the thin blanket grimy with his sweat, and his muscles ached for want of use. They wanted to get up and run, play, do anything but lie there.

They didn't seem to know about the rest of him.

So he lay on his left side, facing the wall – not even a wall, but a cheap, oil-stinking tarp – and squelched the urge to roll over. It was well that he did: soon enough, the stomp of heavy, ugly boots told him that Wally Hen had come back.

"Hey, Ah Che!" the big boy called as he threw back the tent flap. "Sit up and food with me!"

Ah Che pretended to be asleep. No ordinary sleep could last through Wally Hen's ruckus, but Ah Che breathed slow and silently, as if he had gone to the deep place that welcomed him after his seizures, and wished, wished, wished to return there now.

But he couldn't suppress a flinch as Wally Hen knocked him roughly on the shoulder. "Get up, oyami," he said in his clumsy, babyish Maia. "Now is our time for the meal!"

Oyami. *Little brother. That was what Ah Che had called Ah Set, back before the world shrank. It was not a word that this hulking, stinking, turkey-warbling half-boy had any right to use.*

If he and his kind hadn't come to the village last year, there would have been no sickness. If he hadn't found Ah Che, he could have finished dying and joined his family in the Other Lands. If he didn't keep stuffing him with bad food and worse medicine, Ah Che might still be able to get there.

"Up, up!" Wally Hen said. "You won't want to eat cold."

But Wally Hen had done all those things – had stolen Ah Che away from the village and ridden him all the way to this muddy, smoky, miserable tent city and paid some white doctor far too much to hold him here in this world.

Not enough to make the world whole again.

Not enough to bring back Mama and the baby and Ah Set.

Not enough to revive his eyes.

Ah Che's body had long since turned traitor, his stomach growling at the smell of cheap meat and beans, his limbs aching to move and his bladder conspiring to give them an excuse. But he knew how to trick them. He breathed faster, as fast as if he were running full-sprint away from this awful half-life.

Wally Hen must have seen the quickening rhythm of his chest. "Hey!" *he said, rolling Ah Che roughly onto his back – a cruel child flipping a helpless sand-beetle.* "Don't do that! You stop!"

Ah Che didn't stop. He breathed faster and faster still, struggling not to notice the smell of sweat and soot and smoke that told of Wally Hen's day-long backbreaking labor in the silver mine, striving not to feel the fatigue tremor in the older boy's iron grip. He went right on gorging his lungs with air, desperate to trigger that giddy strangeness, that aura of loose, dizzy motion that promised another seizure, another trip to the dream-world, another visit with his family. This time, he would remember his waking-life. This time, he would beg to stay.

But the only motion was a dim, colorless shifting in his periphery as Wally Hen bent down and grabbed him.

"Let go!" Ah Che cried, feeling himself hoisted bodily into the air. "Stop, put me down!"

He pushed and fought against that lanky, rough-shirted body, his struggle punctuated by booted footsteps and the tent-flap dragging over Ah Che's face – just before he caught a whiff of fresh air.

Then he was sinking, a great gray flatness surging up at the edges of what remained of his vision, and he was set down on cold, dry ground.

"You are my brother, oyami," Wally Hen said, his voice sounding near to tears. "My family. My friend. But if you won't try to eat with me or talk with me, then you can't come in my house."

Hot words boiled up in Ah Che's throat. I'm not your *oyami*, they said. A brother isn't turned away because he doesn't do what you want. A brother isn't someone you throw out when you get tired of him. *But they were lost in the retreating stomp of heavy boots and the oil-cloth swush of the tent-flap.*

So Ah Che sat there in the middle of the camp street, as shirtless and exposed as when Turtle had been tricked out of his shell. He smelled cooking-fires and latrine pits and the ever-present sulfurous stink of the mine, heard shouts and talking in the language of rough white men, and through his earth-sense he could faintly feel their rude, clumping footsteps.

He didn't belong here. He didn't belong anywhere. And the only thing more terrifying than the thought that these barbarian strangers might be staring at him right now was the fear that they weren't and wouldn't – that they would step around the poxy blind native boy as if he were a lump of dung in the street, and go right on about their business.

Ah Che hunched over, hot tears running down his face, wild ideas flying through his mind. He would run away back home... but Wally Hen had gone back to find the village deserted, and there was no telling whether anyone was left alive to return.

He would go to the Kaia who lived on the edge of camp, whose language was at least close enough to understand... but they had no reason to want a scrawny Maia boy who might still be sheltering disease.

He would go back to the dream-world and beg Mama to keep him there... but in the deepest, most honest part of himself, he knew that if she'd left him here this long, it was because she either didn't have the power to take him, or didn't want him to go.

Ah Che curled over onto himself, his back and shoulders heaving under the warmth of an unseen sun. He couldn't be here. He couldn't stand it – not for another minute. He pulled his hair and rocked on his heels and bit his tongue until it bled, but all that did was make him cry harder. And the parts of his body cried too – for food, for movement, for everything he'd denied and deprived them of through all these long, wasted days.

It was no good. In spite of everything, his fever had long since abated, his tremors stopped, his blisters healed to fresh, puckered scars. The door to the Other Lands had closed, and he was stuck on this side, in this life.

Ah Che sat there in the street, runny-nosed and wet-faced, as the world went by around him.

He knew the word for 'elder brother'. Ah Set had called him by it before he could even pronounce his given name. To repurpose it now, to give it to that clumsy half-white thief like a pair of cheap shoes, would be a heinous betrayal.

But in a world full of closed doors, he couldn't afford to pass by the one that would still open for him... even if it was a smelly tent flap.

Ah Che rocked forward to a tiptoeing squat. He emptied his nose and wiped his eyes, and then gently scraped and patted the dirt until the earth covered all of what he had given it. He could not reclaim his old life, but his new one would still belong to the Maia. He swore it.

Then he stood and reached out for the oilcloth fold.

"What are your wants, Ah Che?"

Even with broken words, the hard, suspicious voice from inside the tent was awful to bear. He'd never heard Wally Hen angry before.

Ah Che let his hand fall away from the tent. He wrapped it around his opposite fist and held both together under his ribs, trying to force the word up and out of his throat before it choked him.

It was Ah Set's word. A family word. It didn't belong to that gangly stranger in there. It wasn't Ah Che's to give.

But maybe it could be loaned for a little while.

"I'm – I'm sorry, emi," he said. "May I please come in?"

There was a small silence. Ah Che held his breath. Finally, mercifully, the answer came to him in the clump of heavy, ugly boots, and the opening swush *of the tent flap.*

ELIM HAD NEVER had much of an opinion about mountains. They were pretty enough in pictures, seemed well-suited for handing down godly commandments, and they would have livened up the horizon back home. He could approve of mountains on principle, in much the same way as he would lend his endorsement to petticoats, libraries, and the moon.

That was before he'd tried to climb one.

Now, he'd decided, mountains were awful – just the most horrible, hateful, unnatural piles of shameless man-eating lies. This one here kept switch-backing and back-tracking on him, turning easy roads into thigh-slaughtering steep slopes, widening the trail right before washing it clean out, opening gaps in the rock just big enough for whatever midgety crow-men had carved it and leaving him to duck and squeeze and pray to God he didn't put a foot clean through their old rotten bridge-boards. And about the only thing worse than the rocks – the ones in his shoes, the ones in his path, the ones hanging down overhead waiting to crush him like a lizard under a dropped brick – was the absence of rocks. Which was to say the absence of ground. Which was to say the appalling, nauseating drop mere inches from his feet, the yawning abyss of scrubby red earth just waiting for him to put a foot wrong, just waiting to receive his broken body like a window-pane whacked by a cross-eyed idiot pigeon.

Elim didn't look. He didn't look to the side, where the long drop was waiting for him, or above, where the rock loomed over him, and he certainly didn't look ahead, because about the only thing worse than noticing how high up he'd already come was thinking about how much farther he still had to go.

So he kept his gaze on the one safe place – the ground just in front of him – and concentrated on putting one foot in front of the other. It was harder than he could have imagined. There was no way to use his right hand for balance, at least not while he was wearing Hawkeye like a dirty fur coat, and he couldn't get any rhythm – couldn't plan farther than his next three steps. His legs burned, his breath steamed, and the only thing keeping him going was the thought of how much pain his passenger would endure if Elim set him down for a rest.

Elim didn't want to think about what kind of miracle it would take for the a'Krah to fix Hawkeye. He especially didn't want to think about how Sil was keeping up behind him – not wheezing, not panting, not even complaining. He might not have been breathing at all. Elim's master-plan, such as it was, was to pour his brains into his legs, and not think about what might happen to either of his two desperately irregular friends before they got to the top – or what would happen to him after.

Then he noticed the tracks.

They came up from another trail, one that converged from the eastern side of the mountain, and carried on forward from there. It was hard to read anything in the hard, sullen earth, but as Elim's big feet overlaid that other trailsign with his own, trudging on for minute after stooped, sweaty minute, he began to think that he knew those footprints.

Or better to say, he knew the hoofprints.

There probably weren't too many horses out here to begin with. Fewer still with eastern-style shoeing. And Elim would lay down a virgin dollar that there was only one walking around with steel-shod back feet and bare-naked fronts... even if that horse shouldn't be walking at all.

Even if Elim had shot it himself.

He'd seen Actor roll over and die, watched the blood trickle down his forehead and the life leave his big brown eyes. Nothing short of the hand of God Almighty could have brought that horse back up to his feet.

But then again, Elim would have said the same thing about Sil.

"Well, that's something," Sil rasped. God, he sounded like he still had that noose around his neck.

"Yup," Elim grunted. He didn't want to see, hear, or smell his partner just then – but more than that, he didn't want anybody else's thinking encouraging his own.

Because already he was thinking that there were two sets of footprints accompanying that horse, and that he knew who they belonged to. He was thinking – hoping – that that meant that they'd made it through that night at the river alive: that Bootjack had fought off the fishmen, that Way-Say was alive and well-ish, just as Hawkeye had promised he would be. Elim had less idea what to make of the long, continuous scrape-marks that followed them. They might have been poles or sticks of some kind, heavily weighted and dragging behind the horse. Elim couldn't imagine Ax taking kindly to that. Really, he couldn't imagine that he was imagining that Ax was still alive.

"I'm not," Hawkeye said.

Elim just about shit a kitten. For one precarious second, his balance deserted him – which he rectified by positively throwing himself away from the abyss, against the sheer wall on his left. He would have smashed his shoulder right into it, if Hawkeye's backside hadn't kindly intervened.

"Elim, what –" Sil began.

"Hey, buddy," Elim said, forcing some light into his tone. "That mean you're awake now?"

He looked down, to where Hawkeye's head sloped off Elim's left shoulder. He was staring almost philosophically at the ground, filthy and half-blinded by his own hair, and yet as calm and sober as a clerk in church. "No," he said, and commenced picking at Elim's pants-leg.

Elim was irrationally glad to hear Hawkeye's voice again, and yet too nervous to laugh. "If you're allotting on picking my pocket, you're aiming on the low side. Here, how about we have us a little sit-down, let you see the world right-side up for a change?"

"Elim," Sil said again, now close enough that his stink preceded him, "we really don't have –"

Elim's right hand was occupied in pinning Hawkeye's arm to his good leg in a triangle-pattern centered around Elim's head and shoulders. It kept Hawkeye's rifle-splinted leg from bashing up against anything, prevented the rest of him from slipping, and left Elim one free hand to keep from falling to both their deaths.

It was also exactly as uncomfortable as carrying a grown man ought to be, and had been for miles now.

"Sil, he was a hundred thirty pounds *before* I strapped my gun on him, and listening to you don't make him any lighter. I am going to set him down wherever I dang please, so you might as well..."

Elim trailed off as Hawkeye turned his head, forcing his face into the meat of Elim's upper arm. It was a peculiar, unnatural sensation, as if Hawkeye meant to look at something and didn't even realize that he'd met resistance. He stayed like that, his neck twisted in stubborn, senseless rigidity, his pants-picking fingers carrying on perfectly undisturbed.

Elim was disturbed enough for both of them. He set the Sundowner down as gingerly as he could, leaning him up against the wall and watching in vain for any sign of understanding of rationality – even a recognition of pain as his smashed leg touched the ground. "Hawkeye?" When he got no answer, Elim spit on the end of his poncho and stooped to see if he couldn't at least clean some of the filth off the poor man's face.

Hawkeye just looked out over the edge, staring intently at nothing. Sil studied him the way a boy might consider a dead squirrel. "Well, look, he's obviously not – ah!"

Sil's grousing ended in a rusty gasp, punctuated by a vast sandy *whush*. When Elim looked up, Sil was gone – and so was the trail he'd been standing on.

"Sil?" Elim almost couldn't bring himself to look – and then he couldn't look away. "Sil! Holy God, Sil, are you all right?"

From twenty feet down, a big black spot left by the minor avalanche of dirt and stones disappearing down the slope, Will Halfwick's little brother looked up. He was clinging to something, a root or a rock so small that Elim couldn't even make it out, and his frightened, earth-streaked face was almost indistinguishable from the mountain. "NO, damn you, I'm not! Pull me up! Pull me –" His voice broke down into a coughing gurgle, which only put the spurs to Elim's panic.

He had to help him, before Sil lost his grip. He had to save him – but with what?

Elim had no rope, no tools. Hell, he didn't even have a rag to spit on. He could tie his pants to his poncho and lower that down, maybe get Hawkeye's shirt too – but that wasn't going to do it. That wouldn't even come close.

Elim wheeled around, looking for anything, any root or shrub or stick he could rip out and put to use...

... but in the end, the only hint of help he could find were a few dusty footprints and the tracks of one half-shod, questionably-dead horse.

That would have to do.

"Hold on, buddy," Elim called down. "I'm going for help, and I'll be right back for you. Just dig in your heels and hold on!"

He didn't give Sil a choice, or Hawkeye either. He just turned and bolted up the trail, praying to God that the two of them would have the grip and good sense to stay put.

DÍA'S COURAGE DIDN'T fail her. But it could be said to falter when she got to the crows.

They were still perched there in the piñon trees, just as they had been yesterday evening – maybe a few more or less. It was hard to tell.

But there was no mistaking the tufts of brown dog hair nestled like pieces of solstice popcorn in those piney green needles – nor the spots of blood on the ground before them. And there was no telling whether the viciousness of that second attack owed more to the Dog Lady's desperate tenacity, or the crows' anger at rebuffing her trespass a second time.

Día approached very, very slowly. "*Please excuse my return,*" she said in Marín, pinning her hopes less on the words than the solicitous tone that shaped them. "*I'm sorry to bother you a second time, but I have a very urgent errand. Would you please allow me to pass this way?*"

Too late, she realized that she ought to have asked that differently: Día trusted herself to interpret a bird's objection much more reliably than its consent.

Well, too late now.

So she bowed from the waist, wrists upturned and outstretched, and repeated the words Weisei had taught her. "*Kalei ne ei'ha.*" *Please see me kindly.*

Eighteen pairs of beady black eyes stared down at her with varying degrees of interest. Nothing else happened.

Día straightened, willing to give her eyeteeth for a second a'Krah translation. *By which I mean, please let me pass, and please, please, please don't peck out my eyes or dive-bomb my face.*

One crow turned to preen its nearest neighbor.

Día did not know much about crow behavior... but at this point, they could have blessed her eye with a warm white dropping, and she would have read it as a sign of God's will for peace.

So she bowed and turned out her wrists again, even more deeply than before. "*Thank you very much, reverend crows. You have my deepest gratitude.*" And she went walking on...very, very slowly.

It was difficult to force herself not to keep watching them, not to look as if she mistrusted them. Día silently counted out twenty paces, until the cluster of piñon trees was well behind her. Then she let out a stomach-emptying breath.

The Dog Lady had been right, then: Día might have been seen with her, but at least she wasn't considered to *belong* to her. That was a distinction she was eager to keep.

And having now passed those first ominous gatekeepers, Día would lose no time on her quest. She followed the fresh, faint footprints in the dirt – one light pair of eastern boots, and one big, heavy set of moccasins – and only barely kept her pace in check. It might be disrespectful to be seen running in this sacred place... even if it would be downright dangerous to be caught up here after dark.

The cold air dried Día's throat and sharpened her lungs, entreating her to consider how far she might have to go and where her next drink was going to come from. Día's answer lay in those two sets of human footprints, which soon became four and a horse, which led her up a narrow rise and under an especially sinister-looking rocky overhang and around a steep, broken bend –

– where a filthy, earth-covered man sat propped against the sheer sandstone face, slumped over as if drunk or dead.

And was that a *gun* tied to his leg?

"*Hello?*" Día approached cautiously, having never been promised that Marhuk did not harbor thieves or road-agents on his holy mountain. "*Can you hear me? Are you hurt?*"

He didn't answer – which wasn't to say there was no reply.

"Who's there?"

It was a nasty, guttural growl, coming from somewhere down below. Día crouched on the spot, mindful to keep an eye on the first stranger even as she glanced down in search of the second.

He was about halfway down the slope, clinging to something Día couldn't see – and though his voice was monstrous, almost unrecognizable, she knew that tone all too well.

"Elim, are you there? Pull me up, damn you!"

Día put a hand to her mouth. There, hanging twenty feet down, was the very same Sil Halfwick she had accidentally revived back in Island Town.

Well, perhaps not quite same: he sounded awful, and probably looked worse. From Día's present perspective, he was the same black-clad blot he'd always been – a man-sized fly in the ointment of creation. The one who had lied to her, tricked her, stolen her horse and abandoned her. The one who had left her to bake in the desert sun, wandering helplessly like a sun-touched vagrant. The one whose last words to her had been *filthy scorched whore*.

The one Weisei had asked her to save.

"Elim, what the devil are you playing at? Answer me!"

Well, and how was she meant to save him? Día leaned a little further out, just in case she'd missed some hidden path, but no: that looked like a sixty-foot drop, and he was nearly halfway down. There was no going down for him – he'd have to be drawn up somehow.

But Día had no rope or anything like it, and that

poor fellow in the corner looked even more ill-equipped than she. She had her cassock, her belt, her knife, and a powerful disinclination to put herself out for a wretched, selfish, manipulative, hateful young man who had brought her nothing but grief.

But Día didn't live by her own wishes – and thank God for that. She closed her eyes, reaching down past her own pettiness, past everything that she would call herself, seeking the infinite wellspring at the bottom of her heart. *Well, Master,* she thought, *if you want me to help him, show me how. Help me do the right thing. Give me a sign.* Día held still until she had quieted everything inside her – until she knew she could hear any answer that came.

When she opened her eyes again, there was just that same Sil Halfwick, clinging like a fatted tick to the mountain's flank...that same mountain, sheer sandstone walls bottoming out into a dry, stunted forest down below... that same empty space stretching out between them, a lovely, fatal absence of anything but clean, sharp high-desert air.

And in her periphery, curtaining the picture almost as an afterthought, were the swaying, ropy locks of Día's own hair.

Her insides froze.

No.

She couldn't. She couldn't possibly. Her father had made her hair, wanting her to keep it always as a sign of her faith, her connection to both God and His creation.

There was no holy rebuke at that first, most selfish thought – only the pitiless reply of Día's own reason. *And then he wanted you to go out and give yourself in service to the world.*

But her hair was her pride – *a sin* – her beauty – *vanity, another sin* – the one thing that truly belonged to her – *greed, the most odious of sins.*

But her job was to find Elim – she had to save him before the a'Krah put him to death. The Dog Lady was depending on her.

And who better than Halfwick to tell you where he's gone?

But he was so far down – what if she still couldn't reach him?

The answer was as cold and firm as the stone under her feet. *Then you had better give it all.*

"*Hello?*" Halfwick's mutilated voice tried again in Marín. "*Is anyone there?*"

He hadn't spotted her. She could still look for some other solution, run ahead to try and find help...

Except that judging by the tracks, Elim had already done just that – assuming he hadn't gotten fed up and shoved Halfwick over the edge in the first place.

Día pulled her dreadlocks over her face, breathing deep from the rich, subtle scent of her own body's creation. She held fast to their tips, the place where her father had first combed and shaped them all those years ago, and tried to remember the sound of his voice. He had been so big and strong, so full of stern, silent righteousness.

But all she could think of was Fours, her sad, craven *papá*, small and stooped, beaten down by years of fear and duplicity and self-serving compromise. She remembered their last conversation, the day Halfwick had sat up on the slab and obliterated the order of her life.

Papá, she had asked him, *how do you know the right thing to do?*

He had smiled down at his hands, pinching the little scarred spaces between his fingers. *Well, I just think of what I might do, you know, this way or that one, and it's... do you know, the right thing is almost always the one that I am most powerfully anxious to avoid.*

That was how she had decided – right then, on the spot. She could have left Halfwick to his own devices, or given him a horse to use in hunting down his friend. But she had done the hardest thing – she had determined to go with him, just to see that he could have what he said he wanted, could join in Elim's punishment without giving him the means to escape it.

And this was where it had gotten her.

"Please," came the rotting moan from down below. "Please, if you can hear me..."

The world wavered as Día's eyes filled with tears.

I was hoping that you had come to help make things right. That was what Weisei had said. *I was hoping that the Starving God had sent you to help Afvik finish his life.*

He isn't a 'Starving' God, Día had wanted to tell him. *He's just God. He is love and abundance. He is creation itself.*

But that didn't mean he would never ask for a sacrifice.

Día clutched the tips of her hair one last time, a child's tiny fist clinging to her father's hand.

Then she stood and drew her knife.

"Just eat it."

Weisei sighed, as if Vuchak's voice were a pain in his side, and rolled over. "I will, Vichi – after I wake up."

No, not after. Now. Vuchak stood there with the cold

meat in his hands, and prodded his *marka*'s backside with the toe of his moccasin-boot. "Well, split the difference with me. Have some now – just half." Weisei's stomach had to be kept busy, especially while the rest of him was at rest. Food was strength – strength to move, and strength to keep that half-ton of dead horse moving too.

Not that Weisei had any thought for that. He curled over, burying himself deeper in his black-feather cloak, striving to shut out Vuchak right along with the sun overhead. "Leave me alone – let me sleep."

Vuchak glanced about their makeshift camp, willing some hidden source of patience to reveal itself. But there was only the dry copse of juniper and sage just up from the trail – the slow seep Vuchak had dug from the remains of the stream-bed – the horse, lying as far downwind as possible, with the makeshift travois bearing Dulei's coffin still lashed to its back.

Vuchak let out a slow breath through his nose. The sooner he got through this, the sooner he could have his own rest. "I will," he promised, "but I want to make sure that your body-soul doesn't go hungry while your free-soul is out visiting. You've been working too hard, *marka*: you need to replenish yourself. Here, sit up with me, just for a minute – let's share this one."

Weisei sat up, propped himself up on one arm, and lifted the black fold of his *yuye* – but the look on his face promised nothing good. "Vichi," he said, as if explaining something incredibly simple, "I don't want it. That meat is cold and tough and makes me grow old chewing it. My guts are stuffed with it already – I haven't been able to pay a debt since yesterday morning. Leave me alone and let me sleep, and if you really want to do something for me, see if you can find some *koka* berries anywhere around here. I'll eat with you when I wake up."

And he pulled down his *yuye* and rolled back over, folding his holy cloak over himself like a black-feather cocoon.

Vuchak stood there, cold venison in hand, marinating in silence.

He'd hunted down that deer – well, found it, anyway. Wrestled the carcass away from the coyotes. Washed it, butchered it, cooked it, dried the scraps, rendered the fat, pounded the relentless daylights out of the jerky until his head throbbed and his arms ached, and made no word of complaint about any of it. All Weisei had to do was chew and swallow – and that was asking too much? That was reason to order Vuchak out to find something more to his liking, as if he had nothing better to do – as if he weren't absolutely dead on his feet?

Vuchak's grip tightened, squeezing the steak until his fingers trembled, wrestling with the urge to turn and hurl it straight off the mountainside.

He wouldn't, of course. He would master his anger. He would turn it to useful work. And if Weisei wanted to behave like a spoiled child, his ever-faithful *atodak* would be glad to accommodate him.

Vuchak strode right over and sat down on top of him, planting his knees in the dirt on either side of Weisei's frail figure. Then he tore off a handsome bite of venison and set to chewing.

Weisei rolled over underneath him, his eyebrows lifting under his blindfold. "Vichi, what are you doing?!"

"I hear your wishes, *marka*," Vuchak said from

around his mouthful. "If the food is too hard and tiresome for your teeth, then mine will be glad to help you." He kept his tone pleasant and sincere – nothing at all like the words underneath it. *If you expect me to spit food into your mouth like a helpless baby, I'll do it. If you want to act like an infant, I'll treat you like one.*

Weisei pushed and squirmed, raisin-faced with disbelief. "That's disgusting – get off me!"

But it was the easiest thing in the world for Vuchak to swallow the meat, drop his weight on Weisei's stomach, pin his arms, and lean in to make himself clear. "I will, when you can do what I ask of you. My job is to feed you. Your job is to move that horse. Our job is to take Dulei home. And if one of us can't do his job because he decided to put his own wants ahead of his duty..."

The end of Vuchak's thought fell away amidst the sound of onrushing footsteps: soft shoes pounding hard up the trail, and then stumbling to a halt. Vuchak glanced behind him – and realized too late that he had an audience.

"Ylem?" From under Vuchak's armpit, Weisei's voice was an astonished squeak.

Sure enough, the hulking half-man was standing there in the middle of the trail, sweating and sucking air and staring at them.

Staring at Vuchak, who was presently bent over Weisei like a lusty hunter plowing his reluctant wife: hips on hips, hands on wrists, faces bare inches apart.

Damn it.

But if the half had anything to say about that, there was no understanding it: he pointed obscenely down the trail, all but shouting his incomprehensible jabber. "*Komquik – zilzfálenanuigoddagogíddim!*"

What could anyone say to that?

Vuchak had no time to consider it: Ylem cast his gaze wildly about and then dove for Dulei's coffin.

"*Hey!*" Vuchak called, bounding instantly up to his feet. "*Stop that – you stop!*"

The bastard half paid him no mind, molesting the box just long enough to pull off the horse harness they'd used to keep Dulei secure on the travois. By the time Vuchak caught up, the half was bolting back down the trail, pausing long enough for one more point, one more pleading burst of nonsense. Then he was gone.

From behind, Weisei's voice was small. "I think we'd better help him."

Vuchak did not want to help. He didn't want to fight about food, or have to think about Ylem and his murderous holy mother. He just wanted to lie down.

..., but whatever had panicked the half, Vuchak fully intended to go down and meet it before it came up and found them. He snatched up his spear, privately cursing the fishman who had smashed his bow, touched the knife in his boot just to make sure, and spared a glance back at Weisei. "Stay. Here."

Vuchak did not like the edge in his own voice, much less the idea of leaving his *marka* alone and undefended. But any objection from Weisei stayed bottled up inside him, where it belonged, as Vuchak hurried off down the trail.

That was good enough. They would clear things up later. For now, Vuchak was off and running, chasing someone else's problem before it could linger long enough to become his.

* * *

"Wait – wait a minute, please."

It was a choked, feminine voice, one that Sil probably should have recognized. She sounded like she might cry.

Well, that made two of them. He was hanging on to a shelf of barren rock, his boots dangling into empty space, and the thought of what might happen if he fell was only marginally more frightening than what was already happening while he clung on.

The rock was as sharp as a freshly-knapped flinthead, its edge sawing into his flesh. In his first frantic minutes, struggling to get a foothold before he fell, Sil hadn't even registered the scraping, grinding sensation in his right hand. It wasn't until he reached up for a better grip that he noticed the gash in his fingers where the rock had cut through them – saw the dull yellowish-white of exposed bone.

THEN it hurt, certainly – an angry, terrified throbbing. But it didn't bleed, and it didn't end. He didn't lose his grip. He didn't get tired. He didn't even sweat. He just hung there, burying his head in the crook of his outstretched arm to keep the flies from his face, sick with days and nights of barely-suppressed horror, clinging less to the rock than to his failing conviction that he could still be fixed, that this could all still be paid for somehow.

Even if he didn't see how.

Even if he was almost literally falling apart.

Even if the unpromised resolution at the top of the mountain was suddenly so much less tempting than the quick-and-guaranteed one waiting for him at the bottom.

Hurry up, he willed whoever-she-was up there. *Before I lose my grip.*

He could do it, though. He could just let go. Then it would be over – the pests, the stench, the sinister swelling in his belly, that unbearably foul taste in his mouth. All gone in an instant – in a quick, clean finish.

... unless it wasn't.

Unless, god forbid, it wasn't.

Just the idea was so awful that Sil could scarcely bear to consider it. The fall would kill him. Of course it would kill him.

But the hanging hadn't. That long, blistering walk through the desert hadn't. And if the drop didn't... if he hit the bottom and just – just *smashed* like a glass on a flat rock...

The rope that dropped down beside him couldn't have come a moment too soon.

And it wasn't a proper rope – it was made from some peculiar native fiber, black and faintly oily and knotted every couple of feet – and Sil was no kind of climber, and he didn't care a lick about any of it: he grabbed it and held on.

"I've got it," he called as softly as he thought would carry, anxious not to provoke the horrible thing in his throat. "Pull me up!"

"It's too short, and you're too heavy," she called back, her voice thick with exertion. "You have to pull yourself up."

Ugh. Sil glanced up at the vague dark shape leaning down over the ledge – probably an a'Krah woman. If Elim were there, *he'd* have pulled him up.

... well, and if Sil meant to wait on Elim, he might as well throw himself over and have done with it.

Sil thought about warning her that he was going to be absolute rubbish at this – that he'd never climbed so much as a tree. Instead, he sank his efforts into seeking out one toehold and then another, getting one hand above the other, and doing his utmost not to notice the way the rope slid into the gash across his fingers, widening the bone-deep rip in his flesh every time he pulled himself up. But otherwise, the climb matched the rest of his life to date: slow, awkward, more failure than success, probably as dull to watch as it was unbearable to live –

– and over before he knew it. A warm hand closed over his wrist, hauling him the last of the way over the ledge. As Sil struggled to get his legs up and underneath him, his rescuer scrabbled for the rope, gathering it up as if it were a precious, priceless treasure.

Well, certainly it had done him a service. "Thank you," he said, coughing in a feeble attempt to clear that irritating blockage, getting belatedly up to his feet to make a second, fuller start on gratitude...

... but as he got his first proper look at her, his mouth opened for something that started as *Don't I know you*, caromed into *Oh my god*, and burst into a single, bottomless *I'm so sorry* before closing again, speechless and utterly impotent.

He did know her. That was the Afriti girl – Día, as she called herself. The one he and Elim had all but run over, that first day outside Sixes. The one he'd woken to find violating him with her mouth, that morning after the hanging. The one he'd ridden off from and left in the dust, after she decided to play the bossy big sister.

The one who was standing here now, clutching the mass of her own severed dreadlocks to her chest – bald as an egg.

"You..." Sil could scarcely grasp the implications. "... what have you done?"

She looked as if she would cry, or perhaps be sick on the spot. She backed up a step, eyes wide, and swallowed. "I came to help you," she said in a thin, quivering voice. "You aren't supposed to be here."

Normally, Sil would have taken exception to being told his own business. But he absolutely could not fathom how she had gotten all the way out here, much less happened to pass right by here at this exact moment, much less why she would have... done that to herself.

"I know," he said, striving to conjure some coherent answer, struggling not to stare at her denuded head. "But I'm – I told you, I wanted to go with Elim, to try and talk the a'Krah out of killing him. He's here, you know – he was here just a bit ago. He'll be right back." He didn't tell her about his hope of a cure from the crow people – it was a thought too fragile to even speak it.

Día shook her head, sparing a glance for that damned dead-weight fellow Elim had left propped in the corner. "No, I don't mean here – I mean, you shouldn't be *here*. In this world. You don't..." She hesitated, as if groping for the right euphemism. "... you don't belong here anymore."

Sil was no fool. He heard what went unsaid – and even though the very idea was rank nonsense, it scared him terribly. "Ridiculous," he said, with more force than strictly necessary. "I might be ill, but I'm not –"

"You ARE," she said, her lip trembling even as her jaw held firm. "Someone put a noose around your neck and pushed you off a balcony and hanged you, and I'm terribly sorry that it happened, but it did, and it can't be undone. You need to realize that. You have to understand that you're already –"

Sil wouldn't hear it. He couldn't. "Shut up, will you, just shut up!"

Día backed up a step, clutching her pile of hair even as she straightened to her fullest height. "You're dead, Sil Halfwick. You died and you can't –"

Sil bulled forward, possessed by a wild urge to grab the daft bint by the shoulders and shake her until she gave up that heinous lie –

– until she lashed out with a hard kick to the gut.

Something popped. A hideous, feculent belch ripped out of him, the taste bringing up putrid memories of that fruit and cheese he'd taken from Día's private larder – the week-old pilfered afterthought that had been his last meal. Sil bent over to spit, desperate to get the taste out of his mouth...

... and looked down to see a dark stain spreading over his deflating stomach.

Sil stared down at himself, as relieved by the end of that unbearable pressure as he was helpless to understand the rank wetness creeping out over the front of his dirty blue shirt. If he didn't know better, he'd think he had... well, it was as if he'd just... burst.

Someone was choking. Sil looked up.

Día had taken a sharp step to his left, perhaps to keep him from pinning her against the wall, and was now staring at him from a pace or two down the trail, her face as bloodless and gray as it had been the moment he sat up from the slab – and now crumpling with horrified disgust.

Him.

She was disgusted with *him*.

She was disgusted by *him*.

Sil stared at her – at the woman who had ruined

everything. *THIS IS YOUR FAULT!* he screamed – only he didn't get past "THIS" before the rotting paper in his throat finally tore, pulping his righteous outrage into a rancid, meaty gurgle.

Sil charged. He hurled himself right at her, desperate to hurt her – to knock her down, wrap his mangled fingers around her bald head and smash it into the ground until she was *sorry.*

But Día didn't kick him again. She didn't step aside or run or draw her knife or hit him. She might not have even seen him. She had just doubled over to throw up.

Which left Sil crashing into her, knocking her off-balance, pitching them both bodily down the trail-bend – and over the edge.

And as he plummeted down alongside her choking, abortive scream, Sil had just enough time to close his eyes and hope that this time would be different – that this fall would finally finish him.

VUCHAK COULD NOT have said what he'd been expecting to find – but an earth-crusted, half-dead Hakai wasn't it.

The traitorous *ihi'ghiva* was lying propped up in a little wind-sheltered sandstone pocket just past the big bend in the trail. He looked like a man beaten to death, buried, and dug up three days later: his whole body caked with dirt and dried blood, his leg splinted with the half's rifle and torn strips of his own *yuye*, his only human color the wet gap where his mouth hung open. And he was *snoring*, as soft and modestly as if he had only fallen asleep on watch.

And apparently this was not even a point of interest.

The half was pacing back and forth at the edge of the trail, clutching the crumpled harness in his arms, and bellowing like a mother cow bereft of its calf. "*Zil! ZIL! Kañuhírmi? ZIL!*"

Vuchak understood none of it. Nothing in there sounded like an Ardish word for 'mother', which gave him some slender hope that whatever-this-was didn't involve the Dog Lady. Marhuk would have never let her trespass here anyhow.

Vuchak studied the confused mess of tracks, already hopelessly marred by Ylem's clumsy tread. He noticed the fresh, broken stone at the outermost edge, a big triangular gap where the rock must have crumbled away just in the past hour or two: he would have remembered trying to edge the travois past it.

And he certainly wouldn't have missed that sour, lingering stink.

Vuchak leaned over and looked down the sheer drop, at the stark sandstone cliff and the valley of drought-stricken juniper at the bottom. Anyone who had fallen down there was dead, or would be soon, and there was no rope or harness long enough to reach them. They belonged to the crows now.

Which meant that all this, this standing about and shouting, no longer had any purpose. Now his job was to figure out how to get this bellowing barbarian to give up and come peacefully away with him.

He, Vuchak, who had nothing left but stubbornness and anger – who had just been fighting his own *marka* over half a steak.

Vuchak sighed, and made the sign of a sadistic god. This was going to end so badly.

Then he eyed the bigger man up and down, taking in

his bloodless, shaken face, and the death-grip in which he held that harness, and the darting of his eyes as they struggled to gaze into the abyss. He had gone stupid with fear – for whoever had gone missing down there, certainly, and maybe even from the height of the drop itself. He was not rational.

Well, and what had they done to make him go quietly before?

They had assigned him the care of the horse, that was what – given him a useful place to put his energies, a living creature to dote on. What was left of the horse belonged in Weisei's care now... but perhaps Vuchak could enlist a substitute.

He knelt down beside Hakai, and prodded the treacherous slave at the shoulder. "You bastard – wake up."

Hakai groaned, and slumped forward.

Vuchak pushed him roughly back up. "You dirty, shirking old wastrel – I said wake up!" And he slapped him – just hard enough.

"*Hei!*" The half turned at the sound, all full of glowering indignation. "*Donchuhiddim!*"

Vuchak didn't have to know those words to understand them perfectly. He might be a rotten diplomat – but he was also a professional target. He made a shooing gesture at the half-man, and went right on back to excising his frustrations with Hakai. He grabbed him by the shirt and shook him, and Vuchak's growing fear for the *ihi'ghiva*'s wounds was easily quashed by his readiness to pay him back for turning traitor with the fishmen. "What did you think you were doing, you gutless coward? What did they give you? What did you tell them? How dare you even –"

That was as far as he got before Ylem stormed up and shoved Vuchak aside. "*Ahzéd donHIDDIM,*" he snarled, before reaching down and hefting Hakai up over his shoulders. The slave moaned, but Ylem's glower never wavered as he backed up, staring down Vuchak even as he held his prize out of reach. "*Mine,*" he said in Marín, with a defiant up-jerk of his chin. "*Him mine.*"

If Vuchak could feel even mean-spirited pleasure, he would have smiled. As it was, he registered only the satisfaction of seeing things happen in the orderly, sensible fashion in which he'd planned them – for once. He answered with his own lifted chin, picking up the harness with one hand and pointing up the trail with the other. "*Go. Take him to Weisei.*"

But there was no satisfaction from the realization reflected in the half's eyes, from the despair with which he looked over the edge one last time, and the pang of bottomless sadness that crumpled the edges of his expression: whoever he'd lost down there was truly gone, and there was no sensible choice left but to take his remaining friend away for whatever care could be given to him – and to hope that that would be enough. That was the only thing left in his power to affect. That was all he could do.

To his credit, Ylem did not stall or protest. He answered with no words. He only swallowed, wearing the look of a man who didn't even have a hand free to pull the knife out of his own gut, and stooped to begin the climb again.

And Vuchak, the soul-weary avatar of hard truths, pitiless pragmatism and needful unkindness, picked up his spear and followed him.

*   *   *

SIL HIT WITH his shoulder first.

Then his right leg. Then his head. Then there was a tumbling barrel-roll that seemed to go on forever, then branches snapping and scratching at his face, and then a hard, final impact as he hit the ground with rib-cracking force.

Still awake. Still aware. Still completely, unendingly present.

He surged up to his feet, screaming in frustration and absolute bottomless fear – but his right knee buckled, and his left arm hung limp, and all that came out of his mouth were chunky, liquefying pieces of his own throat.

Spitting, gagging, eyes locked forward to keep from having to look at what he brought up, Sil crawled through the bristling brown underbrush with single-minded purpose.

A stone. A good fist-sized stone, if he could get one – or better yet, a big giant boulder, a rock that he could sit up against and just slam his head into, over and over until there was nothing left of his brain, until he was just a smear on a slab in a valley in the desert in the godforsaken middle of nowhere, pulverized and anonymous and *ended*. Anything. Anything to stop this. Anything to keep from having to...

Sil scrabbled heedlessly over anthills and nettles, clumps of blisterthorn and the clawing branches of dead sagebrush – but he stopped still at the sight of the juniper tree.

It was a little bigger than its neighbors, all sun-bleached needles and twisted, gnarly branches. But its nearer side was festooned like a morbid yule tree by a knotted length of thick black rope – by a garland of human hair, dangling like a hangman's noose in the dry, silent breeze.

Día.

Sil forgot the hunt for a stone. He stood up – carefully this time, keeping his weight on his sound leg – and limped forward, struggling to ignore the disjointed sway of his arm and the grinding in his knee and the thick wetness trickling from his stomach and down his inner thigh – to shut out everything to do with himself, just for a little while.

He couldn't call out to her. He had no voice left. So he moved as quietly as he could through the drought-strangled underbrush, sifting the high desert air for a moan, a cry, the softest possibility of life – hope – forgiveness.

As it turned out, Día had found the stone for him.

She was lying on her side in a grove of piñon trees, facing away. Her feet crossed almost daintily at the ankles, the dusty folds of her cassock draped over her still figure, and under the place where her bare head rested on the broken mass of granite, a sprouting creosote bush was fed by a dripping ribbon of blood, its source dark and serene and utterly, utterly still.

Sil took a step back.

He hadn't meant to. He really, honestly hadn't meant to. He wouldn't – not to anyone, especially not to a woman – especially not one who had made the fatal mistake of trying to help him one more time...

Except that he had. This time he really had. This wasn't like the business with Elim at the crossroads – there was no ambiguity this time, no question of intent. He'd lunged with nothing but an urgent need to hurt her, and now she was ruined and he was too, except that she was over and ended and he wasn't – he *couldn't* be – and in the space between the tragedy and the travesty there was no life, no hope, and no forgiveness – only himself – his infernal, eternal self – a shambling inhuman horror that turned and fled into the trees.

CHAPTER EIGHT
CARRIED

AH CHE, A CHILD of ten winters, pinched the needle and drew it through two layers of heavy canvas.

The cloth was coarse and thick, its sweat-starched grain rough under his fingers. This was a simple patch job – the knees always wore out first – and would not take long to finish. But he lingered on the work, half to give himself something to do and half to be seen doing something.

Tomorrow, he would go down the road and ask Mrs. Jameson if she had any clothes for wash. Even if she didn't, she would talk to him, ask him what he wanted from the drygrocer's, and perhaps let him play with the baby. For tonight, he was on his own.

It wasn't a bad life. He was glad to be friendly with the Jamesons, and grateful for their help. For one thing, the afternoons at their house were handsomely improving his Ardish: he understood that 'Wally Hen' was short for 'Wall-Eyed Henry', and that the big boy's name was made differently from most of the others Ah Che had learned. He knew the difference between 'Miss' and 'Missus', and how to order and pay for the things he *bought from the street-men. He could ask for directions and sometimes even understand the answers.*

But he could not get work – not real work, anyway. There were plenty of jobs a blind boy could do, but nobody wanted a boy who might sit down and begin convulsing on the spot, and then spend half the day asleep. It didn't matter that the fits only came once or twice a month: they ruined him for all reliable employment, and made Wally Hen reluctant to take any chances on him. Ah Che was not to go farther than he could walk in five minutes, unless he had someone with him. He was not to do any cooking – nothing with fire at all. He could not even go wading in the creek by himself, even though it was presently so shallow that he had to lie down flat just to wash his hair.

It was not a bad life, but sometimes it felt terribly small.

So Ah Che took his time with the needle, lining up each meticulous stitch, until he heard his reward come clumping through the tent flap. Then he had no more thought for sewing. "Welcome back, emi!"

"Hey, Ah Che." The voice that answered him was bone-weary, and judging by the smell it carried, just shy of drunk.

That was all right. That was fine. Wally Hen worked brutally hard in the mines, pushing barrows full of broken rock through tunnels too small for him to stand up in. But he was part of a crew now, had friends good enough to go drinking with, and Ah Che was happy for him. "Who did they put up tonight?"

Wally Hen did not like to talk about work. It was hard and dull and sometimes there were accidents. But he loved to see the prize-fights, and often Ah Che could get him to talk for the better part of an hour about this round or that one. He would be glad to have him talk about anything, really – anything for the chance to converse in his own language.

But there was no rustling of the tinder-box, no kerosene smell. Which meant that there was no light... which meant that Wally Hen didn't plan on staying awake long enough to need it. "Fischl and Fields. The same." There was a heavy, linen-muffled creak as he flopped down into bed. "I tell you tomorrow."

And that was it. No notice of the diligent work in Ah Che's lap. No appreciation for the freshly-washed sheet smoothed over his cot. No awareness at all.

Ah Che swallowed. He couldn't have a fight with Wally Hen – he owed the bigger boy far, far too much for that – but he couldn't bear another night of silence either. "I patched the hole in your trousers," he said.

Wally Hen mumbled something into his pillow. It might have been a thank you.

It wasn't fair. It wasn't. He worked hard, and Ah Che was grateful for that, but Wally Hen couldn't keep him at home all day like a cooped turkey and then not bother with him.

But if there was ever a time to say that, this was not it. "I, ah... I have something to ask you," Ah Che said, racking his mind for some half-reasonable question.

There was a cloth-muffled grunt.

But all Ah Che could think of were mundane things, chores and laundry and... well, perhaps that would do. "Will you give me the ones you're wearing now, so I can wash them tomorrow?"

There was no answer. Ah Che feared the bigger boy had already fallen asleep.

Then there was a sigh. Then the sound of a heavy boot dropping to the floor, and then another. By the time he registered the sound of a body shifting in bed, Ah Che had already set aside his mending and held out his hands.

A dirty pair of work-pants flew into them with a heavy cloth whump. They stank of smoke and burnt powder. "Thanks." Ah Che turned the legs right way out and began sifting through the pockets, his hands working automatically even as his mind groped for another subject. The coins came out; the dirty handkerchief went back in. The scrap of paper might be important, and the bread-crumbs certainly weren't. And at the bottom of the left back pocket, still warm from being sat on...

Ah Che felt the strange, waxy bullet. He sniffed it, brows furrowing at its faint spicy-sweet aroma. "Emi, what is this? This plug thing in your pocket?"

Wally Hen turned over. Then it sounded like he sat up. "Oh. I forgot. Listen, Ah Che – I have things to tell you."

Ah Che did listen. He heard the tinderbox rattle and smelled the kerosene, and his worry about what might be said was all but drowned out by the promise of a conversation long enough to be worth lighting a lamp for.

"That's a present," Wally Hen said. "Butch Gracie told me to give that for you."

Ah Che dropped the plug. Butch Gracie was one of the alley boys, who made their money on prize fights and alcohol and what Mr. Jameson called 'sporting women'. Nothing good would come from that quarter.

"No, no," Wally Hen said. "It isn't bad. Look at it."

Ah Che felt a distant warmth at his right cheek, accompanied by shadowy movement at the corner of his right eye: Wally Hen was holding up the lamp.

Most people thought Ah Che had been blinded by the pox. That was almost true. The truth was that he could still see a little, but only at the edges of his periphery, and only light and shapes – no colors – and only when they moved. As soon as the thing stayed still, it vanished.

Which meant that his eyes rarely told him anything his fingers didn't already know – which meant that Ah Che rarely bothered consulting them.

But sight was important to sighted people, and Wally Hen clearly wanted him to see this... whatever it was.

So Ah Che picked the plug out of his lap and passed it slowly back and forth beside his right eye. It was dark and faintly shiny, like well-polished wood.

"That's made from a special plant," Wally Hen said, "which the fishmen call it 'tarré'. Butch says it will stop your seizures."

A cold needle pricked Ah Che's heart. He had tried everything the doctor asked, without improvement, and long since given up. But in his most secret thoughts, he had been a little bit glad: his seizure-dreams felt real in a way that ordinary ones didn't. He saw his family there. He could see there – not just moving shapes, but everything. Just last week, he had seen Ten-Maia herself: radiant, beautiful, beckoning to him with a smile and a graceful maidenly hand. She was everything that the stories had said and more: corn-silk dress, squash-blossom hair, sweetcorn jewels of every sacred color – black and white, yellow and red – and real, more real than the waking world, more real than anything Ah Che had ever known. How could he surrender that?

But the only word that came out was "How?"

The warmth of the lamp went away, taking the last of his vision with it. "You shave off a very little piece," Wally Hen said, *"and hide it in your cheek, and hold it there until it goes away. That's all."*

Ah Che could hear the hope in the bigger boy's voice. It made a terrible weight on his soul. "How much does it cost?"

The reply was fast and eager. "I told you: it was a present. Butch feels bad for you, and wants you to get better."

Well, that was stupid. Butch Gracie didn't want anything for Ah Che: he wanted to make money. It was Wally Hen who wanted him to get better. He was the one who felt bad. And though he didn't say it, he was the one who was grinding down his bones in that mine shaft, doing the work of two men while Ah Che scarcely managed half of one.

Ah Che liked to tell himself that he was filling in for the wife that Wally Hen would someday have. He kept the floor swept and the beds made and the clothes mended, and did all those things diligently and well. But it wasn't enough. Nobody would choose a wife who couldn't be trusted to cook or go out shopping or mind a child. Nobody even wanted to pay a laundry-boy who couldn't see well enough to tell whether he had gotten the stains out. Ah Che was doing everything he could, but it wasn't enough.

It would never be enough.

"Ah Che? What's wrong, oyami?"

Ah Che fingered the fragrant, waxy plug. It probably wouldn't work anyway. Nothing else had. And on the off chance that it did...

... well, someday he would join his family in the Other Lands. Someday he might even see Ten-Maia again. It would be selfish to ask for more than that.

Ah Che held out his hand. "Give me your knife."

VUCHAK WATCHED THE blood trickle down Weisei's forehead, and bit his tongue. This was a terrible idea. He should never have agreed.

But as he supervised his prince sitting there with Hakai's head in his lap, eyes closed, head bowed, and fingers threaded through the man's hair as if he would massage his scalp, the part of Vuchak that dearly wished to object – again – was silenced by the part that had already given its well-reasoned surrender.

No, Weisei could not afford to take Hakai's wounds.

No, there was no telling what had damaged the slave's thinking, or how badly, or even how long ago.

But the longer such an injury was allowed to linger, the slower and more poorly it would heal... and Hakai's mind was of surpassing value. It took years to train an *ihi'ghiva*, years more for him to master his crafts. He was a translator, a messenger, a sharp ear and a closed mouth and an invisible pair of hands for whoever was deemed worthy of his service. It would be a grievous loss if he died or failed to recover – and there would be hell to pay if Vuchak and Weisei were found responsible.

So Vuchak sat there under the paltry shade of the piñon tree and watched as his *marka* tried to relieve Hakai of his strange, invisible wound. He hoped it would work. He hoped it wouldn't. He had been telling himself that this was only a token effort to show their diligence, and that it was futile, regardless: Weisei's gift only allowed him to soak up the injuries of his own people – and whatever else he was, Hakai was not a'Krah.

But as the cut on Hakai's forehead disappeared, and the fresh, identical gash over Weisei's brow opened and began to bleed, Vuchak felt suddenly less confident about that.

What if he were wrong? What if Weisei accidentally took too much – damaged his own thinking, or broke his own leg? He had to lead the horse, which meant that he absolutely had to be able to walk. And even if he just overspent himself, used himself all up on this exercise here, it would take that much longer before he *or* Hakai got any real help in Atali'Krah – and that was time nobody had.

No, nevermind what they'd agreed on before: this was too risky. Vuchak opened his mouth to break his promised silence –

– just as Weisei sat back with a sigh. "I'm sorry, Vichi. I can't tell."

"That's all right," Vuchak said, striving to hide his relief. "You did –"

"It's strange, though." Weisei looked down at the unconscious man in his lap and frowned. "His brain doesn't feel like it's been hurt. It's just... used up."

Well, that was incisively unhelpful. Vuchak put his hands to his knees to stand. "Then maybe he'll get better on his own. Come on, let's finish dressing him and –"

Weisei did not look up. "Yes, but he's getting feverish – and see that tremor in his hands, too. What if it's something to do with his old injuries? Are you sure Huitsak didn't say anything about them?"

Thus far, Vuchak had done an excellent job of keeping his attention on Hakai's face. He did not want to contemplate that flabby, scar-puckered bare chest again, especially now that it had been re-seeded with so many fresh cuts and bruises. He especially did not want to think about whatever awful pox lay sleeping in the old slave's bones, or what would happen if it were waking up again. "Yes, yes," Vuchak said, hoping his irritation would finally close the curtain on those questions. "And even if you're right, we can't do anything about it here. We'll give him back to Aso'ta Marhuk when we get home, and let the Eldest use their arts. Now let's dress him: the sooner we get to sleep, the sooner we can get him home."

Vuchak stood and walked past the half, who had already lay down to rest, and retrieved Hakai's shirt. They hadn't been brave enough to untie that makeshift splint, or do anything else to his legs, but it was a simple enough thing to sponge down the rest of him, shake the earth from his shirt and shoes, wash his hair, and salve his lesser wounds. Even as angry as he was with Hakai for absconding back to the fishmen, Vuchak didn't mind doing that much: the *ihi'ghiva* was in no danger of enjoying less than his fair share of suffering... or of having it relieved too soon.

And amidst all these heavy thoughts, Weisei was just sitting there, the hair-tie limp and useless in his hand.

"What's wrong?" Vuchak had to ask – because *What's wrong?* was so much more acceptable than *Why are you making this take even longer than it has to?*

Weisei's thin shoulders slumped. He looked almost as exhausted as Vuchak felt. "I wish we didn't have to go."

Oh, this was going to be a chore. Privately resigning himself to another discussion of feelings, Vuchak straddled Hakai – shamefully aware of how he had done just the same with Weisei earlier – and commenced manhandling him into his shirt. "Why?" He struggled to squeeze some interest into his tone.

Vuchak already knew how this would go. Weisei would give some self-regarding reason next, some anxious fretting about how To'taka didn't like him, how Penten would be disappointed in him, how nobody would want to sit with him, all of which were completely within his own power to amend, if he would only take a hard look at his own –

"It's going to wreck her."

Vuchak stopped with Hakai's arm half in its sleeve.

Weisei cupped his forehead as he confessed himself to his knee. "He's her only son. She's going to be so upset. And then she's going to kill Ylem."

From the other side of the campsite, Dulei shifted in his coffin. He had been still and quiet since they retrieved him, perhaps sensing his nearness to the end – but now he stirred at even this oblique mention of his mother.

And as it turned out, Vuchak still had some empathy left after all. He tried to assemble his thoughts as he finished with Hakai, reaching to provide his *marka* with some helpful, encouraging reason why those things wouldn't happen.

It was just terribly unfortunate that Weisei had chosen this of all moments to be right. His sister would be devastated to learn of Dulei's death – and then she would seek vengeance. And the Eldest had no reason not to grant it: Ylem was not only her son's murderer, but the Dog Lady's favorite child – a rich prize just waiting to be torn from a sworn enemy. Executing him would be perfect, easy revenge.

Vuchak sat down beside his *marka*, struggling to find his new, better self, the one he had confessed to the West Wind that he wanted so badly to become. "It's not your fault," he said at last. "You didn't do anything wrong. Dulei's death and Winshin's grief and Ylem's fate... none of them belong to you. You didn't create them. They aren't yours to suffer. You only have to be responsible for yourself."

It sounded good to Vuchak's ears. It was the absolution he himself desperately wanted to hear. But one glance from Weisei, one look into his hollow eyes, and Vuchak could see his words' callow, vulgar reflection.

Don't bother about other people's problems. Don't let yourself be troubled by their sadness. Just see to your own obligations, and you won't be blamed for anything.

And worse than that was what came after: not offense, not anger, but the sad little crease at the corners of Weisei's eyes – the ones that understood that Vuchak was trying, and that this shallow, pitiful consolation was the best his *atodak* could offer.

"Yes, Vichi," he said. "Of course you're right. We should think of our duty." And he began tying Hakai's hair back with a plain, sensible knot.

This was progress, Vuchak told himself. This was a victory for common sense and compliance and rational, productive behavior – so much better than that embarrassing scene they'd made earlier.

But when all the most needful things were done and he finally – finally! – lay down to rest, Vuchak closed his eyes dogged by failure, and fell asleep searching for a remedy he couldn't name.

* * *

IT WAS A grisly exercise.

Now children, Shea thought as she stabbed the shovel-blade back into the rocky pile, *we're going to practice our sums. Let's say there are twelve of my own kind, plus a baby-faced princess and one overfed fool of a prince. Now we take away the two that were crushed by falling rocks, the four that were buried alive in the rockslide, and the prince, who didn't even have the decency to stay dead. How many of my kin might be left alive, and when should I stop digging?*

Actually, there was another variable, X, which would represent the unknown number of mereaux previously killed by a'Krah arrows or torn apart by an angry canine god-mother... but as weary as she was from all this sedimentary subtraction, Shea couldn't begin to muster the energy to tackle that abominable algebra.

Instead, she swore when she struck a damp spot – at least this one wasn't stuck under a half-ton boulder – and set to her usual pattern of scraping and excavating around and under it. It was hard, ugly work, and there was no-one less suited to it than a wrung-out old mereau with a bad lung and a crick in her back... but it wouldn't be right to just sit and ease herself while she waited for U'ru to return. These weren't the Dog Lady's people, or even her victims. This was not her mistake.

"*Ah, there you are, cousin,*" Shea said in Fraichais, setting the shovel aside when she had finally shifted enough earth to get a good grip on that shriveled, dust-crusted hand. "*Here, let me help you.*"

She dug and pulled and dug and pulled, freeing the body inch by morbid, desiccated inch. To say it was unpleasant would have been a laughing understatement – but this was something that Shea could do, however slow and badly.

She couldn't tell what was happening to Yashu-Diiwa, or how long he might have before the a'Krah put him to death. She couldn't track Prince Jeté – that was U'ru's task now. Worst of all, she couldn't know what had happened to Día. There had only been that slow fading of her mind as she ventured ever farther from the Dog Lady's awareness, and then nothing – a whole day's worth of nothing.

It would be all right, she told herself. It might still be all right – as long as the right people found each other in the right order. Día would find the boy before dark. U'ru would find both of them, once they made it far enough down the mountain. And Jeté... he would find some quiet corner to crawl off and die in, without hurting a soul. Was that so much to hope for?

With one more titanic heave, Shea finally birthed her dead kinsman from the rubble. "*There we are,*" she said, when she'd finally caught her breath again. "*It's a shit life, isn't it? Small wonder nobody gets out of it alive. Now, let's...*"

Shea trailed off as she got her first good look at the body. She'd discovered a few of the Many already, along with some of their pathetic makeshift weapons – the shovel had been one of them. But this was the first one she'd found actually *wearing* something.

Shea turned the body over, puzzled by the bulging sack hung around its neck. Then she dropped to a squat. "*Excuse me, cousin – may I see what you have there?*"

She had no idea what to make of the *tarré*. It was quite a lot to take for such a short trip, and she didn't remember eating anything with that signature smoky-sweetness. More to the point, no mereau would have had any use for that battered old tin: it looked watertight enough, but it was already rusting.

But she did recognize the bag it came in, and the assorted novelty gems inside. They had belonged to that little shy one – oh, what was their name? The one who had been so busy collecting and sorting and re-sorting their tiny terrestrial treasures, the one who had reminded her of a young and still-hopeful Fours.

But they had been easily the smallest of the cohort, and this one here was the biggest Shea had found yet. Tournant, perhaps, or...

Yes, actually, Shea did recall the two of them together – the big one passing morsels to the little one at the dinner-fight, reminding her so much of herself and Fours that it almost hurt to watch. Shea looked down at the broad-shouldered body beside her, its still-open mouth choked with dirt. It could not tell her why it had been wearing its sibling's treasures... but then, maybe she could guess.

In that moment, Shea suspected that she would not find the little geologist in the rockslide – and that Porté had found one more way to live up to their name.

Shea sighed. The big stevedore had carried her upriver on that first day out of Island Town. Carried her supper to her, carried more than their share of all those digging-tools – and now, apparently, they had carried their lost sibling's legacy, all the way up until the moment of their own death.

Shea's own given name had never been so apt. Champagne was a fine, elegant thing, made for merriment and celebration, and her life had been anything but.

But she was still here, naked and dirty and drying out in the dust-shrouded haze of the late afternoon sun. The young ones were gone, killed by the vagaries of a world they had barely begun to explore, and there was no-one but Shea left to look after them.

She could manage that much mothering, anyway.

So she put the tin and the stones back in their bag, hung the bag around her neck, and began the slow, clumsy process of pulling Porté's arms over her shoulders – of getting enough of their withered body over her back that she could begin returning their namesake favor. Shea stooped and bent, her desiccated friend leaving web-footed trails in the dirt as she took her first heavy steps back towards the river. "*Come on, même. Let's take you home.*"

IT WAS A good plan.

Elim would just settle down and pretend to nap long enough for Bootjack and Way-Say to fall asleep. Then he would pilfer some provisions and be off again, down the trail and all the way back down the mountain, if he had to. He'd go get Sil, or whatever was left of him, no matter what.

In fact, it was such a good plan, and he did such a good job of pretending, that when he finally opened his eyes again, the sun had already slipped down behind the mountain.

Shit.

Elim sat up with a start. He'd lost hours. Sil had been lost for hours. His partner was somewhere in pieces at the bottom of a cliff, and Elim had *dozed off*.

And he was starving again.

Elim could have kicked himself – if he'd had the time. But the others were still asleep. He still had a chance. Elim silently picked himself up, grabbed a waterskin and filled it from the little seep, and then retrieved a perfectly-good steak from where some moon-touched fool had left it lying on the ground. He brushed off the dirt and the ants and shoved it into his waistband.

Then he glanced back at Bootjack and Way-Say – a matched pair of cloak-bundled Sundowners sleeping back-to-back under a wizened old tree. Elim lingered on the sight of the crow prince and his knight, reluctant in spite of everything. They weren't his people, he reminded himself. They weren't even really his friends. They would be fine without him. And now that he'd delivered Hawkeye –

He stopped short, scouring their tiny campsite. Hawkeye was gone.

Elim's heart seized; his gaze flicked to the rocky edge of the clearing, and the empty air beyond it. Surely not. Surely, surely not.

He couldn't look – couldn't even make his feet move the two steps it would take to discover the truth. Elim stared straight down at the ground in front of him, willing his heart to slow and his mind to think clearly and the universe to prove that it wasn't just a collection of random, pointless cruelties – that all his efforts hadn't been in vain.

The ground between his moccasins gave him no such assurances. But it did suggest what he probably should have guessed earlier: a lamed man dragging a rifle-splinted leg cut a mighty distinctive track.

Elim caught up to Hakai about a quarter of a mile down the trail. The poor bastard was crawling, if you could even call it that, reaching out with both hands and then pulling his good knee up underneath him, inch-worming along slower than frozen snail-snot.

Which maybe they actually had out here: it was just past afternoon, and already the shadows were getting chilly.

All the more reason to get the man back to camp on the quick side. "Hey, Hawkeye – where you going, buddy?" Elim called ahead, keeping his tone and pace gentle and easy.

Hawkeye stopped and briefly turned to regard Elim with those strange, unfocused dark eyes. "I think that's fairly self-evident." Then he was back at it again, his breath coming in labored little puffs of steam.

Elim quickened his pace. That sounded an awful lot like the Hawkeye he knew. "Yeah, I expect it is," he said as he caught up to him. "But Bootjack's gonna go on the warpath if he wakes up and sees we already left. How 'bout we head on back?"

This time, Hawkeye kept right on going. "You know as well as I do why that's a bad idea."

Oh, that sounded wonderfully like the old Hawkeye – even if Elim didn't have a damn clue what he meant. "Well, you'll get down there a whole lot faster if you let me take you. Here, why don't I –"

Hawkeye recoiled from his touch. "Leave me alone, *emi* – I can do it myself!"

Elim withdrew, and blew out a slow breath. No, Hawkeye's brain hadn't miraculously unscrambled itself. He was just a more articulate kind of addled. And as tempting as it was to let him crawl on and trust that Bootjack would fetch him eventually, Elim had already watched one friend drop off a cliff today. He couldn't live with himself if he let it happen again. "All right," he said, his hopes of finding Sil crumbling like brittle straw. "Maybe I'll see you later, then."

He walked on another ten paces, and then sat himself down and waited. Sometimes you could turn a contrary horse around, if you just let him alone long enough to forget what you'd asked him the first time.

Still, this one made a grim picture. The others had done a fair job of cleaning him up, and except for his missing blindfold and wrecked leg, he looked pretty much like himself again. Which made it all the harder to watch Hawkeye, probably the smartest man Elim had ever met, crawling along like an opium-dazed baby, lost in a world only he could see.

Elim was beginning to wonder if he could see anything. It sure seemed to come as a surprise when Hawkeye's grasping hand reached out for the next step and found Elim's knee instead. "What do you want?" he demanded, turning his head as if to inspect him from the corner of his eye.

"Relax, buddy. It's just me – Elim, your friend. Thought we could sit for a bit, before the boss comes back."

Hawkeye held still, his expression blank and unreadable. But he seemed to cotton to the idea, or at least to the feel of Elim's leg: after some careful rearrangement, he managed to turn and sit down, and Elim likewise collected himself so that they could rest side-by-side, with their backs against the rock. It was all right, as long as Elim didn't look more than three feet out in front of him. Then he held still, and waited to see what his friend would do.

"Can I tell you something?" Hawkeye's voice was quiet, almost childlike.

Elim would take it. "Sure thing. What is it?"

Hawkeye stroked Elim's leg with hot, shaky fingers. "Your pants are filthy."

Elim laughed in spite of himself – in spite of everything. "I, uh – I dunno if you've seen yourself lately, but yours ain't exactly fresh from the laundry line."

Hawkeye smiled, a full-on grin that lit up his face like the glow of a lamp in a living room window – like a beacon welcoming a traveler home. "I'll wash them tomorrow." His smile faded as he ran his hands over his own trousers, furrowing into confusion when his fingers found the torn cloth tied around his thigh. He began to pick at the knot.

Elim needed to pull that up short. "Hey, uh – are you hungry? Why don't we have us something to eat?" He pulled out the steak, wishing he'd been clever enough to take a knife while he was at it.

Hawkeye kept working at the knot.

Well, it wasn't going to be fine dining anyhow. Elim nipped off a bite, wiped it clean, and then touched it to Hawkeye's hand. "Here – see how that suits you."

The translator paused. He took hold of the cold morsel, holding it like a fragile quail-egg. He smelled it. He held it up to the side of his face and passed it slowly back and forth beside his right eye. "How much does it cost?"

It was awful, and yet Elim couldn't help but smile at the absurdity of it all. "For you, it's free." Elim took a bite of his own as Hawkeye consented to try the tiniest experimental nibble –

– and then hurled it straight at him. "That's NOT FUNNY!" Hawkeye cried, and burst into tears.

Elim nearly choked. He swallowed, picked the meat-wad out of his hair, and set down his supper. "What's wrong, buddy? What's the matter?"

But Hawkeye was already heaving himself forward

onto hands and knee, dragging himself away from Elim – and straight for the edge.

"No no no – come on, you don't wanna –"

"Go away!" Hawkeye shrieked, landing a glancing blow to Elim's nose. "I hate you and I want to go home!"

It wasn't hard to wrestle him down, even with all his thrashing. A little trickier to do it without mashing his leg. But to sit on a man who spoke at least three languages, to hold a friend and mentor down like a hog-tied calf while he fought and screamed and sobbed... Elim hunched over, grim-faced and still, pinning Hawkeye's wrists to the small of his back with the soul-withering ease of a man drowning cats in a sack. Something in him went gray in that moment, aged before its time.

And just like that, it was over. Hawkeye went quiet and still, the fight going out of him in one shuddering breath: not a moment too soon, and yet much too suddenly.

"... Hawkeye? What's wrong?"

For a long minute, there was nothing at all. He might have fallen asleep. Then came the slow turn of his head, easy at first, becoming rigid and straining as he reached his limits, as if he were trying to do the owl's trick of looking behind his own shoulders. He fidgeted, his feverish fingers picking at his shirttail, his jaw working a mouthful of nothing.

Then came a tremendous overhead *CRACK*. Elim threw himself over Hawkeye as a hail of stones rained down from above. He gritted his teeth and ducked, tasting limp, greasy gray hair as the rockslide pummeled his back and skull.

And just like that, it was over. Elim picked himself

up, gingerly rubbing the back of his head, staring in stunned wonderment at the heap of rubble all around them.

Shit, but he hated mountains. No wonder the prophet-stories were stuffed so full of them: you needed the Hand of the Almighty pointing straight at you just to survive the trip.

And if God were aiming a finger at Elim just then, it wasn't His first one.

Elim wiped his face. "All right, buddy – how about we get ourselves back to camp before anything else comes clundering down on top of us, huh?"

This time, Hawkeye didn't object. He lay still amidst the rocks, eyes closed, breathing easily – just as he had after the ground gave way under Sil.

Elim picked himself up amidst the gently drifting dust, his gaze switching between the passed-out Sundowner at his feet and the freshly-broken stone up above.

Hawkeye was sorcerous – he knew that much. He found things nobody could see, knew where fishmen were and horseshoes weren't, and could tell Elim exactly how many steps were left between him and his next drink of water.

So maybe he knew something. Maybe that fidgety picking and neck-stretching was his addled way of warning Elim – too little and too late – before something crumbled or cracked. Maybe that was why he'd been trying to crawl back down, saying those peculiar things about self-evidence and bad ideas. Hawkeye was no fool: the mountain was coming apart, and he didn't aim to be there when it did.

Elim might ought to take the hint.

But by the time he'd collected his thoughts, his supper,

and his insensible friend, Bootjack had already come running back for them, his barking jabber stilled by his first sight of that rocky ring of debris, and dirt-showered Elim standing there in the middle of it. He looked every bit as mistrustful as Elim felt... but in the end, Bootjack's hand pointed back up the trail, and Elim's feet followed it.

And on the way back up, he prayed. *Show me something*, Elim asked the deepening light behind the mountain. He knew better than to solicit a miracle – Sil needed whatever of those might be lying around here – and yet he craved *something*. *Give me a sign. Tell me I chose right. Show me you're still there.*

But there was only the path, the peak, and the earth cooling in its shadow. And when they finally made it back to camp, Elim was left to watch in dull-eyed wonder as Way-Say worked his pagan magic: a crow-feathered necromancer raising up what had used to be Actor, a meek and sweet-mouthed drygrocer's horse – *Sil's* horse – and was now a stiff-legged black puppet, an empty-eyed contrivance for the coffin lashed to his back.

Elim's shoulders slumped under Hawkeye's weight. He bowed his head and fell in line behind them as they started forward again: the living bearing the living, and the dead hauling the dead.

THE CROW WAS pecking at her eye.

She swatted it, and it hopped away. Then another peck, another swat. Eventually it switched tacks and started on her ear.

It hurt too much to reach that far. She rolled face-down, waiting for her hair to fall forward and shield her from the pesky bird. A cold breeze tickled the back of her neck.

Then a set of sharp talons alighted on her scalp. She flinched and swatted, feebly jerking. Eventually, when it became clear that her body was not going to be able to manage things on its own, Día reluctantly returned to supervise.

Everything hurt. Lying still hurt. Shivering hurt. Breathing hurt more than she ever thought it could. But it was only when she opened her eyes that she realized what a miracle it was to feel any pain at all.

She'd been out for hours. The world was a dark forest now, the sun an orange-violet glow behind the vast stone face of the mountain. The mountain that she...

No, *he.*

He'd pushed her.

That vile, conniving boy had *pushed* her.

Día had no memory of the drop. She guessed from the scratches on her palms that she must have grabbed something to break her fall. The ground had broken the rest of her.

She began to push herself up, and stopped when the pain in her left arm fountained out into a wave of nausea. Her first gasp drove an invisible knife between her ribs. And her head – in God's holy name, what had she done to her head?

The crow watched her, the sentiment in its beady black eye unreadable. Then it flew off.

Día moved by slow, careful inches thereafter, testing each part as she eased herself up to sit. Her arm was broken. At least a couple of ribs were too. The congealing blood on the stone frightened her until she felt the back of her head: just a cut, thank goodness, long but shallow. She must have rolled the last of the way. And as for the headache...

Día stopped, struck still by the enormity of the gesture – by the reality of her fingers probing her own naked scalp, and the feel of tiny, irregular tufts where her knife hadn't cut smoothly along the skin.

She really had done it. She'd cut it all off.

She looked up and around the shade-swallowed slope, searching the cliff-face and the treetops and the surrounding brush. Had she held it as she fell? Had it snagged on the way down? It could be miles away by now, dangling from some lonely crag.

She'd cut it off for him, and now it was gone and so was he.

Día leaned forward, her good hand sheltering her eyes as she reached out into the silence. *Mother Dog, I need you. I've fallen and I'm badly hurt and I need you to come get me.*

There was no answer, not even a wordless feeling – not unless the Dog Lady was responsible for that churning, bloodless panic in her bowels. *Please. Please, please come get me.*

From somewhere far out in the distance, a coyote howled.

Día folded further in on herself, urged on by the cold air even as she was rebuffed by the lightning-sharp pain in her chest. *Help me, Master.* She didn't even know what to ask Him for, but she pleaded as hard as she ever had. *Help me. Lead me. Save me.*

But the Penitent faith had no earthly gods – at least, not here. They had been left behind in the old world, an ocean away, and were now nothing but a namesake for herbs and holidays. Día had no material spirit to call on, no patron-avatar to advocate for her in the grand order of the cosmos. There was only herself, her own tiny, mortal mind, communing as best she could with a distant, universal creator.

Día was used to that. She knew better than to expect a flash of light and a healing miracle – which was good, because she didn't get one. She was far more likely to find God's help at the end of her own fingertips. So she let Him take her hand and open her veins – let Him mind the drip as anxiety and fear drained out of her – let Him stand in attendance as her tireless, infinite physician.

It was a long, slow bleed. And when it was done, Día could finally think beyond what she wanted to have happen, to what she knew to be true.

It was getting dark. She had no shelter and no water and no clear path in any direction. She had a knife. She could make a fire. The Halfwick boy was gone, and as for Elim...

Some of that cold, unwholesome fear backwashed up through her veins as Día wondered whether she was already too late – whether the Dog Lady didn't answer because she had been ended at the moment of her son's death.

Well, Día wasn't going to find out by sitting here. No, she was going to... she would...

She would work backwards. She knew she was somewhere along the eastern face, that she had been walking up that trail with the cliff on her right-hand side, and that she had seen another trail join up with it just before she found Halfwick. There had been recent tracks coming up from that direction – a horse and at least two people – which meant that it might see regular traffic. If she found that path, she would be much more likely to find help. And if she didn't, she would look for a way down to the southern face, towards the place where she had left the Dog Lady and Miss Du Chenne. She had a vast granite landmark literally looming over her, after all – it wasn't as if she could lose her bearings. All she had to do was start.

Or rather, she needed her body to start. Día sat forward on the cold stone and shivered. It hadn't been her first impact – that would have killed her – but somewhere on the way down, her left side had hit something with bone-smashing force.

She could survive a broken arm. She could live with some cracked ribs, even though they hurt like the screaming pits of hell. But Día desperately needed that ache in her hip to be a bruise, needed to be able to work off that ominous pain in her knee. If she was going to survive the night, if she was going to help herself at all, she had to walk.

And that was where reason passed the torch back to faith. Día sat straight-backed and still, telling herself that God had given her everything she needed to take the next step – that He had seen and sustained her across the desert, past wildfires and raging rivers, through hours up that slope and free-falling seconds back down it, and neither man nor nature nor that twice-damned Halfwick had managed to thwart His design.

He had not failed her yet. She would not doubt Him now.

Día drew in a careful, shallow breath, willing peace to her pain and stillness to her lingering nausea. Then she stood up.

Her knee hurt, but her legs held her. When the dizziness subsided, she took one tremulous step, and then another. Wobbling like a newborn fawn, her feet reacquainted themselves with the ground, her toes closing over sharp grass and dry brush and plain, soft dirt.

Día went slow and deliberately, her every movement planned and prayerful. Miss du Chenne had been right: she was not dressed for this, not equipped or prepared to survive out here. But although that realization had bludgeoned her aching head before, Día now made it a whetstone for her thinking. She cut away her anger at Halfwick, and her fear for Elim and U'ru, and that powerful, irrational urge to go looking for her hair. She had no margin for error now. She would shepherd her steps and mind her time, and make the most of however much of both she might have remaining.

God is my one Master; I will for nothing want. Día bent and ripped up a dead sagebrush plant by its thick, woody stem.

He holds me fast. I shall not waver. He lifts me up. I shall not fall. When her toes found barren earth, she tossed the sage down and stepped on it.

By his grace, I walk to everlasting glory. One fiery burst from the sole of her foot ignited the sage. With painful slowness, Día picked up her torch and walked on into the cold, approaching night.

SOMETHING WAS WRONG with the mountain.

Vuchak didn't pretend to be an expert, especially here on the dry side. He'd lived for two years up there in Atali'Krah, but until the day he and Weisei had set out for Island Town, their adventures had always been on the western slope, where the water was good and the climbing was easy. A shame that getting there from the All-Year River would have required a thirty-mile detour around the roots of the lesser mountains. If Vuchak had told everything he knew about this eastern face, it would have been finished in two sentences.

But the Mother of Mountains wasn't supposed to crack and crumble. He was sure of that much. She had lain down on the third day of the World That Is, and promised to remain until the end, and none of the seer-songs had said anything about random pieces falling off in the meantime... all of which amounted to one more drop in the great bottomless ocean of things that Vuchak was helpless to affect, or even to understand.

He would have liked to talk about that. He would have liked to share an honest word with anyone. But Weisei had to concentrate on the horse – and besides which, talking to him caused as many problems as it solved – and Ylem couldn't speak more than two intelligible words, and Hakai had simply lost himself.

So as day cooled to night, and Vuchak trudged on at the head of their tired, silent procession, he consoled himself by talking to Echep.

I wish you were here, he thought out at his missing counterpart. Echep wouldn't have known anything about the mountain either, but he'd have made a good joke about it. *I wish you could help me. I'm tired of being tired, and angry at myself for being angry, and I can't tell whether I'm doing anything right anymore.*

Vuchak hitched up the carry-sack on his back, the ties digging hard into his shoulder, and listened to the monotone clop of the horse's hooves behind him. He and Weisei had found their better selves again, but when Vuchak thought of himself sitting on a holy son of Marhuk, threatening to force-feed him chewed meat, his free-soul shriveled in shame. *I thought I would be different now. I thought I had changed. But I haven't, and neither has he, and I'm afraid that he never will – that I'll grow old waiting for him to grow up, and that we'll spend our lives disappointing each other.*

Echep had understood that. Dulei was seven years Weisei's junior and already a man, but his boasting adolescent arrogance had cost his *atodak* plenty of sleep. What if he stayed that way? What if Echep had to spend his life serving a selfish lout?

The heavy scraping of the travois poles answered that with funerary finality: that worry was boxed up in a leaking coffin, only hours away from being laid permanently to rest.

And since Echep was almost certainly dead too, Vuchak could entrust him with words that he would never, ever speak aloud.

I wish I didn't belong to Weisei. I wish he weren't even a'Krah. Yes, that was the guilty, sordid truth: Weisei should have been sired by some other god, some other people – someone who would be honored and bettered by his charm and compassion and passionate woman-hearted affections. Someone who knew what to do with him.

Instead, he had been born to Marhuk, to the a'Krah, whose ways were caution and discretion and careful, long-eyed calculation. The mediators of life and death had to keep a balance, a middle-way of living, and Weisei had never managed to find the middle of anything. So the balance-keepers just strapped Vuchak to him to act as a human counterweight, offsetting every wild, thoughtless swing of his *marka*'s sensibilities. That was the solution. That was balance.

It was also an exhausting way to live.

Said the salmon to the bear. Vuchak could all but see Echep's smile. He would say something like that, something clever and funny that would either make Vuchak forget what he was sour about or else think about it differently.

And maybe it wasn't so bad. After all, Weisei wasn't curled up dead in a box. Vuchak wasn't going to have to empty his own veins. Far from it: in defiance of all odds and his own rotten luck, he'd managed to retrieve Hakai, Dulei, and Ylem. He would go home in honor, have the pleasure of enjoying a real rest in a real bed, of eating hot seed-babies and fresh *kohai'Lei*, of sequestering himself in his own land, amidst his own people – at least for a little while. Who could ask for more than that?

Vuchak breathed deep, comforting himself with the familiar, sinus-drying thin air. This was still his place, his heritage, even if he hadn't seen it from quite this angle before. The piñon trees were still giving way to oak and pine, just as they did on the western side, and the jays and woodpeckers were still going noisily about their business, and the fronts of his thighs were still throbbing consolation – reassuring him with every laborious upward step that he was on the right path.

Yes, that was it. He'd collected his companions and done his duty and now they were going *home* again – and the rest of his troubles would look so much smaller from up there.

So Vuchak pinned his hopes on the hidden place just

above and beyond the pine-furred crags overhead, and set his mind to finding it. He went quickly as the trail ambled up into the stunted trees, then more carefully as it swung back out to skirt the edge of the cliff again. Then the wide track narrowed to an overgrown deer-path, scarcely wider than a poor buck's antlers, and he stopped.

"Weisei, wait." Vuchak needed to find some crack or hollow he could duck into to let the horse pass, and then pick up the travois poles from behind. He trusted Weisei to put the horse's feet right – and praised the gods that they didn't belong to a spooky, balking, still-living animal – but the poles were shoddily secured at best, and if the right one slipped over the edge... well, Dulei had suffered enough indignities for one lifetime.

Weisei stopped on the little wooden bridge that filled in the eroded gap in the trail, humming the remembering-song all the while. He stood there, gaunt and concentrating, keeping his head down and his hand cupped around the horse's mouth as if he were feeding it.

Good. Vuchak scouted ahead in the deepening twilight, searching for a safe passing-place. There would be a way through here – he just had to find it.

"*Mister,*" Ylem called forward in his abysmal Marín. His accent was atrocious as always, his voice warbling nervous. "*Mister, please to see...*"

Damn it, what now? Vuchak turned, straining to see back past the horse. "*What do you want?*"

The answer came as a low, rumbling *FRRROAAAAAAAAK.*

CHAPTER NINE
AMNESTY FOR THE DAMNED

AH CHE, A CHILD *of eleven winters, jostled his partner and laughed.* "You will not!"

Wally Hen, who had just declared his intention to father eighteen children and name each of them after one of Ah Che's sins, replied with perfect aplomb. "Well, when Snores-Like-A-Hog-Fart is old enough to understand, I'll tell him you said so."

It took a moment to work out the Ardish words – Wally Hen sounded even more like a gobbling turkey in his own language than he did in Maia – but Ah Che's answer sprang instantly to mind. "And I tell – I'll tell him the story how you" – *What was the word for 'sired'?* – "how you made him with only your right hand."

Ah Che didn't understand why that was funny, but he'd heard enough variations to be confident that it was. And he wasn't wrong: the aforementioned hand, the one that Ah Che held as the two of them walked down the street, curled into a fist, leaving only one finger to stand out straight. "Oh, we'll see about that. You better learn to duck, buddy: I'm gonna have so many woman throwing their petties at me, you'll think you got caught in a cunny cave-in."

And that was how they went: Ah Che holding on to Wally Hen with one hand and carrying their dinner-pail with the other, and Wally Hen leading the way through the bustling streets to work.

It was a wonderful thing. Ah Che had only been hired three months ago, but already he was the best in the sorting-house, better than any of the sighted people: all he had to do was pick up a piece of ore and know, as surely as he knew his own fingers, whether it was pure or mixed or worthless gangue. He wasn't the only one gifted with earth-sense, but his was easily the keenest: the Kaia workers were old, their gifts so worn down by blasphemy and alcohol that they could scarcely tell manganite from lead. Ah Che would not become like them. He would keep the ways of the Maia – well, as much as he could out here – and save his money, and in three more months, when he had worked half a year without a seizure, Mr. Burrell had promised to recommend him for work in the mine proper.

Ah Che was counting the days. It was more dangerous down there, and the work was far harder, but it also paid more. That would be good. The war had helped wages, but it was also driving up prices, especially imported things from back east: the tarré *was already taking half of everything Ah Che made, and he didn't dare try cutting back. Life now was too good to risk it.*

So he and Wally Hen kept their money safe and their paces quick, and played the teasing-game along the way. "– will have you know that I am EXTREMELY handsome," *Wally Hen was saying.* "Really, you're lucky to be seen with me."

"Elmer Wells doesn't say so," *Ah Che retorted.* "He says if I get tired from you, I just shave dog's ass and teach it to walk backwards, and it will be the same thing. He says –"

"Ah Che?" *A man's voice called out from ahead and to the right.* "Is that you?"

The voice was old and familiar and speaking Maia, but Ah Che had no time to wonder about it: there were soft-shod footsteps pounding the dirt, sprinting right for him, and a rush of motion before he was accosted and grappled off his feet.

"Hey!" *Wally Hen cried.* "Let go of him!"

Teetering between panic and shock, it took Ah Che a long, astonished moment to realize that he was being embraced. Then another to remember to breathe. And when he did, his first whiff of the stranger's yucca-scented hair conjured a memory older than words. "Father?"

"I thought I wouldn't see you again," *the man said, his voice thick with feeling.* "I thought you were gone."

Ah Che could have said the same: Father had been away when the sickness came, called back to his own village to attend his mother's death and witness the sharing of her wealth. Ah Che had hoped he was still alive – he'd never seen him in his deeper dreams – but hadn't known enough to tell Wally Hen where to look for him. And now he was here. By every god, he was HERE.

Ah Che's hands closed over handfuls of his father's shirt, his face and voice sinking into the earthy-linen smell of homespun cloth, and the warm, strong body underneath. "How did you find me?" *Ah Che had very little sense of distance – he hadn't left town since Wally*

Hen had brought him here – but he knew that the lands of the Maia were two days away on horseback, on the other side of an increasingly volatile border. He couldn't imagine how Father had braved all that.

"Ten-Maia told me. She came to me in a dream. She's calling everyone back home, and she..."

As he spoke, the hand stroking Ah Che's hair became a gentle pressure, beckoning him to look up – to meet his father's gaze.

"... Ah Che? Don't you see me?"

Ten-Maia must not have told him about that. It was a cruel omission: the flowering fear in Father's voice was awful to hear. Ah Che felt warm, work-hardened hands close over the sides of his head, tilting his face upwards, as if his eyes only needed the correct alignment to remember their purpose.

Well, they still knew how to do one thing. Ah Che blinked back the first tears and swallowed the remainder, overwhelmed by a voice he had long since forgotten. "Yes, Father. I see you very well."

And he did. In his mind's eye, he saw big feet – strong arms – a face that had always delighted in his, and a lap that Ah Che had never outgrown. He saw the ground vanishing away whenever he was tossed into the air, Mama's scolding drowned out by his own infant squeals of delight. He felt, more than saw, the chest that he had so often fallen asleep on, its heart beating faster now than he remembered. But as soon as he touched it, those strong hands arrested his wrists, as if ashamed of what he had found there. "My boy. My son. I'm so sorry. It should have been me. I should have..."

There was a cough, a swallow, and then a metallic rustle and clank: Father picking up the dinner pail.

"Come show me where you've kept your things – we're going home."

Ah Che's spirit flickered. Home, yes... but home was a distant, half-forgotten memory, and here he was standing in the middle of Market Street, embroiled in the pervasive stink of the tannery and the creak and saw of the lumbermen working on the new hotel, thinking about how he was going to be late for work. It was all terribly surreal. "Wait, Father, just for a minute." Ah Che reached out into empty space, groping for someone he had thoughtlessly forgotten. "Emi? Where are you?"

Two stomps of a heavy boot answered his earth-sense even more precisely than his ears: Wally Hen was standing five paces behind and three to his left, probably in the shade of the Magnolia. "Right here, buddy."

He answered in Ardish, maybe so that Father wouldn't suspect him of eavesdropping... but the strain in Wally Hen's voice promised that he had overheard everything.

Ah Che longed to reassure him. "You go ahead," he said. "I come after you." He would find out where Father was staying and promise to meet him there after work, and hopefully Mr. Burrell would understand the delay.

"Sure thing," Wally Hen said – but his boots stayed silent and still.

So Ah Che switched tactics. "Don't worry," he said to his father. "I just need time to talk with him separately, and then we can make plans to leave."

But the word he'd used was ke'dzii, 'we-three', and for a long moment it went unanswered.

"Ah Che," Father said at last, "I have to tell you something that you will not want to hear. The truth is, I came only for you."

It took Ah Che a moment to hear the meaning between the words – and when he did, it jolted him like a rotten floorboard breaking under his weight. Wally Hen wasn't welcome.

"No," he said, struggling to control his upset. "He has to come with us, Father. He's Maia too. His mother – she was one of us, and they took her away, and when she died, his father didn't want him, and he came to live with us, to find his clan and learn how to belong with us. If – if Ten-Maia is calling everyone back, she has to take him too."

A hand clasped itself gently at the back of Ah Che's neck, but what had been a comforting touch now came as a jarring shock – one that retreated guiltily when he flinched. "I know. I'm sorry. I shouldn't have upset you. Let's find a better place to talk, and I'll –"

"No." *Ten minutes ago, Ah Che couldn't have imagined ever seeing his father again – and now he was interrupting him.* "I'm going to work. He's going with me. I'm not going anywhere without him."

"Ah Che." *Father's voice was stern, prodding half-buried memories of childhood petulance and greed.* "I'm listening to what you say. But I need you to hear me too. It's very dangerous for me to be here, and even more dangerous for him to go back with us. The world is bigger than you know, and more complex than we can understand. I'll be glad to share my reasons and answer your questions, but the truth is this: if you care for him, you will leave him here."

"No." *Ah Che had no thought beyond that single, defiant word.* "No, I won't. He's my brother and my friend and I don't care about anyone else. If he can't go, then neither will I."

Father paused. He laid a hand on Ah Che's shoulder, and this time did not withdraw. "That is a very selfish thing to say."

His voice was soft, gentle as always, but it hit Ah Che like a slap. He was four years removed from his old life, but even as a small child, he had learned that first, most basic truth: 'selfish' was the worst thing a person could be.

"No!" he said again, loudly enough for the other street-people to hear, and defiantly enough to assure them that he didn't care. "YOU'RE selfish. You left us. You didn't come when we got sick. You didn't come when Mama was dying. You didn't come on any of the days I lay in bed and begged for you to find me. And if you think you can come here now and take me away from everything, just because Ten-Maia told you to, then... then you're selfish and so is she."

With that, Ah Che grabbed the dinner-pail out of his father's hand and stormed up the street with brash, bullish indifference: anything that didn't want to get hit had better get out of his way.

"I'll wait for you here," Father called after him. "I'll stay until sunset."

But in that moment, with heavy bootsteps running up after him and the steel handle of the old minnow-bucket biting into his clenched fingers and his eyes squeezed shut to hold back hot wells of anger, Ah Che didn't care if he ever saw him again.

VUCHAK DIDN'T EVEN have time to swear.

In the space of a flinch, something huge rustled in the shadowy brush above.

For the length of a blink, everyone hesitated.

Then there was a ground-jarring *thud* as the frog-monster dropped down to land between the half-man and the horse – a dry *swush* as he turned his vast bulk – and a gut-busting meaty *WHAM* as he kicked, catching Ylem right under the ribs with enough force to hurl his overburdened bulk ten feet back into the wall. He and Hakai slammed into the rock and dropped, the stunned, airless silence of the one pierced by the bone-jarring shriek of the other.

Weisei's concentration snapped. He gasped, whirled, and just barely managed to get out of the way as the horse collapsed, a muscular powerhouse of an animal crumpling into a half-ton rotting roadblock right in the middle of the bridge... rolling over onto the shield and spear strapped to its side.

And just like that, in less than three panicked heartbeats, Vuchak found himself trapped and weaponless on the wrong side of a fight.

His spear. He had to get his spear. "Weisei, move it! Move the horse!"

To his credit, Marhuk's son wasted no time. He dropped to kneel beside the carcass, his hand darting to the horse's neck.

The king of the fishmen wasted no time either. He leaped, landing just behind the twisted coffin-bearing travois in the middle of the bridge.

It was a good bridge, as far as Vuchak could tell. Scarcely ten feet long, soundly built – a day's labor for some upstanding a'Krah carpenter.

It was not made to withstand a six-hundred-pound impact. A wood-splintering *CRACK* jolted the frame; the fish-king tensed to leap again before it gave out.

And then the horse kicked him. It was an ingenious move on Weisei's part: he inspired the fallen carcass to strike, twin steel-shod hooves punching into the frog-monster's chest and shoulder with stall-splintering force.

"HROOOOOOOO!" Bellowing in pain, the king of the fishmen reared up, lashed out –

– and with a single angry sweep of his arm, he hurled Weisei over the edge.

Vuchak's heart stopped. For one breathless second, the color drained from the world. He watched in slow motion as Weisei pitched forward – three, four, six feet out into empty space, his entranced expression just beginning to awaken to pain and surprise. And then he fell.

"WEISEI!" Vuchak was at the edge in an instant, staring out into the cold and empty void...

... watching the crow-god's son drift down as gently as a falling cinder, his arms outstretched, his holy black-feathered cloak stiff and billowing around them. "I'm sorry, Vichi!" he called up. "I tried!"

Then the rumpled rusty darkness of the mountain's eastern face swallowed him, and he was gone.

Vuchak was dimly aware of a second *CRACK* as the fish-king leapfrogged over him. He felt the impact through his boot-soles as the monster landed short of his mark and leapt away again. He heard the tortured wooden creak as the sagging bridge swung outwards, its broken maw half-swallowing the coffin. Some distant, still-rational part of him understood that Marhuk's other son was tied between the poles by a few repurposed harness-parts and a great pile of wishful thinking – that Dulei was curled up in his resting-box, with no room to spread his makeshift wings. If he fell, he would not float gracefully to the ground. He would smash like a dropped egg.

And that would serve the frog-monster's interests perfectly. From ten yards ahead, he was turning back again, readying himself for one more devastating leap – and this time, Vuchak saw him clearly.

The king of the fishmen had paid a heavy price to make it this far: he was less a monster now than a maimed, mottled heap. He favored his left front leg, either from the horse-kick or some earlier injury, and dehydration had shriveled him until his scarlet rage was almost lost under flakes of dried mud and vast black patches of dead skin. But there was murder in his clouded amber eyes, and cold-blooded lucidity: Hakai and Ylem had played their part in the fight at the river, but Vuchak had done the killing. The fish-king had come to see that those deaths were paid for.

And if Vuchak were alone and unarmed – if he were anyone but himself – that might have come to pass.

But he was a'Krah – a mediator of life and death – a warrior – a man who fought with every means at his disposal – an *atodak* – a guardian of the children of Marhuk... and there was one such child still left in the fight.

So Vuchak whipped out his boot-knife, hurled it at the monster, and whirled back to the horse. "Dulei, help me!"

Under the wounded roar came a coffin-jolting *BANG*. Then another. Then another. It was a dangerous game, every jerk of the box pulling it another precarious inch further down into the bridge's broken mouth, promising a terrible result if even one of the straps gave out.

But the coffin was tied to the travois, and the travois was tied to the horse, and each kick and shake from Dulei's morbid counterweight shuddered through the poles, pulling the creature's soft, spoiling shoulders just that little bit further upright – giving Vuchak just that little bit more of a chance to retrieve his weapon.

He grabbed his spear-haft and heaved for all he was worth, feeling the edges of the ground bone head tearing through horseflesh like a fishhook pulled backwards through a carp's gasping mouth.

And then he stayed there. Vuchak did not turn or look, did not wait to see where the knife had hit, but feigned ongoing struggle with the spear. He relied on his ears to drink in the fish-king's grunt, let his boot-soles tell him about that last almighty leap. Then he spun, planting the butt of the spear in the ground, bracing it with the instep of his right foot, and angling its head up to occupy the space where his had been only a moment before.

And the monster's chest swallowed it.

WHEN VUCHAK FOUND himself again, he was dying.

Well, perhaps not yet – but he wasn't breathing, and that was soon going to amount to the same thing. There was a horse-carcass underneath him, a broken spear-haft digging into his ribs, and a frog-monster on top of him – and even if his lungs weren't being crushed by that spastic, dying titan, there was nothing to breathe in that grotesque flesh-heap, no room to live. Vuchak kicked and struggled valiantly – but they were feeble, futile human efforts sandwiched between two dead behemoths, and soon he resigned himself to joining them. He was going to die. Starless, luckless Vuchak would end his life as a monument to irony, smothered by his own success.

He could be content with that.

So he dwindled like a candle-flame under glass, panic and guilt ebbing away. Yes, it would be a bit selfish to die here with so much undone... and yet there was something profoundly restful about this warm, airless pocket, a peaceful stillness he'd never found within himself.

And of course he couldn't be allowed that. As soon as he found succor in his imminent death, creation conspired to take it from him: there was a man's voice somewhere out there, meat-muted and indecipherable, and then a pair of strong hands pulling on Vuchak's ankle.

No, don't trouble yourself, he thought. *Really, I'm fine.*

But the universe had traditionally met Vuchak's wishes with something between casual indifference and active contempt, and the present was no exception. Just like that, he was yanked out into the world like a breech-birthed baby: bloody, bewildered, and gasping.

Vuchak wiped the slime from his eyes and looked up, groggily preparing to decipher Ylem's endless gabbling...

"*Ohei*, friend – don't you look a mess!"

... and found himself staring up in open-mouthed astonishment at Echep's lopsided grin.

The other *atodak's* smile fell even as his eyes widened. "Vuchak? By every god, is that you?"

Vuchak had no chance to reply: in one smooth movement, Echep reached down and hauled him up to his feet like a hawk dipping a fish from the All-Year

River. He clapped him on the back, drew his head in to make their foreheads kiss, and then pushed him back by the shoulders, looking him up and down with appalled delight. "By great-grandmother's toothless second-mouth, you are a sorry sight! What are you doing here? And what is that atrocious smell?"

A low, gurgling groan leaked out from behind them. In that moment, Vuchak could have matched it: Dulei had recognized his *atodak*'s voice.

Echep looked out at the mess in growing astonishment: at Ylem hauling Hakai over a great pile of spilled stone; at the smashed bridge and the dead horse and the fish-king's corpse on top of it; at the gore-streaked tip of Vuchak's broken spear peeking out from the monster's shoulder. But when he saw the coffin, he stopped still.

He glanced from it to Vuchak and back again, levity draining from his face as a grievous understanding bloomed in his eyes.

Vuchak closed his mouth, swallowing obsolete words, groping for fresh ones. *I'm sorry. I'm so sorry. I never wanted you to see this.*

Echep found his voice first. "I'm sorry," he said, his voice a strangled whisper. "I'm so sorry. Oh, poor Weisei – how did it happen?"

Vuchak blanched.

It was an old custom, so venerable that it verged on law: the guardians of Marhuk's children were almost universally *a'Pue*: born under no star, possessed of no luck. Vuchak had spent his whole life laboring under the curse. But it was only here, in this moment, that he finally understood the depth of the world's cruelty.

Vuchak looked up at the misdirected pity in Echep's eyes, savoring the last moments of his friend's innocence.

Then he took a breath and steeled himself to speak the words that would ruin him.

It took Elim a little while to recollect how to breathe. A little while more to muster enough air and wherewithal to get back up. Not long at all to amend his list of life-goals: if he never got kicked by a horse, a mule, or a man-eating frog ever again, he would call that a square deal.

Still, that last one might have accidentally done Elim a favor. He looked ahead, to where a good half-ton of rock had tumbled down over the trail – over the exact spot where he'd been standing before those ungodly huge feet had thrown him clear.

He stooped, grimacing at the protest from his aching gut, and bent to collect Hawkeye, who had since excused himself back into a stupor. Elim wished he could do likewise. Not for the first time, he wondered what it would be like to be small and delicate – to get to be carried sometimes, to go through life with options beyond 'walk or get left'.

But as he heaved his rusty, aching bigness back into motion, kicking and nudging at the debris in his path, Elim began to suspect a more dangerous connection between the rocks at his feet and the feverish fellow slung over his back. Somehow the man and the mountain had taken to convulsing in tandem – and worsening every time.

Hawkeye had been getting fidgety again, right before all that happened. Then he'd stiffened, just like those times before. But then he'd started to jerk, curling and clenching in strange, aimless rigors. Elim had called out to Bootjack to try to warn him, and then...

Well, Elim had probably ought to find out what-all had happened after he got walloped by 'and then'.

Fortunately, if you wanted to call it that, the rocks had come from up high, hit where the trail narrowed, and mostly kept tumbling on down the slope. It didn't take too much to knock the remainder down to a pile small enough for Elim to step over. By the time he'd done that and set Hawkeye down to start working on a way over that busted bridge, Way-Say was helping Bootjack up to his feet, talking boisterously in their hardscrabble *ak-ak-ak* language.

Only that didn't sound like Way-Say. Elim squinted in the last of the twilight, and belatedly realized that no, that was some other crow-man – one Elim had never seen before.

He was a textbook specimen, though: tall like Way-Say, pigtailed like Bootjack, with a lean, athletic build all his own. The stranger wore ragged copies of Bootjack's shirt and leggings, and a smile that flashed white in the deepening gloom.

It withered when he caught sight of the coffin. Elim watched, struck by the powerful resemblance between Bootjack and the stranger, as the silence of the one made space for an expression of sad amazement from the other. Maybe they were brothers. Maybe they were friends.

But when Bootjack finally found his voice – strained, hesitant, and smaller than Elim had ever heard it – and the stranger drank in his words, his expression said everything. He gaped, his face aging years as he stared at the battered, tilting wooden box. He smothered his mouth as if he would be sick; his shoulders slackened in helpless astonishment; his strong posture dissolved into a mortally wounded, weak-kneed shudder. And when he spoke, all that came out was a hoarse, hopeless croak. "*Kwenin?*"

Elim needed no translation. It was a question whose answer came in Bootjack's hard swallow... in the big out-spilling explanation as he helped his grief-stricken friend to sit down... in the upturned jerk of his chin – from Do-Lay, the boy in the box, to Elim, the man who had put him there.

And as the stranger's gaze locked on him, Elim felt those watery dark eyes searing themselves into his memory: burning through his conscience, eating through his heart, branding him clean down to his bones. He would remember them for the rest of his life. He would see them again at the moment of his death.

And here, now, he matched that look with one of his own – one that he hoped would convey even a tenth of the remorse that had haunted him through grueling days and sleepless nights, chasing him a hundred hard miles to this place, to the ends of the earth and probably soon to the end of his life. "I'm sorry," Elim said, because the words were pitiful and useless and still couldn't go unspoken. "*O-sento. Me mucho o-sento.* I'm just awfully sorry."

A flicker of recognition lit the stranger's face. His expression wavered, as if he couldn't decide whether to yell at him or cry. In the end, he just slumped forward and buried his face in his hands, his shiny black plaits shivering as he let out a long, wrecked breath.

No one said anything else. Bootjack favored Elim with a baleful stare, and then bent forward to start hauling the coffin back up to solid ground. Elim sat down and began feeling for a way to get Hawkeye across the bridge before the light failed completely. After that, he didn't think any more about sorcerous seizures or falling rocks: there was no telling about the rest of the mountain, but here at least, everything breakable was already broken.

Día's father had always frowned on people who wrote their own epitaphs. He believed the Verses were all anyone needed.

But if she were to break with tradition – and in the increasingly unlikely event that her final resting place was even found, much less marked – her headstone would have to read, 'It seemed like a good idea at the time.'

That was the truth. She had been so sure that she could find the trail by simply following the contour of the mountain, as if she were solving a labyrinth by keeping her right hand on the wall. Maybe she could. Maybe she was. Maybe the path was right around the corner.

But it didn't feel like it. It felt like she'd been wandering for hours in the freezing chill of a high desert night, stumbling through patches of hem-ripping scrub and over fields of foot-biting scree, clambering up rocks and squeezing through gaps as best she could with a broken arm and a fickle torch, which kept burning up and needing to be replaced, preferably without setting the whole drought-stricken landscape on fire – again – until finally she turned some corner or wedged herself through some little pass, only to find herself face-to-granite with a hopeless dead-end slope.

There was no time to waste on crying or cursing.

They would only worsen her headache anyway. There was nothing to do but backtrack, forcing her abused body to reverse all those labored paces until she found the next possible route. And the next one, and the one after that.

There was a way. There would be a way. She just had to find it.

Something rustled in the darkness far ahead of her. Día kept moving, unwilling to lose precious momentum for the sake of a coyote's evening stroll.

Then it came closer.

Día stopped to listen. Not a coyote. A two-legged pace, asymmetrical but steady, moving straight toward her. "Who's there?" she called out.

A reedy groan seeped through the trees.

Oh, no. Día turned left, her hand abandoning the imaginary labyrinth wall, her feet sluggish in spite of her urgency. "Go away!" she cried. "I don't have anything for you!"

But he had never listened to her, not once in the entirety of their short, disastrous acquaintance, and this was no exception: the footsteps picked up speed and followed her, one quicker than the other, both relentless in their pursuit.

Día couldn't match it. Her arm ached monstrously every time she jostled it, lightning-sharp agonies seized her chest with every full breath, and the only thing running was her nose. "Leave me alone!" she called again. "I can't help you and I'm sick of trying. Go find someone else!"

She'd spent ages looking for the way up, and yet it took less than a minute to find a way down: opening out in front of her was another steeply rolling slope, one whose bottom her pitiful smoking brand couldn't begin to illuminate. She halted and turned as that unholy foul smell washed back over her, roiling her stomach and hardening her resolve: if push came to shove again, Día would do the pushing. She would not give him another chance to hurt her. She would not go through this again. "God Almighty, what do you want from me?!"

But as the horror that had once been Sil Halfwick dragged itself to the edges of the firelight, the only answer was a piteous, broken wheeze.

He was a ghastly sight – shocking even to Día, who'd seen him just hours before. He was the color of a sick bird's droppings, a horrible blotchy grayish-greenish-white, his hair matted with dirt and trickles of some sinister fluid where the left side of his skull had been flattened by the fall. One arm hung limp, his opposite knee hitched with every shambling step, and dribbling down his chin and over his chest and soaked all through the front of his shirt were dark patches of stiff, dried gore.

And Día cared not one whit for any of it. "Well?"

Halfwick didn't answer. Perhaps he couldn't. He came three steps closer, his expression unreadable, his stench overwhelming. And just before Día would have hurled the torch at him and run, he dropped to his knees, silently beseeching her with pleading, mismatched eyes.

"You're sorry?" Día said, her queasiness undercut with naked incredulity.

Frantic nodding. Fearful eyebrows.

"You're sorry," she repeated, stupid with astonishment. "Not before, when I met you outside Island Town, and you treated me like an idiot child. Not after, when I turned myself inside out trying to help you, and you betrayed me. Not today, when I – when I *mutilated* myself to get you out of a bind, and you tried to kill me. NOW you're sorry. NOW you feel badly."

Bowed head. Slumped shoulders.

Righteous indifference. "Well, that's a terrible shame for you, Sil Halfwick, because I've got nothing left. I don't know how to fix you. I don't know how to get out of here. I can't even feel sorry for you anymore. You're just a selfish, thoughtless, stupid boy who only bothered to realize that when your outsides finally turned as rotten as your insides always have been. And now you're ugly and broken and helpless, and it's too late to do anything about it. You can't even..."

It was a wicked, exhilarating sermon, full of everything Día had spent her life schooling herself not to think, let alone say. But as the wind picked up and a cold breeze knifed through her, her spiteful passion fizzled into a dizzy haze.

Día swayed, fighting fog and nausea and a terrible, lightheaded malaise. After a concerted effort, she scraped together enough presence of mind to take a step forward, away from the edge.

Halfwick was watching her with yellowed eyes, his gross features knotted in perplexity or concern.

She'd been in the middle of a thought. What was it?

"... and... and I think that speaks for itself." Día paused, struggling to find a point and make it. Nevermind the proofs – what was the conclusion?

She needed help. Yes, that was it: she'd been going for help, and time and steps were precious, and her task was to do everything she could to make it out of this alive.

And here as proof of God's peculiar providence was the principal cause of all her miseries: the one who had brought her nothing but grief, who had been the very antithesis of help and succor, who always seemed to be exactly as ill-equipped to render assistance as she was obliged to require it...

... the one who owed her, and knew it.

Día closed her eyes, feeling the flickering heat on her cheek as the burning branch in her hand dwindled toward extinction. She'd need to replace it soon. "So that's why you're coming with me," she said. "Not because you deserve it. Not because I forgive you. Becaush... because you're the reason I'm out here, and my *papá* is worried sick, and God help me, you're my best chance of getting home. You keep me alive until we find help. That's why you're here. That's your job now. Do you understand?"

Halfwick answered by using his good hand to pick up his limp one, clasping both together at his chest.

Well, it wasn't much of a promise, but it would have to do. Día held her breath, steeled her nerve and walked forward to help him to his feet, all but wincing in anticipation of his cold, slimy grip.

She was not expecting him to kiss her hand.

As it turned out, his lips were no more pleasant than the rest of him – even if that was far and away the best use he'd put them to. But as the two of them started off into the dark, Día tried to find her better nature under the roiling unrest in her stomach, and the growing ache in her skull.

After all, it was easy to love the loving, a simple thing to be good to the good. And so damned difficult to find compassion for the damned and the difficult.

* * *

VUCHAK HAD NO idea what to do next. He couldn't begin to imagine what to say.

"It's not my fault," Echep repeated. He sat and stared out at nothing, as hollow and purposeless as a broken drum. "I did everything right. I didn't... I wasn't careless. I didn't travel by night. I didn't make a fire. I just – they shot me. They stole my horse and shot me!"

His hand went again to the aging wound at his neck, where the bullet had plowed up his flesh as it passed through him, probably missing his jugular by a feather-width. Vuchak didn't doubt that it had taken him weeks to make it here. It was a wonder he'd survived at all.

"I believe you," he said. "The broken men robbed us too."

But Echep might as well not have heard. "All those nights I spent crawling through the desert... all those days I spent fighting vultures over carrion... didn't he even miss me?"

Vuchak spared a guilty glance at the coffin. Dulei had been so glad to be rid of his *atodak* for awhile, to do as he pleased without Echep looming over him, cautioning him to moderate himself and mind his responsibilities. When he didn't return, Huitsak discreetly dispatched a search party – and when that turned up nothing, he told Dulei that Marhuk had come to him in a dream, that the Eldest had given Echep a new, sacred duty, one far more important than merely delivering Huitsak's ledger.

Dulei had never thought to ask why the dream wasn't given to him personally.

And now here was Vuchak, struggling to conjure some face-saving excuse, acutely aware of Ylem standing there not ten feet away, blind and shivering in the dark, probably wondering when they were going to get moving again.

"Of course he did," Vuchak lied, and nodded at the coffin. "Isn't that so, Dulei? Didn't we discuss that very thing? You were so confident that your *atodak* had done his duty, so sure that he had stopped to do someone else's too, so proud that he trusted you to mind yourself, no matter how long he was away..."

Echep glanced up, shaming Vuchak into silence.

Mind him for me. Those had been Echep's exact words. *Keep him out of trouble, don't let him get behind the bar, and make sure he doesn't go to Oyachen's after work.*

Well, damn it, Vuchak had done all that, on top of reining in his own *marka*'s wild fancies. Huitsak was the one who'd ordered Dulei out that night, and Ylem was the one who'd shot him. He was sorry for Dulei, and for Echep, but he was not about to start blaming himself for either of them. And if they didn't appreciate his attempts at consolation, then... well, they could get in line behind Weisei, to start with, and Vuchak would gladly return to his own duty – which had nothing to do with exchanging awkward sentiments and everything to do with getting *this* stinking box and *that* two-colored delinquent up there to Atali'Krah for someone else to decide about and dispose of.

Vuchak said none of that, of course. He drew a deep breath and made the sign of an inscrutable god. "Well, the important thing is that you're here now. Come on, brother – suck your teeth. Let's get your poor *marka* home to his rest."

And just like that, the lingering resentment in Echep's face melted into fear. "No – I mean, yes, but not just yet. Look, you see – it's full dark, and the half-man won't be able to see a foot in front of his face. And besides which, it's freezing, and I've been hiking up the north face all day – really, Vuchak, I'm dead on my feet. Let's just stay here for tonight, and start again in the morning."

That was a bag of excuses, and they both knew it. Vuchak frowned. He had already reconciled himself to the futility of going back down for Weisei, just as he had for Ylem's missing mystery-person: they had no supplies to reach a stranded man, no clear idea of where to look – and with Hakai in mind, no time to waste. The best thing to do now was to hurry through the last hours to Atali'Krah, and mount a proper search from there.

Vuchak did not trust Echep to care about any of that just then. "We can make a light for the half, we'll stay warmer if we keep moving, and you can..."

He stopped just short of a disastrous finish: *you can rest when we get there.*

Yes, of course he would. When they got to the top, Echep would make his apologies, dictate his wishes, and then he would sit down and kill himself. Since the moment Vuchak had learned of Dulei's death, he had known that Echep's life was over too – and yet it was only here, looking down at his pleading, fearful face, that the reality finally sunk in: Vuchak was talking to a man who would be dead by this time tomorrow. He was witnessing his friend's last hours of life.

And Echep – strong, handsome Echep – clutched Vuchak's leggings like a needy child and begged. "Please. Please, just let me have tonight."

Vuchak couldn't look away. He didn't need to. He already knew that Hakai was badly hurt, and the mountain was unstable, and Weisei was out there somewhere in the freezing dark, without food or water or even a flint for fire. The hours until morning were hours they didn't have. Staying here was the worst possible thing they could do.

From somewhere away and to the north, an owl hooted.

They were horrible creatures, owls – rapacious, crow-eating, bone-vomiting opportunists. Their pellets brought bad luck for the one who found them, and their cries portended death. Echep cringed at the sound.

And Vuchak – practical, duty-bound Vuchak – gathered his resolve, surrendered his judgment, and made the worst possible choice.

"... all right. Come on, let's find a place somewhere out of the wind."

After all, Hakai would live – or at least he wasn't actively dying. The Mother of Mountains might chip a little, but she wouldn't fall apart under their feet. And as for Weisei... well, this was Marhuk's home, and he was Marhuk's son. He would be fine.

After all, Vuchak was betting his life on it.

SO ELIM PICKED up Hawkeye and followed behind the two crow knights as they carried Do-Lay's box between them, to a place where the rock stuck out enough to offer a break from the north wind. That was fine.

Then they hunkered down and started on a light. That was fine, too. Better than fine: it was colder than the Sibyl's tit out here, and darker than the very pit of her back-premises.

But when the scraping of the flint finally threw a spark, and the spark caught the tinder, Elim realized with the first flare that that wasn't a torch – it was a fire. A sit-down sing-a-long boil-your-supper fire.

Elim could do with about three suppers just then.

Bootjack motioned for him to put down Hawkeye, which Elim swallowed a grumble as he did – because honestly, just getting the poor bastard up and down was as tiring as all the toting in-between. Then he waited to see what would happen next.

Maybe the stranger was waiting here, while Bootjack went out to look for Way-Say. Maybe they would make some fancy smoke-signal with a blanket, though God only knew what good that would do at this hour. Maybe someone would tell him what the dickens was going on.

But no: Bootjack just waved for him to sit down, and then he and the stranger set to making camp: unpacking this, unwrapping that, making stilted conversation between them.

Elim did not sit down. He stood there, making himself just as big and awkward as he could possibly be – and when Bootjack finally looked up, Elim had his Marín words ready. "*¿Way-Say dóndeyestá?*"

Irritation flashed across Bootjack's dark face, tainted with something that might have been guilt. "*Abaho,*" he replied – whatever that meant – with a downward motion of his upturned fist. "*Abaho, y regresa.*" Two fingers became walking legs, climbing up through the air, finished with a chin-jerk at the fire.

All right. So Way-Say had gone down – fallen down, maybe – and was going to climb back up. His best buddy here sure didn't seem too worried about that.

Elim copied the chin-jerk, this time at Hawkeye. "*Regresa Hawkeye,*" he said, making the climbing-up motions head up toward the top of the mountain. "*Pronto.*"

Bootjack scowled. "*Luego.*"

Well, whatever that was, it was a hell of a long way from 'yes'. "He's sick," Elim snapped, "and he's getting worse. You understand? He might even be –"

"So fix him!" the stranger barked.

Elim just about flinched himself to death – and then barked right back. "HOW?"

The stranger bounded up to his feet, and for one giddy second Elim wondered if he was about to eat a Sundowner's fist. "You dog-woman child, idiot! You heal him! Or only you are for killing?"

"*Hsst – trankilo, echep,*" Bootjack soothed, beckoning his friend back to a seat.

The stranger reluctantly returned to his place by the fire, glowering at Elim all the while.

Elim said nothing, his surprise at hearing Ardish out of the stranger's mouth shredded to a meaty pulp as the words delivered their brutal, mangled payload.

Or are you only made for killing?

Elim stood there for a minute more, being roundly ignored by the two Sundowners. Then he gave up and went to go sit with the one who couldn't refuse his company.

"Hawkeye," he said, drawing the translator's head and shoulders up into his lap, "do you reckon we could have another chat?"

There was no objection, of course – just closed eyes, slack mouth, and those insidious trembles, which Elim knew better than to hope was anything as natural as shivering.

"You were saying a few days back, about how I was good with handling Ax – you know, right when he was starting to take that queer turn. And you might've suggested that keeping him going was me being sorcerous somehow. And I, uh, I know I took some exception to that, because I don't... I didn't want it to be that way. I wanted to make him right just with my own know-how." Elim was grateful the firelight didn't stretch far enough for him to have to keep looking at his results. "But if there's something I could do to make you right, I wish you would tell me. Even if it might not work. Even if I'm not – even if it's not what I'd call church-regular."

There was no answer from Hawkeye, of course. He was just a presence, as comforting as a warm cat in Elim's lap – even if the warmth was a rising fever, and he didn't so much purr as shake, and both of those things were a sharp reminder of just how much more help he needed than Elim had to give.

Elim had *something*, though. He must have. The stranger had called him a dog woman's child. That bastard Champagne had said he was the son of the 'Dog Lady'. And the monster herself sure seemed to act like it.

And somebody had taken away all his scrapes and cuts, that arrow-wound at his side, the ugly sunburn on his back. He'd woken up as clean as a licked calf – apart from being half a monster himself. Was that in him? Could he do it for someone else?

... and would he maybe already have an answer for that, if he'd just shut his trap and listened?

Elim smoothed Hawkeye's gray-threaded hair back from his face. He kissed his forehead. He said the night-prayer, keeping his voice low and soft, and if he'd had a candle, he would have made the sun-wheel over it before he snuffed it out.

But none of those things were magical. They were just

the things he knew how to do, because Lady Jane had done them for him. That other mother probably did things too – powerful, arcane things – but Elim couldn't begin to guess what they were. They didn't belong to him, and neither did she.

He was still thinking about that when a pair of dirty, battered moccasin-boots came to visit.

Elim looked up at Bootjack, the great avatar of austerity. His face was an unyielding mask, his bloodstained shirt and leggings and – well, and everything, really – still as hard and solid as ever. He bent and handed Elim a warm, bundled cloth... and whatever was inside smelled *wonderful*.

Elim looked from his supper over to Hawkeye, and then back up at Bootjack. "I don't know how," he confessed. "*No se.*"

Bootjack's pigtail-framed expression softened just slightly; he cast a glance back over his shoulder at the stranger still sitting by the fire. "Soon," he said. It sounded like a promise. Then he went away again.

Inside the little pocket were half a dozen grease-glistening hot balls of... well, of something edible, anyway. They looked like fruitcakes and smelled like meatloaf, but they were studded through with something else, nuts or tiny dried things, like good raisins or bad mushrooms. Elim was well ready to find out.

But he hesitated even in spite of the raging, ravenous emptiness he'd been beating back for two days now. This wasn't like the rabbit he'd shot or the steak he'd purloined from earlier – not a simple thing taken straight from hand to mouth. This was *made* food. And that was dangerous.

He looked back over his shoulder, tempted to call

out and ask about his oats, his peas, that half-round of cheese – the good, safe food he'd brought with him.

But on recollection, he'd eaten the last of the peas and cheese already, polished off the oats with Ax... and if the Sundowners were feeding them from their own stores, it was almost certainly because there was none of his own food left to give him.

So Elim was left with a hot pile of temptation in his lap. No, this new food probably wouldn't poison him, but that didn't mean it was safe. All its parts had grown here, died here, been transformed and finished here according to some unwritten recipe passed down through hundreds or thousands of indigenous hands. It had been steeped in place and ripened in time. It belonged here, to this old, wild world. What would it do to a visitor, a foreigner who put it inside himself? Would it change him – or worse yet, anchor him?

Elim looked down at Hawkeye and back at the little bag of gleaming heathen meatballs. If it did change him, maybe that would come in useful. And if it anchored him... well, it wasn't like he'd ever had much chance of leaving here anyhow.

Elim closed his eyes, listening to the soft hooting of a nearby owl, wishing with all his heart for the taste of Lady Jane's honey-butter biscuits. Then he dug in.

KEEP ME ALIVE. That was what she'd said. *That's your job now.*

It had seemed simple enough at the time: all Sil had to do was show her the trail he'd found, and they'd be well on their way.

And he had, and they were... and yet he was beginning

to despair of keeping his promise. Día had been sick twice already, and had taken to stumbling like a Sunday drunk – and slurring like one too.

"... an' sho Harding advised against the c-consumption of copper-cooked fat, which lied leddle – which led Lyle to ban the use of boiling pans for his expedition, which meant that hish men ate their vegetables fresh, rather than reduced, preversing their health."

Sil had no idea what she was going on about. He didn't care. His good arm held the smoldering nub that could only charitably still be considered a torch; his bad one was a leash for Día, pulling her along behind him with barely-restrained impatience. She might move faster if she saved her breath for the climb, but he needed her to keep talking – and could just about convince himself that that was for her own benefit.

"... inspired De Zavala's experiments," she gasped. "By reppecating Lyle's results, he p-proved the antic... antiscor*b*utic propeties of cabbages. He conquered scurvy, shaving countless lives and, and, and permently reducing the balance of human misery. Do you see what I mean?"

He didn't, no. He saw about six inches' worth of road in front of his feet, and then a whole god-damned sea of darkness. He squeezed her hand.

Día paused to take the next big step up, swaying in place for a long, agonizing moment. It was all Sil could do not to yank her bodily forward. *Come on, hurry up – you don't have much time.*

Then she swallowed hard, shivered harder, and continued on. "S-so, so, I'm saying... what I'm saying... invidually, we can relieve shimple suffering – starvation, poberdy, neglect. But *collectily*, we can make unvoidable suffering avoidable – we can change the nature of suffering itshelf. Izntit beautiful? Izntit miraculous?"

No. Beautiful would be the sight of dry forage, some fresh kindling he could use to keep that fire alive. Miraculous would be finding the a'Krah before Día collapsed in a heap. Sil squeezed her hand again, urging her to go on, irrationally convinced that as long as he could prompt her mouth to keep working, the rest of her would follow suit.

"... and that's why I do it. Books and, and spearments and all. I want to be part of that. I want to belong to that. I want..."

With a cry of dismay, Día lurched forward. Sil instinctively held the torch away as she fell, before realizing that she wasn't falling at all – she was grabbing for it.

The branch had burned all the way down to his fingers, crisping their edges to a black char. But Sil was apparently too wet to catch – and with nothing else to sustain itself, the fire dwindled down to a smoking cinder, and died.

"No!" Día cried, wrenching herself from his grip, pulling the dead nub from his hand. Sil was happy enough to let her have the useless thing – but when she dropped it and stepped on it, he had to intervene.

No, come on, he thought, grabbing her hand again for an insistent pull. *Let it go. Keep moving. You don't have the heat to spare.*

After all, Sil was a Northman. For him, the cold was a distant suspicion – something that might be happening to someone else. But he could feel the trembling of Día's hand, all but hear the chattering of her teeth, and needed no thermometer to tell him what was going to happen to a barefoot Afriti girl who was bleeding heat with every step. There was nothing else he could do for that: he'd already given her his jacket, but couldn't manage to wrestle his boots off his grotesquely swollen feet. Sil pulled her again, frantic to get her moving.

"No," she repeated, stubbornly rooted in place. "No, I can't – I can't anymore." And she dropped like a gut-shot deer.

She hadn't passed out, though. She was only sitting – sprawling, rather. "I need... tell them I need a treven – a trephination. One to t-two inches for a closed head wound. No sssedative. And if they can't, tell my *papá* that, that I..."

Oh no. He wasn't about to let her start dictating a will. Sil jerked harder, crushing her hand until his grip turned wet with his own foul juices. She cried out, but made no move to rise. "Le'mi 'lone!"

Move. Move. Move, you ashy slag. You snotty god-bothering twat – get up! He shouted at her in his own head, called her every nasty name he could conjure – but one pop from his shoulder warned him that he was going to come apart like a picked-over chicken carcass before she so much as budged.

Well, fine – but if she thought he was going to stand here and let her die on his conscience, she was dumber than any concussion. Sil let go of her hand and grabbed at her head, fully intending to haul her to her feet by whatever remaining tufts of hair he could catch...

... and was answered with an ecstatic gasp. "Oh!" Día cried, eagerly seizing his hand and guiding it over her scalp, to the back of her head. There was a nasty cut back there, frosted with dried blood. "Yes, there – just there – oh, you're so cold... please, please, just hold it there..."

Her head felt like a shorn sheep. Sil felt like a huge fool. He couldn't stay like this: every minute they delayed was a minute Día didn't have. If she wouldn't move, he'd have to go on alone.

Alone, in the dark, up a mountain, with no tools and no torch and half a rotting body that might give out at any minute. Sil couldn't see a foot in front of him – one wrong step and he'd be... no, *Día* would be done for. She'd freeze to death before morning.

From somewhere to the north, an owl hooted.

Sil glanced out at the sky – a black bowl pierced through with the light of a hundred thousand beautiful, useless little stars. Día probably had some grand theory about God's will as revealed through observational astronomy.

Well, if he was up there, he was a right prick.

But he could probably still be trusted to let the moon rise sometime in the next hour or so. Then they might be able to make some progress without breaking their necks.

So Sil reluctantly folded himself down to one knee as Día leaned into his touch – a frigid benediction given to a huddled supplicant, and paltry interest paid on a huge and looming debt.

"– AND THE TIME he decided to play a trick on Tadai?" Vuchak said then.

Echep grimaced in rueful delight. "How could I forget? Tadai had gone upstairs with... what's her name? The pink one with the big tits. And I was sitting there at the bar – I swear, Vuchak, I was JUST taking my first sip, thinking about how strangely pleasant an evening it was, wondering why I was in such a fine mood –"

Vuchak smiled. "– and then Weisei and I heard that chicken-scalding shriek, and when I stuck my head out to see, there was Tadai tearing down the hallway, wide-eyed and bloodless, his half-standing penis waving like a little white flag –"

Echep snorted. "– and then the thump, and then the bang, and by the time I made it upstairs, there they were –"

"– an angry naked white woman kicking the mischief out of Dulei with her shoes still on, yelling hell the whole time –"

"– *until I actually had to fish the little shit out from under the bed!*" Echep finished, roaring with laughter.

Vuchak winced at the sound, and cast a guilty glance over at the soft nonsense-noises coming from the right. Ylem was bent over with Hakai's arm slung around his neck, trying to cajole the *ihi'ghiva* into bearing his own weight for the length of a piss. It was a sorry sight, and an uncomfortable reminder.

I promise that we will keep him well, and return him safely to you. That was what Vuchak had said to Huitsak, the night they left Island Town.

See that you do, the master of the Island Town a'Krah had replied, *or I will break the other side of your face.*

No, this wasn't the time or the place for such raucous merriment. They shouldn't have stopped here at all.

But by every god, it felt good to laugh again.

Echep heaved a huge, cleansing sigh, and then threw a pebble at the coffin. It hit with a reproachful *plick*. "You always were an unbearable trial."

It was a crass thing to say, and yet Vuchak was glad to see Echep finally talking to Dulei. There was a difference between knowing the person in the box was his *marka*, and actually believing it... and believing it would make tomorrow's task that much easier.

Vuchak leaned his head back against the cold stone, and drew his cloak tighter. "I wish we had some wine."

"Say it again!" Echep swore, glaring up at whatever crows might be roosting in the trees above. "Listen, Grandfather – if you're going to throw a man's life away, you could at least offer him a drink first."

That was a bit more than a joke. Vuchak sucked his teeth, choosing his next words carefully. "You won't be thrown away," he said after a moment. "You'll be laid to rest in honor beside him –"

"*FUCK him!*"

Vuchak flinched. There was no teasing in Echep's face now – just raw, righteous anger.

Well, maybe he was just lancing a boil. "I know the feeling," Vuchak said, and thought of how to get back to sound footing. "Remember the time he and Weisei decided to –"

"Am I wrong?" the other *atodak* interrupted, his long plaits swaying as he sat up straighter. "Am I missing something? Why should I waste my life just because he couldn't hold on to his? What good does that do anyone?"

Oh, this was a bad road to go down. Vuchak took his time in answering: if he was going to have to defend the order of things, he'd better not do it sloppily. "It safeguards our work, and our oath," he said at last. "We swore to defend them with our lives. What would that mean if we could just walk away? Who would ever take a bullet for someone when he could choose to save his own skin?"

"Mothers," Echep spat. "Fathers. Lovers. People

make a gift of their lives all the time – and they do it willingly. Selflessly. They do it for love, not because To'taka Marhuk is standing behind them brandishing an axe. What's a gift if you're forced into giving it?"

Vuchak frowned. He understood the sentiment, but this was blasphemy. "Echep, we took an oath, when we became men –"

"We were TAKEN from our families when we were six years old! What choice did we ever have?" His eyes were rimmed with white, and his breath smelled of deer-fat. "They told us that it was for our own good – that we were the children of intemperate mothers – that we should be so lucky to spend our lives minding his black-feathered brats!"

"Well, what else do you want?" Vuchak snapped. "He didn't make your mother open her legs during the fallow-month. He didn't tell her to wait until the Pue'Va to drop you out into the world. Blame her if you want to blame anyone – she's the one who set you up for this."

That might not be strictly true, of course. Every a'Krah woman knew when to shut her husband out, so that her child would not be born during the five starless days of the year... but sometimes mothers fell sick or met with accidents, and sometimes children were born too soon. That was just the way of the world. You might as well complain about a club foot or a lazy eye.

Maybe Echep had the same thought. He leaned forward, lacing his hands behind his head and contemplating the thin spots in the soles of his shoes. He'd need new ones for the winter.

... would have needed, rather.

The wind blew. The fire popped. It would need feeding soon.

Presently, Echep sat up. "Vuchak, come away with me."

Vuchak stared, waiting for an understanding that didn't come. His friend's eyes were wild, earnest, his face lit by some weird, precarious hope. "What?"

Echep's gaze flicked to the coffin; he lowered his voice, as if to keep Dulei and the West Wind from overhearing. "I'm serious. Let's just go away and start over – be masters of our own lives."

He was mad. Just hopelessly, blasphemously mad. Vuchak's mouth hung agape, unable to even begin to reply.

"Don't think like that," Echep admonished. "It sounds bad, but you know I'm right. My *marka* is dead, and yours will be better off without you. What good are we doing here?"

Vuchak could not have been more astonished if Echep had pulled a knife and stuck it in his eye. "That's not – that isn't true!"

Echep's answer came with a serious, penetrating stare. "Isn't it? Dulei is seventeen, and already a man. I'll be twenty this year, so you're what, twenty-one? And your *marka* is older still. Men our age are building cradleboards, Vuchak. Teaching their sons to walk. Why, look at Otli – he's younger than both of us, and already he has a fat wife and two children. And then there's Weisei, still wearing his hair down like a bare-bottomed boy, even while it falls in his wine, even while it hangs in his sex-pleasured face –"

"Shut up," Vuchak snarled. "That's none of your business or anyone else's. He'll take his vows when he's ready. And when he does, he'll be better than either of us – better than you, Dulei – because he'll be old enough to understand what they mean." After all, Weisei could easily live two hundred years – what should it matter if he spent an extra ten in childhood?

If Echep took offense on his *marka*'s behalf, he didn't show it. There was only cold, unpleasant rationality – the same look Vuchak had given Ylem when the time came to turn him away from his futile calling down the cliff. "How many years have you been telling yourself that, Vuchak? How many more will you cling to it? He doesn't plait his hair. He doesn't use men's speech. He doesn't have to become an adult, because he knows you're there to do it all for him – and as long as you're around, he never will. Now you have to decide: are you willing to make him wait the rest of your life to grow up?"

This wasn't how it was supposed to go. Only hours ago, Vuchak's imagination had made Echep the voice of patience and good-humored optimism. Now he was hearing all his own worst thoughts articulated with terrible precision, every sensible strike hitting with devastating accuracy. Echep hadn't even said *are you willing to wait* – because then the answer could have been a noble and self-sacrificing *yes*. It was *are you willing to make him wait* – as if Weisei's course was fixed and unchangeable, and Vuchak himself was the rut he had gotten stuck in.

Vuchak pressed the heels of his hands to his eyes, groping for some reason, any reason, why Echep was wrong.

Beside him, the voice of temptation turned warm and honey-sweet. "Come on, brother – you've done your time. You've given him everything. Why, if I hadn't come along just when I did, you would be lying dead under the Grandfather of Frogs back there, and Weisei would be already bereft. It works out to the same thing in the end."

Vuchak felt ill. He reached for the branch and poked the fire, urging it brighter so that Weisei would see it more clearly, and come back that much faster – before his fickle *atodak*'s heart failed him.

"I don't... what would be the point?" he said at last, his voice weak in his own ears. "Where would we go? What would we do? We're still a'Pue. Our wives would be unfaithful to us. Our children would die. What other life is there?" Vuchak had envied the happiness of other men, but it was the same envy he would feel on watching a bird in flight. That fate wasn't his.

"How do you know?"

Vuchak glanced over, as mystified as if Echep had asked him to count the stars. "What?"

Echep tipped his head left and right. "I said, how do you know? I thought about this for days when I was lost out there in the desert. You know, the Eldest like to frighten us with those rotten stories about Madap and Ko'lit, but do you actually know anyone those things have happened to? Can you even name one *atodak* who's tried?"

Vuchak might have been able to conjure a name if he thought long enough. Echep didn't give him the chance.

"What if it's not true? What if Marhuk has just been tricking us into minding his children by keeping us too frightened and superstitious to have any of our own? Really, Vuchak, what if all of this is just one big self-serving lie?"

Vuchak couldn't hear this. He just couldn't. "No. It isn't – you don't get to question the dice just because you lost your throw. I'm sorry for you, and I'm sorry for you too, Dulei, but we're not Eaten-people. We don't just bumble through life satisfying ourselves like thoughtless fatted hogs. All of us have a place and a purpose and a duty, and they don't change according to how we feel about them. We're a'Krah, and if we aren't that, then... well, then we aren't anyone. I would rather spend the rest of my life being Weisei's miserable *atodak* than run away and look for happiness as a nobody, and – and nothing else you say is going to change my mind, so you might as well save yourself the effort."

They were some of the hardest, truest words Vuchak had ever said. He had no idea where they'd come from.

But they had an edge to them, and it cut Echep deeply. He stared at Vuchak for a long moment, and his eyes were open wounds. "Remember me, Vuchak," he said at last. "When you're lying in your bed, old and stiff and useless, listening to your fresh-faced *marka* drink and sing the night away in the next room... remember me, and what your life could have been."

Then Echep pulled his cloak more tightly around himself, turned his back, and lay down.

Vuchak made no reply. He didn't need to. Let Echep have the last word: by this time tomorrow, he would be dead or fled. He'd wanted one last night of company, and Vuchak had given it to him. There was no point in troubling himself any more about the sacrilegious delusions of a condemned man.

But as the night passed and the fire dwindled, Vuchak had no one to confide in but his own murky thoughts, and freshly-unsettled recollections of the day he had been an uncle.

* * *

THE SCREAMING HAD *gone on for hours.*

It was awful, just soul-searingly unbearable, made all the worse for knowing that that was Vuchak's sister in there, that she was in unutterable pain – and that he was powerless to help her. There was nothing he could do but draw and erase the spirit-lines outside the house, over and over, hour after hour, misdirecting evil things to keep them from finding their way to the laboring woman inside.

It wasn't supposed to happen that way. Vuchak wasn't even supposed to be there. His place belonged to Suitak – the husband, the father – but he was halfway down the mountain, cutting wood for the cradleboard. The baby had come much, much too soon.

But Yeh'ne was in there, trying with everything she had for the child's life – and Vuchak had to try too.

So he drew the sacred lines with the milk-blessed end of his spear, soaring arcs and swirls punctuated with the rhythmic stomp of his heels. He recited the graces until his mouth went numb, blending the words into endless, meaningless sounds. He prayed wordless prayers there in the gray light before dawn, asking Yeh'ne to finish her work quick and bravely, begging the Ripening Woman to see her safely through it. He willed his strength to her.

Then the pulsing, contracting howl died down again, and did not return. There was a long silence. Vuchak drew and erased with feverish sweat-beading panic. What did that mean? Was it done? Had the baby survived? Had she?

Then a woman's sobbing – and underneath it, a tiny kitten cry.

The bottom fell out of his stomach..His spear wobbled

in the dirt. It was done. Yeh'ne had done it. She was a mother.

Nobody had told Vuchak how long to keep going, but he wasn't about to risk stopping too soon. He went on through the motions, dizzy, unfocused, thanking every god and spirit with ears to hear him, thanking his own starless, luckless birth. After all, who better to safeguard a confinement than a man who drew every nearby misfortune onto himself?

Then the door-curtain parted, and the midwife came out – holding a swaddled bundle in her arms.

Vuchak's spear clattered to the ground. He backed away, a blistering oath on his lips. "What are you doing?!" The baby wasn't supposed to be exposed to the outside air until its cord-wound had healed – and it certainly shouldn't be anywhere near him!

But the midwife's age-lined face only crinkled a little at the corners of her eyes. "It's all right. She can't stay."

Vuchak scarcely dared to look, lest he ruin the baby with his gaze... but as the old woman unfolded the blanket and he caught his first glimpse, his fear dried up and fell away.

Yeh'ne must have swallowed a grain of sand, or dreamed of needles. Maybe she had been cursed by a witch. Regardless, the cause was as mysterious as the result was final: she had made a tiny, beautiful daughter, fawn-colored, wrinkle-faced, and freshly dried all over... except for the glistening red-purple blossom at the back of her head, where her brain had flowered out of her skull.

The baby didn't seem to know that. She only squirmed and smacked her lips, as if idly wondering about breakfast.

"Mother thought you might like to meet her." And before Vuchak could begin to understand, the old woman came closer, and the blanket-creature shifted into his arms, and suddenly he was holding a freshly-made little person no bigger than his forearm – a perfect, tiny life.

Vuchak's breath deserted him.

Somehow, in the face of all that pain and wonder and heart-crushing sadness, Yeh'ne had thought of him. In a handful of minutes, she had gone from agony to ecstasy and back to agony again. Then she had wrapped up her joyful, impending sorrow and made it a gift. She knew Vuchak would never have children of his own – that he would never dare touch a child who had any chance of life. She knew what this would mean.

Vuchak couldn't object. He couldn't even see through the wet strangers in his eyes. He could only stand there, stunned to utter stillness by the wondrous tiny weight in his arms. What else was there?

"This one is special," the old woman said. "It's rare that such children are born awake."

Special. Well, of course she was! But Vuchak had no idea how to honor that. What good was he to her? How could he better a life that would be measured in hours?

He looked up, wet-faced and helpless. "What do I do?"

The old woman smiled, patience incarnate. "You could start by saying hello."

"Hello," Vuchak stupidly repeated to that sleepy, ruddy face. "Good morning," he said to the intoxicating smell of her wispy black hair. They were silly, meaningless sentiments: a baby didn't understand words, and even if she did, how would she know what morning was? She hadn't been here long enough to even...

Vuchak paused, seized by a sudden epiphany. No, she wouldn't be here long – but she was here now. She was awake, outside, in the world. This wasn't just his chance: it was hers, too. He looked up. "May I walk with her?"

The old woman's eyes softened in fondness, as if she had been waiting for him to ask that very thing. "I think Mother would be grateful if you did."

Yes. Yes, of course. Vuchak couldn't keep her here among the living – but he could show her the joy of being alive. He could show her how wise she was to be born a'Krah.

"You and I are lucky people," he said as they started up the road. "Has anyone told you that? Yes, it's true, and I'll show you so…"

So Vuchak and his niece went walking up the hill together, co-conspirators absconding with a precious pocket of time. On the way, he showed her the stars that Grandmother Spider had hung in the sky, and the first warming light on the horizon, where Grandfather Marhuk had moved the sun to make a place for people to live. He showed her the great valley behind them, the banks of the All-Year River lit up with the watchfires of thousands of a'Krah in dozens of towns and villages, and pointed out Morning Town, where their family belonged. And when they reached the top, he showed her the wonders of Atali'Krah: the great calendar, which had been raised on the place where Marhuk fell to earth, and would stand until the end of days – the Spirit Towers, whose sky-reaching wooden platforms made a rest for the dead – the huge stone Giving Hands, where the bodies of truly exceptional a'Krah were offered up with prayers and feasting. He explained how her body would be laid atop the Tower of Innocence, and how her mother and father would bury her cord under the floor of their house, so that her free-soul might find its way back to them. He told her that she was loved and wanted, and would be warmly welcomed back, if she chose to return. He promised that she would have a good life, even if he wouldn't get to see much of it.

And when she grew weak and fretful, Vuchak walked her home again, the spring breeze cool on their faces as they left the world behind.

AND THAT WAS how Vuchak passed the night: sitting alone before the fire, an old saddlebag nestled protectively in the crook of his arm as his thoughts dissolved into a treasonous, unspeakable fantasy.

CHAPTER TEN
CREATURES OF EARTH AND FIRE

AH CHE, A CHILD of twelve winters, pressed himself against the bars as the cage door slammed shut.

The iron was grimy, slick with years of palm-grease and dust, but it was still better than being wedged into Orv Orson's armpit on the ride down.

"God damn, Mag," Orson swore. "You getting paid by weight?"

The old liftman grunted. "If I was, I'd kick your fat gut down the shaft and retire." Then came the bells – two and three – and the jolt of the cage as it descended. Then there was nothing but the sound of De Puerta's wretched cough and the stink of Orson's gin-sweat as the whole lot of them sank five hundred feet down into the mine.

Ah Che had learned to savor these moments, even cramped and nervy as they were. Standing in the cage was standing, not pounding or crawling or heaving or hauling. It was rest, albeit of the most brief and begrudging kind.

It was like being eaten. Every descending second swallowed them deeper into that foul, unnatural air –

hot with the work of two hundred sweating men, humid with the constant seep of water through the walls, and perennially stinking, acrid and sour from that peculiar admixture of spent powder and stressed human bodies.

All too soon, the cage jerked to a stop and the door opened, and then the day's labor began. Ah Che followed the men through the damp, narrow gallery, his hand trailing the rough limestone wall even as his ears strained to pick out individual footsteps over the clang of hand-drills and sledges and the soggy violence of De Puerta's putrid hacking. There weren't supposed to be any tools or timber left out where people could trip on them – but then, there were a lot of things that weren't supposed to happen down here.

So Ah Che tracked the tunnel edges with his fingers and the bits of debris by the skittering thuds they made when Orson kicked them to one side or the other. He kept his head turned, gleaning every precious bit of light and movement in his periphery, and focused on making it to his worksite unnoticed and unbothered. That was getting harder to do.

He suddenly sensed a body in front of him – just in time to take a hard shove to the chest. "Watch it, part-timer."

Go break your neck, ditch-pig, Ah Che thought. "Sorry," he said.

Six months ago, near-misses like that didn't happen. Six months ago, his earth-sense was sound enough that he could feel the hobnails on a man's boot soles, even if said man were standing twenty feet away, picking his nose in perfect idle silence. Wally Hen had hammered his into perfect triangle-patterns so that Ah Che would easily find him on his first day down the shaft. Now it was all he could do to make out the striations of a rock with his hand right on it.

Of course, he would be fired in a heartbeat if that got out. So Ah Che kept his ears open and his movements careful and his step-memory sharp, avoiding the little pits and snags in the floor almost as cleanly as if he could see them.

Unfortunately, he had no such strategy for avoiding the people he had to work with.

"Hey, Achoo!" *Monk Farley's odious voice rolled through the gallery like stink off a wet dog.* "Off for another long day of playing with yourself in the dark?"

Ah Che kept walking. "Yeah. Lucky for me: if you spent half as much time pounding rock as you do thinking about pounding me in the ass, we'd both be out of a job."

The consumptive laughter that boiled through the tunnel completed his picture of the other miners. Four in the big stope just ahead and to the right – muckers picking up the broken stone left by yesterday's blasting, sifting chunks of valuable ore from piles of worthless tailings. Orson and De Puerta had set to work filling in the smaller, exhausted stope farther up and to the left, packing it in with their neighbors' waste. Up ahead at the end of the gallery, Farley and some other fellow were drilling holes for the blasting powder that would be set to blow at the end of the shift, advancing the tunnel another ten feet, leaving piles of rubble for tomorrow's muckers to sift through.

"Don't flatter yourself, chief," *Farley called back.* "Runty ratboys ain't my type."

There was no heat in his voice – it was all a game to him, dim as he was – but Ah Che hated it all the same.

He hated speaking their language. He hated that he'd let himself get good at it – that he'd even started thinking in it. He hated the crude sex jokes, and he especially hated that he understood them now. He hated the damp, and the dust, and the ear-savaging noise, and the collective unspoken fear of what could happen to any of them, at any moment. He hated to think that he'd once wanted to be here.

But as he reached the familiar hole and sat to climb down, the bootsteps approaching from the end of the gallery paused to give his arm a friendly nudge – and for an instant, Ah Che sensed triangle-patterned iron nails. "Good one, buddy," Wally Hen whispered. Ah Che hadn't even realized he was down here – it had been weeks since they worked on the same level.

Then Wally Hen went clomping on, adding his voice to the general clamor. "De Puerta! You pilfering weasel – what'd you do with my bar?"

It was the most fleeting, passing moment, hardly arrived before it was over – but somehow it lightened the weight of all those uncountable tons of earth hanging overhead, and banished Ah Che's foul temper like a sharp breath extinguishing a sullen flame. He sat at the edge of the winze, his legs dangling down into the hole, savoring this stolen moment of serenity. Then he climbed down and got to work.

When Ah Che had first started down the shaft, he was certain he'd be assigned with the speculators and geologists: the easiest, best-paid work in the mine. Ah Che could read the rock as well as any of them – better, even. He could sense where the gold-bearing veins would intersect, knew by a touch where to find the richest beds of silver ore. You couldn't buy that kind of talent – not on this side of the border, anyway – and he could learn the rest faster than a hummingbird could blink.

But although Mr. Burrell had been perfectly delighted with his talents, his authority ended at the sorting-house door – and the shaft boss, Mr. Rutledge, would have no truck with 'heathenry and devil-dowsing'. He made it clear that Ah Che would have to earn his way up alongside his paler peers – and under twice their scrutiny.

So Ah Che became a ratboy: a child miner squeezing through passages too narrow for grown men, wedging himself into gaps and crevices like a rat crawling up a drainpipe. This month, he was working a bed of galena: too thin to blast for, too valuable to leave behind. So he lay on his back with mallet and chisel in hand, hammering up into the stone scant inches above his head, his mouth and eyes tightly closed to keep the grit out as he pounded away. Whatever else they said about him, Ah Che was worth his weight in unspent candles.

He didn't dream about being a geologist anymore. It was too late for that now. His earth-sense was growing twisted, blunted, polluted with the brutality of his work. The delicate, lovely layering of crystals and carbonates, folds and faults, had faded to nearly nothing – replaced by the itch of chisels, the throb of heavy sledges, and the ache of powder-pulverized rubble. Ah Che had tried to atone for his daily sacrilege with ever-more-fervent orthodoxy: he grew his hair out and tied it in the keshet, *refused bacon and sugar and coffee, spoke only Maia at home – as if by acting more like one of his own people, the earth would be fooled into forgiving his depravities.*

When that didn't work, he just used more tarré.

Tarré *was his constant companion now, his morning ritual, his evening release. He had taken to buying the crushed leaves, because they were cheaper than the plugs, and smoking them, because the high lasted longer. He told himself that it was to help him work more efficiently, undistracted by the phantom pains of the mine or the ordinary ones in his own body... but any extra money his 'efficiency' made him went right into buying more* tarré, *and the truth was that he needed it less to soothe his senses than to deaden his mind.*

He wanted not to feel the ache in his arms and shoulders, the damp muck soaking his back and behind until he shivered in spite of the heat, the rocks dropping on his face or chest or gut when he misjudged the faults or missed his strike. He longed to avoid the silent, stifled throughline of every miner's fear: at any moment, there could be a fire, a cave-in, an explosion, and the only prospect worse than dying instantly when the mountain bit down on him was being sealed in its closed mouth and left to suffocate.

More than anything, he needed not to hear his father's voice.

Ah Che paused to wipe grit from the hollows under his eyes, and then gave the chisel one more hard strike. A fist-sized piece of ore dropped three inches from his head with an angry leaden thunk, *like a piece of bone-bark ripped from the skin of the World Tree.*

"That is not good work," *his father had told him that day last year.* "That is not a thing for human beings to do."

Ah Che had not been able to hear that then. He heard it now. That grave paternal tone echoed out from every stone-mutilating strike of his mallet, from every petty violence he did to the rock up above. He felt it in his diminishing senses – in the constant cacophony that blunted his hearing, in the casual sacrilege that was poisoning his gifts. And he knew as surely as if his father had told him so that it didn't matter how scrupulously he minded his diet or tied his hair: he had refused the call of his family, his goddess, and his own conscience, and all his efforts to behave as if he still belonged to them was simply the sad, self-serving pretense of an overgrown boy struggling to fit into the half-rotted garments of a person he hadn't been for five years now. Ah Che wasn't keeping the ways of the Maia – he was only profaning their remains. And if he ever wanted to live that life again, he would have to go home... before it was too late.

Soon, he promised. I'll come soon. He had to stay with Wally Hen just long enough for him to find someone else to share his life with – just long enough so that Ah Che wouldn't be leaving him alone. The bigger boy – man, now – had been the one to convince Ah Che to go back and see his father again, that one evening on Market Street last year. Wally Hen, who had no family of his own, had been the first to remind Ah Che that that chance was not one to be cast aside in a moment of anger – that his father should be seen and heard and respected, even if he could not be obeyed.

Ah Che had made up his mind on the spot. Perhaps it was true that the two of them could not live well together – that the great violence on the other side of the border would kill Wally Hen just as surely as the greedy peace on this one was draining Ah Che. But if that was so, then he would stay until he wasn't needed – until his volunteer brother, his self-selected family, had found a family of his own.

That was his mind's one pleasant roost. This spring, Wally Hen had taken to courting Flory Hayes, one of the girls working at the Magnolia. She was witty and kind and never said coarse things, at least not around Ah Che, and seemed every bit as happy to overlook Wally Hen's two-colored face as he was to disregard what he called her 'upstairs work'. He had confided to Ah Che they were both saving to buy out her contract, and when they did, he would ask her to marry him.

Ah Che would stay at least that long. Then he would break the news, as gently as he could. Then he would go, following the directions his father had given him, hoping that the world and Ten-Maia would forgive him for all that he had done in the meantime, and see him safely home.

In the meantime, he hammered and shivered and sweated in the stuffy, suffocating dark, doing his best to focus on strikes and angles, faults and fractures, on cleaving the beautiful cubic galena from the brittle, amorphous beds of limestone, all while packing his soiled conscience and stifled claustrophobia deeper down into his gut. And when at last his trough was full, Ah Che turned over, laid his tools in it, and slid his feet through the loops on either side, dragging it behind him as he crawled back towards the winze. There would be a drink of water waiting for him there, and a chance to stretch his aching limbs.

They talked to him more now than they used to. Even tarré *couldn't numb the stirring unrest inside his own body – bone-pains, new hair, the growth of his appetite and the awakening of a new one. He wouldn't care so much about Monk Farley's crude jokes if they weren't true – if they didn't make him ashamed of what he did when he was alone. That was unhealthy thinking, and Ah*

Che knew it. He knew that he had entered the autumn of his childhood, and that winter was coming. He knew that the blood of girls and the seed of boys were special things, connected somehow to the sacred mysteries, the rites of passage that would initiate them into adulthood. But he didn't know what happened when the men took a boy down into the kiva for the first time, or when it was right to spur himself to creation, or what to do with the result. So he had no rebuttal, no holy bulwark to keep his thinking from being tainted by these perverse people and their great love of guilt and secrecy and shame.

What he did have were exquisite, unspeakable thoughts about Flory Hayes – about how she always smelled like fresh lavender soap, and how she laughed so brilliantly, and how she'd felt that one time she hugged him, a single memory of softness that had provoked his body into opposition more times than he could count. Sometimes Ah Che even thought about John Samson at the bar, who told good jokes and gave him haymaker's punch for free. He was always careful to put the glass into Ah Che's hand, which wasn't really necessary, but Ah Che encouraged it – partly because he was hungry for any human touch that didn't happen in a shaft cage, but also because John Samson had big, soft hands, with long shoulder-squeezing fingers that lingered in his imagination every time he...

Ah Che's pleasant fantasy evaporated in the midst of unfamiliar territory. He patted gingerly at the floor, sensing ordinary limestone – but there were none of the familiar pits and ripples to guide him. He put his hand to the ceiling, hunting for traces of his own handiwork – but the galena here was undisturbed, run through with pyrite and quartz.

Ah Che had never found quartz down here.

He froze in place, mentally backtracking through each past movement – but he hadn't been paying attention. Had he passed the half-moon bump already? Had he just veered a little too far to the right, or turned himself in some other direction entirely? Should he try moving straight backwards, or would that only compound the error?

Ah Che's heart beat faster; his sweat turned cold. He listened in vain for some sound from above, any little noise that would tell him where the winze-hole was. But under the tightly-controlled panic in his own heavy breathing, there was nothing but endless, cavernous silence. He was lost.

SOMEONE WAS PULLING Día's hair.

She flinched and groaned, adrift on a stormy dark ocean. No distractions. She had to keep afloat. She had to stay awake.

Awake...

A harder pull. A small, sharp pain piercing the aching swells. Just noticing it was an effort. Opening her eyes was another. Remembering was another.

Halfwick. Kneeling there in the moonlight, a speechless, deathless horror. Why was he still here?

"Wake," Día mumbled.

A third pull, the hardest yet – putrid fingers pinching the scant tufts of her hair. Día flinched out from under his grasp, sprawling backwards as a wave of nausea threatened to sink her. Too much. Too long. She'd taken on too much water.

And Halfwick just knelt there, his arm sinking slowly, as if by concerted effort.

They had to get up. Día groped for his hand, missed, tried again. Her fingers found his forearm, the flesh under his sleeve no longer rotting-soft, but as tough as an iceboxed steak.

Frozen.

They'd stayed too long. The night had caught up with him. His eyes didn't even follow her, but remained locked on the place where she had sat, congealed into a fixed, unblinking stare.

"No," Día croaked. She needed him to get up – to go get help. Why did he always have to be useless right when she needed him?

Fire. He needed fire. Just enough to limber up his joints – just enough to get moving.

Día fumbled for something to burn. No wood. No plants. Too weak to tear her cassock – but she had his jacket. She pulled it from her shoulders and wadded it up between her feet, a clumsy crane incubating a filthy denim egg. The wind knifed through her. She shut it out, riding dangerously low on the dark waves as she sought out the tiny sun inside her, kindling it for one last burst of heat and light and love.

Nothing happened.

Not a singe, not a smolder, not even a blush of warmth. Her hair was all gone – her strength was all gone – and Día was nothing now but a wickless wisp, dwindling to extinction in a pool of cooling wax. Her body was failing, and soon she would die.

But Halfwick wouldn't. He couldn't. He was her accidental resurrection, God's obnoxious miracle. She had made him, however inadvertently – had supplied and abetted him at every turn of his journey. And if that wasn't just a series of fatal mistakes on her part – if she was going to keep believing that she had acted well and faithfully, that her life had served a worthwhile purpose – then she would have to serve him one more time.

Día sank down to lay her head on her knee. She guided his hand to her temple, every inch an effort for his frozen shoulder. Then she closed her eyes and waited.

"Go on," she said, her voice almost a whisper. "Do it."

He was a Northman, after all – one potent enough to freeze the noose around his own neck. But freezing was merely the withdrawal of heat, and some book or rumor or dim, ancestral memory suggested that his kind had used people this way before, back in their harsh winterlands across the sea – that they were a race of pallid heat-thieves, blue-eyed vampires who sustained themselves *in extremis* by draining the warmth from their thralls, the way her own desert-born ancestors might survive by drinking mare's blood. And if that was so – if the Northman boy and the Afriti girl truly didn't belong here, if their two old-world souls were not fit to survive here in this vast, wild other-land – then their only hope was to collapse themselves down into a single, viable self... and Día was fit only to collapse.

"Do it," she urged him. "T-take it. I wan-WAN'chu to." Human beings were creatures of earth and fire, after all. He would take her fire, and then she would return to the earth. It was the most natural thing in the world.

Día didn't let herself wonder what it would feel like. She admitted no fear. Only her toes curled a little as she readied herself for the end.

We move as You have moved us,
We love as You have loved us,
We live as You live in us,

And die in Your grace perf –

The hand on her temple, kept limber by the warmth of her scalp, closed into a fist, its knuckles just brushing her skin. Then it disappeared.

No. No. Damn it, he had to. Didn't he see that? Día forced herself up, beating back the swirling dark tempest by sheer force of outrage. She'd asked him for one thing. One simple thing! *I hate you!* she cried – except that it came out as a blurry, half-formed "haychu."

He didn't apologize – not even with his eyes. He couldn't. He just stared straight ahead, one bloodied eye and one jaundiced one fixed in agreement on nothing especially. But he held his arm in place, and from his closed hand, one index finger extended – a morbid compass needle pointing the way up the trail.

"No," she moaned. "Can't." She was so cold, and everything hurt so badly, and she was so, so tired of trying.

Nobody objected. Nobody tried to tell her otherwise. There was nobody to help her now but herself: Halfwick had squandered himself into total uselessness.

"Haychu," she whimpered, pushing away from him. "Hate you." She tipped back to a dizzy squat. "I HATE you!" She forced herself up, the frigid dark tides swelling and rolling over her as she staggered to her feet and left him there, one hand clutching the ache in her side, the other hanging limp as she lurched and tottered, step after giddy half-blind step.

Help me, Master. Right foot. *Save me, Mother Dog.* Left foot. *Kalei ne ei'ha, Grandfather.* Right foot.

Help me, Master. Save me, Mother. Kalei ne ei'ha, Grandfather.

Help me. Save me. Kalei ne ei'ha.

Help me...

Día went on like that, measuring her progress in steps and seconds and bleary, unanswered prayers. At long last, her foot found a crevice, and the ground rushed up to meet her, and finally, mercifully, she sank beneath the waves.

VUCHAK DIDN'T THINK he had fallen asleep – and yet the tapping at his ankle came as a surprise.

The night was growing old, and the fire had nearly died, but Vuchak didn't need the glow of the embers to see Ylem crouching before him, patting at his leg with child-like delicacy. *"Hcht – Butchak. I go. Time I go."*

Vuchak sat forward, equally bemused by the saddlebag in his arm and the half-man at his feet. By every god, it was *freezing*. *"What?"*

Ylem gestured to the left, where Hakai sat shivering, feeling over the ground like an infant discovering mud. *"Go. Hawkeye makes we go."*

Vuchak got the main idea, but couldn't find the urgency behind it: if the man was well enough to wake up and move, where was the rush?

Well, maybe there was someone fluent enough to tell him. "Hakai, what are you doing?"

The *ihi'ghiva* paused at the sound of his name. *"Tsi'do o'otna wahne biida."*

Ugh. Just what this party needed: a fourth language. It sounded like one of the builder tongues – Kaia or Maia or one of the Ohoti – but that was as much as Vuchak's ears understood.

"Hakai," he said in Marín this time, pitching his voice more sharply. *"Explain yourself."*

The slave's hands came together in a shaking anxious wad, his gaze wandering aimlessly in the dark. "*I'm lost*," he said, enunciating as clearly as if he were giving instructions at the bottom of a well. "*I need to find the way out.*"

"*Wígoddago*," Ylem added, having apparently used up all his prepared Marín words. "*Hes – hiimaitgit-zík, anthén thurlbi anuter urtquek. Rokzlit. Rox?*" His hand reached up into a fist and then came down, as if pulling the earth and trees down on top of his head.

That got Vuchak's attention.

He reached behind him, never taking his eyes off the half, and slapped at Echep's arm. "Echep. Echep, wake up."

"What?" came the groggy voice from behind him. "What do you want?"

Vuchak didn't look back. "Tell me what he's saying. – *Say again*," he added for the half's benefit. Echep's Ardish was far from fluent, but he'd at least made a proper effort to learn.

Then Vuchak pressed himself back against the wall, leaving a clear line of sight for the other two to understand each other, and glanced up at the steeply-sloping rock.

It seemed stable, even ordinary. There were a few pine trees up there, and judging by the white stains running down the stone, it was probably a favorite roost for crows. They might be watching even now.

Watching Vuchak sit idle through the night, leaving one son of Marhuk to ripen in his box, and another to fend for himself a few hundred feet down. Watching a priceless *ihi'ghiva* drag around a shattered leg and a broken mind, as if he were a toddler to be kept quiet while his mother gossiped. Watching a half-man explain... something.

Echep frowned, and shook his head. "He's talking nonsense," he said. "He says that the *ihi'ghiva* is going to have a taking – a seizing? – and it will make the mountain fall apart." This, punctuated with an incredulous snort.

A chill prickled up Vuchak's spine. "How does he know?"

Echep stared at him as if he'd just emptied his nose in the stew. "Are you touched? He's obviously not –"

"Ask him how he knows!"

That earned him a sour look, but the stress in his voice apparently convinced Echep to play along. Vuchak's gaze flicked between the *atodak* and the half-man, studying every gesture and steam-frosted syllable for an understanding that might already be too late.

"He says there have been three already," Echep began. "And that they started after he found the *ihi'ghiva* crawling out from under a hill. He says they get bigger each time. He says... hold on. *Uat-chumín 'sichur'?*"

Vuchak could only recall one: earlier that day, when he'd found Ylem standing bewildered and filthy in a ring of freshly-fallen stones, with Hakai slung over his shoulder. But whether the others had been real or merely something of the half's imagining did nothing to answer the more pertinent question: why was this two-colored fool waited only bringing it up *now*?

Or rather: what would have happened if Echep hadn't shut him up when they first made camp here – if Vuchak hadn't let him?

There was no answer from the half. He had stopped to watch Hakai – who had himself stopped to look at something over his shoulder, his neck turning until it popped.

"Hakai?" Vuchak ventured.

The gray slave twitched.

And as if on cue, everything fell apart.

"*MOVE!*" the half-man cried – an Ardish word that Vuchak understood perfectly – as he bolted up to his feet and scooped up Hakai. His wide eyes found Vuchak's; his chin pointed at the coffin. "*Do-lay! Git do-lay!*"

"*Wait! You stop!*" Echep surged up likewise, standing fast to block Ylem's path.

Vuchak could have told him that was a bad idea. Ylem bulled forward, knocking Echep aside with one mulish shove of his shoulder – just as a precarious piney creak sounded from overhead.

Vuchak looked up as the tree began to topple, its fall announced by a downpour of disturbed earth, a clamor of beating wings, and a white rain of droppings. He grabbed for Echep and dragged him back before the trunk crashed down on top of the remains of their fire, scattering still-glowing coals amidst a bristling cloud of needles.

"An earth-prince," Echep gasped, fighting off Vuchak's hands as he scrambled back up to his feet, staring in horror at the half-man backing up on the other side of the fallen tree. "You've brought an earth-prince here to ruin us!"

There were half a dozen things Vuchak could have said in reply: that Hakai had no night-marks, that he clearly didn't have the wits to do anything deliberately, that even a prince of one of the earth-shaping tribes couldn't do such things spontaneously and alone.

Echep never gave him the chance. He grabbed his

bow and Vuchak's quiver, whipped out an arrow, and took aim at the half – who tightened his grip on Hakai, turned, and bolted up the trail.

"Echep, don't –"

Vuchak's hard yank on his collar spoiled Echep's first shot. The arrow went wide, and for a fleeting moment, Vuchak hoped the other *atodak* would turn to argue, or even to fight.

But of course, he wasn't that lucky. In the time it took to curse, Echep vaulted over the tree-trunk, tore off up the trail, and disappeared into the night.

"– do that. *Dammit!*"

A week ago, Vuchak would have followed him. He might even have led the charge. But now it was as if he were an old man watching the person he had used to be – the ignorant, impatient one, the one so blinded by his own paranoia and first half-guessed impressions that he couldn't see the truth in anything. By Marhuk's pinfeathers, how had Weisei ever put up with it?

If only he were present to ask. But Weisei was gone, and Ylem and Hakai too. Vuchak had no one left to vex – and no one to disturb him if he decided to lie back down and hibernate until spring.

That would be the surest way to reassemble them all: just roll his weary bones up in a blanket and sincerely wish to be left alone to rest. They would be pestering him again by morning.

And if Vuchak were young and foolish, or old and helpless, or responsible only for himself, he might have done exactly that. It was viciously tempting.

Unfortunately, somewhere in the last few days, he had sunk into that terrible middle-place of life: old enough to know better, and young enough to do something about it. He sighed, uncountable years escaping in a single steaming breath, and glanced over at his last companion.

"Well, Dulei – I suppose it's just the two of us now."

This wasn't how it was supposed to be. It wasn't what either of them wanted. Vuchak should have been minding his own *marka*. Echep should have been carrying Dulei. And Dulei – well, he should have been working his shift at the dice table, annoying but alive.

But as the saying went, you couldn't fill an empty stomach with excuses. Dulei's death couldn't be undone, and it couldn't be paid for with apologies or protests or cowardice, either. Man for man, life for life, the World That Is had to be brought back to balance – and mercy meant doing it quickly.

So Ylem would die, and his death would pay for Dulei's. Echep would end himself, if he knew what was good for him: gracefully close a life that no longer served any purpose. And Vuchak...

Vuchak would knot up that harness, lift that leaking coffin onto his back, and do his part to set the world right, just as he always had: one slow and excruciating step at a time.

AND AS THE tree fell and the crows scattered, the largest among them tucked its gleaming black wings and dove for the root of the mountain.

CHAPTER ELEVEN
A MAN IMMINENT

AH CHE, A CHILD of twelve winters, cowered in the great alien silence of the galena chamber, and counted the ways he might die.

There was a reason he was down here alone. This place had been an unexpected boon for the company: a rich, ore-bearing natural gap in the rock, found too late to intersect the digging of the galleries above and below, sandwiched too closely between them to risk triggering a collapse by widening it... and yet too tempting to leave unplundered. Nobody had properly explored it, much less made a map. Why bother, when it might split and twist and go on for miles, inaccessible to anything larger than a garter snake? Why trouble, when all those rich minerals were right there for the taking? Far easier to drop a line, bore a hole, and send down a boy who would not cost much to replace if he didn't come out again.

A disposable boy. A compliant boy. A thoughtless, sightless, drug-addled fool of a boy who had been too busy thinking lustful thoughts to pay attention to his work – a boy who had now lost all sense of direction.

Ah Che thought he had not turned. He thought that if he backed up, he would arrive back at the spot where he had been working, or close enough that he could find his way from there. If he was right, he would be out in five minutes. If he was wrong, he might never emerge.

No, that wasn't true. Ah Che held himself there on hands and knees, spinning assurances to quiet his rigid-limbed terror. He could call out, and someone would hear him. Even if they didn't, someone would miss him. And even if they didn't, Wally Hen would notice when he didn't come home that night, and go back to look for him...

... long after the shift had ended, the miners had emptied out, and all those dozens of powder-crammed fresh holes had been set to blow.

For one lightheaded moment, Ah Che thought he would be sick. Then he thought he would have an accident. Then he reached into his pocket for his sachet of tarré, desperate for anything to numb that dry-mouthed, bowel-purging fear.

No, wait. That was what had gotten him into this mess. Too much easy tranquility – too much cheap chemical comfort. He needed his senses now. He needed to be awake.

Ah Che lay down, pressing his hands and forearms and the left side of his face to the rough grit of the rock, as if more contact would rouse him that much more quickly. He lay still, telling himself that this was only an exercise in self-sufficiency – that if he really had to, he could call out and someone would definitely, definitely hear him – and that he was choosing to prove himself. He lay quiet, asking his breathing to slow and his muscles to relax, coaxing the earth into revealing its contours, or at least its freshest wounds, so that he could find the way out.

Minutes marched by – hours, maybe. Nothing happened.

Was it too late? Had it left him while he wasn't looking? Ah Che had been using more and more tarré to keep from having to feel pain – his own, or those in the earth – but he'd been doing it for so long and so relentlessly that he wouldn't have noticed if something had disappeared behind that constant, cloying dullness. What if it wasn't just temporary? What if he'd permanently destroyed his earth-sense?

What if he'd blinded himself all over again?

Ah Che stared out at nothing, no sooner having asked himself the question than rendered mute with horror by the answer. He reached out again, struggling to rekindle his old friendship with soil and stone... but if he had ever been a friend before, that time was over.

Of course it was. He was a paid parasite now, a little brown maggot burrowing ever deeper into the flesh of the earth, his crude grubbing abetted by the infernal genius of all maggot-kind. He was one of the Eaten now – one of those who set fires in the ground, crammed powder into every molested crevice to blow rock more conveniently, pumped groundwater out like malicious surgeons suctioning blood from an ever-widening wound. His kind ate the rock out of the earth, gobbling up gold and silver and shitting the remainders right back into the ground. They allowed themselves to be swallowed, buried alive for the promise of a life, for the dream of something wholesome and real – fleas feeding on leeches feeding on egg-swallowing salamanders, simultaneously eaters and eaten.

Ah Che curled onto his side as the weight of unfathomable tons of stone seemed to press down on him. Bad enough for the Eadans to pillage the world. That was almost expected of them. So much worse for him. Ah Che had trespassed into this holy stone grove, this precious untouched pocket in the earth, and despoiled it. He had ripped out every piece of that galena knowing that it would be refined into silver, which would be cast into bullets, which would be used to wound and kill the gods and children of gods. He had justified it to himself by saying that they were meant for the a'Krah, for the Lovoka, for the old, wild scourges of his own people. He had convinced himself that the foes of the Eadans were foes of the Maia too. He had fancied himself a secret ally, even as he had made an enemy of his oldest ancestral friend.

The air seemed to grow thicker; the heat of his own body was unbearable. Ah Che swallowed his voice, unable to bring himself to test his last, most feeble self-assurance, and struggled to find purchase above the rising tide of his fear.

He wasn't trapped. He wasn't hurt. This wasn't one of those nightmares where he grew and got stuck, or fell asleep and got left, or struck the chisel too hard and made the rock overhead start bleeding semen. He was awake, alive, and himself, and if he couldn't count on his gifts to help him just now...

Well, how would an Eadan get out of this?

They would think of something clever. They would use what they already had to help them get more of what they wanted. They were good at that – always hunting for new things, new ways to use old things. Ah Che felt around him, groping for inspiration – and found it in the skitter of a tiny pebble, a disturbed crumb of earth.

Of course. Of course. Here he was, crying for a trail of breadcrumbs to lead the way home – and dragging a whole box of bakery-sweepings behind him.

In a flash, Ah Che was twisting around, freeing his feet from the rope loops and digging through the trough for the tiniest bits and flecks of ore. He threw one far out ahead, and listened as it bounced away into nothing. Another one, this time out to his right, found the same fate. Another one to his left ricocheted off the ground – and then hit a wall.

Ah Che crawled for it as fast and fiercely as a trout swimming upstream. It might not be the right wall, but it was a wall – a landmark, an endpoint, proof that the space and silence didn't truly stretch on forever. He felt the ceiling and the floor, and when he found nothing familiar, he started again: a stone thrown out ahead of him, another one behind. By his third iteration, he was getting a vision for the shape of this part of the chamber, and by the fourth, he had found the spot where that one chunk of pyrite had nearly concussed him last week.

Ah Che's stomach sagged in full-body euphoria. He grabbed his trough and crawled for the winze, scraping and dragging and absolutely overjoyed by the first intermittent sounds of Monk Farley's lewd recollections.

"... put her hand all the way... until I thought I would... and so I said to her, get this... after my gold teeth, I can think of easier ways to get at 'em!"

Someone else laughed. Ah Che's hand met the wall. Wally Hen was saying something. Ah Che pulled himself up to stand – by every god, it felt good! – and pushed the trough up out of the hole. He reached up to push himself up and out likewise –

– just as a deafening double boom blasted through the rock.

THERE WAS NO plan. There wasn't even really any hope. Elim's world had shrunk down to the size of three facts: the stranger was shooting at him, Hawkeye was calling rocks down on his head, and if he stopped moving for even a second, one or the other was going to kill him.

So he ran blind and headlong into the dark, straining to see over the feverish shuddering body in his arms, praying for a fix he couldn't even picture – for some divine intervention that would keep him from being shot or crushed or pitched off a cliff the moment he put a foot wrong.

If the hand of the Almighty was present, Elim sure as hell couldn't see it. But as the wind picked up, the frigid goose-prickles over Elim's flesh turned into patches of fine brown hair, and the steaming clouds of his hard-charging breath grew just a little more robust, and the growing disagreement in his vision became a lifesaving boon: one eye remained steadfastly human and useless, even as the other took an equine interest in greenish-yellow shapes and edges that now stood out beautifully in the moonlight.

And as the shouts from behind him grew farther and fainter, overshadowed by the crumbling cacophony of the rockslides nipping at his heels, Elim ran on, following the bolting horse's creed: whatever-it-was back there might kill him – but it would have to catch him first.

*   *   *

IN THE DREAM, Shea was swimming in a choppy freshwater ocean, fighting the tide to get to a black heap lying on the beach.

In the waking world, she was being shaken awake.

It was wickedly cold. Shea struggled up through confusion and torpor, as certain that she had been waiting for something as she was powerless to recall what it was.

It was night. She was cold. She had retreated to sleep in the little pool in the tiny stone valley where she had first brought Yashu-Diiwa to heel with a healthy dose of royal hemlock. There wasn't enough water to breathe, but at least she wouldn't be ambushed by one of Jeté's surviving kin.

Jeté. It hit her sluggish mind like a pillow-muffled punch. He was gone – Día was gone – and U'ru had set out after them. Shea dragged herself out of the water, the deathly chill wrapping weights and chains around her every movement. There was a reason mereaux didn't live at this ridiculous altitude.

But she would have had to be downright comatose to miss the enormous furry feet waiting for her at the water's edge. She looked groggily up – and up, and up – at the Dog Lady's massive moonlit splendor: an ageless canine queen standing robed in brown fur, and crowned with a circlet of twinkling stars.

Well, perhaps not literally. But the view from Shea's ant's-eye vantage point never failed to impress, no matter how many times she saw it. The dark silhouette above her was the deathless mother, the great lady, the stunning immortal justification for everything Shea had done and suffered on her behalf. This was the Dog Lady she had fought so hard to revive. This was U'ru of old.

Who was apparently wearing something new. As U'ru bent to collect her amphibious servant, the black mass on her shoulder flinched, flapped, and let out a disgruntled caw.

The bird was huge, even bigger than a raven. Shea squinted and stared in the dark, scarcely able to credit it. That was a royal crow – a child of Marhuk by one of his feathered consorts. It studied her with shrewd bright eyes.

And it sat perched on the shoulder of a blood enemy. To see the crow-god's herald at the Dog Lady's side – why, Shea would have as soon expected to see a cat birthing mice.

"Mother?" Shea searched the great lady's canine face for answers as she felt herself lifted off the ground. "What's going on?"

The reply was vague, blanketed by questions for which U'ru herself might not have answers – but as she folded Shea into the infinite warmth of her arms and started her long, swift strides up the side of the mountain, her mind's voice was as calm and certain as Shea had ever heard it. *We are invited.*

AH CHE, A CHILD *of twelve winters, was falling.*

He took a breath to cry out, but there was no breath, no air anywhere at all – just a hand over his nose and mouth as he fell sideways through an ocean of sand.

Calm. A foreign feeling bloomed in his mind – a strange, overpowering bliss. Safety. Love.

That was when Ah Che knew he had died.

He still had an urgent need to breathe, though, and when the sand and the hand and the feeling fell away, he was gasping clean, sweet-smelling air – and being carried on a woman's back.

His hands clasped themselves over her delicate collarbones, his knees pressed at either side of her shapely waist, and for one wild moment he thought of Flory Hayes. Then she turned her head, brushing Ah Che's face with a perfect whorl of soft, squash-blossom hair, and he knew that he knew her – that she had come for him once in a dream.

Her amusement rippled through his mind. Naughty. He was a rude, thoughtless boy to make her wait so long – to make her come all this way.

Ah Che couldn't argue. He had been rude and thoughtless and so much more. He hadn't meant it. He'd tried to choose the right things. Now his body was lying lifeless and buried under a half-ton of rubble, and it was too late to fix anything.

No, the great lady answered – a thought that felt like it came with a smile. It wasn't too late at all. This wasn't the end. It was the beginning – the first day of his new life.

Ah Che must have misunderstood. She had come for him. Ten-Maia herself had come for him. What was there to do now but carry his spirit to the Other Lands?

No, she thought again, with the greatest delight. His spirit was nestled safely in his body, and his body was safe with hers.

Then Ah Che realized that yes, actually – there was wind in his hair, which meant that he still had hair, and flashing shadows in the corners of his eyes, which meant that he still had eyes, and his clothes were plastered and *flapping against his skin, which meant that he didn't even want to think about how fast they were going. But where?*

Home, *she answered. Then suddenly his senses opened. Through her ageless eyes, Ah Che saw a brilliant blue sky over green-furred mountains, felt beds of gypsum and sandstone running underfoot, understood stone-splitting roots and fresh autumn grass and a deer-track that would become a path that would become a road that would take them all the way home to where the holy songs of the Maia raised white-earthen walls and dug soft seed-keeping furrows –*

Too much. Too much. Ah Che shut his eyes and pressed his face into Ten-Maia's shoulder, holding his breath as he begged himself not to vomit down the back of her cornsilk dress.

Then, mercifully, his second-senses went away, replaced by a sweet, soft chagrin.

Sorry, *the great lady thought. But underneath it was that same boundless delight: a missing child was coming home again. His empty place would at last be filled.*

Ah Che let her joy wash over him. He breathed deep from the hollow of her neck, relaxing into the smell of fresh soil and sweet corn, and hugged her shoulders closer. It wasn't too late. He wasn't ruined. He was safe now. Everything would be all right.

But he was forgetting something. There was a reason he hadn't gone home yet – something undone, something he'd been waiting for. What was it?

Nevermind, *Ten-Maia thought. Much better to rest his mind on harvest songs and hot curling-bread fresh from the stone, on holding a pot up to catch warm autumn rain, and pulling blankets close to sit before the sweet mesquite smoke of the feast-fire. His aunties were waiting to fuss and exclaim and make him fine new clothes, and his father would teach him the things he needed to make himself worthy of a wife –*

Wife. Ah Che held that thought and followed it like a silver-bearing vein. *Marriage.* He was waiting for a marriage – for Flory Hayes – for Wally Hen.

The bottom dropped from Ah Che's stomach. What about Wally Hen?

A conspicuous emptiness lingered in his mind – and then reassurance rushed in to fill it. Wally Hen didn't need Ah Che to worry about him. He was with his own people.

No, Ah Che thought. *That wasn't good enough.* If Wally Hen was hurt, then Ah Che needed to help him, and if he wasn't, then he needed to tell him what had happened. No matter what, he had to find him. He couldn't just vanish.

"Stop," Ah Che said aloud. "I have to go back."

Ten-Maia did not stop, but the eye-watering speed with which she glided over the ground slowed in deference to Ah Che's distress. *I'm sorry.* Her thoughts were slow, as if she were hand-picking each word from Ah Che's mind. *There is nothing to go back to.*

And through the touch of his hands on her shoulders and her bare maiden's feet on the ground, their combined earth-sense ran all the way back through the earth, through dozens of miles of trackless wilderness, to the mountain, down the shaft, to the galena chamber where he had been working. To a collapsed gallery. To a wall of rubble. To fresh limestone dust drifting down to settle on broken rock and broken tools and still, broken bodies.

Ah Che stopped breathing, speechless with horror.

It couldn't be. There was no reason for it. It was too early in the day – the powder hadn't been set. There was nothing different, nothing out of the ordinary.

Nothing except Ten-Maia.

Ten-Maia, who had beckoned to him in his deepest dreams, before he smothered them with tarṛé. *Ten-Maia, who had sent his father to fetch him, and would have seen him return empty-handed, bearing stories of a two-colored brother who could not be left behind. Ten-Maia, who was the maiden mistress of the red earth and all its fruits – who must have realized that Ah Che would not leave of his own will – who could shatter stone as easily as Ah Che would crush a dried leaf.*

NO. The word echoed like thunder in his mind. She loved him. She would never hurt him, nor anything dear to his heart. She had waited for him, even as he defiled himself, even as he joined in the rape of the mountain. She sent her messages and messengers, and when he refused, she waited with grace and patience for him to finish with his white life – and now he had. The chamber where he had been working was gone. The hole he had been climbing only seconds ago was a rocky ruin. The grave of Ah Che's old life was marked by a rope-looped trough, smashed to flinders under four tons of limestone.

But all he could think about was how Wally Hen had left his bed unmade that morning. "... how?"

Ten-Maia did not have his understanding of the mine – but her earth-sense told him everything. A thin hole drilled into limestone, stuffed with sulfur and charcoal and saltpeter. An iron drill twisting inside, digging out the foreign substances. A strike from the iron, igniting the contents of the hole first, and then the drum beside it.

Ah Che's heart forgot its rhythm. The black powder. Monk Farley and Wally Hen were working that wall. They must have thought it had misfired at the end of the last shift. They must not have realized that it was still potent. Ah Che wanted to rail and scream, shout at them for trading their coarse, silly jokes instead of being careful with their work. They weren't supposed to use iron tools – they were supposed to have copper-coated ones for safety. They were supposed to dig a fresh firing hole. They were supposed to keep the powder kegs at least twenty feet away.

Ten-Maia couldn't tell him which of the men had made the fatal mistake. It didn't matter. Through her earth-sense, Ah Che found the last of his answers: a pair of triangle-pattern hobnail boots, lying fifteen feet apart under the rubble.

Ah Che buried his face in Ten-Maia's shoulder and cried.

And the great lady received his grief, his tears disappearing into her skin like rain soaking into fresh earth. I'm sorry, *she thought again, full of empathy and understanding.* I'm so sorry.

Ah Che clutched her tighter, sobbing until his breath came in shuddering, lightheaded gasps. "Why did you take me?"

He was distantly aware of Ten-Maia slowing, her steps degrading from an effortless glide to a labored loping gait. But in that moment, the feel of her cheek caressing his was infinitely more real.

I love you, *she answered. Ah Che was important. He was a survivor. He was Maia. And she would not be satisfied until all of the lost ones found their way home again – until all of the people were together again.*

Ten-Maia suffused him with her compassion and conviction, her sorrow for his sorrow and her need for him. She showed him his link in the sacred, unbroken chain of thousands of generations past and future, of all the great-great-grandparents who had brought him into being, and all the great-great-grandchildren he would bring in turn. She showed him his place in the fragile, precious, irreplaceable part of creation that knew itself as Maia. She saw him as he had never seen himself: as a man imminent, complete and worthy – as a person of vast, unutterable value.

Ah Che did not know how to think of himself in that way. He repeated the ideas to himself, making the thoughts into discrete words. He was alive because he was important. A survivor. Maia.

Yes, she answered, her heart brimming with gladness at his understanding, even as her back stooped under his weight. Her bare feet carried two people – over wooden planks, by the sound of it – and from somewhere down below came the sound of rushing water.

She wobbled, and Ah Che instinctively circled his arms more closely around her neck, even as her thoughts strove to reassure him: they were safe, and soon he would be home. His father was waiting to see him.

Father. The idea sprouted in Ah Che's mind, roots and tendrils striving in half a dozen directions. The strength in his hands. The stern, sad tone in his voice. The words that had broken Ah Che's heart. If you care for him, you will leave him here.

Ah Che was alive because he was important. A survivor. Maia.

Wally Hen was not important. He was not Maia. So he had not survived.

Slowly, almost absent-mindedly, Ah Che's arms tightened around Ten-Maia's neck.

Be calm, *she thought, reassuring him with blooming, effusive certainty: they were almost across the bridge, and everything would be well.*

The truth is, I came only for you. *That was what Father had said. That was what Ten-Maia had done.*

She could move mountains and shift the earth, but there was no room on her back for Wally Hen. She could have dissolved that blasting powder into three-colored sand – but there was no place in her world for two-colored Maia. She could have done anything... but she had chosen to do this.

Ah Che pulled on his elbow, crushing delicate flesh in the hollow of his bony arm.

Ten-Maia staggered. STOP, *she commanded, her voice ravaging his mind like boiling water poured over an anthill. But it was daytime, and she was mortal – and her feet, perched weakly on nothing but a few planks of dead wood, had no purchase in the earth.*

Ah Che's old words welled up fresh in his mind; his grip turned iron-tight. If he can't go, then neither will I.

She dropped his legs to claw at his arms – but that only left his whole weight to hang like a hundred-pound albatross from her neck. She threw her head back, her squash-blossom hair beating his face as soft and gently as a powder-puff. Her tongueless mouth choked. Her shapely knees shook. And when she finally collapsed, Ah Che found himself falling again – not sideways through sand, but straight down, through empty space and the distant roar of water.

* * *

"COME ON, BUDDY," Elim grunted, struggling to divide his breath between reassuring the man on his back and feeding the hunger in his lungs. "Come on – hold tight. We're gonna make it."

Really, he was talking to himself more than anything else. This part of the trail was far too narrow for his liking, with a mound of soft, treacherous dirt on one side and a long, long drop on the other. He wouldn't have liked his odds even at high noon, in his own clothes, with only himself to watch out for. Now he took every step in the dark, in slippery-soft moccasins, with an extra hundred-thirty-pound weight on his back – one whose next jerk or kick promised to kill them both.

"*Bzi'daa ast, emi,*" Hawkeye mumbled. He was burning hot, and already awake again – a bad omen for sure.

But at least that meant that Elim could shift the load a little, make Hawkeye cling to his back instead of keeping him slung over his shoulders like a top-heavy sack of suet.

"You got that right," Elim said, choosing to assume that what Hawkeye had said was Sundowner for *Isn't this a mother.* He pressed his weight to the wall, but not too hard in case he jostled his friend's bad leg, and took another big step, but not too big in case he slipped, and calculated the next one with his night-friendly eye, but not too long because there was almost-certainly still a crazy crow-man out looking to shoot him, and no telling how close he was to catching up.

For a brief, evil moment, Elim longed for his gun.

Then he took another step, and another one, and another, until he was too witless to think of anything but the ground and the wall and the huge, yawning drop waiting to eat him –

– until the next clumsy wall-clutching grab of his hand brought down a rain of earth.

Elim threw himself into it, cringing into the inevitable rockslide – and when none came, he was left with only his own momentum, rebounding off the wall just as hard as he'd bulled into it. He took a single backward step, the heel of his foot hanging out into nothing.

Nothing.

It was nothing. No rockslide. No collapse. Hawkeye hadn't even twitched. Elim had just loosed a little dirt – not even enough to fill his shoes.

It was no comfort. He stood rooted to the spot, heel hanging out into the dark abyss, dizzy with remaindered panic and sick-hearted certainty: if he moved a step, an inch, he was going to fall.

The mountain was going to eat him.

He was going to die.

Then Hawkeye's hot arms circled almost protectively around his neck, his good knee pressing gently into Elim's side, like a rider prompting his mount to move forward. "Don't worry, sir," he said, his voice a warm puff in Elim's ear. "She won't hurt you."

Elim had no blessed clue who 'she' was – but it didn't matter. He was 'sir' again. Which meant that Hawkeye was *here* again. The mild-mannered translator, the soft-spoken sorcerer, the smartest man on this or any mountain had scraped together enough brains to take a look at things and assure Elim that no, he really didn't need to get himself in a fix. They could just go on their way, just like anybody would, and maybe settle in for a leisurely work-shy smoke at the end of it.

That was all Elim needed.

The drop didn't get any kinder, and the wall didn't get any firmer, but the distance from his left foot to his right got longer, and then shorter, and then longer again, and just like that, they were past the choke-point and back out onto safer ground, the path stretching wide and straight ahead of them.

Elim let out a breath his bollocks had been holding for the last half-mile, and patted Hawkeye's knee. "Gonna make it, buddy," he said again, cheered by the faint, rosy glow of the eastern horizon – so much prettier in his right eye than his left. "You and me – professional survivors."

Hawkeye didn't answer.

Elim glanced over his shoulder, just to be sure there weren't any head-turning dire portents going on back there, and checked his surroundings in what was fast becoming instinct. The trail was wide and gentle for another handful of yards. Then it switch-backed, disappearing up into the trees above their heads, and from there it was anyone's guess. Lots of dirt, and a few trees. No boulders, except the odd few at ground level. And no guarantees that Hawkeye wouldn't drop said ground out from under Elim's feet, the way he had with Sil.

Elim forced away the thought of Sil. "Ain't that right?" he said, anxious to keep Hawkeye talking as they hurried on. "Ain't you a survivor?"

Hawkeye's only answer was the tightening of his arms around Elim's neck.

"Hey, go easy," Elim said, bolstering his hold on Hawkeye's good leg to assure him that he wouldn't fall off. "Don't..."

His mouth might have kept moving, but no more air came out. The arms garlanding his neck suddenly became a stranglehold, a feverish fleshy vise throttling him on the spot. Elim dropped Hawkeye's leg to yank on his arms, but that left the man's whole weight hanging from the forearm digging like an iron bar across his throat.

Elim staggered, the world swimming in his periphery. Down. He had to get down – get the weight off. But the ground was pitching and yawing under his feet, the edge swelling and lunging at him, waiting for the one off-balance step it needed to swallow him whole.

Elim staggered and dropped to one knee, his vision blackening around the edges. He had just time to think of turning, whacking Hawkeye's broken leg against something to force him to let go. Then his eyes rolled back, and his brain gave up.

And then his body fought back. Even as Elim's grip on Hawkeye's arm began to go slack, his right hand stretched and hardened, crushing the Sundowner's forearm in a massive mailed fist. Even as he swayed and lolled left toward the precipice, his kneeling-foot bulged and ossified likewise, growing and growing until with a stitch-popping snap it burst his moccasin open and held fast there amidst the ruined leather – as a godly huge hoof, a titanic doorstopper holding Elim back from the edge. His entire self changed like that: bones popping, muscles rippling, his whole body swelling up like a superhuman allergy to death. He didn't even have to pull Hawkeye off him: the burgeoning taut cords of his neck broke the Sundowner's grip like tree-roots bursting through an old pipe.

And as Elim sucked in his first unfettered breath, Hawkeye gasped and dropped off him like a blood-fatted tick. Which left Elim free to kneel there and suck wind, glutting himself on endless draughts of cold, dry, sweet mountain air.

Until something flitted by his ear and skittered away over the edge.

Until another one zipped past right afterwards – an arrow that stuck and trembled in a dirt-and-stone crevice not five feet ahead.

Until Elim realized that Hawkeye hadn't miraculously come to his senses and decided to let go. He'd been shot.

Elim stared at the black-feathered shaft sticking out from his friend's back, its head buried deep in his kidney – a malicious bullseye already enlarging a target around itself, seeping a dark second-prize ring through Hawkeye's dirty shirt.

Elim whipped his head around, closing his human eye to let his horsey one show him the enemy with uncluttered certainty: a dark crouching man-shape in the muddy green-and-yellow night-world, his every movement a predatory beacon – his arm already preparing another arrow.

Elim had had enough. He surged up to his mismatched feet with a shout, with an enraged *STOP* that emerged as a deafening foghorn bellow. The stranger startled, ducked, but he was fresh out of chances: Elim bent and wrenched up the arrowed stone behind him, tearing the hundred-pound rock out of the mountainside as if he were pulling up a potato, and hurled it down the trail.

He aimed it a little low, anxious in spite of everything not to add another body to the weight on his soul, but didn't wait to see the result: the trail ahead was too long, too straight, and too narrow to have any hope of avoiding another shot. He was going to have to improvise.

So as the rock thudded and rolled, Elim bent and snapped off the arrow in Hawkeye's back, his oversized fingers trying to keep the head undisturbed while breaking the shaft as close to the skin as possible. *Sorry about this, buddy*, he thought – right before he picked up the translator and pitched him up over the dirt-packed wall. He couldn't see where the trail would switch back exactly, but at least there were trees up there – some kind of cover.

Hawkeye hit with a cry, and Elim lost no time following him: he threw himself at the big earthy roll and climbed, his gauntleted fingers driving into the dry soil like so many railroad spikes, his iron-hard hoof kicking in every second toehold, his breath billowing out like a human steam-engine until he was up and over and up again – picking up Hawkeye again – and running, crashing through the trees with no certainty save that in that moment, Elim was exactly who he was supposed to be.

God willing, that would be enough.

IF SHEA WERE human, her place in the Dog Lady's arms would have been just perfect: warm and soft, a furry makeshift pocket to fend off the chill. But there was no moisture in that warm-blooded embrace, nothing to help the desiccating dry air.

Shea made no complaint. She held still and waited, saving her energy, striving to stay awake. Día was out here somewhere, and Yashu-Diiwa, and Prince Jeté, and whether and which of them found each other first would spell the difference between hope and disaster.

Then she felt U'ru's ground-eating strides change

course – with an accompanying burst of enthusiasm.
Puppy!

There was a faint, foreign echo after that, a mental
aftertaste of surprise and disapproval at this sudden
shift in direction. Was that the crow?

Well, nevermind: they were apparently close enough to
Yashu-Diiwa that U'ru could find him even here, at the
very seat of Marhuk's power – which meant that he was
still alive, which meant that the a'Krah hadn't caught
him, which meant that this might still be salvageable.
Shea felt her stomach unclench as U'ru stopped and set
her down, and she took her first tentative steps on some
sort of wide mountain path –

– and all but tripped over a shapeless dark heap.

Shea couldn't see worth a damn in the dark, but the
feel of cold flesh, thin cloth, and shorn wool told her
everything she needed to know. That was a body.

A human body.

Día's body.

Puppy? The great goddess knelt to make her own
inspection, a new, tentative confusion just then rippling
through her mind. Shea dropped to a stunned squat
and let her, marveling at their perfect triple complicity:
Día had become one of the Dog Lady's children, Shea
had allowed it to happen, and true to form, U'ru had
destroyed her.

SIL COULDN'T DO it. Of course he couldn't. Leeching heat
from Día would have killed her. And who knew if it
would work anyway? Why should he think he had any
of his talent left, when the rest of him was rotting away?

Anyway, it was done and she was gone – long gone –

and now there was nothing left but to endure his own second-guessing: to listen to the little voice that said it wouldn't have mattered anyhow – that she was already dead, and that he was responsible, and that now he'd lost his only chance at saving himself – and passionately exhort it to shut up.

But in its place was only silence, and that was the worst of all. There was nothing he could do now, literally nothing, but sit in frozen solitude and fight the rising tide of raw, existential terror.

What if it never ended? What if he was just stuck in his own consciousness, watching his body decay into a putrid pile of bones? God, what if he was doomed to exist forever?

He wasn't. He wouldn't. He couldn't possibly. Weisei had said that Marhuk would help him. Día had said that he'd gotten stuck somehow – that he'd died between day and night, between the age of a boy and a man, on an island between two lands. Surely the old crow could mend that. Surely he could jostle Sil back into his proper place somehow, like jimmying out a sticky nickel caught in a brass tobacco-dispensary.

At this point, Sil didn't even care which side he fell out on. He just needed it to be over.

But until then, he was left kneeling there in the cold and lonely dark, raging at creation.

Why me? he demanded of the universe at large. He hadn't sold his soul to the Sibyl. He hadn't lost a gamble with a Sundowner shaman. He hadn't made any infernal bargains at all – nothing to warrant this extraordinary torture.

Why not? came the imaginary reply, its tone laden with the infinite indifference of the world.

Because I don't deserve this, he said, his mind's voice full of righteous anger. *I was a good person. I was trying to do the right thing.*

What then? What answer could there be to that? Sil turned the chess board and tried to imagine it, staving off stark raving terror by playing both sides.

Prove it.

Well, that was easy enough. *I was trying to make money for the Calvert family*, he said. *Going to exceptional pains to undertake a generous act for my neighbor.*

But he had scarcely set down the white piece before the black one demolished it. *Fallacious. You wanted to make a name for yourself. You even fancied poisoning the remainders to save face.*

To restore my family! Sil corrected. *To do honor to my parents – to revive OUR name, not mine alone.*

Disingenuous, said his other-self. *Would Father have approved of you hazarding your neighbor's money? Would Mother like to see the way you lord yourself over everyone else? Have the courage to be honest: you covet their name, their pedigree, the wealth and prestige that used to attend it – but you've never lived their values.*

Suddenly it wasn't a game anymore: not a chess match, but a court case... one he absolutely couldn't afford to lose. *Because their values drove them into penury!* Sil snapped back at himself. *Too much soft living, too much soft-hearted lending. I did it all the hard way – MY way. Why, I risked everything to rescue Elim, got myself killed trying to get him out of his own mess!*

Irrelevant, came his other-self's pitiless reply. *He wouldn't have needed your help if you hadn't blackmailed him across the border. Everything you did for him was for your own conscience and concern, a reckless losing streak you sustained trying to correct a mistake of your own making. Admit it, Halfwick: you accrued no moral credit. You gambled it and lost.*

No, that wasn't true. It wasn't. He did good things all the time. He had given Weisei his belt back, when he won it at cards, just to be kind – he had refused to take ownership of that tongueless white boy, just because it was the right thing to do – he had taken Elim out to eat at the fair, just because he knew Calvert's mule desperately wanted to go.

But he'd made the mistake of letting out the nasty, self-critical voice in his head, and now there was no silencing it. *To reiterate: you courted favor by refusing a useless novelty, and kept your hands clean by declining an opportunity to free a slave, leaving your crowning moment of selflessness as the time when you begrudgingly consented to escort your partner to a supper that cost you nothing. Is that it?*

No, it wasn't – not at all – but even as he racked his mind for something to put on his side of that swiftly tilting scale, Sil could dredge up nothing that wasn't either a stillborn intention or compensation for some previous error. He'd tried so hard, tried all his short life to *be* someone, to amount to something – and yet there was nothing, absolutely nothing to show for it. He reeled like a perjured witness on the stand, groping for something to help himself. *I want an advocate,* he moaned, clutching at the conventions of his lonely artifice. *I have the right to an advocate.*

You had one, came his own instant, pitiless reply, *of the most constant and selfless character –*

– Sil tried to shut that thought down, already knowing that its end would ruin him –

– and three times you refused her, the last even in violence –

– but of course he could no more prevent the terrible conclusion than halt a bolt of lightning –

– and now she's gone, and you'll have no other.

There was nothing to say to that, nothing to reply with. In that moment, there was nothing but the galling memory of Día coming to him with the horse and the dog, the packs and the bags, having readied herself to accompany him on his quest – daft, bossy girl! – and whatever might come after. What could he have done if he hadn't squandered all that?

What could he have done, if only he had lived?

I need another chance, Sil said, retreating further into frantic fantasy, imagining what he would say to a hypothetical god, one real enough to exist and omnipotent enough to intervene and aware enough to devote even a tenth of his attention to the pleadings of some wretched wisp of a soul that had gotten itself wedged and forgotten between the couch-cushions of creation. *Please – you have to let me try again.*

Why should I? God would reply – because if he was anything, he was a bored speculator, doling out lots ranging from lavish to execrable and watching with anemic interest to see what his creatures would do with them... and if Sil was anything, he was a prodigal son who'd already lost what little he'd been given.

Because I have POTENTIAL, Sil would say – and THAT he could make a case for. *I'm clever, and charming, when I put my mind to it, and bloody persistent. Before we left Hell's Acre, I'd already educated myself. Before Elim picked up his gun, I'd already made enough on those horses to return Calvert ten times his asking-price, and mint my reputation. And then I would have made my way back east, gotten a job as a clerk somewhere, worked my way up to run the business or build one of my own. I would have become the master of hundreds and then thousands. My industry would have clothed and fed and housed more men than all the tithes of all the churches together. I would have restored my family, left my children a grand inheritance to continue my work. I would have been a boon to my nation, an example to my race, and a credit to your investment in me. I would have...*

What came next was a strange, incongruous thought, born from the smallest, deepest part of himself.

I would have saved him.

Yes, that was it. That was the right answer. If Sil could have just gotten here a little sooner, if his body had just held out a little longer, he would have been able to advocate for Elim – bargain with the a'Krah to let him go. That was his case. Sil deserved another chance, because Elim deserved to go home.

By what means? the Infinite Underwriter would say. *I gave you everything you needed to put things right. I gave you a miracle itself. What more can you ask me for?*

LIFE, Sil replied, plumbing his memories for some sacred precedent, some justification in that old book of holy case law. *I have another one, a second life. It's promised to us all, explicitly written right there in the contract... and I want mine now.*

Yes. That was it. He knew he was right about that much: there was no guarantee how much his would be worth – that was determined by what one did with the initial loan – but it was the right of every human being, and Sil would cash his in for whatever it might still be worth, clean out his divine trust for just one more spin of the wheel. *Please*, he said, in what might legally constitute prayer, *let me have that much. Let me live, and I will profit you more than any man ever has. Or if I haven't the chips for that, give me whatever I'm still worth – give me life enough just to finish this, and I'll ask for nothing more.*

There was no answer, of course. There was nobody there. God was imaginary or indifferent, and the earthly spirits of the Northmen were all dead or left behind in the old world, and the new one was fast paving over its pagan remainders, blasting through ancient ways, jackhammering its way to futurity. Any half-intelligent creator had long since since given up answering the screams of the willfully deaf.

So Sil, who had never been much for listening, who had spent his life waiting to reply, was finally left begging to hear any voice but his own. He was nothing now but a madman trapped in a ruined house, waiting for some ancient pagan caretaker to come clean up his mess, passing the time by raving at phantoms in the dark.

And in the world beyond his frost-glazed eyes, life was going on without him, the sky already brightening with the promise of dawn.

DON'T BE SAD, *Water-Dog. We'll fix her.*

Shea said nothing. She did nothing, because there was nothing left to do. She sat on the ground, unmoving, unshivering, and waited for the cold to take whatever was left of her mind.

And the Dog Lady went back to work, arguing with the crow all the while. Shea couldn't hear the other half of the conversation – to her, Marhuk's child spoke only in vague impressions – but it hardly mattered.

Because this one is mine, the Dog Lady said. She knelt on the path, having reduced herself to nearly human size, and gave Día's arm a hard, bone-setting wrench.

The crow perched on a nearby stone. Doubt.

Mine by choice – her choice. U'ru turned Día over and did something to her side.

Shea could have snapped off a hard reply to that: what choice had U'ru ever given her? Instead she sat still, Porté's sack of stones hanging heavy around her neck, and counted her slowing breaths.

The crow shook itself. Irrelevance. Haste. Urgency.

I don't care, U'ru was saying. *This one is mine too, and I won't leave her. It will go faster if you help.*

Perplexity.

Yes, you can. Make a hole here, at the back. Crack the bone – the blood needs to come out.

Disbelief.

Shea privately agreed with the crow: U'ru had been a peerless healer, famous for her ability to rekindle even the tiniest spark of life. But that was at the height of her power, with potency flowing into her through the lineages of hundreds of Ara-Naure. Now she had no descendants left, no source save for an ignorant mixed child – an Eaten boy too stupid to even know her name. What could she possibly do now?

I will try.

U'ru might have been talking to Shea. Or it could have been a promise made to Marhuk's messenger.

Regardless, the crow fluttered down to alight on

Día's shoulder – and began pecking at the back of her denuded skull.

Shea half wanted to stand up and swat it away, to shout, to ask whether the girl hadn't already suffered enough for one lifetime – to rage and scream at these alien resurrectionists quibbling over a broken human doll.

Instead, she closed her eyes, and wished she could do likewise for her ears. She flinched once as the cascade of tiny wet tappings turned hard and grim – as that pitiless black beak pecked down through hair and flesh, and started on bone.

What else was there to do? After all, Shea had never gone out of her way for Día before. It seemed a bit silly to start now.

But perhaps it wouldn't hurt to say something spiritual and reverent, or at least to think it. God didn't exist – at least, not the benevolent source of order that Día so cherished – but Shea had certainly put up with Him long enough. She might as well wring some use out of all those ass-taxing hours in the pew. How did that one go?

We move as You have moved us,

We love as You have loved us,

We live as You live in us,

And die in...

Wait – damn. Nevermind. Nothing about death. Something nice and uplifting.

God is my one Master; I will for nothing want.

No, not that – Shea had a list of wants long enough to hang herself with.

The one about waking to an unpromised day... except that it wasn't day, and Día hadn't woken, and the only tragedy more galling than the possibility of her death was the reality of her life: she'd lasted not even twenty years, and spent all of them cloistered in a sweet, meaningless fantasy – swaddled in sanctimonious horseshit.

Shea splayed out her toe-stumps, huddling down into herself like a ruffled hen. *Oh, bless us, you pompous old prick.*

And having exhausted her supply of piety, Shea hunkered down to weather the ghastly cornucopia of noises that heralded the surgery in progress: morbid, meaty pecking, bone-setting pops and wrenches, and a whole slurping surfeit of dog-kisses.

Which ended – miraculously, or perhaps inevitably – in a great groundswell of joy. *Look, Water-Dog!* U'ru enthused. *See how she nurses!*

Shea did not care to look. Even if she did, her poor eyes wouldn't be able to see. But the anxious knot inside her loosened its hold, leaving the cold, numb thing that might have been her soul free to awaken again, like a foot too long sat on, with sharp little pinpricks of anger. "Splendid," she said, her torpid wits groping to justify her efforts to heave her stiff old bones up to a stand. Where were they going again? What was the rush?

U'ru answered with equal confusion. *Why aren't you happy?* Día was alive! She had been saved!

Shea eyed the great lady: a wondrous vision, a majestic, godly silhouette rising up to blot out the stars – and yet also a dog circling expectantly after its trick, waiting for some promised morsel.

Well, to hell with that.

"Because I have nothing to be happy about," Shea snapped. "She's alive? Yes? Well, forgive my indifference, but she was alive when I saw her this morning, and every time before that. It's not much of a novelty."

U'ru's reply brimmed with hurt. *But I fixed her!*

The crow croaked from its place on her shoulder, anxious to be off – but it was damned well going to have to wait.

"No, you didn't," Shea retorted. "You healed her wounds, but have you even asked yourself how she got them? Did it even occur to you that someone DID that? Do you realize that she was assaulted and beaten, probably raped, mutilated" – and that was exactly the word to describe what they had done to her hair – "and then left out here to freeze? You can't fix that! You can't – someone tore out her innocence, and you can't put it back!"

It seemed not to occur to U'ru that she could squash Shea like an insolent snail. She just shrank back, perhaps clutching Día more tightly to her breast, her mind overflowing with hurt. *I didn't do it,* she whimpered. *It's not my fault.*

She might as well have been seeping rage into the water. "No, of course not," Shea sneered. "It's NEVER your fault. It wasn't your fault that you dragged her halfway across the god-damned desert while you were hunting for Yashu-Diiwa. Not your fault that you made her a murderer, that you left her to drown, that you resisted every effort she made to apologize on your behalf, that you sent her up here after I TOLD you she was in no shape to go. And don't think about telling me that that was her choice, either: you asked, and she answered. You've used her every step of the way, and she's paid the price. So go ahead and congratulate yourself for having just managed not to add one more death to all your hundreds and thousands of others, but don't expect me to stand here and applaud."

It was a vile, exquisite monologue, an absolute masterstroke of cruelty. Really, the only thing missing was a haughty flourish and a stormy exit.

But Shea was here, halfway up Marhuk's freezing sphincter, as blind as a cave-newt and twice as helpless.

Well, let it be: it wasn't as if she was any use to this lot. U'ru could rage and kill her or storm off and leave her here to dry out and die, and it wouldn't make a lick of difference. Shea had done what she set out to do: she'd brought the Dog Lady back into the world, and now she was done.

There was no telling what the Dog Lady herself was thinking just then. Her thoughts disappeared as cleanly as if she'd drawn a curtain around them, leaving Shea with nothing but her own weary fatalism.

But apparently U'ru wasn't done with her. The great lady bent and grabbed her up with one arm, as briskly as if Shea were a toddler throwing an embarrassingly public tantrum. Then she set off again for who-knew-where, following the flight of the crow.

Still, perhaps Shea could guess: by the looks of things, the Dog Lady was gathering up her toys and going home – more specifically, to Marhuk's home – and the gods only knew what sort of tea party they were in for.

AH CHE, A child of twelve winters, awoke to find himself lying on wet rock. For a moment, he thought he was back in the galena chamber. But the air was not dusty, and the rock was not flat, and as he pulled his aching body up to sit, he began to think that the wetness was not water.

There was water, though, rushing all around him. Ah

Che had never heard such a mighty river. He reached out to either side, feeling for the edges of this little bit of land. But he was as earth-blind as before, and all his fingers could tell him was that the rocks were sharp, broken, and covered in something sticky.

Ah Che sat still, punchy and lightheaded, waiting to see what this peculiar dream would bring him. He watched the water rushing past, making sparkling fluid patterns in his periphery. He sniffed at the thick slipperiness on his fingers. And then, as much to clean himself as for idle curiosity's sake, he tasted it.

It was sweet – wonderfully rich and sweet. He took another taste, marveling at the sublime flavor. He would have called it corn syrup, but under that delectable sweetness was a rich, meaty zest, a savory tang unlike anything he had ever known. Ah Che licked between his fingers, over his palms, up his left arm and was starting to suck it out of his sleeve before it even occurred to him to wonder where this wonderful substance had come from.

Then it began to burn.

It started at his lips, seared his mouth, scorched a path down his throat and into his stomach. Ah Che's eyes watered; he lunged for water, desperate to drown the pain –

– and hit a human body.

No, not a human body. Ten-Maia's body. Ah Che's trembling hands found a sodden corn-silk dress plastered over sprawled, still limbs – a head bobbing face-down in the water, limp whorls of hair trailing in the current – a shapely maiden's figure impaled on the rocks, lying in a pool of seeping, sticky sweetness.

Ah Che threw himself into the river. He drank until

he vomited, and then drank more. It didn't help. Her blood was in him, part of him, boiling up through him as if he were a stoppered glass pipe about to burst. His earth sense flooded out in every direction, assaulting him as a million gallons of rushing water crashed over his jagged edges, as a hundred thousand animals crawled and burrowed and rooted through his flesh, as human hands pounded fenceposts into his bones and ripped his hair out by its helpless tuberous roots – as his mind dissolved into a woman's keening, endless scream.

CHAPTER TWELVE
THE WRECK OF HEAVEN

IRABEI, A CHILD of ten winters, crouched in the underbrush and nocked her first arrow.

It was stupid. The whole thing was stupid. There was no good reason for a proper young lady to be squatting in a clump of onions at daybreak, freezing her toenails off.

No reason except that her brother was hopelessly lazy, and every time Mama sent him out for a turkey, he came back with some empty-handed excuse. *There aren't any*, he would say. *I saw one, but it ran away. I shot one, but then it fell in a ravine. I caught one, but then a cougar stole it.*

You must have eaten it all yourself, Irabei had replied. *Because everything that comes out of your mouth is a pile of its droppings.*

But when Mama grew tired of scolding him, Irabei was left with the obvious conclusion: if she wanted turkey feathers for her new dress, she was just going to have to get them herself.

So she laced up her best winter boots, donned her heavy wool dress and *serape*, and marched down the

Mother of Mountains' eastern face to make good on her threat, warming herself in the frigid crystal stillness with the thought of carrying her prize back to Atali'Krah, equal parts smugness and triumph. Then she would have the pleasure of plucking the feathers all out, and sorting them into neat piles, and choosing the best ones to lay along the collarline. Then Mama would make Otatak clean the carcass – women's work – as punishment for his laziness. Then –

Something rustled in the trees. Irabei held her breath.

It came closer – the sound of a fleeing feathery ground-bird, with heavy, lopsided footsteps lumbering close behind it.

One of the men must have flushed it out. Well, if Irabei killed it, he would have to share it with her. She drew back the arrow and sighted down the shaft as the turkey burst out of the brush in a running, flapping, wattle-quivering panic –

– and then she saw what came after it.

That wasn't a man. It wasn't even human. It was HUGE – a hideous mangy giant, its rag-draped flesh a grotesque mix of brown hair and naked white patches, its arms crushing a bloodied, writhing man to its chest... its left eye gleaming green with reflected dawn-light as it spotted her.

Irabei dropped her bow and fled.

WHEN DÍA WOKE, it was to the most marvelous, pleasant confusion. It was like waking in her own bed in Fours' house, with the window open and a cool spring breeze refreshing the room, and wondering what was so uncommonly pleasant about that – and then remembering that she'd gone to bed still miserably sick, and now woken to find that her nose was clear and her throat was sound and her appetite was already wondering about breakfast.

Yes. That's what it was. This was the first day of health after a long illness, and every ordinary sensation was the most exquisite pleasure.

... even if there was nothing terribly ordinary about finding that her bed was crooked, furry, and moving.

Día opened her eyes and looked up, as awed to find the Dog Lady's half-canine features above her as she was to see the ground so remarkably far below her.

It was a strange, sacred world, one Día's river-valley sensibilities could never have imagined. The Dog Lady walked between spindling pine trees, their green needles glittering with a hint of frost, their slender shadows just beginning to appear in the gray light behind them. The air was cold and clean and almost supernaturally quiet, its stillness broken only by the great lady's soft, gliding footsteps. It was nearly dawn.

"Mother Dog?"

U'ru looked down at her and smiled. *Hello, puppy.*

"Well, it's about time," a familiar voice interrupted – and it was only then that Día realized that U'ru had taken on other passengers too. Miss du Chenne was hunched up in the crook of her other arm, bedraggled and dried-out and somehow even less cheerful than before... and above her, perched on the Dog Lady's shoulder, was the biggest crow Día had ever seen.

"And what happened to you, girl? Who did that to you?"

Día heard the anxiety in Miss du Chenne's voice, felt a second pang of sadness on touching the faintly tender spot at the back of her head and finding that no, her dreadlocks had not miraculously regrown... and yet she couldn't look away from the crow. It favored her with a one-eyed avian stare.

Kalei ne ei'ha, Grandfather, she thought – about half a second before the significance hit her.

Grandfather Marhuk was *here*. The Dog Lady was here. Which meant that the hand of God had to be here too: what else could have brought two immortal enemies together to save her?

Yes, Día realized with newborn gratitude. She had been saved. She had done the right things, and the great forces of creation had converged to reward her for it. She had...

"Halfwick," she said, almost absently. She'd left him there on the trail, helpless and frozen. She looked up to the Dog Lady, and the crow on her shoulder. "Mother Dog – Grandfather – I need you to go back with me. There's someone who needs our help."

She was answered with an indignant flap of the crow's wings, and a faint, foreign pang of disapproval.

Can't, U'ru said, and lifted her chin up at the mountain's nearing peak. *Loves-Me waits.*

Oh, of course: she had to find Elim. Thank God it wasn't yet too late!

"Halfwick?" Miss du Chenne repeated, incredulous. "HE took advantage of you?"

Día belatedly returned her attention to the old mereau, and mirrored her confusion. Who had taken advantage of anyone? "No, no," she said, flushing as she caught Miss du Chenne staring at her baldness. "I – I did it to myself. It was a gift. Nobody hurt me." *At least not while they were in their right minds.*

And as she saw that sharp-toothed mouth open for a more thorough interrogation, Día forestalled it. "Please, I'll tell you all about it later, but I need to get down – I have to go." And she tried to picture it for U'ru's sake: how she urgently needed to go down and help Halfwick, just as she'd once gone up to try and help Elim, and how important it was to bring him to Grandfather Marhuk so that he could finish his life, and how eager she was to do that and then go straight on to be reunited with U'ru and Miss du Chenne.

"Go?!" the mereau said, almost speechless with incredulity – but U'ru was already bending down, and Día was already climbing out from her grasp, a baby opossum discovering life outside its mother's pocket. "You can't go. What do you think you're doing?"

The first touch of her feet on the burning-cold ground, and her first tentative wobbling efforts to bear her own weight, gave Día a moment's pause. Did she really propose to do this? Go tearing off after Halfwick *again*, even after every previous effort had invited her closer to catastrophe?

Yes, she realized. Yes, she would – because she could, and because she had been far too blessed a receiver not to go back out and give in turn, and because she had already been through the worst and survived it. God and U'ru and Marhuk were with her, and not even Halfwick's rotten contrarianism could mar that.

"I'm doing the right thing," Día assured Miss du Chenne – and U'ru too. She was following their example, after all: moving heaven and earth to save a lost soul.

The Dog Lady approved. *Good girl.* She straightened again, a voluptuous robed giantess lingering just long enough to give Día a pat on the head – and a mental picture of the path she had taken since collecting her during the night.

It was winding and difficult, with places too steep for a human-sized person to climb – but as Día called out her farewells and promises and then set off following the great godly footsteps in the earth, she worried not at all. She would find Halfwick again. She always did.

ELIM HADN'T MEANT to spook the girl – but he sure as hell couldn't blame her. Every second was a horror, every step a quickening disaster: Hawkeye was going funny again, and though Elim hadn't seen any falling trees or smashing rocks, the spreading wetness over his still-human hand assured him that every back-arching jerk and shudder of the man in his arms was shredding his insides on that arrowhead.

So Elim bolted after the girl like a hound coursing a hare, hoping to God that the crow city was close, and that Hawkeye would be spent by the time the girl went to ground. He charged up and forward, clearing tree-roots and earth-rills and the toe of his own heavy horse-foot, needing not to think about what would happen if he tripped and fell on the burning-hot body he carried.

And then he ran clean out of mountain.

As he crested the last rise, the ground opened out into a great clearing scooped into the top of the peak – into a little terraced town too small to be a city, too elaborate to be a village, and too busy for anyone to miss the shrieking panic of the girl running headlong into their midst.

It was a tiny, living world, full of diamond-patterned cabin-houses with fire-lit windows, dotted here and there with strange stone monuments, and criss-crossed with foot-worn streets busy with people.

People shouting in astonishment and alarm. People fleeing at Elim's approach. People crying out in the universal language of surprise as one of the five sky-scraping wooden platforms on the western slope tilted and crashed into its neighbor, spilling piles of something whitish-yellow-gray all down the mountainside.

Too late, Elim looked down and realized that Hawkeye's seizure hadn't stopped – its range had just gotten bigger. Even as Elim turned to retreat, a barn-sized sinkhole opened up to his right, swallowing half a street full of houses and gardens and shocked, screaming people. Even as he ran back to the left, a huge, ruinous *boom* brought down a ten-ton stone slab, crushing an adobe building like a boulder dropped on a dried mud pie. Even as he spun to find a way back into the trees, the mountain's highest peak began to crumble, belching out a sky-blackening mass of crows like hornets from a stone-pelted nest.

It wasn't ending. Hawkeye wasn't stopping. He just kept convulsing in Elim's arms, blood pulsing from his back, sinister leafy-green veins crawling up his neck, his bulging eyes and straining muscles fit to burst as his rictus expression darkened to an air-starved choking blue.

This couldn't happen. It just couldn't be. Elim was supposed to save this one – he was supposed to get him here alive, and somehow that would make everything right. He turned and turned in horror-stricken circles as the holy crow city collapsed around him, pleading for an intervention. *Help!* he shouted at the billowing chaos. *Someone help us!*

But as the screams and dust and crow-shadows enveloped him, all that came out of his mouth was a frantic bellowing bray.

AND THAT WAS how Día went: running between the trees and down the slope and through the drought-stricken brush, following U'ru's footprints just until they led her to the faint man-made wrinkle in the mountain's eastern face, a little track far too steep and narrow to admit anything but single-file human feet. Then she helped herself down, step by step, pace by careful ground-gripping pace, anxious not to slip and kill herself even as she longed to keep going fast, to keep her fire stoked and furnace-hot for Halfwick's sake. She would keep an eye out for good kindling, once she had arms free to carry it. She could try burning his jacket again, but it would make an ungodly stench, and the cloth might go too quickly to thaw all his joints. And if that didn't work... if he just absolutely fell apart... well, then Día would simply bring Marhuk down to him, once his business with the Dog Lady was done. Yes: one way or another, she would see this finished. She could do that. She had that power.

And Día was so alive with that power, so potent and brave and wonderfully, ferociously *certain*, that she almost didn't hear the footsteps pounding up from the other side of the bend. She halted on the spot just before the two of them would have collided –

– and found herself staring at a far more perfect Halfwick than nature had ever first allowed.

He was brilliant to behold there in the first fiery light of dawn – just absolutely immaculate, all fresh-milk skin and spun-gold hair and ice-blue eyes, without a shadow or a smudge to mar them. He stood and stared at her in open-mouthed surprise, positively radiating youth and health and *life* – so much life that if he hadn't still been wearing his reeking gore-stained rags, Día would have taken him for an imposter.

As it was, she could only gape, stunned to utter speechlessness by the manifested miracle before her.

Fortunately, he didn't seem to know what to do either. "Día," he said – a clear-voiced confession of the obvious. "I – er, I meant to say... you know, that I'm sorry."

God had apparently made Halfwick flawless, but Día was still painfully, imperfectly human. "I know," she said – an awkward compromise between *I forgive you* and *as well you should be*.

They stood there like that for a moment, locked in an uncomfortable little pocket between untruth and unkindness. Then his sapphire eyes flicked their attention up to the path behind her. "We should go," he said. "Elim might... I still have to fix everything."

"Yes," she said, her voice distant and faintly silly in her own ears. "Of course. Come on, I'll – I can show you the way."

And before her doubts knew what she was doing, Día took Halfwick's hand one more time, gratified to feel his cold, answering squeeze as they turned and hurried up the path together.

SHEA STILL HAD precious little idea what the hell was going on. Día had rabbited right off again – shameless, wicked, ungrateful child! – and U'ru's mind remained a cold wall of silence.

It was a bit awkward, being carried by someone who wasn't speaking to you.

But the crow had no shortage of sentiment: it grew increasingly anxious and irritable, cawing admonishments before finally giving up and flying off.

After the first tremor, Shea didn't wonder why. The ground shook hard enough that she could feel it even in U'ru's arms, and it came punctuated with a resonant *boom* – as ominous and profound as a bookcase falling in a distant, empty room.

Then came the crows – a great black-winged geyser fountaining up into the sky. Then the first faint sounds of chaos, of human fear. By the time they crested the last rise, U'ru's anxious, tightening grip on Shea all but admitted it: they had delayed too long. Whatever Marhuk had wanted the Dog Lady to prevent had already come to pass.

Shea was left to discover the rest on her own. U'ru scarcely bothered to bend forward as she dumped her out on the ground, and she scarcely needed to: the great lady was already diminishing with the sunrise, and she knew it. She hurried on alone, leaving Shea at the edge of town.

Or what had been a town, anyway. It was a war zone now, a collapsing crucible of misery and human fear. Its heart was obscured by a great blossoming cloud of dust, a toxic earthen miasma that assaulted Shea's already painfully dry eyes and throat even from this distance. But as she loped forward into the blinding chaos, the rest of her senses filled in all too well: she couldn't miss the smell of burning pitch and pine, or the roar of the fire gouting up through the buckled roof of a nearby broken log-house, or the wailing of children and adults alike, their cries needling through the heavier sounds of breaking stone and caving earth.

And in the middle of it all were the Dog Lady and her son.

Yashu-Diiwa was himself again: a lopsided equine juggernaut, offering up a bloodied, spasming figure like a child handing up a broken toy for its mother's mending. If he said anything, Shea couldn't hear it.

But she didn't miss the outraged cawing above and behind her – and when she turned, even her poor eyes couldn't miss the stranger, the a'Krah archer, standing not twenty paces away: feet apart, bow drawn, and steel-tipped arrow aiming straight at the Dog Lady.

Or Yashu-Diiwa. Or the man he'd just given her. Shea couldn't tell, and had no time to wonder. She bolted forward to block the shot, already cringing as she prepared to complement the fading bullet-scar under her arm, to add a crow-feathered arrow to the top of the list of outrages and indignities she'd suffered on behalf of that wretched, incorrigible boy –

But Shea's martyr complex went begging as the arrow clattered and skidded to a halt before her foreshortened feet – as the stranger cried out, fell, and vanished in a black cloud of dive-bombing crows.

And then things went quiet.

Not silent, of course: there was no stanching the noise from a disaster of this magnitude. But whether because the nearest a'Krah had stopped to wonder what their kinsman had done to incur Marhuk's collective displeasure, or because the man in U'ru's arms had finally gone still, or because the world had simply stopped tearing itself apart, the result was a strange, fleeting moment of tranquility.

One that Shea should probably make use of. Coughing and wiping her eyes, she went to go see how the family reunion was proceeding... and was positively astonished to recognize the bloodied wretch in U'ru's arms.

"Ah, Mister Hakai," she said, in that old, scolding voice that had belonged to her lovelier human persona. "What have you gotten yourself into now?"

Yashu-Diiwa glanced at Shea, apparently recognizing the name, but then went right back to fretting over its unlucky owner.

As well he should. Hakai looked *terrible*: his face ashen, his lips blue, with a sinister, unnatural greenish tint creeping up through his bulging veins. His breathing came quick and shallow, his eyelids trembled with barely-suppressed apoplexy, and even as U'ru held him, some hidden wound watered the ground with drips and sprinkles of blood. And was that a *gun* strapped to him?

He broke his leg, and there's a metal tooth in his back, U'ru said. *And he ate Ten-Maia.*

Shea understood the first, had just started on deciphering the second, and had absolutely no idea what to do with the third. "I... what?"

But U'ru's power was ebbing by the moment, her shrinking figure already bathed in daylight: if she was going to do anything for Hakai, they had to work fast. *Help me take it out, Water-Dog. Use your fingers to pull it.* And she knelt down to roll him over, so that Shea could see the wound: a blood-soaked wet stain over the right side of his lower back, with the broken stump of an arrow-shaft jutting out from the center.

So maybe that archer had already found his mark.

Well, regardless: this was going to hurt like a whelping mother, and bleed like one too. Shea sucked her teeth as she prepared to do the necessary thing, thinking of how much more handily Hakai could have done this himself. She told herself that the arrowhead was a poetically appropriate way to pay him back for the bullet he'd so kindly relieved her of, and wished she at least had something for him to bite down on.

The answer hit her square in the chest.

Shea glanced down at the bag hanging from her neck. "Wait, Mother – wait just one moment." Then she was pulling it off, dumping the rocks out, handing the bag itself over for U'ru to give him as a teether... and ripping out the arrowhead before she could think herself out of it.

His scream was the gut-wrenching cherry on a whole apocalyptic cake – and he hadn't even finished it before U'ru was rolling him over, pulling his shirt away to expose his torn, gouting flesh.

There was not much of the dog left in the Dog Lady by then, and Shea did not care to watch what that steadily-humanizing face did to close the wound.

Which gave her plenty of time to notice that rusty yellow tin of tarré lying amidst a heap of novelty rocks. No mereau would use such a water-weak container... and the House of Losange had probably pickpocketed Hakai after they swarmed over him in the river that night... and Shea had known him to enjoy a smoke, of an evening.

She sat back, staring at the bloody, shuddering spit-flecked wretch before her, pursing her lips at the implications. She'd heard the withdrawals were hell, but this...

... well, better late than never.

"Come on, you old goat," she said, and set about

prying the tin open. "If you can't have a pipe, be grateful for a chew, eh?"

It was a sad state of affairs – pitiful, even. But as Shea worked his mouth open and tucked a generous pinch of the spice under his tongue, she declined to judge him: at least among his present company, Hakai's addiction was more honest and wholesome than any of them.

ELIM DIDN'T KNOW what to do with himself after that. The dog-woman seemed to know how to tend to Hawkeye, and the fishman had apparently found some medicine for him. At least he wasn't wrecking things anymore.

Not that there was much left to wreck. Elim looked out at the carnage all around him, dumbstruck by how completely everything had fallen apart. Maybe half the town was still whole, at least the parts that he could see. Another quarter had tipped or buckled or fallen over, and the rest was just... gone.

He stared at the sinkhole, at the place where houses and furniture and yards and people had been just minutes ago, before the ground swallowed them. Could anyone still be alive down there? Would it do any good to get close enough to look?

Elim hesitated, torn between the urge to make himself useful and the fear of somehow making things worse. The handful of ashen-faced a'Krah who had stopped to stare at him weren't helping... but then again, neither was he.

"Elim!"

A familiar voice rang out, clear and strong. He spun to face it, forgetting that one foot was heavier than the other, and stumbled, ending up on his backside with an impact worthy of one of Hawkeye's aftershocks.

But he hadn't imagined it. That was Sil coming for him, running up with a bald a'Krah fellow in tow – and he was *stunning*.

No, more than that: he was a living miracle. As he approached, Elim stared at his partner in helpless astonishment, too stupid to understand anything except that the Sil Halfwick he knew had never, *ever* enjoyed even half so much health and vigor.

He still stank like a dead man, or maybe that was his clothes. Regardless, as his cold blue gaze darted to Elim's face, his hand, his foot, his everything, Sil's expression matched Elim's just about perfectly: each man just too plumb gobsmacked to do anything but stare at the other.

Which left all the conversation to Sil's native friend. "Elim, thank heavens – we didn't want to think what might have happened to you."

And Elim, who thought he had found the bottom of his own ignorance, apparently hadn't half scratched the surface. He closed his horsey eye and squinted, his disjointed vision already brewing him a double-rectified headache. No, that wasn't a Sundowner, much less a man. That was... was that *Día*?

What could she be doing all the hell way out here? And what on earth had happened to her hair?

Elim didn't have the voice to ask, and she offered no answers. There was just Sil and Día, smudging to a pair of sharply contrasting blurs as Elim's eyes filled, offering their hands there in the middle of a settling dust cloud.

But as their dual hot-and-cold grasp reached down and helped him up to his feet, something in him fell out or got left. Elim sagged forward between his friends, ebbing, softening, draping himself over their shoulders like a two-quart drunk as his strength drained out through his soles.

As it turned out, Elim had been wrong all these years. Here he'd been thinking he was different from other fellows, that he would live his whole life too tall to fit and too big to carry – when the whole time, it was just a two-person job.

Thank God. Thank every god. Elim hung there in helpless gratitude, in a relieved echo of the posture he'd once adopted when tied between a pair of sun-roasted streetposts: head down, knees weak, arms outstretched across the backs of two people who had gone to the ends of the earth to find him.

One of whom ought to be dead three times over... while the other shouldn't have been there at all.

Elim glanced over and down at Día's almost-barren fleecy scalp, dumbstruck all over again. "You came," he said. "You came to get me." And after the way he'd treated her – after that terrible silence he'd given her, when she'd come to break the news about Sil's death...!

She might have glanced over at Sil just then. The two of them were mostly a pair of heads sprouting from Elim's armpits, so it was hard to tell.

"Of course she did," Sil said. "We both did. Now come on, old boy – let's make ourselves useful."

Of course. Right. They were standing mid-catastrophe, and it was going to take a whole lot of able bodies to clean it up.

So as Elim stood there, his pants and lone moccasin-shoe loosening under a cloud of gently drifting horse-hairs, he slowly found his own feet again, and the three of them set to work.

They helped man a bucket brigade to put out what

remained of the housefire. They lifted up one wall of a fallen home, so rescuers could get to the old man inside. They joined the rope-pullers working to haul people still trapped in a pit of deadly-fine sand. It didn't make them many friends – the a'Krah plainly didn't trust any of them, and Elim least of all – but every task was a small, vital help, a collective effort to scab over the worst of the disaster.

And it was such good work, and Elim was so glad to finally have some simple, ordinary use for himself again, that it took him completely by surprise when a grim-faced a'Krah man beckoned him forward.

"He says you're to come with him," Sil translated, his expression struggling to paper over his anxiety. "He says it's time for them to decide about you."

For a moment, Elim wondered what there could be to decide about. Then it hit him with a pang of shameful dread.

Oh.

He looked around, appalled at his own forgetfulness. Where was Do-Lay – and Bootjack, for that matter? Had Way-Say come back? Had anyone?

Unfortunately, the only certainty was the one waiting in the man's baleful stare. After all Elim's long journey, after every hazard and obstacle, there was finally nothing left between him and his penance. The sun was rising, and judgment day had come.

FOR AS LONG as he could remember, Vuchak's obligations had been endless. *Mind Weisei. Read the ghiva. Spar. Cover for Weisei. Attend the blessings. Shoot. Pick up after Weisei. Learn the graces. Wrestle. Apologize for Weisei.*

Now, on the last stretch home, his list had dwindled to a single entry: *Don't quit.*

That was it. That was all he had to do. And it might still be too much.

He could have carried Dulei well enough if he were alive and injured, or even freshly dead. Vuchak had vigor and strength, and Echep's *marka* hadn't filled out to a man's weight yet.

But if there were a harder, more unnatural way to carry another human being than tied in the fetal position and boarded up in a wooden box, Vuchak never wanted to find out. No wonder infants were born so small – what mother could tolerate them longer?

As it was, he was bent nearly double, his fingers numb with trapped blood where he'd stuffed them under the repurposed horse harness in a mostly-futile effort to keep the straps from digging into his shoulders. The coffin on his back weighed as much as he did, and there was no straightening, not even an inch, without it pulling him over.

And the rockslides weren't helping. Every stone in his path was a mandate to stop, put Dulei down, clear the way, and then somehow find the strength to lift him again.

At least the cold was helping with the smell.

Vuchak went on like that, step by impossibly heavy step, each one a new item on the list of things he didn't have to worry about just then.

Ylem and Hakai were gone – someone else's problem.

Echep had run off to kill them – someone else's problem.

Some unnatural power was trying to break the Mother of Mountains – a problem so far outside

Vuchak's responsibility, the stars were sending it smoke-signals.

And as for Weisei... well, he might still technically be a child, but Vuchak was just going to have to trust that his *marka* was enough of a man to handle himself out there. And he was. Vuchak had seen those glimmers of greatness in him more times than he could count.

For now, Vuchak had to concentrate on his own greatness, or at least his own adequacy. He had to take the next step, and the next one, and the next one, and when the trail switched back and grew too steep for his feet, he had to lean forward and crawl on hands and knees, a creeping child straining under the weight of its cradleboarded cousin.

This side of the mountain was too dry to see much ice, but the freeze had made wet places dangerous. Vuchak stopped when his hand met glazed rock, and looked up to find a safer grip. There was a tree root just above it. He reached up to take hold of the gnarly bark.

Too far. For one weightless moment, Vuchak held himself perfectly, precariously upright, an accidental model of good posture. Then the weight on his back overbalanced him, and sent him tumbling backwards, head over heels over neck over box, to land at the bottom of the hill with a meaty wood-splintering crash.

Vuchak gave up.

He lay in a heap at the bend in the trail, a mangled mass of agonies trapped in the wreckage of a dead man. *Help me,* he thought, when he finally had enough air and sense to think beyond pain. *Give me your hand. I can't do it anymore.*

But there was nobody there to help him – not even anyone to wish at. Weisei was gone. Echep had turned his face away. And Dulei was almost certainly frozen stiff. Vuchak had no-one but himself – and that wasn't nearly enough.

Vuchak was no son of Marhuk, no extra-potent godchild. He had no superior well of strength, no divine favor at all. He was only an ordinary person – less than that, even. He was *a'Pue* – born under no star, possessed of no luck – and he couldn't do this.

Vuchak lay still, closing his eyes against the lancing light of sunrise, and waited for nothing.

Maybe it was inevitable. Maybe this was how it always had to be. After all, the World That Is would continue only as long as *atleya* held it together – only while people lived the ways of order and righteousness – and nothing could last forever. Already people were abandoning their duties. Cowardly Echep. Irresponsible Weisei. Faithless Vuchak. Three poor specimens in a whole world full of callow men, frigid women, and insolent children. And who could blame them, when even the gods themselves had failed? Some greedy Eaten swine had killed Ten-Maia, and so her sisters had abandoned their husbands to wander and weep and scream. The Lightning Brothers got no satisfaction from their mourning wives, and so they gave none in turn: their storm clouds rolled resentfully on, and refused to seed the earth. So there was no rain, and so there were no crops, and so the toiling men of the earth abandoned their work and turned on each other. The stag ate his brother, and the doe mounted the wolf, and the fawn starved. And what arrogance did it take to imagine that he, Vuchak, could somehow stand against that? What had he ever done but officiously wash his hands in the wellspring of a poisoned world?

It was a comforting thought for a man craving rest: if Vuchak could do no good, then he could safely do nothing. After all, what value could there be in such a lonely, hopeless life? Why try at all?

Vuchak had thought that way once before. He had looked into the eyes of the tiny infant girl in his arms, struggling to understand the value of a person who would exist only as a pause between labor and grief, to discover the purpose of a life that would be measured in hours. He had found the answer on this very peak, on a morning much like this one.

Vuchak wanted not to remember it. He wanted to lie still and rest. He lay on his left side in the frozen dirt, distantly registering the trembling of the ground and the faraway *boom* of a falling stone. His heart slowed, his breathing quieted, and his dull gaze drifted to the mark of the *atodak* on his inside wrist.

They had called it a sign of honor and service when they put it on him. He saw it now for what it was: a tattooed curse, warning away any woman who might intend him for a husband, killing his children before they were born.

What if it's not true? Echep had said. *What if all of this is just one big self-serving lie?* Then it wouldn't matter what they did. After all, the mark only had the meaning people gave it. Why couldn't the same be true of the starless days on the calendar? If they meant nothing, there was no reason for starless people to spend their lives deprived and toiling for the greater glory of the Marhuka – no reason to hold themselves apart from the joys of the world.

But then, if there was no such thing as *a'Pue*, there was no cosmic force conspiring to make him miserable

– no reason to lie there like a sack of spilled potatoes. And if he weren't an *atodak*, if the mark on his arm had no meaning, then he was only himself: Vuchak, the son of Seitak – an a'Krah man of twenty-one years, who had once run naked through the smoking-house on a dare, and liked his corn cakes with green chile sauce.

And if he were just himself – a man, free and complete – and he could do anything he wanted... what then?

The question itself was a treat, a priceless untasted luxury, and Vuchak lingered long over the answer. If he owned himself, had mastery of his own life...

He would have a bath, first of all – a long, hot, extravagant soak.

Then he would sleep in a real bed, for at least three days. Then he would go Oyachen's and eat until his teeth gave out. Then he would say hello to Lavat's daughter.

But first he would finish what he started.

Vuchak's hands and knees found each other first, and then the ground, encouraged by every small, painful good omen. His back hurt, but he hadn't broken anything. Dulei's coffin had taken a battering, but it hadn't burst. The world was decaying, but it wasn't dead.

Vuchak, son of Seitak, crawled one foot forward.

Vuchak, son of Seitak, son of Atlip, crawled another.

And he went on like that, every pace a proud reiteration of himself. Not because he was *a'Pue*, and not because it was his duty, but because he chose to do it – because his was a lineage of men, human men and women, who had taken ownership of their lives.

He was Vuchak, son of Seitak, son of Atlip, son of Totolit the Odd-Footed, son of Henat the Endless, the daughter of Shrewd Soshei – and shrewd Vuchak likewise paused to ground his left foot before reaching for that faithless tree-root – who was the third daughter of Liswei, son of Huigash, son of Chugash Who Died Twice, the son of Unyielding Pitat – and unyielding Vuchak likewise refused to let his aching knees buckle – the only daughter of Yagwei, the son of Tasutak, the son of Tsidagash, the son of E'hiyat the Ever-Ready, the daughter of Vo'ono Who Kept Her Name...

Vuchak climbed his lineage all the way to the top, defiantly delighted to run out of steps long before he had run out of ancestors. He relished the first scent of sweet burning pine, rejoiced in the gracefully arcing crow-shadows on the ground, and hurried to unharness himself, to set Dulei down and enjoy his first glimpse of home.

But as he looked out onto that familiar terraced slope, Vuchak's breath deserted him, fleeing his lips to dissipate out amidst a vast settling dust-cloud.

Too late. He had come too late. Vuchak, son of Seitak, had returned home at last – and Atali'Krah lay in ruins.

CHAPTER THIRTEEN
THE BLACK MASS

AH CHE, A CHILD of *twelve winters, did not awaken. He only lay there on the rocks, open-eyed and unthinking. The empty sachet of tarré lay beside him, a few sweet-smelling dried flakes still scattered on the ground around him, clinging to his lips and wedged between his teeth.*

By the light of the full moon, he could just make out a few telltale sparkles in his periphery, as the river began to wash away the maiden-shaped mound of corn beside him. He lay quiet, wishing for nothing. He lay still, waiting for an end.

But the corn attracted crows.

The crows brought crow-feathered men.

The men took Ah Che.

And by the time they had carried him all the way back to their nest, Ah Che, a child of twelve winters, was neither a child nor Ah Che.

THE CALENDAR OF Atali'Krah, which was without equal, divided the year into four seasons, and each season into five months, and each month into eighteen days –

a horology that Vuchak had relished explaining to She Who Was Born Awake.

Today is the day of the eye, in the month of the new grass, he'd said, showing her the intricate designs carved in the great stone circle that represented all the heavens. *And here above it is the bell star – see up in the sky, how it presents itself to you!*

He had explained to her how that meant that she was a belled-shoe daughter, destined to be beautiful and brave and demanding, lucky in love and graceful in manner. He'd told her about *atleya* – about the great natural order of creation, and the sacred place she occupied within it. He'd taught her how to read the heavenly cycles and convergences, so that she could find her way back to life.

The calendar of Atali'Krah, which was without equal, lay shattered on the ground.

The House of the Last Twilight, where his niece's body had been prepared, had been smashed to rubble underneath it.

The Tower of Innocence leaned like a lightning-blasted tree, spilling her bones out over the western slope.

And the house where she had been born, where Yeh'ne and Suitak'had buried her cord to help her find her way back to them... it was simply gone.

Vuchak stared at the sinkhole, at the great earthen abyss that had swallowed up the entire street. Every touchstone, every place that Born-Awake had seen or known – they were all gone, wrecked or broken or simply eaten by the earth. She had no conduits left now, nothing she could recognize. If she hadn't already returned in the two years since he'd left for Island Town, she never would.

Vuchak thought he might weep. He thought he should

sit down. He did neither, helpless to take his eyes from the cold carnage before him. The damage had been done hours ago, and by a force he couldn't imagine, much less name. Now the legacy of a thousand generations lay in ruins before his eyes. What was left for the new one to inherit?

"Vuchak, stand fast and answer!"

He was already standing. But if he hadn't been, he would have leapt to his feet at the sound of that blood-freezing feminine command.

She was stalking straight for him, like a cougar on the kill – and if Vuchak had spent a year and a day on the journey here, it still wouldn't have prepared him for the living terror that was Winshin Marhuk.

In that moment, she was the avatar of Atali'Krah itself: a ruin of power, a wreck of beauty, and a tempest of grief. She had torn her blue-shining black hair all out from its braid, leaving it to snap and tangle in angry waves behind her. Her black-feathered holy cloak cramped and clung over her arms, sticking and pulling as the daylight tried to loosen it from her, and her own ravenous need kept seizing it fast to her skin. Her hands curled into crow-talons, her eyes shone with murderous purpose, and the painted diamond shapes around them now ran in tear-tracked white streaks down her furious midnight face as she all but spat the question. "WHAT HAVE YOU DONE?"

Vuchak flinched, a mouse freezing under a raptor's looming shadow. "*Markaya*, I didn't –"

He got no further: an air-cracking *snap* rang out behind him, half a second before the back of his thigh burst into agony. His leg buckled, dropping him to one knee as he tried to turn to face the shot –

– just in time to take a roundhouse kick to the neck.

Atodaxa, of course, were only human: they had none of the divine longevity of the god-children they served, and their mortal features easily betrayed their masters' true age. But as Vuchak lay sprawled out on the ground, bright spots flashing over his first glimpse of Ismat's weathered face, his first free-floating thought was that arthritis must not have caught up to her yet.

And it probably wasn't going to manifest in the two seconds it would take her to finish him off.

It promised to be a shameful end: Ismat was old enough to be Vuchak's mother, but harder than his manhood ever had been. Her ruthlessly firm figure made a mockery of all the months he'd spent growing soft in Island Town; her dust-smeared bloody clothes pronounced him guilty of loitering while Atali'Krah fell. Ismat was everything Vuchak should have been: fierce, fit, and unbreakably faithful.

She wouldn't kill him, though. She couldn't. Winshin's *atodaka* could get away with shooting his leg out and kicking the daylights out of him, but no-one had any right to take his life – not unless Weisei was dead and Vuchak had been convicted of treason.

Surely not. Surely, surely not.

And maybe he was right to be optimistic: in a sign of the universe's ongoing grace and good will, Ismat didn't reach for the knife in her boot. Instead, the gray woman whirled her whip-sling casually, almost teasingly, its stone payload having already been delivered to the meat of his leg. Then she stomped on his gut. "Get up."

Vuchak did the next best thing: he rolled over, clutching his stomach in a stunned, airless world.

"I SAID –" she snarled.

But he was down on the ground, which apparently afforded Winshin an unfettered view of the battered, leaking box behind him – of the container for what had once been her son. And whatever else Ismat was going to say was drowned out by her mistress's first grieving scream.

It was a keening, seemingly endless ungodly wail – a sound Vuchak could absolutely believe had once inspired half a dozen murdered a'Krah to crawl up out of their profane graves and take revenge on their Ara-Naure executioners.

That was more than twenty years ago – but Winshin's voice had lost none of its potency. The coffin creaked and rocked. Ismat flinched back.

Vuchak seized the chance to roll up to his hands and knees. "Don't," he gasped – not that he expected either of them to listen. "Please, *markaya*, don't call him – you won't want to see him."

As he predicted, Winshin did not swallow her voice – but Ismat found hers again.

"What she wants?" she spat over that terrible banshee cry, whipping Vuchak across the back with the sling. "She WANTS her son back!"

Vuchak covered his head just in time to take a whip to the face with his arm instead.

"She WANTS her city back!"

Vuchak grabbed for the sling, missed, and curled over as it cracked against his side.

"She WANTS your confession!"

The coffin jolted again, this time with a muffled interior *BANG*: Dulei might have frozen overnight, but hours of being carried on Vuchak's steaming back had apparently limbered him up enough to answer his mother's call.

With a burst of initiative he wouldn't have guessed he had left, Vuchak seized the sling and ripped it out of Ismat's hand, hurling it away with a hard fling of his arm. "Confess what?" he coughed, rolling up to a crouch in spite of the blaring pain in his leg, tracking her as she circled him. "That Dulei's death wasn't my fault? That I've been through unholy hell bringing him back? That I carried him here, myself, alone, after his own *atodak* abandoned him?"

Ismat was lean and trim and lithe in spite of her age, as graceful as a dancer and as deadly as a thirty-year veteran – which she was. Beaten and exhausted, Vuchak had no hope of besting her in a fair fight.

So he would not fight fair. He ducked sideways as she lunged for a kick, reaching to whip out his boot-knife and drive it into her calf –

– except that the knife wasn't there.

It was lying at the bottom of a cliff somewhere, or buried in a frog-monster's eye. And his split-second confusion was all the time she needed to stop, spin, and kick him in the back of the head.

"Confess that you failed your promise to keep him safe," she hissed as he hit the ground chin-first. "Confess that you brought an earth-prince here to destroy us – that you tried to kill Echep when he intervened – that you abandoned your own *marka*, traitorous wretch that you are!"

No. Absolutely not. Echep must have gotten here already – must have filled their heads with lies – but Vuchak's own head was spinning as he curled up and covered it, his poor brain desperate to keep from taking even one more hit.

And the coffin was cracking. Winshin's grief-song

carried on without pause or punctuation, underscored by every answering *BANG* from the reanimating ruin striving to answer its mother's call. Even as Vuchak glanced up, the bottom of the box broke open, evicting a black gout of flies, a stomach-withering stench, and the first mottled, weeping glimpse of something that might have once been a foot.

Vuchak couldn't bear it. He couldn't bear to witness the breaking of that poor battered grave egg, or to see the hatchling horror inside. "Please, *markaya*," he tried again, cringing in anticipation of Ismat's next inevitable hit. "Let him rest! Let him be!"

There was no reply – which wasn't to say there was no answer.

"Winshin, STOP!"

And she did. Everyone did. Ismat paused in mid-kick, and even Vuchak couldn't help but look up to see if he was mistaken in recognizing that voice.

The rising sun reduced the figure on the terrace above to a bright-edged silhouette of a man – tall and splendid, fine and fearless, his cloak and hair flaring with the force of his great resonant command.

Then he jumped down, and was Weisei again. "I mean it, big sister!" he said as he strode forward. "You leave my Vichi alone right this minute or I am TELLING."

Winshin stood tentpole-straight, her whole body stiff and quivering – as if she couldn't decide whether to laugh, cry, or kill someone.

In the end, she just covered her face and let out a hair-raising, heartbroken moan.

"Wait," Ismat said, forgetting everything as she hurried to comfort her mistress. "Wait for me, *markaya* – come, let me grieve with you..."

Vuchak didn't wait to see how long that peace would hold. He staggered up to his feet, dizzy, head spinning, his whole body screaming. Then he retreated to leave the two women far behind – to drown every pain in Weisei's waiting arms.

As a rule, men of the a'Krah did not embrace. That was a thing for children.

Fortunately, Weisei was no man of the a'Krah. He had never made his declaration of adulthood, never plaited his hair. It spilled loose and free down his back, smelling of yucca soap and happiness as he enfolded his *atodak* like a willow tree winding over an oak.

"I'm sorry," Vuchak said into his prince's feathered shoulder. Sorry to have left him, and sorry for disappointing him, and sorriest of all that he couldn't return Weisei's ebullient embrace – that even now, years of honor and practice and shame-fearing tradition kept Vuchak standing there in some sad, battered attempt at stoicism, pretending that he had neither heart nor arms.

"You have nothing to apologize for, Vichi," came the warm, earnest reply. Then Weisei stiffened just a little, and the back of Vuchak's neck started to tingle where his *marka*'s hand clasped it, and his pains began to leave him, drained away by a gentle thief.

Vuchak meant to protest. He shouldn't allow such things – not when his wounds weren't serious, and especially not when he had trained his whole life to soak up the world's punishments on Weisei's behalf.

But by the time he found the thought, and then a voice to speak it with, the work was done, and there was nothing left in him but gratitude and endless, soul-sucking weariness. "I'm sorry," he said again.

"I'm not," Weisei said, and withdrew to take him

by the hand. "Come on, Vichi. We just have to do one more right thing, and then you can rest."

Yes, of course. He'd promised himself one of those, hadn't he?

Vuchak asked no questions. He did not look back at Dulei or his mourning mother. That work was finished. Now he had only to let himself be led through the broken streets of Atali'Krah, trusting his *marka* to tell him the secret that would let them mend the world.

It PROBABLY HAD been a beautiful city, before Hakai got to it. Shea could believe that much.

Now it was just a terrific pain in the ass. All those lovely terraces were a beast to climb, especially when she was helping to hold up half Hakai's weight, because apparently Great All-Seeing Grandfather Marhuk insisted on having the poor bastard dragged all the way to his lair for his own personal inspection.

So Shea and U'ru carried the wretched man between them, up the terraces and through the entrance of a little stone temple. Inside, an impossibly old woman sat atop a high dais like an moldering peach, asleep or dead or maybe both, given whose door she guarded.

U'ru led the way around and behind her, Shea struggling to hold up her end of the dead-weight bargain between them, to another, smaller doorway at the far back of the room. The diamond eye carved over the top might have been an icon or an irony or just a'Krah for 'watch your step'. Everything inside was pitch black.

But that was apparently where they were meant to deliver this hopeless human heap, and it would only take longer if Shea balked. She hefted his right arm over her shoulder again as the three of them were swallowed up into the darkness.

Shea had been blind before. River-bottoms tended to do that to a person, especially at night. But at least then she had her water-sense to warn her before she crashed into something. Now there was nothing but cold stone underfoot, and the soft, padding rhythm of two sets of bare footsteps... and as they went deeper into the mountain's core, a steadily growing sinister smell.

And heat. And light, distant but nearing. And a peculiar buzzing, almost like a strange organic hum. By the time Shea got close enough to make out the shaft of sunlight beaming in through the huge, fresh hole in the ceiling, and to understand what it illuminated, there was no turning back.

The whole cavern was *seething* with crows. Every near-vertical surface in that vast, ageless chamber was a black curtain of preening, feeding, shitting, bickering birds. The floor was a reeking midden of droppings and feathers and the remains of old meals and older relatives – thankfully less so here on the grand boulevard, where surely some loyal acolyte came regularly to harvest all that fresh fertilizer.

And the heat was incredible. Tens of thousands of energy-burning little bodies all crammed in here together, every twitch and flutter stoking the fetid furnace. After the brutal dry chill of the outside world, Shea would have luxuriated in it – if only she didn't have to think about how quickly this mass of scavengers could skeletonize a foul-mouthed mereau.

Her foot kicked a stone shard, its skittering retreat instantly swallowed up by the endless avian clamor.

Go around, U'ru said of the fallen-in ceiling pieces blocking their path. *Lay him in the sun.*

At another time, Shea might asked whether U'ru intended Hakai to sprout. Now, she picked her way around the rubble in awed silence, and did as she was told.

And when at last they had dragged the man into the fat shaft of light there in the middle of the chamber, U'ru turned, gathering her furry brown robe, to kneel before the thickest part of the great black mass. Shea hastily followed suit, her knees bitching about the imposition.

But she must have looked respectful enough, because when the voice of the collective spoke, it deigned to resonate in her mind too.

Well, child. The words prickled up through Shea's nerves like a march of primeval spiders, sending a frisson of dread through her old bones. *Better late than never.*

SIL COULDN'T HAVE said how it started, except as a succession of modest yet miraculous urges.

He'd wanted to blink, and then he'd blinked. He'd wanted to breathe, and so he'd breathed. He'd wanted to scratch his cheek, and was actually amazed less by the sight of his own immaculate hand than the sheer ordinary joy of having an itch to scratch. Everything after that had been a discovery of himself, a phenomenal sequence of granted bodily wishes. He'd just been learning the joy of running – and it had never, ever been any such thing previously – when Día all but collided with him. Things had spiraled out from there.

Now, though... now he was here, among the a'Krah, preparing to do what he'd told himself was his new, exclusive reason for being. Now he wanted to save Elim – but that was a power yet to be tested.

Which meant that at the moment, his best asset was Weisei – standing beside him, hands knotted, feet tight together, eyes roving up and down the length of Sil's body, as if he still couldn't believe he was real.

Sil wasn't sure he believed it either.

"*And that is the Last Word,*" Weisei said, nodding up to the apparently mummified old woman sitting atop the dais. "*Her name died long ago. Now she lives as Marhuk's human voice.*"

That was putting it poetically. To Sil's crude eye, she was nothing but a mass of feathers and wrinkles, a crone so old and withered and shriveled and frail that Sil couldn't believe that she'd set herself there by her own power – much less that she'd ever been human. Sparse, brittle yellow feathers draped over her stick-thin bones and sprouted from hands wizened into arthritic talons. Her eyes were gone, her toothless jaw had collapsed to make a gaping beak of her nose and chin, and through the mottled rash of pinfeathers and broken white hairs on the left side of her scalp, Sil could just make out an earless, wax-crusted hole.

Was that where he should direct his appeal? Did she understand Marín? Could she hear at all?

Sil was about to ask when a shadow darkened the doorway. At first he expected Elim, who had volunteered to stay outside until he was needed. Sil hadn't asked whether that was to avoid the claustrophobic confines of this strange, sinister little edifice or simply to enjoy what might be his last breath of fresh air. Día was out there with him, certainly doing a better job of consoling him than Sil ever could have.

But this wasn't either of them. This was one of the biggest a'Krah Sil had seen yet. He was easily as tall as Huitsak, but with none of his fat: older, perhaps in his fifties, with broad shoulders and white streaks in his long black plaits, and a keen-eyed stare leveled on Weisei, whom Sil could all but feel shrinking beside him. Vuchak, still standing guard at the door, made the peculiar wrist-offering bow that Weisei had shown Sil earlier, and did not straighten until the newcomer had taken a seat at the foot of the Last Word.

"*That's To'taka Marhuk,*" Weisei whispered, without looking at him. "*He is the – the honor-father for the children of Marhuk, our duty-parent.*" Sil could hear him fumbling for a translation, and guessed at the meaning behind it. "*And since the grievance concerns two of us – my sister and her son – he will be the one to decide.*"

Sil inwardly winced. So the magistrate was the godfather of both the plaintiff and the victim. Hardly an impartial judge. "*What is my best chance of persuading him?*"

Weisei glanced up, confused. "*What is there to persuade him of?*"

Sil began to feel as if he'd missed a step on his way downstairs. "*That Elim is deserving of mercy, of course... or have I misunderstood something?*"

"*Of course you have,*" Vuchak snapped from behind them. Sil turned in surprise. The man had looked absolutely dead on his feet since they got here, but now apparently found the strength to come forward and castigate him – albeit at a church whisper. "*You people always do. What arrogance you have to presume –*"

"*Vichi!*" Weisei scolded.

"*– that you will even be asked to speak! What do you have to do with anything? Did you seal his fate with the Azahi? Did you bring him here? By the Starving God, Halfwick, you have been absent or inconsequential to everything from first to last, and you have the nerve to invite yourself here now, as if you have anything of even trivial importance to add –*"

"*Veh'ne eihei.*" To'taka's resonant command echoed in the temple – the first words spoken at full volume since Sil had arrived.

Vuchak shut his mouth, offered his wrists again, and retreated back to the doorway.

Weisei swallowed, and presently ventured another whisper. "*What my* atodak *wants you to understand,*" he said delicately, "*is that there is no case for you to make. Marhuk has already learned the truth from Dulei, and To'taka from – from me.*" But his gaze had dropped to the floor again, and his voice trembled, and Sil didn't dare guess why.

"*Weisei,*" he said, forsaking all prudence as he took the thin magician by the shoulders, demanding eye contact even as he enunciated his next words with grave precision. "*What did you tell him?*"

Weisei met his gaze, his dark cheeks somehow flushing darker still. "*Only what is true, Afvik! I spoke of all the good things Ylem has done for us: how he saved Dulei from the fire, and gave me the last of his water when I was ill, and took such care of our Hakai, and – and returned to us here of his own choosing, when he could have run away a dozen times. I promise: I said only what was good and true.*"

Sil wanted to believe that. Certainly he believed that

Elim would have done those things. But truthful people didn't sweat and stammer and stare at their shoes, and he didn't have to know what Weisei was leaving unsaid to hear the gaps it left in his speech.

"*What aren't you saying?*" Sil said, stifling the urge to shake the truth out of this fumbling equivocator. "*Why are you afraid of me?*"

Strangely enough, Weisei's gaze went not to his shoes, but to Sil's hands on his shoulders. Then the space between his words changed their shape. "*You... do you like me, Afvik?*"

"*Of course I do.*" The answer was dumb, automatic. What did that have to do with anything?

But Weisei fairly beamed with delight. "*Oh, I'm so glad. Forgive me, please – I'm sorry I ever doubted you.*"

And before Sil could ask what that was all about, another shadow spilled over the old stone floor, and admitted the oddest fellow yet.

Judging by the black-feathered cloak at his shoulders, he was another of Marhuk's children, young and fit and not displeasing to the eye. But that was where his resemblance to other royal men of the a'Krah ended. He wore what Sil could only think of as a deerskin dress, its hem falling to the ankles of his boots, its sleeves spattered with blood and dust – the first reminder Sil had seen of the disaster outside. The man had painted white diamonds over his eyes, which seemed to look kindly on Weisei in spite of his grave face, and every step made his waist-length single braid sway and sweep the air behind him. Following behind him, almost as an afterthought, was an old man who might have been a future-vision of Vuchak: he held fast to a spear and shield that he couldn't possibly wield with any purpose, his twin plaited pigtails snow-white and shaking as he made his way to the dais at a palsied shuffle. Vuchak's eyes seemed to linger on him long after the old warrior had taken his place behind his master.

Sil had already put his hands away, eager not to be seen manhandling a son of Marhuk – who didn't wait to be asked for introductions.

"That's Penten Marhuk," Weisei said, *"the youngest of our Eldest. I asked her to join us because she's good at getting people to be reasonable, and because To'taka doesn't know much Marín, and because I thought she might... there's a small chance she might be able to change his mind."*

Sil didn't understand how the person he was looking at could be a woman, or why any man OR woman would want a geriatric bodyguard trailing after them. But his curiosity crumbled like cigarette ash in the face of that last dreadful suggestion: that the magistrate's mind was already made up.

Sil glanced up at the three of them there on the dais: great masculine To'taka and strangely feminine Penten, both sitting authoritative and serene, with the Last Word perched high and silent between them.

Sil swallowed. He didn't know their customs. He couldn't speak a word of their language. He didn't even know what justice was to them. How had he ever thought he could handle this?

"Weisei, what am I going to do?"

The question came from his mouth only, as his eyes were still fixed on that dire tribunal, and his brain was already bracing itself for the worst – perhaps only – possible outcome.

But his hand raised no objections as Weisei picked it up and pressed it between his warm, slender fingers. "*Do as they tell you,*" he said, his face full of a calm, earnest wisdom. "*Listen. Speak only when you are invited. Be patient. Assume nothing. Make your manners, as I showed you. Trust in your god's favor. Have no expectations. Pray. And remember that I am at your service in everything, Afvik, that I –*"

Then the last newcomer announced itself, not with a shadow, but with the foul smell and dragging gait of an unnatural four-footed creature.

On Sil's side of the border, it would have been gentlemanly to help the two ladies with the box they carried between them. But this was as far from his side of the border as he'd ever been, and he would not be caught presuming anything about their status as ladies, much less his role as a gentleman, and even if he did, he absolutely did not want to get anywhere within ten feet of that ripe, ruined coffin. It looked like it had been beaten half to pieces, and it smelled like...

... well, like him.

Its bearers set it down at the foot of the dais: an egregious, unmissable Exhibit A. Then the athletic-looking older woman went to flank the other side of the door – a neat, haughty counterpart to Vuchak's bedraggled glower. The other remained with the box.

Sil didn't need to be told who that was. One look at her fierce, haggard features – her hard-set mouth, the tear-streaked white makeup running down her face, and the naked hate in her eyes – told him everything he needed to know.

In another time, in another life, Sil had once stood on the streets of Sixes, confidently assuring himself that the pearls in his pocket would buy him the understanding of half a dozen grieving mothers. As it turned out, he couldn't even meet the eyes of one.

Weisei squeezed his hand, and let it go.

"*Our children are present,*" Penten said, his – her – voice as calm as its register was confusing. "*Our witnesses have gathered. Where is the offender?*"

No-one moved.

Sil glanced over at Weisei, who gave a suggestive lift of his chin at the door.

Well, all right, then.

Sil had entered the temple expecting to lead the defense. He left it as a delinquent jailer, with no more authority or plan than to fetch Elim inside for what might be his last hour of life. And for all his lately-manifested perfection, Sil had no faith in the miracle it would take to get his partner out of there alive.

YOU ARE LATE, *U'ru,* came the voice of an old, cold soul hidden somewhere in the teeming mass of crows. *Perhaps too late.*

Or maybe it was coming from all of them. Shea didn't think it was supposed to work that way, but what did she know? There was a living god kneeling beside her and another one probably leering at her from some shit-stained perch up above, and apparently a third one stuck in Hakai's craw, however that had happened. Who knew anything anymore?

I fixed him, U'ru said, her homely face lined with anxiety as her eyes darted from point to point around the chamber's living contours. *You said I would have my son if I fixed him.*

Let us be clear now, came the admonishing reply. *We said you would SEE your son, whole and alive – and so you have. We shall regard that bargain as complete, and turn our thoughts now to –*

No! she cried, realizing the trick far too late. *He is mine, he is mine – give him back to me, he is mine!*

Shea cringed. U'ru could never have matched wits with Marhuk, not even at the height of her power. And here, now, when she was nothing but a dim, struggling flicker of her former self... oh, he was going to humiliate her.

And what have you done to deserve him?

But she was already riled by his deceit, and snarled with flat-edged teeth. *I have done EVERYTHING –*

You have wrecked everything, came the deathless rebuke. *You have betrayed your allies. You have slaughtered innocents. And now you have truly forgotten yourself.*

I have not forgotten! she cried, shoulders stiffening under imaginary hackles. *I am U'ru the mother! I am good! I am love!*

Something small and dark fell into the midden ahead, but Shea couldn't see well enough to guess what it was.

You were good, the crows replied, and then their voice was as soft and grave as a terminal diagnosis. *You were love. But in your loss, you stopped being loving. And soon, perhaps, you will be nothing at all.*

Shea flinched, gut-checked by the implications. She glanced back up at the simmering hot walls, at the thousand glittering eyes perched like an executioner's axe over their heads, and for the first time, it occurred to her that this conversation might not be about Yashu-Diiwa or even Hakai. U'ru might be answering for her own life.

The great lady quailed at the thought. *Grandfather, you wouldn't...*

He could, though. He might. Marhuk was one of the Old Ones, if you believed the stories – one of the gods who had climbed up from the wreckage of the old world, who had shaped the new one into a place where life could flourish. U'ru and Ten-Maia and the rest were infants by comparison, lately-born children of a soft, earthly nursery... and Shea imagined precious little paternal affection coming from a creature who measured his thoughts in geologic time.

Hakai groaned, and Shea lay a hand at his throat. His pulse was weak and thready.

We are not discussing what I will do, came the loveless reply. *We are discussing whether I am your grandfather.*

Whether all those thousands of crows should recognize her, in other words. Whether there was any reason they should not swarm this foreign irritant and finish her on the spot.

And even then – even with her own life on the line – U'ru could not resist a nervous backwards glance at the tunnel leading back to the world of human concerns. *But my baby...*

Shea cringed at this fatal inattention – but no feathered hurricane descended.

Instead, the chamber rippled with wry amusement. Condescension. Pity. *Now you see, U'ru, this was always your trouble. Always a nursemaid to daisies and mayflies. Even here, with our own sister-spirit in agonies before you, you have no thought for anything but your own trivial offspring. He is nothing –*

HE IS MY SON! she cried with a tongueless howl of outrage.

He is MORTAL, replied the great consensus. *He is disposable, replaceable: you had a thousand others before him and can have a thousand more after, and he will age and weaken and die regardless.*

Another small, dark something fell to land a stone's throw away, and this time there was no mistaking it. That was a dying crow, its wings flopping in erratic, soft-bodied convulsions. Soon it was still.

Shea could feel the retort brewing in U'ru's mind long before it was formed enough to voice. *Is that what you will tell your grieving daughter?*

It is what she already knows, said the great black mass. *We will kill or let die any of our children before we hazard their shared purpose. Your thrall there understood that. It tried to prevent you from martyring yourself for the sake of that one foolishly-begotten boy, and spirited him away for your own good. How awful it must have felt to see you squander its sacrifice by gutting your alliances, plundering your future, hurling yourself at enemy spears for nothing – for a mere morsel of life.*

For the record, Shea was not a thrall or an 'it'.

She was also not about to say anything of the sort. She kept her mouth shut and her eyes down.

So you destroyed your own people, the merciless reckoner continued, *and thereby reduced yourself to a mere dumb animal, which is what you will become again – for good, this time – if we decide to let our daughter have her way, and put an end to the last son of the Ara-Naure.*

But U'ru had already found the bottom of her fear, and now there was nothing left but defiance.

Then do it! She hauled herself violently to her feet,

her blazing eyes alighting on one indifferent bird after another. *I would rather be a mindless dog than a childless mother!*

The silence in Shea's mind grew all the more terrible when it finally ended.

Then certainly we can oblige you.

IT BEGAN SIMPLY enough. Penten lifted her chin to recognize each of the three foreigners in turn, and Sil made a mental note not to point at anything.

"*Who is here and why?*"

Día went first, with a graceful wrist-turning bow. "*My name is Día, Eldest. I'm an ambassador for the First Man of Island Town, who has sent this man here for your judgment.*"

Penten nodded, and switched her gaze to Sil.

"*I'm Sil Halfwick,*" he said, because he could at least manage that much, "*his partner and friend. And his name is –*"

"*May it please you, Eldest,*" Día interrupted, with a sidelong glance at Sil. "*He wishes to speak to you himself.*"

Taken aback by this brazen interruption, Sil's temper flared: as if he needed any help looking like a superfluous idiot in front of this lot!

But he shut up and gestured graciously – and was amazed when Elim took it upon himself to speak in Marín.

"*My name is Appaloosa Elim,*" he said, his accent atrocious but his voice unfaltering. "*And I am here because I killed Dulei Marhuk.*"

Día must have taught him that while they were waiting

out front. He couldn't string three words together by himself.

Then again, at this time last week, Sil would have bet money that Elim couldn't have done this without buckling like a trick knee. And here he was: standing front and center in a foul, crowded little room, bearing up under the stares of half a dozen angry strangers intent on his death.

Penten tilted her head in acknowledgment – *her*, Sil confirmed to himself – and translated for To'taka.

Día used the time to give Sil a nod, which he returned: yes, actually, that had been a good opening gambit. It was important for Elim to make a good first impression.

"*And what was the reason for his death?*" Penten asked then.

Día began to translate for Elim, and Sil resisted the urge to spring forward with an answer. It was bloody difficult, doing nothing – hard not to feel like the third wheel Vuchak had called him. He had to contribute something, but what?

"I don't rightly know," Elim said, apparently unclear on whether to say it to Día or the a'Krah judges. "I was drunk, and I can't recollect anything about it. I think he must have – I think I must have mistook him for a rustler coming to plug me. I'm awfully sorry."

"'*I don't know,*'" Día faithfully rendered. "'*I was drunk, and I don't remember it. I believe I thought he was a thief who had come to kill me. I'm so very sorry.*'"

Even Día's translation beat out anything Sil could have done, with a natural eloquence that he envied.

All right, so he wouldn't play interpreter. He would study the people instead.

"*And what fate do you believe you deserve?*" Penten's

voice was soft and fluid, her heavy jaw relaxed. Her makeup made it harder to read her eyes, but Sil privately commended Weisei for bringing in an extra voice of reason. Elim needed all the help he could get.

"Well, I know – I know by rights I should die," he was saying, his composure flaking just a little. "But I was hoping you might let me live."

To'taka sat impassive and silent while this was expressed to him, as he had for the entirety of the interview. He kept his arms folded across his chest – a bad sign for someone Sil hoped to persuade – and yet his aura of disapproval seemed to have no focus. Was he just exasperated at having to sit through this? Could it be that he was more vexed at being called away from the chaos outside to arbitrate some trivial execution? Just how exceptional was all this, anyway? It was enough to make Sil wonder just how often demigods dropped dead around here.

One glance at Winshin was enough to stop that thought cold.

"*Why should we?*" Penten asked – a reasonable, dangerous question.

"I, uh..." Elim's hands made an anxious wad of the front of his poncho; the sole of his bare foot pressed itself over the top of his moccasined one, and he looked for all the world like a child about to embarrass himself at the blackboard.

Then he looked to Sil. "Sil, will you tell them for me? Explain to them about Boss and Lady Jane and... you know, and the rest of it."

That was a terrible idea, and Sil opened his mouth to tell him so. These a'Krah weren't like the people back home: Elim wasn't going to legitimize himself by hiding behind a respectable white name, and any sympathy anyone might have had for his family particulars was going to be swallowed up and spat back as pure venom by the mourning mother right there in the room.

Then again, it was Elim's life – and if he were going to lose it, he'd better do it on his own terms. Sil shut his mouth and stepped forward into a wash of déjà vu. He had done this before, on a hot morning in Sixes, readying himself to answer Twoblood's mistrustful glower before a circle of two hundred gawking Sundowners.

This time, though, he would get it right. This time, it wouldn't matter whether he was appealing to a wolf in trousers or a crow in a dress or to the Sibyl herself. This time, Sil would be Elim's advocate.

Sil made the wrist-turning bow before he spoke, and shared his attention equally between Penten and To'taka. "*He wishes for you to know that he is not asking for mercy for his own sake. He belongs to an older man and his wife, citizens of good standing in our town. Their daughters are gone, and they have no other family to help them in their work, or to care for them as they age. If it pleases you, he would ask to be allowed to return to them, because although by the law he is their slave...*" Sil cringed in anticipation of the last words, but one look at Elim's earnest dirt-streaked face guaranteed that no, damn it all, there was really no other way to end it: "*... by their usage, he is their son.*"

There was just time enough for Elim to recognize that last word, *eho*, and for Sil to savor the appreciation in the big man's face. Then came the inevitable reaction.

"*And what of MY son?*" Winshin cried, pushing forward. "*What of MY child? Why –*"

"*A very good question,*" Penten smoothly interrupted.

"*Let's ask him. What do you think, Dulei? You've traveled all this way with him. Shall we spare this man's life?*"

Every eye in the room locked on to the dilapidated box at the foot of the dais. Even Winshin held silent, waiting – but for what? The boy had been dead for a fortnight. How was he going to think anything, let alone say it?

And if Sil was wrong about that, he went utterly uncorrected. The coffin sat motionless on the ground, and the only sound in the room was Weisei's dismayed sigh.

"*Then we will offer the decision to a higher power,*" Penten said. "*Ene vitsa nihani, Taivape?*" She directed the question to the decrepit woman serenely decomposing up above.

But the Last Word elected not to live up to her title: she made neither sound nor sign, and after a suitably respectful waiting-time, Penten began to confer with To'taka.

Sil didn't need to understand the words to know how to take that: Winshin's satisfied silence and Weisei's grim anxiety said it all. The evidence was all in, the witnesses had declined to testify, and the judge was about to render his verdict.

It would come as no surprise – at least, not if Sil had been paying attention. *The man-price is at the election of the family,* Twoblood had told him at the crossroads. *This family will accept only blood.* Why, even lying, treacherous Faro had said as much, as he blithely poured the coffee that Sil would drink to commission his own murder. There was no chance of appealing to mercy. There never had been.

And Penten's vaguely-regretful expression confirmed it even before she opened her mouth. "*We appreciate your candor, Appaloosa Elim, and salute your courage. We believe that you did not intend the death of our dear child. We are sorry for you, and for your family. However –*"

Sil's restraint snapped. "*Wait!*" he said – before realizing how rude that was, and hastily making a bow. "*I mean, please forgive me – please, just hear me out.*"

That got him a collage of shocked and dirty looks – but nobody stopped him, and Sil didn't wait for someone to try. He'd known all along that Elim's tack was the wrong one: the a'Krah believed in taking an eye for an eye, and if that was the case... why, if that was the case, then you simply had to offer a superior eye.

That was it. That was what Sil had been brought here to do. His body had been restored, so that it would make an attractive offer. His life had been returned, so that he could give it away.

"*I just – I wanted to say,*" he began, struggling to polish his egregiously tardy moment of inspiration, "*that if your wish is to honor Dulei with a life-gift, there is none more suitable than mine. I belong to one of the great houses of the Northmen; I have many exceptional talents, and – and I have earned special favor with my god, as Weisei will be glad to tell you. Please consider it, respected elders: I am the last of my line, the son of an old and noble family, and far better suited to answer for the death of a beloved prince*" – this with a deferential nod to Winshin's scowl, and a gesture at Elim's dirty bulk – "*than any poor horseman's son.*"

As he said it, Sil's gaze lingered on the brown spot over Elim's eye. Too late, he remembered that the

Calverts' mule was someone else's son too – and he hadn't accounted for her at all.

Well, someone else was going to have to take up that mantle: Sil didn't have the first idea about any of it, and he'd probably ventured too much already.

Still, it was gratifying to see interest, or at least hesitation, from the people who had been perfectly resolved a minute ago.

"*Excuse us, please,*" Penten said. "*We will discuss it. Winshin, Weisei, kui' hagat ne.*"

And as the two younger royals approached to confer with their elders, Sil let out a nervy breath, and tried to temper his expectations. There were no guarantees. It still might not work. But if it didn't, he would spend the rest of his life – however long that was meant to be now – glad for having tried. And yes, he might have phrased that last bit better, but –

Then Elim accosted him. "WHAT DID YOU DO?"

He was pale under his spots, suggesting that this was a rhetorical question – that Día had already translated.

"Don't worry, Elim," he said in his most soothing undertone. "I've got a plan to –"

"Yeah?" Elim retorted, with a disturbing absence of gratitude. "You had a plan last time too, and it got you killed!"

Oh, for pity's sake. Sil threw up his arms, gesturing expansively down at himself. "Yes, and then I got over it! Look, just –"

"No, YOU look," Elim snarled, grabbing Sil up by his bloodstained shirt-front. "I have spent this whole god-awful trip thinking you were dead and beheaded, or sick as a whiskey-shitting pig, or dropped off a cliff, or I don't even know what anymore. And if you make me spend even one more second wondering if I gotta go home and tell Will and Nillie how I let their baby brother get himself beefed out here, so help you God, Sil Halfwick, I will knock the resurrected snot out of you."

Sil frowned. God Almighty, leave it to a rustic to look a gift-horse in the mouth and then start flossing it for corn. "Listen, you ungrateful shitkicking son of –"

"GENTLEMEN," Día said, rolling her eyes pointedly towards the assembled a'Krah – who were politely awaiting a resolution, or perhaps a knockout.

Elim let go. Sil jerked his shirt down. The tribunal proceeded.

"*We... appreciate your efforts to speak to us in the language of our loss,*" Penten said delicately. "*And we have learned from Weisei how exceptionally your god has blessed you.*"

Sil looked to him for some signal of how this was about to go, but Weisei was staring at the floor, his posture maddeningly ambiguous.

"*Therefore, we will invite you to demonstrate the power of the Starving God, who strives always to compound our sadness. If you successfully invoke him to prevent Winshin's knife from entering Appaloosa Elim's heart –*"

Winshin drew a bright blade from her boot, the flash of silver panicking Sil back into action.

"*Wait,*" he stammered again. "*I want – I meant – it doesn't work that way. I'm offering you my life in trade for his, not –*"

"*His life is not yours to barter with!*" Penten snapped. "*The First Man of Island Town sent him to us –*"

"*– and would be pleased,*" Día interrupted with a nervous curtsey, "*very gratefully pleased, if in your* *great wisdom you were to choose to reciprocate the gesture by returning Elim to Island Town – a gratitude that the First Man will gladly express with –"*

"– *with what?"* To'taka barked, rising to his feet in rage. *"With disrespect? With fool-regard? Does he give and expect we refuse? Does he insult by giving gift that make him angry when we accept? Then go and make him happy, woman, and tell that we return his man as same he return ours – in stinking wooden box! Winshin, vaika u!"*

Marhuk's daughter needed no second-prompting: before Sil could draw a breath to protest, before Elim could even guess at what had been said, Winshin curled her fist tight around the dagger's hilt and rushed forward to slam the blade between his ribs.

BUT THE DOG LADY could not hold such a horrible thought for more than a moment: it had scarcely even escaped her mind before her face crumpled and her defiant stand turned into a stricken, aimless stagger. *No, wait,* she pleaded, hand to her mouth as if to smother a sob. *Please don't kill him. I'll do anything, but don't kill him!*

The walls erupted into raucous, shrieking caws. *And what will you do? How will you answer for what you've already done?*

I don't know! U'ru cried, burying her face in her hands. *Everyone is angry with me. Everything is different now, and I can't understand – I can't decide anything.*

It was a pitiful sight – one that needled Shea's conscience as she remembered the scorching accusations she'd leveled at her after they found Día. Now, here, watching her plead with someone else, it was easy to see U'ru for what she was: a dog begging for an end to the withdrawal of affection, one whose sins had already escaped her short memory, and for whom there could be no worse punishment than uncomprehended hostility and indefinite loneliness.

The crows fell silent as she cried.

Then I will decide, they said at last, *and you will obey.*

The great lady looked up, her wet face wild with hope. *Yes, Grandfather. Just tell me what to do. Tell me how to make you like me again.*

Accept that you were wrong, U'ru, came the admonishing reply. *You are a spirit of love, but you let it become selfish, childish, and shortsighted. You were a greedy mother and a bad leader, and the new world has no room for such weakness. If you want to survive here, you will have to grow up, and you will have to do it quickly. Do you understand?*

Shea eyed the black mass, privately longing for a slingshot. U'ru hadn't been as bad as all that. And what did this old corpse-eater know about love anyway? His own birds were dropping around them, probably from the unbearable heat of their convergence. Even as Shea watched, another crow toppled off its perch and into the shit-heap on the floor, its fall unremarked by any of its neighbors.

But maybe Marhuk had more power than Shea gave him credit for. And maybe his point was well-taken. Regardless, there was no more crying, no angry rejoinder – just a rich, ripe silence.

... yes, came the tiny thought from behind U'ru's crumpled sleeves. *I was wrong. I am sorry.*

Very good. Now think outside yourself for a change.

Look there at the great gift you have brought us, and think: how shall we restore Ten-Maia?

U'ru obediently looked down to the frail, sweat-drenched man before her, his tremors finally swallowed by a deep, drugged sleep.

So that was the game. That was why Marhuk had sent his messenger down to fetch them yesterday, after all the years of bad blood and silence: he must have discovered that Ten-Maia was tangled up with Hakai somehow, and that he was going to need help in separating them. Apparently he was counting on one problem to solve another – for one lost spirit to restore another.

A cunning plan – provided U'ru had any idea how to do that. Shea looked up at her patron-mother, her hopes dim.

Ten-Maia was the Corn Woman, the youngest of the Three Sisters. People in Island Town said that the drought had begun with her death. Shea knew better than to put money on that: the truth was a lump of sugar stirred into a whole pot of gossip and piping-hot superstition, where the earthly gods were concerned. But she also knew just how little rain they'd had since the Maia collapsed... and how little faith she had in the Dog Lady's ability to change that.

U'ru put her arms down. She took another long look at Hakai, her brows furrowing as she gazed through him. *She is not awake,* she said at last. *But she is still too big for a human body. All the years he's been holding her inside – see how she's aged him!*

Shea had always taken Hakai for a man on the far side of forty. But as the last of those sinister leafy green veins receded from his neck and jaw, they left just his own soft, golden-maple features behind – and left Shea wondering how many of those white hairs and crow's feet he'd earned by his own merit.

U'ru smoothed his hair back, her expression pensive. *Now she kicks and struggles and will destroy them both if we let her wake up. She is like a baby that wants to be born.* And she looked up into the fetid air, seized by the thought. *Maybe if we could help her be born... maybe if he would sire a child...*

A cawing chorus rippled through the chamber then, like creaky guttural laughter. *It always comes back to babies with you, doesn't it? Well, let it be: we'll search our holdings for a young woman of the Maia, if there are any still left. And what about him? Can we trust you to care for him, and keep him alive in the meantime?*

Alive, yes. Shea suspected that the *tarré* had done the hardest part of their work for them. But how much of Hakai's mind had survived would be hard even for U'ru to know.

Yes, she said. *I will keep him safe. I'll do my best to make him well. But please, will you keep your promise? If I take care of this one for you, will you let me have my son?*

The answer was long in coming.

You know he does not love you, U'ru. He does not even understand what you are.

Oh, but he will! she assured him. *My Loves-Me will love me again – I only need a little time!*

The birds had gone quiet. From the long, dark tunnel behind her, Shea could just make out the sound of human shouting.

Well, the voice of the crows said at last. *He has cost us one son already, and perhaps we are soon to lose another... but that is the way of things. Go and have yours, then, and do with him what you will.*

I will, U'ru pledged. *I'll explain everything to him. I'll make him love me again, and then I'll make him new brothers and sisters, and together we'll –*

No.

She looked up. *What?*

Not a twitch, not a peep – not one sound from all the thousands of crows around them. The thick, stinking air had gone deathly still. *The scales are not balanced, U'ru. Your debt is not paid. You were not a fit leader of your people – and now you have no people. You were not a good mother to your children – and so you will have no children.*

U'ru's face crumpled in horror. *No – Grandfather, you can't –*

But the voice that answered her was the voice of certainty, of authority, of pitiless worlds-old finality. *You left it for me to decide. It is decided. Do as you will, but know this: from this time forward, nothing you plant in your own soil will live. Nothing you do for yourself will last.*

It was as good as a death sentence. The earthly gods lived only so long as they had a people – a culture – a human bloodline of their own. The Ara-Naure had been killed or dispersed, and if U'ru could not have any more children...

Shea's gill-plumes prickled as U'ru's gaze came to rest on her. For a weightless moment, she felt herself the sole object of the great lady's attention – saw herself through a wise, warm-blooded lens. And then the Dog Lady shared a thought with her – a vital realization born from their fight over Día's unmoving body – a frail, hairless epiphany she had apparently been nursing all night long.

U'ru had been counting on her progeny – on her son, on the siblings she would give him, and on the grandchildren they would give her in turn. But they would not be enough. They would never have been enough. Yashu-Diiwa had the bloodline, but he had never learned the ways of the Ara-Naure – and U'ru could not teach them all. She had no tongue to impart their language. Diminished as she was, she barely remembered the old ways.

But Shea had been awake all these years. Shea still remembered. And if she – who was not the Dog Lady's child, who was not even a human being – had been made Ara-Naure, had belonged to the people, had accepted the name they gave her... what was to prevent her from taking her place as a teacher of new people? What was to prevent her from fostering others like herself?

Age, Shea thought at once. *Patience*. Too much age, not enough patience. She had been a terrible teacher in her own right, a failure of a foster-mother – and that was when she still had health and vigor on her side.

That was when she was alone, the gentle second-voice corrected her. Shea and U'ru had both done terrible things, when they were alone. Together, though... together, softening and tempering each other's excesses... together, as they had been before...

Shea had ruined her vision long ago – one more sacrifice in the quest to find that misbegotten boy. But she was seeing herself now through U'ru's eyes: not as the withered, mutilated, cynical old wretch who looked back at her from every pond and glass, but as the one who was *still here*. The one who had singlehandedly kept her mistress's legacy alive for twenty years and more. The one who had swallowed every cruelty and survived. The one who had come with her here, to the end of the world, to stand with her as she answered for her past crimes – as she stared into the abyss of her own future.

The Dog Lady had one child left. She would not survive without him.

The Dog Lady had one friend left. She would not survive without her, either.

So U'ru knelt down before her old companion, and kissed her hand. Not on the back, as a suitor would, but three times, at the crevices between her fingers – one for each of the faint scars where the webbing had been cut away and burnt. And at this close remove, even Shea could not miss the trembling at the corners of U'ru's mouth, the wet shine in her eyes, as she forced herself to let go. *Will you stay with me, Water Dog? Will you help me do the right things?*

It was a small, humble question, not meant for Marhuk's hearing.

And it could have only one answer. *Of course, Mother. We'll do them together.*

That was the answer. That was the way forward. If U'ru could not have any more children, then she would have grandchildren. And Shea would teach them.

Perhaps that was what the old crow had intended all along.

Then I will do for others, U'ru said to him at last, *and my son will do for me. Come, Water Dog! We are going now – we are going to fix everything.*

Freshly resolved, the Dog Lady rose and began to collect Hakai for the long walk out. Freshly inspired, Shea hauled herself up to follow her.

She knew better than to set her hopes too high: Yashu-Diiwa was still a big ugly question mark, and so was Hakai, and... well, and so was she. After all, she wouldn't be around forever. There would come a day when U'ru would have to get along without Shea.

But that day was not today. Today, U'ru had one child, one friend, and two great tasks ahead of her. Today, Shea was welcome and wanted – and tomorrow, together, they could finally start setting things right.

But in spite of the radiant heat of Marhuk's manse, its occupants saw them off with precious little warmth.

We shall see.

"HE LIVES."

The voice, if it could be called that, was little more than an articulated death-rattle. Vuchak looked up in astonishment. He had never heard the old woman speak, and tended to dismiss those who claimed they had.

But the Last Word was exactly that, and her croaking edict halted Winshin's momentum, if not her mouth.

"WHY?" she demanded. "Why must he live, when Dulei is gone? By what right –"

"Be quiet," To'taka commanded. "Those are not your questions to ask."

Vuchak folded his arms and watched as the foreigners gawked and wondered at this last-second reprieve. Nobody bothered to translate for them.

Instead, Penten's brow creased in sympathy; she gestured to beckon Winshin closer. "Come, love, and be consoled: you may still have some satisfaction. Have the white one instead. He is a rich and fitting prize."

A pebble skittered over Vuchak's foot. He glanced over, where Ismat stood guard opposite him, on the right side of the doorway – and Echep crouched down just outside it.

He looked *awful*, as if he'd been mobbed by a flock of rutting turkeys – but the intention in his eyes and the jerk of his head might as well have spoken aloud.

Come on – let's get out of here.

Vuchak couldn't believe it. Echep should be in here, dealing with this. Vuchak should be out there, hurrying to find out whether he still had a sister. Dulei's faithless *atodak* had managed to be forgotten about in the chaos, and now he was hiding in the bushes like some delinquent wastrel, urging Vuchak to cut and run too. By every god, what had happened to shame?

"Isn't that so, To'taka?" Penten was saying. "Shouldn't we consider this second offering equal to the first? He's obviously a valuable person, even if he doesn't have any manners."

To'taka was fed up with it, of course. Half of Atali'Krah was in ruins, scores of people dead, and he was stuck here, spoon-feeding Winshin her promised vengeance. The law was clear: justice for a child of Marhuk took precedence over everything but the lives of others – and she had taken full advantage of it.

So To'taka did the expedient thing, sat back down, and nodded. "Yes. Take that one. Do it now, before he talks again."

Vuchak glanced ahead at Halfwick, and made no effort to hide his scowl. The Eaten boy should not be here, at the seat of Marhuk's power – not dead, not alive, not anything in between. He had been a fine enough young man before, but now his purpose was clear: he was a tool of the Starving God – and his presence, his entire being, was a dangerous outrage against nature.

"No, you can't!" Weisei cried, shriveling Vuchak's nerves with the first sound of his voice. "Afvik didn't do anything to Dulei, and everyone knows it!"

"Weisei, hush," Penten said. "Winshin, go ahead and –"

"No!" Weisei said. "This is not right. It is not just. And I won't – and I won't allow it to happen!"

Shit.

Vuchak bit his tongue, shamefully aware of the stares of the other two *atodaxa*: Winshin's in haughty smugness, Penten's in grandfatherly disapproval, and both in perfect agreement – that was no way for a son of Marhuk to speak to his elders.

"Weisei, be quiet," To'taka growled, speaking Vuchak's part for him.

Another pebble. Another head-jerk from Echep. Another reminder of the case he had made last night. *Weisei will never grow up,* his pointed gaze said. *He'll spend his life chasing his appetites and embarrassing his company – just as he's doing now.*

And he might even be right.

"No," Weisei said, his petulance fermenting into full-fledged revolt. "I'm tired of this. I'm tired of all of it. We hold ourselves in such high regard – we look down on all the rest of creation – but look what we do. Look how we treat people!" He was ranting, flinging his hand out in a borderline-obscene gesture at the three bewildered foreigners, working himself up to a fury – and it was all Vuchak could do not to throw law and caution to the wind and march up there to clamp a hand over his mouth.

"Well?" Weisei demanded. "Is this justice, or is it

a meat market? Are we here to swap and barter like old women haggling over a pile of intestines? 'Oh, that one's no good, I want my money back' – 'Well, take this one instead, and I'll throw in a –'"

Fear finally bested prudence. "Weisei, by every god SHUT UP!" Vuchak shouted, giddy with dread.

"I WILL NOT!" Weisei roared back, livid with righteousness, proving Echep wrong in one heedless instant. He *was* a man – a man about to do something really, irreversibly stupid.

To'taka rose to his feet again, his face darkening, his lips a tight, dangerous line. "Weisei Marhuk, your next word will find you guilty of treason."

This was bad. This couldn't happen. Vuchak glanced over at Echep one more time – not beckoning or gesturing anymore, but crouched there staring out at nothing, his face an astonished eavesdropping reflection of the fear curling around Vuchak's gut.

"Then let it be treason!" Weisei swore, tearing his holy cloak off and hurling it to the floor. "I would rather be nothing than belong to this!"

That was it. He had said it. It was done.

The sadness in Penten's eyes was nothing next to the sorrow in Vuchak's heart. "The punishment is death," she said gently – as if he didn't already know.

Weisei lifted his chin, the edge of his anger blunting just slightly on her kindly tone. "Yes, and as a child of Marhuk, no-one has any right to my life. I'll accept my exile gladly, and –"

Vuchak swallowed, floating on a wave of everything – of clarity, of regret, of wry, poignant consolation. Weisei hadn't meant it. He still hadn't realized it yet – didn't see the hole in his reasoning. Leave it to him to hurl down his cloak in a single great act of misplaced bravery, and never feel the hair spilling loose and free down his own back.

"The punishment," Penten repeated, "is death."

Vuchak locked eyes with Harak, who still stood at attention behind her. The ancient, decrepit *atodak* was a white-haired emblem of duty – the very portrait of a life spent in service. He was old now, useless now, probably kept more for loyalty and sentiment than anything else...

... but the old man's rheumy eyes held Vuchak firm and fast, and in them lay a vision of perfect, unflinching clarity.

Then To'taka's gaze locked on him; he beckoned him forward with a lift of his chin. "Vuchak, are you prepared to serve?"

It wasn't supposed to be like this. Nobody had intended it to come to this. Everything had just happened too fast.

Come on, Vichi. We just have to do one more right thing, and then you can rest.

But there was still enough time for Vuchak to make his decision and step forward, offering his wrists to the assembly, and receiving theirs in turn. Then Ismat stepped up behind him, her knife scattering sunlight as it flashed in his periphery, and opened his throat.

CHAPTER FOURTEEN
THE END

AT THE TIME, it had been an odd bit of trivia.

It's a most curious practice, Faro had said, regaling Sil with some arcane fact about Marhuk's children. *Their companions share in all the best... except that when the little godling should misbehave, it's his playmate that gets the smacking.*

But then, as now, Sil had more pressing matters on his mind: he found an angry white-streaked face in his vision, and then cold steel in his gut.

FOR A MOMENT, time slowed down – and then everything snapped forward.

Día didn't see what was happening behind her, and by the look of it, Weisei didn't either. He'd surged ahead, hot on Winshin's heels as she rushed for Halfwick – and too late to keep her from burying her knife in his belly.

"Afvik, watch out!"

Día felt Elim go rigid beside her, heard the surprised little *ah* as Halfwick took the hit – as Winshin twisted the knife in his gut, pivoted sharply around in a malicious parody of a waltzing twirl, and then rammed the hilt, sending Halfwick stumbling back into Weisei's arms as she ripped the blade messily free.

Weisei looked up at his sister with such a singular, murderous fury in his eyes that for that one instant, their faces were interchangeable.

Then he caught sight of something behind her.

"*VICHI!*"

It was a scream that echoed beyond human pitch as the room held its breath – as Weisei understood that he'd made the wrong choice.

He dropped Halfwick, leaving Winshin to fall on him like a wildcat on a wounded stag, knocking the Northman boy to the ground as she stabbed him over and over in a flashing, furious tempest of rage.

And all the while Vuchak just stood there in the doorway, bright rills of blood pouring from his throat as he offered his wrists out – and Winshin's handmaiden slashed them open.

To Día's ignorant eye, there was no malice in it. It looked like a precise, ritual cut, almost the natural answer to the traditional a'Krah gesture of respect whose meaning she had never thought to question.

And if that was a fatal definition of respect, then what happened next was a cruel act of love. Penten had stepped down from the dais, calm amidst all the horror and commotion, and caught Weisei as he tried to rush forward. Her masculine arms held him effortlessly in place, her face sad but serene as he struggled uselessly in her grasp – as he reached out, one hand straining to close the gap separating him from his life's companion.

For his part, Vuchak seemed to understand that he had not been given permission to fall: he stood and stood, steadfast and faithful in spite of his own bubbling wet gasps, in spite of the blood making a crimson livery of his clothes, until at last his limbs lost their strength, and he dropped to his knees in a puddle of his own making.

And still Weisei reached, his dark skin darkening further, his grasping fingers trembling as a mirror gash opened across his own throat, weeping a delicate red necklace as his face contorted with effort.

Día knew that Marhuk's children performed his work as mediators of life and death. She did not know how effective a mediator Weisei would be – especially here in daylight, ten fatal feet away from the object of his attention, with his holy cloak lying cast off behind him.

Vuchak seemed to come to the same conclusion. He leaned forward in slow, graceful prostration, his arms slackening as he folded them across his middle, his forehead sinking gently down to rest on the cold stone floor, folding his body as neatly as a finished newspaper.

And Weisei reached to his very limits, fingers sharpening into talons, the cords of his neck standing out iron-stiff, sweat beading over his furrowed brow as his companion's body twitched, shuddered –

– and sat back up.

But there was no feeling left in those slack features, no humanity remaining as that empty face gazed up at Weisei, its eyes devoid of light or reason.

"*AIAH!*" With a screaming, wordless cry, the accidental puppetmaster broke the spell. Vuchak's body collapsed into an awkward heap, motionless save for the slowly spreading pool underneath. Weisei simply collapsed, weeping.

Which left Día, holding fast to Elim's arm as the two of them stood as far as possible from the carnage...

Penten, her arms a loving buttress for Weisei's first hysterical sobs...

And Winshin, who had apparently, finally exhausted herself.

She might have stabbed Halfwick fifty, a hundred, two hundred times. Now she straddled his body with arms red to the elbows, heaving, sweating, wearing a look of almost post-coital satisfaction.

For a long minute, there was only Weisei's broken weeping, and Winshin's heavy breath.

Día did not want to look at either of the two bodies on the floor – or anything else for that matter. Her nerves couldn't bear one more shock or wonder or brutal sudden horror. She closed her eyes and leaned in at Elim's side, one helpless bystander sheltering with another, and was grateful when the big man put his arm around her.

Then that cold, familiar voice cut the air.

"Are you quite finished?"

Winshin leapt up and away like an electrocuted cat – leaving Sil Halfwick free to sit up and climb laboriously to his feet.

He coughed and spat, the wet red result instantly lost upon the bloodied stones. But that was all. Even as Día watched, the single stray slash over his face closed, healed, and vanished, leaving him exactly as immaculate as before – albeit in considerably more ventilated clothing.

To'taka stared down at him from the dais, regarding what must look like the 'Starving' God's own chosen son with equal parts awe and mistrust. "... *what you want?*" he said in his rough Marín.

Halfwick swallowed down a rattled demeanor and

matched him, stare for stare. He pointed at Elim. "*I want to leave with him. Whole. Alive. Now.*"

To'taka frowned, sniffing for treachery. "*What else?*"

Halfwick faltered, and Día began to suspect that he'd been badly frightened. Certainly he was having to improvise. "*And I want... I want supplies, enough food for us to get back to S – to Island Town.*"

To'taka lifted his chin. "*What else?*"

Halfwick thought for a long moment – long enough even for Weisei to pause and look up at him with hollow-eyed wonder, or perhaps expectation.

If Halfwick noticed, he didn't show it. He folded his arms. "*And that's all.*"

To'taka grunted. "*We will see.*" He beckoned Penten and Winshin to him, leaving their old warrior-guardians on silent watch as their seniors conferred. Weisei was left alone to drop to a stunned, graceless seat at Vuchak's side.

Día's heart ached for him. She had understood none of the terrible shouting match that had preceded the great violence, nor what Vuchak could possibly have done to merit his execution. But she was confident of one thing: if anyone here had had a plan when they walked in, it had long since been snapped in half and stomped on.

"... what's he saying?"

Elim's voice was hoarse, almost whisper-soft. He had gone deathly pale, his face a mix of milk white and blanched brown, and his gaze stayed riveted on his partner, as if one careless blink would see him killed all over again. She hoped he wasn't about to faint.

"He's asking for your life," Día said, though perhaps 'asking' was too soft a term. "Do you want to sit down?"

Elim's answer was a vague shake of his head. She didn't blame him: blood was running between the floor-stones like batter spreading out through a waffle iron, the air had grown thick with sweat and fear and fermented death, and the urge to run was overwhelming.

It was almost a relief when Penten finally turned back to address them. "*Well,*" she said to Halfwick, her voice calm, yet colder than it had been before. "*The gods have made themselves clear. Marhuk has spoken for your Appaloosa Elim,*" and this with a bow to the Last Word above and behind her, "*just as the Starving God has spoken for you. We acknowledge and honor these decisions. You are free to go, and we will provide for your leaving.*"

Día let out a breath that came from the bottoms of her feet – quietly, of course. She wouldn't interrupt to translate, but gave Elim's hand an encouraging squeeze.

"*However,*" Penten continued, "*It is now time for the a'Krah people to speak, and this is what we have to say. This is our home, our most sacred place, and we will give no shelter to the heralds of unwelcome gods. For now it is day: our time to sleep, and your time to leave. When night comes, it will be our time to rise, and we will not treat kindly any trespassers we find lingering here on the Mother of Mountains. Are these words clear to you?*"

That was good. That was better than they could have asked for. Día wadded the folds of her cassock at her sides, hoping that Halfwick would have the sense to be gracious.

He answered with a bow – but this time in the Eadan style. "*Yes, reverend elder,*" he said. "*We understand and thank you for your tolerance. We'll leave at once.*"

That was probably supposed to be 'forbearance', but nevermind: Día took the cue and curtseyed, nudging Elim to likewise make some small gesture of respect. She couldn't stomach the wrist-bow, after what had happened to Vuchak.

The a'Krah received the courtesy as well as could be expected: Penten nodded, To'taka grunted, and Winshin stood quietly aside, sullen or perhaps just spent.

"*Then let's make it so,*" Penten said, after a moment's aside. "*Go away down this road, following it left to the edge of the city, to the place where the trees begin. Don't stray or linger or speak with anyone on your way. Wait there, and we'll see that you're provided for.*"

But as Halfwick turned to obey, the kindest of the a'Krah continued, her tone switching from the voice of consensus to a more personal inquiry. "*Please tell us, though, before you go... what is the reason for this? Why does the Starving God care for him?*"

Día could feel Elim flinch as he caught Penten's nod. Sil looked back at his partner, and seemed to stifle an ugly thought. "*He doesn't,*" he said. "*I do.*"

Then he turned and went, beckoning Elim and Día to follow, and his expression was absolute business. "Come on," he said, with a jerk of his head toward the door. "Don't speak, don't touch me, and don't do anything stupid until we're outside."

Día chose to assume that that last wasn't directed at her. But it was terribly hard to follow the other two in stepping around Vuchak's body, and impossible not to notice the stunned, hollow expression on Weisei's tear-stained face as he looked up – as Halfwick walked past without so much as a downward glance.

Día should say something. She should keep going. She

should help him somehow. She shouldn't do anything that would jeopardize Elim's freedom.

In the end, the decision was made for her. As she reached the threshold, To'taka's voice called out from behind, arresting her on the spot. "*Not that one,*" he said. "*The ambassador, she stays here.*"

SHIT.

Of course. Of course it couldn't be that easy. Sil turned, straining his anxiety and anger and the lingering memory of that god-awful knife through a mental sieve until he could reply in something approaching a sensible voice. "*What do you mean?*"

This time it was Penten who replied, her tone as ambiguous as her sex. "*She speaks for the First Man of Island Town, doesn't she? And he is our ally, isn't he? It would be foolish of us to waste this opportunity for a visit.*"

Horseshit. They'd been denied Elim and deprived of Sil, and now they were settling for the next best thing: sighting down the crosshairs at Día.

To'taka might be reading his thoughts: his gaze drilled into Sil, daring him to object. "*Unless we are not worth her time?*"

Shit, shit, shit. Sil racked his memory, but no: he had spoken only for himself and Elim. He hadn't said anything about Día.

"What is it?" Elim asked, right on form for choosing the absolute worst time to start belching ignorance. "What's the matter?"

"Shut up – let me think."

But in the time it took to say it, his time was up: Día

curtseyed again, and her voice was as smooth as freshly-poured cement. "*It would be my privilege.*"

Penten might have smiled. Or it might have been a trick of the light as Sil stood there on a sunlit doorstep, squinting back into the dim recesses of the charnel-house.

"*We are pleased by the gift of your time,*" she said, and stepped down from the dais. "*Come and let us make you comfortable.*"

Prison, then. They meant to make a prisoner of her: circumstances questionable, confinement indefinite, purpose unclear. "Día, d'you not want me to see if I can –"

"*I would be honored by your hospitality.*" She didn't so much as glance in his direction.

And just like that, she'd made herself their hostage.

"Right," Sil said. "That's that. Elim, come on – just the two of us for now."

"What?" Calvert's mule brayed, looking back and forth between his two minders. "How come? Día, ain't you coming?"

"It's all right," she assured him, though the quaver in her voice gave that up for a lie. "You go on ahead. I'll follow after you."

Which ought to be enough for a man holding a reprieve not even five minutes old... but one look at the furrowing of Elim's dusty sweat-streaked brow said exactly how much that mattered to him now. "No," he said, with a stubborn shake of his head. "No, I'm not going to leave you by yourself – not with them, not for any –"

"Elim, MOVE ON," Sil snapped, acutely aware of the fragility of their pardon. They were burning daylight and good will, and he would be god-damned if this balking fool was going to ruin a good deal *again*.

"The hell I will!" Elim retorted, utterly indifferent to the fact that he was literally blocking the door. "She came all the way out here to get me, and I'm not going to –"

"Elim, for God's sake will you go away and let me do my job!"

It was a shrill, panicked demand, so surprising that both Sil and Elim stopped to stare at the source.

Día stood inside, stiff-backed and press-mouthed and perhaps those were tears in her eyes, which she covered with a hasty dip of her head. "And – and please, when you get there, tell Fours where I am."

Sil couldn't have said whether it was belated good sense, or simply that Elim hadn't built up a tolerance for being shouted at by women. Regardless, Calvert's mule surrendered with a half-turn and a nick-of-time duck to keep from being brained by the stone doorframe.

Which left Sil with enough of a view to glance briefly back, just to assure himself that she really would be all right somehow... but by then the a'Krah were gathering around her, blocking his view, and there was no sensible course but to turn and get out of there, double-counting every one of his hard, ugly blessings.

BY THE TIME Shea and U'ru finally made their slow, belabored way back through the black corridor, the faint sounds coming from up ahead had long since died away. There had been some great commotion up there, but the echo of the stone passage distorted everything to distant, senseless warbling.

So all Shea had to go on was U'ru's continuing elation: she had made peace with Marhuk, and had a new puppy to take care of, and both of the others were safe, unhurt – even if they were frightened and sad.

"Sad about what?" Shea grunted, shifting Hakai's arm higher up on her shoulder for what felt like the hundredth time. She didn't blame Yashu-Diiwa for being afraid – he'd probably escaped the axe by the skin of his goose-pimpled ball-hairs – but Día had been fearless, positively euphoric when she'd run off earlier.

It's complicated, U'ru answered. In other words, she didn't understand.

Nor did it get any clearer when they finally emerged back out into the temple – or better to say, the slaughterhouse.

The moldering old woman still sat up there on her perch, presiding in mummified serenity over the carnage below. The whole place now reeked of week-old rotting flesh, the bodies on the floor lay sprawled heedlessly on top of each other, and there was blood *everywhere*.

"*Merde alors,*" Shea swore, hastily coordinating with U'ru to set Hakai down. "What is this? What happened?"

... *it's complicated,* U'ru said again.

But as Shea stepped gingerly around the dais, taking care to avoid the biggest of the drops and splatters, the first startling hint of movement suggested that she'd been mistaken. There was only one body on the floor. The one on top was alive.

"*Ak aku?*" It was a man's voice, thick and hoarse and heartbroken.

Shea quickened her pace to see if he was hurt, squinting against the harsh light from the open doorway – and realizing only when she was almost on top of him that she knew him.

That was Weisei – from Island Town, from La Saciadería – and the corpse he cradled was his friend – that dour, irritable fellow whose name Shea couldn't recall.

Well, they made an awful pair now. Weisei was a ghastly sight, nothing at all like the merry drinker Shea had left behind. Thin and frail and spent, with blood smeared over his clothes and sticking in his hair, he looked up with such an abyssal mask of horror as could only belong to a living body operated by a broken soul.

It was all Shea could do to keep from flinching at his gaze. "Weisei, what happened?"

But he wasn't interested in her. He was staring at the Dog Lady's approach, watching her step heedlessly through the drying crimson slick, leaving eerily clean bare-stone footprints behind her.

"Great lady?"

U'ru came towards him with compassion and sadness in her eyes, and Shea could feel her domesticated heart swell with pity for this poor lost crow-child who had fallen out of the nest.

Weisei's attention flicked back to Shea, suddenly animated by a spark of desperation. "Fishman?"

She startled as he clutched at her ankle with a hot, sticky hand, his pleading bloodshot eyes rooting her to the spot. "Help me, please. Tell me how to pray to her. Ask her to heal my Vichi..."

Thankfully, Shea was spared having to tell him the truth. U'ru came and knelt down beside him, easing him gently away from the dead man in his lap. Weisei's expression crumpled as he began to understand.

And U'ru folded him in under her arm with the grace of ages: a mother-dog fostering a frail bird, soothing him as he cried.

It was a hard thing to watch.

Among human beings and their earthly gods, Shea would always be something of an outsider. She'd made her peace with that long ago.

But if she were human, and had some supernatural talent, she would have wished for the power to conjure other people – to fill this grisly room with everyone she had cheated and used and manipulated over the past twenty-odd years, point at the scene unfolding before her, and say, *This. This is what it was for.*

She didn't expect them to understand. She wouldn't ask for their forgiveness. But it would have been nice to show this to Fours, to Día, to the poor souls of the House of Losange whose bodies were currently drifting downstream – even to good old Henry Bon, the bounty hunter who'd given himself so lustily to the cause. It would have been nice to be able to repay them, at least in part, with the knowledge that they had helped to accomplish something of unknowable importance. They had brought back the Dog Lady, the living avatar of love and healing and the simple creature comforts that made life worthwhile... and the world had been a poorer place without her.

Instead, Shea crouched down on U'ru's other side, her skin darkening in sympathy with Weisei's as she settled in like a torpid newt on a sun-drenched stone, basking in warmth after a twenty-year winter. *This* was the U'ru she'd held out for. *This* was the one people would lay down their lives for. Here again at last was a joy for the joyless, the mother to the motherless, the great lady who had looked out on a world falling into war and slaughter and tried to love it whole again.

It had been worth it, Shea decided – everything she'd done over these long, lonely years of waiting and hoping and hunting for that boy. Not necessarily right... certainly not well-executed... but worth it.

She was just sorry that this moment had come at Weisei's expense. Because although he still lived, his hiccupping sobs diminishing as he wrung himself dry on U'ru's shoulder, Shea already knew that the person he had been was gone. A hundred miles to the east, a rowdy border-town bar was already missing its most vivacious regular, a sparkling prodigal host who had so zestfully entertained all comers – a gentle, delightful, once-in-a-generation exceptional human soul.

He should have been the Dog Lady's child, Shea decided. Love and healing and creature comforts, the both of them... a loss for the Ara-Naure, and a waste for the a'Krah.

Perhaps U'ru thought so too. When the last of his sadness finally dissolved into an exhausted slumber, his head slipping down to rest in the hollow of her neck, U'ru made no move to rise. She stayed, safeguarding him as he sank deeper into sleep – probably the last good one he would have. Only when Hakai began to stir did she reluctantly relinquish Weisei, easing him back down to lie with his fallen friend.

Where is his bed? U'ru asked as they rose, her distressed gaze roving over the charnel-house around them. *He shouldn't stay here.*

Shea climbed stiffly back up to her feet, feeling as old as that comatose crone in the chair. "I don't know, Mother. We'll have to find out."

Tonight, of course, it would be a simple thing for U'ru to scoop up Weisei and take him to a more wholesome place, or to carry him all night long, if it pleased her. For now, it was as much as they could do to carry a single broken man between them. And wasn't that always the way of the world? Too many wounded people crying to be picked up, and no arms big enough to hold them.

THAT COULD HAVE gone better.

Sil led Elim down the road, grateful at least that he didn't have to tell him not to gawk: the big lunk kept his head down and his attention on the ground six inches in front of his feet, as if he didn't want to see or hear or think about one thing more than he absolutely had to.

That made two of them.

Still, the sun was up, the worst of the calamity seemed to have passed, and it was a tremendous relief to have finally emerged back out in the fresh air. By the time they reached the edge of town, Sil had mastered the worst of himself, and managed to handle their business with something approaching civility.

Not that he needed to do much. As eager as the a'Krah had been to get their claws into Día, they seemed even more anxious to be rid of Sil and Elim. Like ants establishing a supply line, the gift-bearers came, set their bounty down on the ground without ever meeting Sil's eyes, and hurried away again. It was an impressive cornucopia: berries and corn-cakes, fresh pemmican, roasted nuts, jerky and some kind of dried fruit patties, blankets, a knife and hand-axe, flint and tinder, packs to carry it all, and skins with water enough for two days at a time – parting gifts all delivered with the alacrity of hosts whose overstayed visitors could not possibly leave a moment too soon.

In the end, their only deprivations were a replacement for Elim's lost shoe, and his rifle. When it seemed that nothing could be done about either of those, Sil cut his losses and made ready to leave, acutely aware of the shrinking shadows on the ground: he didn't have to know how long it would take to make it down and off the mountain by nightfall in order to know that he didn't care to find out what would happen if they didn't.

So he shouldered the lighter half of the load and gave Elim a nudge. "Come on, then – let's get going."

Elim, who had been resting with arms folded over his updrawn knees, lifted his head with a look of bleary confusion. "Ain't we camping here?"

Sil was annoyed for all of the two seconds it took to realize that no, he really hadn't told Elim anything. "Er... no, actually," he said, as kindly as he could. "We'll camp down at the foothills. We have to be off the mountain by dark."

Elim's face dissolved into the horror of a struggling pie-eating contestant who'd just been served a fresh, quivering mountain of mincemeat. "I can't," he said – and then, before Sil could get sharp with him: "No, I mean it. I believe you, buddy – I'd do it if I could – but I spent all yesterday and half of last night running and climbing and hauling Hawkeye and dodging rocks and getting shot at and dumped on and frog-kicked into a wall and I can't even recollect what-all else, and then with all this up here, and all that just there, and I just – I'm just used up, Sil. I can't."

Which would ordinarily have been Sil's cue to start in

with a righteous red-hot bollocking, full of *How dare
you* and *D'you have any idea what it cost me to get you
off the hook* and the perennial classic, *God damn your
ungrateful spotted hide...*

... but he couldn't miss the cracks in Elim's voice, or
that look in his eyes. It was the frightened expression of
a downed animal, one every bit as aware of the circling
vultures as it was powerless to rise.

He wasn't, though. He wasn't. Elim had walked down
this very road not even an hour ago, with no difficulty
at all. He hadn't broken his leg or stepped in a bear
trap – he was just overwhelmed thinking of how far he
still had to go.

Sil groped for a new tack, a new angle to use in
cajoling him up to his feet. This would be so much
easier if he could just provoke Elim back into that...
that monstrous thing he had been before. No shortage
of strength in that fellow.

Well, never mind that: how had this mixed idiot found
the energy to get himself up here in the first place? He
was just as poorly back when Sil had found him in the
foothills, and there hadn't been any balking then. Why,
Elim himself had led the charge, nattering on about
how they were cursed men, how he had to go finish
settling up for Dulei. He'd even taken it upon himself to
go haul a half-dead man out of a mountainside.

Yes. That was it. That was the problem here. There
was no Dulei anymore, nobody needing to be rescued
or found or dug up and toted about like an oversized
chew-bone. Elim didn't have anyone left to help – and
apparently helping himself didn't count.

"Sil?" Elim was staring up at him, fear settling into
confusion at this uncommon silence.

Now there was a capital suggestion, inadvertently proposed by Elim himself.

Yes, that might just work.

"Sorry," Sil said, hurrying to spin out a convincing line. "I was just thinking – just realizing, actually. You don't have to go anywhere. You can stay here and rest, if you like."

This was a dangerous gambit, not to mention a flagrant lie: the a'Krah had commanded them both to be gone by dark, or else.

But Sil could see the relief on Elim's face as the weight of necessity dropped off him, and pressed on. "It's just me they don't want here, and I was only hoping – you know, as dangerous as it was on our way up here, I would have felt safer for having you with me on the way back down. That was all." And he shouldered his pack again, as if to see himself off.

Elim frowned. "What? Why? How come you can't stay here?" He nodded back towards the temple. "It ain't like they can hurt you..."

Trust me, it hurt like hell.

Sil bit back his first sharp remark, sidestepping around the crack in his composure. "I know, but they could still keep me in prison, or – or do violent things to me," and oh, God, the light in that woman's eyes as she'd gutted him, "and I just... honestly, Elim, I just want to go home."

That last bit started out as a convenient way of salting the oats, confessing something for himself that he knew would resonate with Elim's own motives. Still, there was more of the truth in it than Sil had expected. He was restored, yes, hale and hearty and apparently unkillable... but he also hadn't slept in a week and a half, and there was no telling how much time he had left – no way to know when his miraculous second-life might expire – and when it did, he wanted to be at home, in his own bed.

Maybe Elim understood that more than Sil had given him credit for. He rose to his feet, swallowing down some faintness or nausea as he did. Then he picked up his pack, an effortless weight now that it belonged to someone else, and committed. "Sure, buddy. Sure, I understand. Let's go take you home."

And that was all it took. Elim, who could do for others what he would never manage for himself, fell in line behind Sil, who could make a breadcrumb trail of his own wants long enough to stretch from here to Hell's Acre. The two of them shared a glance, just long enough to draw on the last dregs of their own peculiar talents, and then headed down the trail: borrowed time escorted by lent energy as they started off in search of an ending.

EVERYTHING WAS A bit of a blur after that.

Día had enough sense to follow the a'Krah graciously as they escorted her out. She had enough presence of mind to ask about Weisei, while managing not to imply that the rest of them were heartless savages for leaving him there alone with the body. And she had just enough prudence to listen to Penten's double-sided answer: her words were kind, assuring Día that he would only be left long enough to compose himself and share a private moment with his companion, and yet her tone evoked an exasperated parent whose child had embarrassed himself in public, and was now being left to finish his tantrum alone.

It didn't seem right, but Día couldn't risk putting a foot wrong. She went quietly thereafter, full of grace and gratitude as Penten showed her to a small one-room house, and promised that she would have every comfort provided to her before they met again tomorrow morning. Día had no difficulty hearing what went unspoken: she was a guest of the a'Krah now, and she was not to leave her room unescorted.

Perhaps the proper term for that was 'house arrest'... but at the moment, she didn't care.

When the door finally closed on the last pleasantries and promises, Día stood still for a bit, assuring herself of the door and the walls and the flue and the lone westward-facing window – mentally marking off her new perimeters.

Then she sat down in the middle of that small, safe, quiet space, and let out the breath she'd been holding for a week.

She would be all right here. They recognized her as a representative of the Azahi, an indispensable ally. They had no reason to treat her poorly. And she trusted the Dog Lady not to leave without her.

So for the first few hours, Día was content just to dwell there in that peaceful little pocket-world. She admired the fine stonework of the diamond-shaped walls, and the beautiful multitude of eyes painted upon them. She ate the strange but savory food they brought her, and drank sweet, clean spring water. She wrapped herself in the great pile of furs and blankets that dominated her snug quarters, having never in her life lay in such luxury. And when the afternoon sunlight began to disappear up the eastern wall, and the modest warmth of the day ebbed away again, she took a cord of fresh pine from the generous stockpile beside the pit, and made herself a fire.

But even though she had been confined to a room scarcely ten feet square, her thoughts now had infinite space to expand, evaporating and diffusing like an uncorked bottle of ether.

She shouldn't have shouted at Elim like that.

She should have said something to Weisei.

She was going to be in trouble when the a'Krah found out that the Azahi hadn't actually sent her – that he didn't even know she was here.

And as for Halfwick...

Día had been blessed to wake up in the Dog Lady's arms and see her faith rewarded – to imagine the hand of God working to bring U'ru and Marhuk together for her own personal restoration... even if the bloodbath in the temple had thoroughly disproven Marhuk's interest in any single human life.

But it was impossible not to see the direct, divine intervention that had brought Sil Halfwick to radiant immortality without feeling... what? Jealousy? Bitterness? Disgust?

Regardless, it was a terribly selfish, unhelpful sentiment – and yet impossible to ignore. Why on earth should such a miracle be manifested for one of the most obnoxious, least-deserving people she had ever known? What could he possibly have done to merit that? He'd been arrogant and useless from first to last, compounding every error and sometimes contriving to inflict new ones. He hadn't even saved Elim: Marhuk's verdict had done that for him. In the entire tenure of their very-short acquaintance, Halfwick's singular accomplishment had been a string of gross, protracted, seemingly effortless failures to die.

But as she sat and stared into the flickering light of the fire, this prideful exercise opened a much darker doorway. Because if Halfwick had been superfluous – why, Día had been completely useless.

She hadn't restored the Dog Lady at the end of that long walk through the desert, nor saved her from the fishmen. The landslide had done that for her.

She hadn't rescued Elim, as she'd so staunchly promised U'ru and Miss du Chenne. Far from it: she'd had to be rescued herself.

She hadn't even helped Halfwick finish his life, as she'd promised Weisei she would. If she hadn't stopped to help him there as he dangled from that ledge, why...

... why, he would have fallen, just as he had anyway, and God would have restored him in His own good time, as He did anyway.

Día pressed her hands over her mouth, stunned.

All of that, all of this – for nothing.

She could have kept right on walking.

She could have spared herself all that pain and trouble.

She could have saved her hair.

Día ran her hand over her plundered skull, but there was no miraculous restoration there for her – not even a quickening of the follicles.

She'd cut away her life, her strength, her *connection*, for a boy who'd taken one look at them and shoved her off a cliff – and for his trouble been raised up by the hand of God Almighty.

And now he was gone.

Día sat there for a long, long time afterwards. The sounds of a distant human world carried over the breeze as night fell, and Atali'Krah woke up.

When the fire grew hungry, she pulled out her knife

and cut off little pinched bits of her remaining hair, evening out yesterday's crude, futile handiwork. She threw each one into the flames, breathing deep from the acrid stink. When it was done, she was left with a more-or-less even quarter-inch cut: not much for warmth or protection or a spiritual connection to the cosmos, but at least she would look presentable for tomorrow's interview.

Then she got up, eased herself, washed, and went to bed, reciting her usual prayers about gratitude and blessings as she did – even if they were recitations only. Even if the only blessing ready to hand was the absence of a mirror.

IT WAS A sick bit of irony.

Here was Elim, who had probably spent his whole life striving to be treated like a full human being, and who was probably going to have to try even harder to square that with himself, now that it had turned out to be only half true...

And here was Sil, who was now treating him like a mule – like an actual, four-legged mule.

And it *worked*.

"There we are – mind that step, now. Good! Here, d'you want some more nuts?"

Of course he did. He always did. Sil could feed him every five minutes from now until doomsday, and Elim would never not be hungry. And thank god for that!

Because Sil could see the brutal exhaustion in the man's spotted face, noticed the wide white roll of his eyes every time he caught a glimpse down a drop or gap, or even just took a sideways look at the sprawling, scorched desert vista beyond. And Sil, no horseman himself, had partnered with this one at least long enough to have learned a little about how to keep a spent, spooky animal moving.

"No, nevermind that – look here, you can hold on to the root while you step down. Steady on... there! Well done!"

Needless it say, it was awful. Sil was the absolute worst fellow in the world for this work: to have to treat a more-than-grown man like a toddling infant or a dumb brute was a day-long exercise in humiliation. Elim should have had someone like himself for this part, someone gentle and patient and understanding.

Too bad they'd left her with the a'Krah.

So Sil kept doling out carrots and kindness all day long, an endless stream of encouragement and little feedings designed to keep Elim from seizing up on the narrow bits, slipping up on the steep ones, or sitting down and giving up altogether. That was the one rule: they could stand and catch their breath for a bit, take a drink or eat a handful of something while leaning up against a tree, but nobody was to do any sitting until they got to the bottom. Those were the terms. That was the bargain.

And it still might not be enough. Elim held up his end admirably – steadfastly soaking up every one of Sil's awkward, ham-fisted efforts to coax him along – but their progress down the less-ruined side of the mountain was still horrendously slow. As the sun sank behind the mountain, Sil found himself hurrying them along with redoubled vigor: he didn't really believe that a mob of crows would magically appear at sunset to peck their eyes out – but he also didn't need to be proven wrong about that.

And honestly, Sil was beginning to tire too.

"Come on," he said, for the hundred thousandth time that day. He'd never been so weary of the sound of his own voice. "Not much farther now. Let's just get to that big rock down there and then we'll –"

Elim took him up on it much too quickly. His first step down was fine, but the second failed to clear: his toe caught on a gnarled root, pitching him to the ground with a grunt and a *whump* as he tumbled and slid down the steep trail – thirty feet in three seconds – to land in a dusty heap at the bottom.

"Elim!"

Sil dropped his pack and leapt down with an agility scarcely twelve hours old, skidding down after him, just waiting to find out that the lumbering ox had crippled himself somehow. "Elim, are you all right? Can you hear me?"

But though Calvert's mule lay exactly as he'd fallen – on his side, pack still shouldered, with one arm crooked over his filthy serape and the other outflung beside him – his only difficulty seemed to be in keeping his eyes open.

"Yep," he mumbled with a conspicuously long blink, as if even that was an effort. "'m fine."

"Here, get up," Sil said, grabbing his hand and giving it a hard pull. "Get up, come on – no time for lying about."

"Sure," Elim said, making no move to rise. "Sure, I can do that." Another, even longer blink.

"Do it, then! We have to go!" Sil pulled and tugged, but it was like hauling a side of beef. He shook his shoulder hard enough to earn one more blink – but there was no reason left in those aimless brown eyes, and soon they closed.

Sil glanced up at the darkening twilight sky, and back down at Elim. He felt over his head and limbs, just to be sure the poor clod hadn't broken or cracked anything. He watched his breathing, until the rise and fall of his chest grew slow and deep and regular.

Then Sil gave up. "Right. Well. Perfect place to camp, wouldn't you say?"

It wasn't. It wasn't watered or sheltered or even flat, and more importantly, it wasn't safe: they had made it to the mountain's root, or something like it... but was that close enough to count? Did the a'Krah really mean to kill them if they stayed here?

Well, probably not. They had their own concerns. Regardless, there wasn't much Sil could do about it now.

So he collected their things, pulled off Elim's pack, and spread a blanket over him and another one underneath. It was a poor job, but Sil didn't have it in him to fix a fire just then.

In fact, he began to think he didn't have much left at all. Sitting here alone in the still evening air left him with nothing to distract him from the deepening stillness in himself – nothing to do but listen to the burring of the crickets, the hooting of an owl, and the rhythm of his own heart.

One-two one-two one-two...

He wouldn't mind having company right about then. As usual, all he had was Elim.

He snorted. "Some help you are."

With Día, though – now there would have been a conversation worth having. There was so much he wanted to tell her... but by the time Sil had something worth saying, he'd had no voice left, and now it was too late.

One-two... one-two... one-two...

The slackening beat inside him was unnerving, and he couldn't resist another glance at that red glow on the horizon. The dark contours of the mountain gave the light an irregular edge, as if Sil and Elim were ants sheltering in the shadow of a great pile of smoldering coals.

What if this was it? He'd begun at dawn – what if he were going to end at dusk?

He'd asked for enough time to do this one thing, to see Elim safely delivered. Sil would have thought that meant getting him back to Hell's Acre... but that was the trouble with those dark-night-of-the-soul bargains: never any fine print.

One... two... one... two...

Sil pushed himself over to sit with his back against a flat stone, frightened and yet resolved. He didn't want to think of it – didn't want it to be over – but then, he'd spent his life as a sickly, impatient boy, coughing and wheezing as he clawed at greatness, hedging his bets against an end that he'd always known could come at any time.

And if now was the time, and this was the end... well, what was left to say?

Sil looked over at Elim, wrapped up like a fish supper and already beginning to snore, and smiled in spite of everything. "Not bad for a day's work, eh?"

No, not exactly splendid – certainly not how Sil had imagined it – but not bad.

One...

CHAPTER FIFTEEN
A MAN OF THE A'KRAH

THE CHILD, AH Che, faded away again – a ghost twenty-four years departed.

The goddess, Ten-Maia, toppled back into the abyss of chemical sleep.

The man, Hakai, began the long climb back to the world.

AND AFTER ALL that, there was finally time to rest. Shea took her cue from the a'Krah, drawing the curtains on the morning and sleeping the day away. It was just a bit awkward, turning to the people who were practically still sifting through the rubble for their aunties and grandmothers and saying, *pardon me, but could I trouble you to draw me a bath?*

But the water was clean and wonderfully warm, at least to start with, and by the time it wasn't anymore, the sun was setting, and it was time to get back to work. U'ru was anxious to go, sad not to be following Yashu-Diiwa as he and his little death-friend made their way down the northern side of the mountain. But the a'Krah had Día, at least for the time being, and of course there was no leaving without her.

So as night fell and the great lady grew magnificent once more, Shea found other things for her to do.

They picked up the largest of the fallen pieces of Atali'Krah, first of all. They helped prepare for the mass funeral that would be held at dawn. Then they climbed down into the great sinkhole and lifted out bodies, a sad work unexpectedly lightened after Shea's blind fumbling found a missed survivor lying under a broken roof.

It was hard to guess how much U'ru remembered of the heinous violence she'd done to their elders in the years before. Certainly Shea had been horrified to hear of the Ara-Naure slaughter of the a'Krah delegation, of the hostages meticulously executed and profanely buried, one by one, in a futile attempt to win the return of her missing child. Regardless, it seemed appropriate now to be digging out their counterparts, lifting them out of the ground and giving them over to their surviving kin – readying them to enjoy their own preferred ending, the one that waited for them at the top of those sky-reaching wooden platforms above. Shea didn't pretend that this would singlehandedly atone for all that had happened before... but U'ru seemed happier for finally having a fence to mend.

And when that was done, the great lady very graciously walked down the mountain to help Shea finish her own mending.

It didn't take long to find Jeté. The body of a six-hundred-pound mereau prince was a hard thing to miss – even if the desiccating mountain air had reduced him to a gaunt husk of his former self. But Shea couldn't help but feel a little sad in spite of it all, having privately held out hope that the great fool would have come to his senses and quit while he still could.

Which wasn't to say that there was no-one left alive.

Shea felt it after she had waded in to help U'ru ease the body into the river, swimming far enough out to be sure that the course was deep enough to keep Jeté from catching on the rocks. She couldn't see worth a damn, even with the moon, but her water-sense told her of a kindred shape hiding in the shallows, not even a dozen yards downstream.

No, she realized with astonishment – she hadn't imagined it. One of the Many had survived.

"Hello?" she called out in Fraichais. "Who's there? Are you hurt?"

The answer was *yes*, albeit not spoken aloud: as the survivor swam tentatively closer, Shea sensed its arcing, lopsided rhythm, as conspicuously wrong as a sea-turtle missing a flipper.

What's wrong? U'ru stood there in the current, her great arms holding Jeté's dried body as if preparing to baptize an infant.

There was one left behind, Shea thought in answer – not wrong, per se, but a different kind of sad.

The two of them held still, waiting amidst the churning lap of the frigid moonlit water, until a plumed head broke the surface, and spoke in a small, quavering voice.

"... what happened?"

By now, the survivor would have seen the other bodies they had dragged to the river. It might even have been watching from afar. There was no need to tell it that the rest of its cohort was gone – but that didn't make it any easier to explain.

Shea glanced back at Jeté, half a dozen replies jostling for preference. He'd been run through, his life ended on the point of an earth-person's spear. He'd crawled out of the landslide that had consumed his siblings, and refused to return to the river. He'd decided vengeance was more important than survival.

"He made the wrong choice," she said at last. And then, after a suitably respectful silence: "Would you like to show me your wound? The great lady here can heal you."

That might or might not be true. But U'ru took that as her cue to make herself available: she set Jeté gently down in the water, and held out her arms to encourage her newest prospective puppy to swim to her.

The survivor held still, laboriously treading water. It made no move to pursue Jeté's body as it sank and began to tumble gracefully through the current, nor to come any closer to the Dog Lady.

If Shea were further downstream, she would surely have smelled the survivor's distress. If she were here during the day, she could have read its mournful, angry colors. Instead, its pain came through only in its voice.

"Why did you do this to us?"

That hurt. *It's not my fault*, Shea mentally protested – except for the parts that were. They'd kidnapped her. She'd manipulated them. They'd abandoned her. She'd caught up and lied to them. They'd used her to bait their trap. She'd used them to spoil it. Somehow or other, her need to bring back the Dog Lady and their wish to secure a courting-gift for their prince – two well-intentioned, poorly-pursued ends – had left the two of them here at this sad crossroads.

The least Shea could do was own that. "For her," she

said, gesturing up to the great lady behind her. "All of it was for her."

U'ru didn't move, but Shea could feel the corners of her mind crumpling. *Water-Dog...*

"You can come with us, if you want," Shea added. "We can bring you back to the Etascado, and the current will take you home."

The survivor was tiring, the river pushing it farther downstream. Its reply was labored and small, almost lost amidst the churn of the waves. "But what then? What will I say? What will I do?"

They were hard, bleak questions. Shea would have liked to tell that other mereau to count its blessings: after all, it still had its tail and toes and youth – its whole life ahead of it. It still had a house to go back to, a mother, other relations that would fold it back into the family and soothe its grief. It should take Shea up on her offer and go back, grateful that it still had somewhere to go back to.

But to return as the sole survivor of its cohort, what earth-persons would call an *only child*, bearing the news that the House of Losange had just lost an entire generation... oh, there was no wealth in the world that would have convinced Shea to trade places with this sad, maimed remainder.

"I'm sorry," she said at last. "I don't know."

She could feel U'ru longing to wade further in, vexed by that irrepressible mammalian urge to scoop the other mereau out of the water and press the sorrow right out of it. To her credit, she held still, her mind overflowing with stifled wants.

Say that for me too. Say that I'm sorry too.

Shea could do that much. And she did. But the current

kept running tirelessly on, widening the distance between her and her audience, and any answer Shea received was lost as the water's endless roar finally swallowed the last of the Many.

THE FIRST KNOCK startled Día.

For a strange, half-woken moment, she was at home – her first home, or at least the first one she could remember: the tiny one-room cabin she'd shared with her father, just outside the Sixes churchyard. It was still night outside – no good hour for anyone to be knocking at the door – which usually meant that someone had died. Her father would get up and shuffle on his shoes, leaving her to roll over and settle back in to the warm pocket his big body had left in the bed, enjoying the exquisitely human pleasure of sinking back into an unfinished sleep, and trusting that he would be back by morning.

No, her waking mind said. This was not their cabin, that was not her bed, and he was not coming back.

Now she was the adult, and that knock was hers to answer.

So Día reluctantly evicted herself from the warm folds of the blankets, shuddering as her bare feet touched the cold stone floor. She didn't fear the caller – the door had no lock, and anyone with ill will could have walked right in – but it was hard to imagine what anyone would want with her at this hour. "Just a moment," she said, pinching the dried sleep from the corners of her eyes, taking a bite of bread and a drink of water to freshen her mouth. Then, hygiene and beauty answered for, she opened the door.

And as it admitted a fresh yellow-orange wedge of lantern-light into the room, she was amazed at how thoroughly Penten had put Día's ten-second ablutions to shame. None of yesterday's dirt and dishevelment was any more in evidence – far from it. He – she, she – was now the very avatar of style, grace, and composure: her hair pulled back into a sleek, glossy blue-black braid, her strong features highlighted with perfectly geometric yellow and white marks, her smooth black skin and tall, athletic figure complemented by a white dress and a few light touches of silver. In short, she was a beauty, albeit one of a kind Día hadn't met before.

And the finishing touch was the soft white flash of a smile as she greeted her guest. "Ambassador, I'm terribly sorry to have disturbed your rest: I had meant to call on you later, but it seems we're to begin our funeral ceremonies earlier than I'd thought. Would you be willing to walk with me?"

Well, there was only one answer to that – even if Día didn't especially relish the idea of taking a stroll in the freezing dark. "Of course, Eldest – I'd be honored." It couldn't be any less pleasant than her last one, anyway.

But her thoughtful host had brought more than a lantern, and presented Día with some kind of brightly woven outer-garment – a fuller version of the *serape* Elim had worn, and one she was glad to fold herself into. Shoes would have been even better, but Día could at least warm her own feet.

"I wanted to apologize for the, eh – that unexpected sadness yesterday," Penten said as they made their way up the little path. "It wasn't something we wanted to happen, especially not in front of visitors. It must have been terribly distressing to watch."

Well, there was an understatement for the ages. Día dipped her head, struggling to shift back in to her role as a representative for the Azahi, and to offer assurances without endorsing the incident in question. "No, don't worry. I'm..." ... *sorry you had to resort to ritual murder? Sure you had a good reason for executing an innocent man?* Día longed to ask what had happened to Vuchak, prevented less by politeness than by her certainty that no answer would satisfy her. "... I'm aware that we were all working under exceptional circumstances." By heaven, it was too early for this.

But if her host was feeling at all guilty, Día would not let it go to waste. "I'm glad you mentioned it, though, because I did want to ask: how is Weisei? Will he receive visitors?"

Penten's discomfited expression said it all. "He is... he is resting. And your concern speaks highly of you – really, we are gratified by your compassion – but I'm afraid I can't arrange a meeting."

Día wasn't all that surprised – and yet *I can't arrange a meeting* was leagues distant from *he doesn't want to see anyone*. "I understand, and won't press you further," she said, preparing to do exactly that. "It's just that he was – he was tremendously kind to me when I was in dire need. It pains me to leave him in grief."

Penten stopped, and Día feared she had said too much.

But as Marhuk's broad-shouldered daughter looked around, to the small lights dotting the still-living parts of the city, and the distant chat and clamor of people at work, Día realized that she wasn't vexed: she was looking for privacy.

So she followed her off the road, walking aside to stand

under the nearest terrace wall: Día with hands clasped, Penten with arms folded. "Let me tell you something, ambassador. I know what you must be thinking. I'm sure our ways must look strange, even cruel. But I'm not going to try to explain them, because... well, because some things aren't made to be shared. Our business is ours, and our friends respect that."

In other words, *don't put your nose where it isn't wanted*. Día glanced down, duly chastised. "Of course. I'm –"

"Well, but wait. Let me tell you something else now – something not for ambassadors to know. Something made to be shared between Penten and Día." The other woman's gaze was roving, hunting for eavesdroppers in the dark. It returned to her with a calm, unblinking gravity. "Vuchak was not murdered. He was not executed. He stepped forward of his own will, in order to... to save Weisei's life, let's call it. That was a hard thing for both of them. Vuchak is safe now – his place is assured – but Weisei is in a dangerous position. He is angry and questioning and vulnerable. His wounded heart is beating on a knife's edge, and we don't know yet which way it might fall."

Which is exactly why I want to visit him, Día thought.

"Which is precisely why we can't let you visit him," Penten continued. "See yourself as we see you, Día. It's clear you have a noble soul and only the most selfless motives. But you don't know him, or us, or the ways given to us by our holy parent. And if you with your great and loving nature were to inadvertently sow a foreign seed in his mind, accidentally imprint one of your own god's truths onto him – if you were to cause Weisei to see what happened yesterday through YOUR eyes..."

She shook her head. "We can't risk contaminating his thoughts, or spoiling Vuchak's gift – and we would hate to let that noble soul of yours suffer a wound inflicted by your own good intentions."

Too late. Those last words were kindly meant, yet only galvanized Día's need to do *something*, anything to avoid just – just stepping over Weisei on her way out the door.

Anything to avoid being like Halfwick.

But Día understood, or at least better comprehended the scope of her ignorance. So she surrendered with a grateful bow of her head – and one last effort at securing a concession. "That's very kind of you. I understand. And if it wouldn't upset anything... could I perhaps leave a letter for him? For you to read and give to him later, if it seems prudent?"

Día hung everything on the *if* – the one that would ease her conscience, and hold Penten to no obligation. She didn't ask whether Weisei could read Marín.

Marhuk's daughter smiled in the lantern's warm glow – a nice gesture, albeit one that didn't reach her eyes. "That we can do. But please, try not to worry. He and I..." She frowned. "It's a hard path, but not one he has to walk alone. I promise I'll look after him."

Día would have expected a *we* just there – but the *I* was infinitely more reassuring.

"And speaking of the path – let's get back to it. There's a good place up ahead for seeing the sun rise."

Día followed her host's gesture back to the road, surprised at how the blue-violet glow in the east had already crept up on them. "Thank you," she said as they resumed their stroll. "I truly appreciate it. And if it's appropriate, please tell Winshin that I'm sorry too. About her son." About her everything, really.

Penten swallowed a grimace. "Try not to think too badly of her. Dulei was all she had left of her husband, and he in turn was all she had left after her sister was... well, there's no point in rehashing ancient history. Let it be enough to say that her service for the a'Krah has cost her dearly, and her life isn't what it should have been."

Not for the first time, Día wished there were a graceful second-tier version of *I understand* for moments like these – for the times when she wanted to convey the depth of her fellow-feeling, even though she would never, ever understand.

Not for the first time, it seemed a strange, cruel omission, that Ardish and Marín used *widow* to name a husbandless wife, and *orphan* to describe a parentless child, and yet had no word for a childless parent. How could anyone survive such an intolerable deprivation when there wasn't even a name for it? How could anyone else even try to grasp it?

Día wanted to ask if ei'Krah had a suitable word.

She wanted to ask whether Winshin had had any say in Dulei's going to Island Town.

She wanted someone to tell her that this was all for a reason, or at least not a waste.

Instead, she admired the scenery. "It's beautiful," she said, as by that time they had climbed to the top-level terrace, and it was light enough that she could look back behind them and see all of Atali'Krah.

And it was beautiful, even with all its fresh, traumatic irregularities. She could see now that there was a plan to the city, its terraces laid out like rich, living tiers of a wedding cake baked over a thousand generations. Yesterday, the collection of little wooden towers scattered amidst the ordinary buildings had seemed odd and pointless – poorly placed for defense, and too small for even a single watchman. Some were lit up now, and as Día noticed the arrangement of the lights, she realized that she recognized that pattern: that was the constellation Passer Austrinus – the Southern Sparrow, which was even now crowning the sky overhead.

Penten must have caught Día glancing from the earthly lights to the heavenly ones. She smiled. "It is. I was sad when I first came here, you know. Atali'Krah can feel small and stuffy sometimes, so dense and cluttered with history. But now it's hard to imagine living anywhere else."

Well, it had certainly been relieved of some of its history. Día couldn't begin to guess at the significance of the great stone disk, or the distinctions between the five burial towers, or the purpose of those great stone hands rising in supplication out of the earth... but all of them had been severely compromised, if not outright destroyed. "Were there very many people killed?" Día asked, regretting it as soon as she'd opened her mouth.

"Oh, no," Penten said, with a kind of ageless sigh. "Not many at all, in the greater order of things. Actually, though, that was what I was hoping to speak with you about."

Día stopped gawking at the city-lights, and hurried to remember her duty. "What's that?"

Penten paused to help her up a steep step – the first of many that seemed to wind around and behind the mountain's peak. "Well, ordinarily we would never ask an honored visitor to do our message-toting for us, but..." She smiled with some rueful humor. "Do you know, of the five a'Krah we have here from Island Town, two are dead, one has run away, another is comatose, and the last is... well, is Weisei. So if it wouldn't disagree with you, we were hoping to send you home with a message for the First Man of Island Town."

Oh, thank goodness. This was going to be so much simpler than she'd expected. "I'd be glad to," Día said, preparing herself to commit the next words to memory. This would probably be some intricate business about trade, or improving the roads, or –

"Ask him to be on the lookout for a woman of the Maia – one of childbearing age. We'll pay top price."

Día stumbled on the next step.

She hadn't heard that correctly. She hadn't.

"I'm sorry?" she said. "I don't – could you say that again?"

The Azahi would never deal in human beings. That had been his very first edict: from the day he'd taken office, there were to be no slaves in Island Town.

But Penten continued on ahead with a blithe wave of her hand. "Yes, I know it's an odd request – I'm not quite sure what the urgency is myself. But it's very important to Grandfather that we find one, and they're terribly scarce these days. Anything the First Man could do to secure one for us would be most appreciated."

Día had to answer. She had to open her mouth and make words come out, and save her private horror for later. "Yes," she said, though it sounded distant in her own ears. "I'll be sure to ask him about that."

Oh, would she ever.

But Día was a rotten liar, even when she was technically telling the truth, and whatever expression she wore was enough to stop Penten at her first backward glance.

"You didn't know," the bigger woman said. It was not a question.

Well, there was no use denying it. "No," Día said. "I don't – I can't believe he would do that."

Penten clasped her hands with a pained look. "Would it help if I told you that he doesn't personally oversee the business? We have our own people for that."

"No," Día said again, as pleasantly as if she'd been asked whether the seat next to her was taken. "Not even a little bit."

Penten pursed her lips, her handsome figure silhouetted against the graying northern sky. "You must think we're terrible barbarians."

No, of course not. That was the polite, correct thing to say. That was what the Azahi would say. *You've been wonderful hosts and valuable friends, and even though we do things differently, we have the utmost respect for your traditions.* That was what Día would have said last week, yesterday, even an hour ago.

But that was then, and this was now, and now found her standing on a frigid mountain path on the wrong side of dawn, having just been casually informed that the great golden moral compass of Island Town, the earthly authority in which Día had placed her absolute trust, was nothing more than a fence for human flesh.

And now there was no measure to use in deciding what the Azahi would do or say, no pretending that she was equipped to act on his behalf – no-one left to represent but herself.

"Well – well, yes, a bit!" Día said, throwing out her hands in a rude, spontaneous confession. "I – you know, I watched that woman open up Vuchak like a steer for slaughter, and I watched Winshin just – just brutalize Halfwick with that knife, and I watched YOU stand back and let it all happen, not lifting a finger except to be sure that Weisei couldn't reach his friend in time to help him, and now we're strolling along like the best of friends, even while half your city's wrecked and scores of your own people have been killed, and, and, and you're just standing here picking out a mail-order slave!"

Día stopped herself there, hearing the cracks in her voice and the thickness in her throat – but her eyes went on without her, lingering on those bone-laden wooden platforms. A blanket of crows had already descended in anticipation of the feast.

Penten said nothing, her face an indecipherable mask. She followed Día's attention to the sky-towers below, and then glanced over to the east.

There was a long, heavy silence, one that Día refused to break. She'd said her piece.

"You know," Penten said at last, "I'm sure you've seen plenty of sunrises before. Perhaps we should stop here." And she sat down on the spot.

Día had no idea how to interpret that – but it didn't take long to come to her senses. "I'm sorry," she said, feeling properly foolish as she stood there with steaming breath and burning ears. "That was coarse and uncalled-for. I shouldn't have said anything of the sort."

Penten didn't look at her. She just tipped her head, left and right – an a'Krah shrug – and kept her attention on the tiny lights down in the great valley below.

So they weren't speaking, then... and yet the interview wasn't over.

When Día could think of no graceful alternative, she sat down too.

It was miserably cold, and seemed appallingly pointless. She'd gotten the message from the a'Krah – the bizarre, sordid, vile message – and now there was nothing left to do but take the filthy thing back to Island Town and drop it at the Azahi's feet. Everything else was just posturing and formality, a thin, smiling pretense at papering over the moral abyss between them. Día should never have let herself be left behind yesterday. She should have admitted the truth straightaway – the Azahi had not sent her here, and she had no right to conduct any business on his behalf – and headed off with Elim and Halfwick.

God, there was a thought: even Halfwick looked nobler by comparison, now. He had never traded human beings under the table, at least not that Día knew of. More to the point, he had never presented himself as anything but what he was: a smarmy, boorish lout whose empathy didn't extend past his own nose. What did it say about the state of the world when a man like that could hold the moral high ground?

But the world, notoriously indifferent to human critique, kept right on turning. As it did, the sky lightened from black to violet to gray to blue, shrinking the darkness to just those long shadows that reached westward from the mountains – and then revealing the splendors within.

Día had never seen such a lush, green landscape. She had never imagined that such a color could still exist. And yet there it was, laid out in endless rolling riches beyond and below her: pine-furred mountains and neatly-cultivated fields, lapis-like river tributaries winding all around and through the hills and valleys and ageless rumpled peaks, their slopes all but glowing with orange-pink mineral luster. And strewn all through it, like delicate flecks of light-scattering quartz in raw green copper, were the marks of human beings: tiny lights along the riverbanks and between the fields, birthing delicate wisps of smoke into the cold, sweet mountain air.

It was a world apart – a vision of paradise opening up before a woman just then discovering that she had lived her entire life in a rain shadow.

And while Día marveled at the dawn spreading out over the horizon, Penten had apparently been watching the one lighting up her guest's face. By the time Día noticed and looked over, Marhuk's daughter was smiling. "You had me worried. I was beginning to think you'd never see it."

Well, Día would try to make up for lost time. Her night-blind eyes drank in the great vista all over again, helpless to comprehend the scope of it all. "How?" she said. "The drought, it's – how can anything live here?"

Penten shifted closer to her. "The Lightning Brothers brought the rain. They've scorned the earth ever since the Corn Woman died, their beds neglected by her grieving sisters. But the North Wind brings snow, and the Ripening Woman coaxes it to melt, and we build the dams and channels that carry it out for the earth to drink. You've endured so much of the deathly side of our domain. I thought you should also have a chance to see some of the life."

It was a thoughtful gesture, and salve for a dry soul.

Yet even here, amidst the wonder of a lush, pristine world, Día couldn't help but look down at the place where one of the burial platforms had crashed into its neighbor, its yellow-gray bones now spilled down the slope like a rancid raw egg dribbled down the front of an exquisite emerald dress. And even now, she could find nothing in those pretty trees and valleys that would explain or erase the carnage of the temple.

"I appreciate that," she said at last. "It's just... hard to see the connection between them. Hard to see how the one is anything but a detriment to the other."

Penten must have noticed the object of Día's attention. She nodded down to the bones below, and then to the crows gathering on the still-standing towers. "I know it must seem terribly uncivilized, to think of children of Marhuk eating each other. But the other way to see it is that we feed each other. We sustain the crows with what we leave behind. And they do likewise, as we take their shells and feathers and droppings yes, their dead, and use them to enrich the land that sustains us in turn."

That was a nice sentiment, but Día had never accused the a'Krah of practicing unsound ecology. She nodded.

"And it's true that – you know, I wonder sometimes about what we miss up here, with our bird's-eye view of the world." The a'Krah woman tipped her head again, watching the lights in the valley below disappear one by one. "We tend to take the long view, and when you're used to seeing things from high and far away... it's easy to miss the details. To not notice the people who fall through the cracks, or not miss them when they do."

Día looked over at Penten Marhuk, and wondered how much of her was Penten, and how much was Marhuk.

"But I hope – we try to make sure that everyone knows themselves to be a part of something bigger and greater, even though none of us can see the whole design. To be honest, I don't know why Grandfather allowed our calendar to fall and so many of our people to die, but I believe he made that choice deliberately, and in our own best interests. I don't know why he wants a woman of the Maia, either, but I trust that it's for a good purpose. Maybe I'll understand the grand design someday... but regardless, I plan on doing my best with my part of it." Penten glanced over at Día, unsmiling but earnest. "I'm glad it afforded me the chance to meet you."

And there at last was common ground firm enough to stand on. "Me too," Día said, warmly and without hesitation. "I'm just sorry the circumstances weren't better."

Penten nodded and smoothed the lap of her dress. "So am I. Hopefully your next visit will be a happier one."

Which implied that there would be a next visit, and perhaps that this one was nearing its end. Día groped for a polite way to ask. "Was there anything else I should take home with me?"

Penten smiled and rose smoothly to her feet. "Some of our chokecherry wine, I think, and as much honey-cake as I can persuade you to carry. I'll have it brought to you directly."

Día returned the smile and accepted her host's proffered hand. "Thank you," she said. "I'm sure the Dog Lady won't mind helping me bring them home. Have you seen her, by the way?" U'ru's mind had faded out of Día's awareness almost as soon as she was out of sight yesterday, but that was apparently an expected consequence of their presence here at the heart of another god's domain.

Penten's expression faltered as she helped Día to her feet. "Ah... I think she's already gone. I saw her walking down the eastern slope with her mereau friend a couple of hours ago. Were you waiting for her?"

Día had been sitting too long, or else stood up too quickly.

Mother Dog? Do you hear me?

No... of course not. How could that be a surprise?

U'ru would have gone after Elim again. He was her real 'puppy', the one whose first surfacing was reason enough to leave Día to drown. And as for Miss du Chenne... well, she'd walked off twelve years ago, and Día was more than old enough to know never to count on that terrible old witch for anything.

"No," she said, countering the sickening lightness of her bare head with a hand on the wall. "No, I suppose not. But if you could... if you would be so kind as to direct me, on how best to get back to Island Town..."

... *because I seem to have been stranded out here.*

That must have been written all over her face. Certainly it was reflected in Penten's eyes. "Of course," Marhuk's daughter said. "We'll get you a horse and supplies – everything you need."

"Thank you," Día said, bringing her entire short lifetime's worth of social conditioning to bear as she formed each word. "I'm so much in your debt."

And all philosophical differences aside, she did owe Penten considerably: for her kindness and patience, her compassion and professionalism, and now, apparently, for an expensive array of parting gifts as well. But Día was most profoundly grateful for the way Marhuk's daughter neglected to let go of her hand as the two of them started back down the path... not because she feared a fall, but because her next dizzy glance down at the sprawling verdant valley below assured Día that she no longer had mass enough to hit the ground.

OREKUT CHEATED AT dice. This was known.

And Sakat would have done well to remember that last night. But as the saying went, every backward glance was a mirror – and now it was too late. Sakat had lost the bet, and so he was going to have to do the dirty work.

And oh, was it ever.

He could smell it as he made his way down the hall – a sour bouquet of body odor and fermented cherry vomit that only grew stronger as he approached the door at the end of the corridor.

Still, the quiet was unnerving. There was no weeping now, no screaming or sobbing or stupefied alcoholic snoring – an eerie silence that prickled Sakat's neck-hairs as he approached.

What if the disgraced wastrel had actually done it? What if he'd decided to redeem himself by following his *atodak* in feeding the crows?

Probably for the best. A waste, to be sure, but not much of one.

Still, it took Sakat a moment to steady himself, mentally preparing for whatever he might find as he took a last silent footstep and peered through the half-open door.

But no, there was no body on the floor, none hanging from the beams. There was only that same swaying drunkard standing there on the far side of the room, his back to the door, a bowl of water on the table – and a knife in his hand.

Sakat swallowed. This was a more difficult thing. He couldn't stand here and watch like an eavesdropping woman while a child of Marhuk emptied his veins... and yet he didn't relish the idea of disturbing a wine-soaked madman with a weapon.

But even as Sakat stared, the prince's free hand gathered up the long unwashed tangles of his hair, holding them in a fist at the back of his neck. He pulled his hair tight, making a taut, greasy black ribbon. He held the knife against it, as one would press a blade against a hostage's throat.

Sakat swallowed, transfixed. A man might lose his plaits if he were defeated in war, and an enemy cut them away for trophies, or if he were convicted of treason and cast out – permanently unrecognized. But no sane man would willingly take a knife to his own hair. He might as well be saying he wasn't a'Krah.

The prince stood, swaying, looking down into his reflection in the water-bowl, his body tensing with intoxicated resolve.

Then, with a furious, frustrated cry, he hurled the knife away with such force that he lost his balance and toppled to the floor, the thud of his body punctuated by the discarded clatter of the blade. He groped on all fours, weeping like a day-old widow, pawing through the gourds and bottles littering the floor until he found one with some substance left, and tipped it straight up to stopper his mouth, stanching his hysterical grief for the length of five frantic swallows.

Sakat let out his breath. Back to business as usual, then.

So he announced himself with a loud shuffling of his feet, and turned his wrists out into the *ashet* as he entered the disgusting room. Best to get this over with.

"Pardon me, *marka*," he said, careful to skim the contempt from his voice. "I'm sorry for disturbing you. Our reverend To'taka Marhuk sent me with a message."

The prince turned with a slow, clumsy effort, struggling to prop himself up on one hand as he met Sakat's gaze in a sickly, dull-eyed stupor.

When it seemed there would not be a reply, Sakat

continued. "He says that Dulei's *atodak* has taken the craven path, and fled to exile. He says that he has decided to make this an opportunity for you. He says that if you care to find Echep, and if he will serve you, his death-obligation will be excused. He may continue to live in honor, as your own *atodak*." *As one selfish coward in service to another.*

The prince stared at Sakat in silence for a long moment: his stained shirt shifting with every heavy breath, his lip quivering over a dribble of wine, his eyes bright with glazed, glittering hate.

Then he pitched forward and began to retch.

Sakat flinched, scarcely able to conceal his revulsion as he stood there in the wasted remains of a room more splendid than any his family would ever know. Priceless plush rugs stained red with drink, and now filling with streams of hot vomit. A luxurious bed of down feathers and master-woven wool, now a piss-reeking rumpled heap. Broken crockery, spilled wine, spoiled food and ruined clothes – a festering midden of luxuries mindlessly swallowed and then joylessly disgorged.

Sakat stayed long enough to see that the prince did not choke or black out. He stayed longer than that, even – until the prince resumed his hands-and-knees hunt for liquid solace, having either forgotten about Sakat or elected to ignore him.

When it was clear that there would be no answer, Sakat made the *asket* again. "It will be as you have said, *marka*." Then he excused himself, all too glad to leave the spoiled, crying child crawling in squalor through a mess of his own making.

*   *   *

DÍA WOULD BE fine. Everything would be fine. She was by herself, a hundred miles from home, and barely knew how to sit a horse, but she would be all right... somehow.

It wasn't so hot now, for one thing, and she would take something to shield her from the sun. Even if the horse ran off, she could still walk home, as long as she had enough food and water.

Even with the drought.

Even despite the thieves, and those monstrous things she'd stopped with the fire, and whoever had sunk those corpses in the oasis at Yaga Chini.

No, she'd just... well, she would just take it one step at a time, that was all. She would just put one foot in front of the other until she was all the way back in her *papá*'s arms.

Yes, that was it. Día forced away all thought of Halfwick and Weisei and the Azahi, pushed aside her doubts, and aligned the needle of her moral compass with Fours. He loved her. He was missing her. He would be desperately worried about her, and no-one here could say anything to the contrary. She had cleared away all the rest of her obligations, and now her only task was to return safely to him.

By the time the knock came, Día was ready to go. She answered the door with questions prepared for Penten or whoever she'd sent in her place, ready to secure everything she would need to have or know or do to help herself make it home alive.

She was not prepared for Winshin Marhuk.

The a'Krah woman might have been drinking. She had certainly been crying. But compared to yesterday, she was a marvel of composure: her hair neatly braided, her makeup fresh and unspoiled, her sharp features innocent of everything but sincerity as she gathered her outer-robe in her hands – and curtseyed.

"Ambassador. Forgive me for disturbing you – I heard you were leaving soon, and I wanted to come by to apologize."

Día could not have been more astonished if a cougar had rubbed up against her legs and mewed. "Oh, you don't... really, that's not necessary," she said, struggling to gather her wits. Had Penten put her up to this?

If she had, Winshin didn't let on. She dipped her head in polite disagreement. "No, it is. Yesterday was – it was one of the worst days of my life, and I would hate for that to be your only impression of me. I'm so sorry."

Her Marín was as smooth as her youthful features, and Día had to remind herself that she was speaking with a woman old enough to have an adult son – old enough to have fought in wars that had ended before Día was even born, and perhaps to have negotiated a peace or two.

Día would try to keep up. "So am I," she said, and had no trouble meaning it. "About your son, I mean. I see how much you love him."

Winshin glanced down, but not before Día saw the fresh well of pain in her reddened eyes. "Thank you," she said, her voice just a little thicker. "It's... he was my only one."

And what was Día doing, keeping a grieving mother standing here at the door? She ought to invite her in, give the poor woman some relief... even if she was the same person who had made a bloody applesauce of Halfwick's torso yesterday. Día glanced down, noticing how Winshin's hands were hidden in her over-robe. "I can't imagine how much you must miss him," she said, racked and stalling with indecision.

Marhuk's daughter looked up. "Do you have any children?"

Día flushed. "Oh, no. I'm – I've sworn myself to chastity." Hang it all, this was no conversation for an open door. "Wouldn't you like to come in?" She stepped aside, acutely aware that she had just invited the other woman across the literal threshold.

Winshin followed her in, though there wasn't really anywhere to sit, or room for comfortable conversation: just the table and the cold fire-pit and the plush pile of bedding on the floor. Was it appropriate to offer that as a seat? Would Día look hopelessly vulgar if she tried?

"Chastity? That's very selfless of you," Winshin said, her tired eyes innocent of suggestion. "But why would you do that?"

Out. Definitely should have invited her out. Día clasped her hands awkwardly, squelching the urge to tug on dreadlocks she didn't have. "Well, so that I may better serve my god. As a grave bride, I –"

Winshin made a peculiar clucking noise. "Oh! I'm sorry – I wasn't clear. I do understand your occupation. What I mean is, why would your god want *you*?"

Día froze.

She searched Winshin's face for maliciousness, any hint of understanding for what an appallingly tasteless question that was. But the a'Krah woman's expression wore nothing but a look of the most serious inquiry, as if Día were some sort of newly-discovered paradox. And it would not do to accuse a daughter of Marhuk of deliberate insult – not when Día was a lone foreigner among the a'Krah, begging charity enough to get home with.

"... why wouldn't he?"

Winshin lifted her eyebrows in surprise. "Why, for

the same reason He wouldn't want me either. We are marked as inferior."

Oh, thank goodness. Día had heard that one before. "Actually, that's not quite accurate. The word *maculata* doesn't refer to dark skin – it simply means something impure. So the people of Tam Shen –"

"Yes," Winshin said, the very portrait of a serious student, "but I wasn't referring to Tam Shen. As you know, the Curse of Misraim condemned his children to wander the desert as 'servants of servants', and the sun blackened them –"

"But that was a curse laid by his father, not by God," Día gently interjected, "which means it can last no more than seven generations." Even if people had been using it to justify making slaves of the Afriti for far longer.

Winshin frowned. "Then how do you account for the Blood Prohibition?"

Día blinked. "I'm sorry?"

The a'Krah woman cast her gaze up to the low stone ceiling, as if bringing the words down from the attic of her memory. "'Defile no holy office with the slave woman's son, nor any of his issue: no, not for a score of a score of generations; a single drop of bonded blood bars him.' –That's the Third Order of Meniah, but I'd have to look up the verse."

Día had never heard of Meniah. That sounded like something from the Lex Rubia – a part of the Verses she didn't have. She swallowed, loathe to admit the extent of her ignorance, especially in her present company. "Your command of the scriptures is impressive," she said. "Where did you study them?"

Winshin eyed her, but did not remark on this convenient shift of subject. "Marhuk tasks us to learn the ways of our enemies," she said. "I spent my youth studying your god's word, so that I would understand how to destroy him. But since we aren't enemies anymore, I have no more need of this –"

She stepped forward, her hands moving under her robe, and Día instinctively flinched back –

– as Winshin withdrew a beautifully bound gold-edged book.

But one look at her face promised that Día's recoil had not gone unnoticed, and the a'Krah woman's expression cooled on the spot.

"I'm sorry," Día said. "You just startled me. I didn't –"

Winshin tossed the book on the bed, reached into her robe again, and brought out her knife. "Was this what you expected?"

Día's eyes darted from the blade to the book, frantic to excuse herself. "Oh, certainly not. Is that a copy of the Verses? It's beautiful."

"It's yours," Winshin said, her voice dead of warmth.

"I couldn't possibly," Día said, not least because she'd just managed to insult the giver. "It's far too dear, and I don't have anything to give you in return."

"Oh, I'm sure you do," Winshin said, tossing the knife in her hand, watching the glint of the metal as it spun, catching it expertly each time.

Día would not let herself cringe again – but she wouldn't ignore the weapon either. She swallowed. "I'm sure I can find something. Could you – would you mind putting that away?"

Winshin's gaze slid back over to Día's face. She caught the knife, the hilt meeting her hand with a solid *thap*, and did not toss it again. "Why, ambassador, what do you have to fear from me?"

"Nothing," Día hurried to assure her. "Nothing, of course, but if it accidentally slipped –"

Winshin folded her arms, fixing Día with a heavy-lidded stare. "'Fear not the sword nor the lash nor the arrows of the infidel, for nothing may touch you who walk under the grace of heaven.'"

Día knew the verse. And now she understood the game. Winshin meant to slip that knife between Día and her devotion, prise her out from her professions of faith like a thief working a jewel out of a monument's eye.

Well, let her try. Día's lips pressed to a hard line; she lifted her chin and straightened, her bare feet warming the floor. "'Look fast to your weapons, faithful men of God, and pray no help until you have exhausted your own right arm.'"

Some of yesterday's anger rekindled in Winshin's eyes; she took a step forward, the knife bright at her side. "'Hypocrites, pretenders, affectors of piety, martyrs in word and liars in deed – quit My sight, ye cursed; I turn my face away.'"

"I am no hypocrite!" Día cried. "I am a faithful servant of God!"

And Winshin smirked. "A pity, then, that your great faith didn't encompass the reading of your own holy book. I made up that last verse."

Día took a step back, the hem of her cassock brushing the wall behind her, her face burning in anger and shame. "A blessing, then, that your son didn't live to see his mother's capacity for wickedness."

That hit home. Winshin's eyes widened; her jaw tensed. "And what do you know of my wickedness?" she hissed, pressing forward, brandishing the knife, forcing Día to the corner.

But Día would not give her the satisfaction of seeing her fear. She stuffed it all down in her stomach, keeping her gaze on the other woman's face and her voice steady with the weight of conviction. "Only that you will be called to answer for it."

"Will I!" Winshin barked. "And will you be rewarded for your righteousness? If I drive this knife into your gut right now, will God restore you, as he restored the Northman boy?"

No. Día felt it. She knew it. She might be saved – but she would have no miracle.

Winshin smelled her weakness like blood from a gut-shot deer, and closed in for the kill. "Or could it be that you're just a deluded little girl playing dress-up – that you've lived your whole life in ignorance – that all your devotions and pieties matter *nothing* to a god who has saved his favorites and left you here to live or die or crawl back to your church and spend the next fifty years trying to seduce him with your shrivelling virgin cunt!"

"No," Día said, aloud this time – but it was a weak, wavering word. *Come get me, Mother Dog, please come get me –*

"No?" Winshin repeated. "How do you know that? Did God tell you so? Did he speak with you personally? Is he any more real to you than this knife?"

Día's first instinctive glance at the blade betrayed her.

"Then scream for help," Winshin said, "and let that be your gift to me. Scream, and confess that the god of the Northmen loves only the Northmen. Scream, and admit that he holds your dark face and mine equally in contempt. Scream, and let me hear that *you are afraid of me.*"

Día was afraid. She was absolutely terrified of the mad, wicked woman before her, and even as faith told her what became of those who renounced God's name, reason assured her that this was not going to be like Halfwick lurching at her in a clumsy rage: Winshin was a veteran warrior with a deadly weapon, and any fight she started here would end in one second, with that blade somewhere in Día's body.

And Fours was waiting.

Día swallowed, took a breath, and opened her mouth. "I –"

"Please your pardon, ambassador," said a soft, thickly accented voice at the door. Winshin whirled, affording Día a view of a small, hooded a'Krah man standing there, offering his wrists out in the traditional bow. "For you I have a message."

In the time it took Día to blink, Winshin made her manners, the knife disappearing in a single courteous flourish. "Well, I've taken up too much of your time already. Thank you for a lovely discussion, ambassador – do have a safe trip home." There was nothing but pleasantness in her face as she turned and walked out, leaving Día no room for doubt: Winshin had finally taken her pound of flesh.

Which left Día, standing there in the corner like an unruly schoolgirl, and the a'Krah man at the door, who was even now straightening to regard her with a mischievous gleam in his dark eyes, his hood falling back to reveal his baldness – and his dark skin brightening to a pale blue-white.

Día stood there, helpless to understand. "... Miss du Chenne? What are you doing here?"

The old mereau answered with a sharp-toothed

grin – which just as quickly turned to a scold at this most obvious question. "Why, coming to get you, you ungrateful ninny! What, did you think I was just going to keep wandering about naked in broad daylight? Now collect your things and let's be on our way – U'ru is waiting."

Día didn't move. She didn't need to. The world was already swaying under her feet.

"Día?" Miss du Chenne's voice took on a note of concern – a single deadly pinprick of compassion. "What's wrong?"

Nothing, Día said. It started as a word, emerged as a moan, and ended with a cry – with Día buckling, covering her face, and sobbing helplessly into her hands.

"Well, I never!" said the oncoming patter of footsteps, punctuated with a damp hand at her arm. "What happened to you, girl? What's the matter? Did you think we'd left without you? Come here, come down here this instant – you have the Sibyl's nerve, crying where I can't reach you..."

But although Día folded herself down to sit with her old teacher, weeping freely into her lap, she had no answer – no name for the thing that had burst inside her, skewering her insides on a hundred thousand mirror-glass shards.

IRABEI WAS GOING to miss her doll.

She was getting to too old for it, she told herself. It was time to start thinking of other things – of the work proper for the young maiden she already was, and the bride she would someday be.

But it was impossible not to be sad as she stood

there in the giving-line, clutching Blueberry Lady in her anxious, sweaty hands. She hurried to memorize the soft beaded contours of that little woolen dress, the crinkle of the corn-husk body underneath, the slightly blurry blueberry-juice smile that Father had painted and repainted over the years. As the line moved forward, she frantically savored the little burned spot on the doll's foot, where Irabei had once left her too close to the fire, and the cherry stain that had never quite come out of the back of her skirt, and the indentations of tiny toothmarks on her head, from when Irabei had teethed on her.

But it was still her turn far too soon. Irabei kept her posture straight and her face serious, striving to appear composed and mature as she followed her mother's example: walking forward with solemn purpose, repeating the sacred words of gratitude, and setting her doll into the growing pile of gifts in the pit before the dead man.

He was naked, of course, sitting cross-legged in a great pile of wildflowers – violet harebells, scarlet paintbrushes, and white nodding onions. He had been positioned to lay forward over his lap, his freshly-washed, brushed hair flowing freely down his back, still kinked from having been plaited. He had his arms out and upturned in the *ashet*, and as she caught side of the twin slashes across his wrists, one cutting through the mark of the *atodak* to show the end of his service, Irabei was at once fascinated and frightened – and glad she couldn't see his face.

It was still hard to leave Blueberry Lady there with the body of a stranger. But Irabei understood that this was a different, more special kind of funeral. The man had willingly given up his life in service to the a'Krah people – and so each of the people would give up something for him.

She tried to keep her mind on that as she filed past him and took a seat with her family on the grass beyond. Later there would be a great feast, with dancing and smoking and gossip. For now, everyone was silent, save for the repeating of the ritual words, and the occasional shriek and babble of the babies.

So as the air cooled and the sun set, Irabei watched the gift-pit fill with offerings from the twin streams of people filing past the body: tools and weapons and intricate carvings from the men's line; pottery and clothing and beautiful jewelry from the women's. The lines crossed just once, when Yeh'ne and Suitak met before the dead man. Her face was haggard and swollen from crying, but she betrayed no other feeling as she traded her new baby for her husband's knife, cut off her hair with one sharp sawing motion – Irabei gasped to see it – and tossed her braid into the hole. Then she cut a tiny lock of the baby's hair and bent to set it in the dead man's open hand. Suitak threw in the knife, returned his cradleboarded child to her mother, and then the three of them went into the crowd together.

Irabei had heard that the dead man was Yeh'ne's brother. She knew for a fact that their family's house had been eaten by the sinkhole. And although none of the adults seemed to have a straight answer, the story circulating among the children of Atali'Krah was that the man had died fighting the giant horse-monster who had come to wreck the city. Irabei's one glimpse of that terrible creature had been more than enough to convince her that the *atodak* had earned his hero's funeral.

So she inwardly thanked him for his service, and tried not to think about Blueberry Lady as To'taka Marhuk came forward to light the fire.

There would be talk about that tonight. A shame that a man had died so selflessly, and so young – a travesty that his own *marka* did not even attend his funeral. As the people rose to their feet, a single sideways glance at Yeh'ne's frozen, hollow stare told Irabei everything she needed to know.

There wasn't much she could do about that. But as the fire kindled to life, and the people began to sing the grieving song, she clutched her mother's hand, and tried to make up for it by adding her voice as tuneful and beautifully as she could.

In the springtime of happiness, you were with us
In the summer of toil, you were with us
In the autumn of plenty, you were with us
In the winter of grief, you left us

The twilight air soon filled with sweet pine smoke as fire spread through the stacked wood under the gifts, the heat making a shimmering mirage of the great stone Giving Hands beyond. They had been damaged in the earthquake – two of the fingertips had broken away, and there was a crack running up through the left wrist. But the Eldest had inspected and declared it still sound in spite of that, and now – for the first time since Irabei's family had been called to Atali'Krah – the ancient supplicating hands would lift up an offering.

In the springtime of your memory, we honor you
In the summer of your house, we sustain you
In the autumn of your people, we follow you
In the winter of the world, we will join you

The fire leapt up brighter, making odd smells as it

began to eat the gifts, and Irabei's eyes watered as much from the smoke as from the thought of her doll burning up.

But then there was a disturbance, a parting of the assembly as someone new came forward. Irabei stretched and ducked, trying to see between the forest of arms and bodies, even as discordant whispers snuck through the air behind her.

"Who is that?"

"Surely it's not –"

"He wouldn't dare."

Irabei didn't recognize the new man, or have any idea how he could be so brazen. He wasn't one of the Marhuka, because he wore no holy cloak, and he wasn't one of the people, because he'd brought no gift, and he wasn't the dead man's missing *marka*, because that disgraceful truant was a child, and Irabei understood at her first glimpse that the person striding towards To'taka Marhuk was a man.

Not a very splendid one, to be sure. He was terribly frail, almost gaunt, and looked as if he hadn't slept in a week. His clothes were rumpled and ill-fitting, and his plaits hung unevenly at his shoulders, as clumsy and lopsided as if he'd never braided his own hair before. But he moved with sober, single-minded purpose towards To'taka, leaving a ten-foot-wide swath of parted people behind him, their wary eyes meeting each other as the song faltered.

The man made the *ashet*. The fire burned brighter.

He spoke words that Irabei couldn't hear. The parted people hesitated.

Then To'taka bowed to him, and stepped aside to let the new man lead the song.

Irabei had no idea what had just happened. She couldn't begin to understand it. But one look at Yeh'ne's solemn, uplifted face dissipated her doubts, and she was relieved to see the parted people close back in together, assuring the new man's place among them as they sang with renewed vigor and harmony.

We will be with you as you leave us
We will be with you as you go
We will be with you as the nights grow long and lonely
We will keep you always with us

And as the new man held out his arms to harness the song, the power of the assembly flowed through him, shaped and wrought and focused to a single noble purpose. The body of the *atodak* rose gracefully, walked through the shimmering sacred smoke, and climbed up to rest in the great stone cradle of the Giving Hands – a hero of the a'Krah raised up in honor by the united, undying gratitude of his people.

CHAPTER SIXTEEN
THE LONG WAY HOME

SOMETHING WAS SHOVING Elim's shoulder.

"... UP, I said..."

And kicking his ribs.

"... you son of a..."

And slapping his face.

"... god damn you, if you don't..."

And when he felt his head drop back down, his eyes snapped open all on their own – just in time to show him a livid, absolutely furious Sil Halfwick readying another strike.

"– you whoreson obstinate son of a bitch, GET UP!"

Elim's first flinch jerked him the rest of the way into wakefulness – into a world of curses and beatings and confusion and such a deep god-awful malaise that he could just as easily have been back in Fours' barn again, ruinously hung over and freshly made a murderer.

But he was here, lying on the ground at the root of a mountain in broad daylight, frantically mustering up the wherewithal to stave off the next blow. "Going," he grunted, his voice as thick as winter mud. "I'm going – just wait a tick..."

"Good," came the acid reply. "Then you'll have no difficulty catching up." Sil rose and left without so much as a backwards glance, his boot-heels rapping a receding tattoo as he stalked off down the rocky trail and disappeared.

Which left Elim to push himself blearily up to a sit there in the middle of a pleasant mountain morning, the sun shining, the birds singing as he rubbed the sleep out of his eyes and wondered what the hell had just happened.

UNFORTUNATELY, HE GOT no closer to finding out. Sil just kept on like that, walking a quarter or a half or even a whole mile ahead, and he didn't stop for anything.

Which left Elim limping on behind, doing his bare-footed best to keep up. He followed along all that day as the foothills leveled back out into miles of rolling, scrubby red-brown earth. He followed across the bridge that spanned the great river, its endless gray-green rush trapping a fishman's bloated body in the hollow of a rocky spit. He followed down the wide, broken highway, marveling at how the vast fire-blackened wastelands to the south were already sprouting with tiny green shoots of new life.

Elim would have liked to stop and see more of that. He would have liked to try and find the remains of their wagon, or the dug-out little ditch where he and the Sundowners had survived the night by the toasted skin of their teeth. He would have liked to pause there and picnic with someone, just sit back and savor the new hints of greenness together.

But his native friends were all gone – dead or sick or just plain wrecked – and as for Sil...

Elim had no idea what had happened to the kindly fellow who had helped him down from the mountain yesterday, or even to the garden-variety irritable one he'd traveled with on the way out from Hell's Acre. All he could think of was what he'd said on that last morning they'd spent together – about how the two of them were cursed men, and nothing was going to get better for either of them until they hiked up that mountain and dealt with it.

Elim thought he had gotten clear of his curse. Maybe Sil was still working on his.

He would have asked about that, if the sour-faced son of a bitch would slow down long enough to let him. As it was, all Elim could do was try not to let the distance between them get any wider – and when it was getting dark and he couldn't keep up any more, Elim hollered ahead at his partner one last time.

"Sil, you bastard – stop! Just stop, will you!"

But he was so far ahead – hardly more than a black blot on the darkening horizon – that Elim couldn't tell if he'd even heard, never mind listened.

Not that he could do anything about it, regardless. After days of pushing himself past his limits and smashing through all manner of new ones, Elim was spent, wrung out – just hopelessly stove in. His last act was to walk a little ways off the road, flop down, and pass out in the dim hope that tomorrow wouldn't find him waking up alone.

PROGRESS WAS SLOW, to say the least.

U'ru could only carry them at night, and Hakai couldn't sit a horse, nevermind walk, and Shea had to rest in water.

But as they came down the mountain, Shea was glad to see that the last of the Many – Bombé, as it turned out – had decided that yes, in spite of everything, it wanted to go home. And U'ru, who was never so happy as when she had her arms full of babies, was perfectly delighted to add one more puppy to her pile.

So they took the long way back to Island Town, following the All-Year River north and then east to Limestone Lake, where Shea was irrationally disappointed not to find any trace of Henry Bon. As one-night stands went, he had been a good one.

But after they made it across the great dry stretch from Limestone Lake to the Calentito River, and sent Bombé off to start the long swim home, Shea and U'ru were left with just their two human charges, neither of whom were much for company. Hakai was coming back an inch at a time, and all Día wanted to do was sleep.

So the mother and the mereau sat together by the riverbank as the sunset made warm, bright ripples in the current, watching their fosterlings enjoy a few last restful minutes before it was time to move again.

Don't fret, Water-Dog. She will feel better.

To Shea's unfocused eyes, Día was a black shape on the ground, curling around Hakai's muddy gray-brown. Like a weanling puppy with a hot water bottle, his peculiar sleep-terrors seemed to abate when he had someone else lying beside him – a comfort that Día had been glad to provide.

Of course, Shea answered. She hadn't been able to get much out of Día herself, as every question yielded the same complaint: she was just tired, and wanted to go home. But U'ru had raised enough children to know a distressed worldview when she felt it. This had been

Día's first time leaving the nest, and if it had been more difficult than most... well, she was cloistered to begin with, and had probably seen more of the world in the past week than in all her nineteen years combined. It would have been a hard coming-of-age for anyone.

But you're still sad, U'ru said. It was neither a question nor an accusation.

Shea glanced over at the Dog Lady's soft features, and made no effort to deny it.

Of course she was sad. Sad to see Día so distressed, no matter how inevitable it was. Sad to know that Fours wouldn't get his daughter back, at least not as she'd been before. More than anything, Shea was sorry that she couldn't give her any real help or comfort – that she not only didn't have the girl's trust, but didn't even know her well enough to understand what had gone so wrong.

I'm sorry about Yashu-Diiwa, Shea thought – just in case that hadn't already been said. *If it makes you feel any better, I've made plenty of other mistakes since then.*

Some were reasonable, even inevitable. After Mille-Feuille's suicide, Shea had been anxious not to let anything happen to Fours – to do whatever it took not to become the last surviving mereau in Sixes. And after the two of them had helped to sabotage the town, digging that tunnel down through to the river, sneaking the gates open to let the invaders in... well, Shea had told herself that they were only following orders – that they were helping to right a wrong by returning the island to the Sundowners, from whom it had been stolen in the first place. But the work had withered something in Fours. And after that last, violent night of the siege, he had been so taken with the Afriti child he found in the ruined church, so animated by a vigor and passion that Shea hadn't seen from him in years, that she had gone along with it. She was afraid of what would happen if they took the girl – but in the end, she had been more afraid of what would happen if Fours gave up... if Shea were left alone.

So their slapdash little family had been born of bad circumstances and worse decisions – only one of which Shea really regretted.

I wish I hadn't tried, she said. *I would have hurt her less if I had never even tried.*

U'ru's plump, ageless face softened; she wore the expression that would accompany a dog's whine. *I think you would hate yourself more if you hadn't.*

She wadded her furry robe in her lap, her hands ever anxious to hold some small, soft, delicate thing, and looked down at it. *I think I tried too hard, or not in the right way. And I know things would be different, if we had chosen differently.* She glanced over at Día. *But they're still here, alive and in the world, and so are we. We can choose new things, and so can they.*

Shea heard the hope blossoming behind that, and shied away from it. She nodded at Hakai. *What about him? What did he choose?*

U'ru frowned. *I don't know. Ten-Maia was confused and hurting, but she didn't seem angry. Whatever he did, I don't think he did it wickedly. I don't think he even knows she's there.*

Well, he certainly couldn't have failed to notice her death. Even Shea had heard how quick and completely the Maia had collapsed after that – their lands plundered, their people killed, enslaved, or dispersed. She hoped for Hakai's sake that he hadn't been at fault, or hadn't known it if he was. The guilt would have been crushing.

Regardless, he was paying for it now. Marhuk had given him to U'ru's keeping, trusting her healing arts to keep him alive – and perhaps trusting him to keep her safely occupied. That was a shrewd maneuver. But while U'ru's diminished power worked well enough on fresh wounds, most of Hakai's had been left to fester for days. She had mended his leg, but there was no telling whether he would get any use out of it. The *tarré* had put Ten-Maia back to sleep, but there was no telling how much she'd left of her human host.

Or whether she could be born back into the world.

Or whether that would bring back the rains.

Shea stood and popped her back in the red light of sunset, eager to get in one last soak before night fell and it was time to move again. *Well, he's in the right place now.*

Yes, came the warm, answering certainty. *Now all we need is Loves-Me.*

Shea didn't answer. She didn't stop walking, either. She kept her worry and her pessimism to herself, and submerged them in the salty-coppery depths of the Etascado. And when she'd sunk all the way down to the slow, murky bottom, she gave the river a private message to carry on ahead: after fifty years, the Dog Lady was finally returning to Island Town – and if her son ever wanted to return to his old life, he'd better not be there when she did.

AND THAT WAS the pattern. The next morning, Elim was kicked awake just after dawn, and spent the day trailing after his silent, tireless ass of a partner. It was the same the day after that.

And maybe it would have been the same the day after that, too. Elim was halfway to finding out when he was awakened in the middle of the night by a gunshot.

Even then, with a lead-busting blast cracking the air overhead, it was his body that woke up first. By the time his brain pulled itself out of that deep, exhausted black pit, it found the rest of him climbing automatically to his feet, too stupid even for fear.

"Elim, get DOWN!" Sil barked.

It was dark. Galloping hooves were bearing down on them, accompanied a horrendous foul smell. And Sil – God almighty, Sil was charging right at the oncoming strangers, hollering bloody murder and... was he throwing a *rock*?

"Bugger off!" he cried, his voice wet and ugly. "We don't have –"

More gunfire, and by now the moonlight and Elim's eyes understood each other well enough to see the riders bearing down on Sil, who waded right on in to a hail of gunfire, staggering as every successive round plowed into him.

But of course, it was going to take more than a bullet to shut him up. "– anything for you, and even if we did you wouldn't have it, so take your guns and GET FUCKED!"

And by now the three riders were on top of him, and Sil didn't care a lick about that either: he grabbed one man by the leg and yanked as he rode past, pulling him halfway out of the saddle – and leaving Sil right in the path of the next oncoming stranger.

"Sil, look out!" Elim hollered, rising up in spite of all

better advice, watching in helpless horror as the horse crashed into Sil, the rider cried out in untranslatable surprise, and all three went down in a tangled half-ton heap.

Which left one rider struggling to right himself in the saddle, and the other coming straight at Elim, shouting in a language he couldn't recognize.

But the whinny undercutting it was instantly, perfectly clear.

Elim halted dead on the spot, dropping his fear in one incredulous hot second. "You son of a bitch, that's MY HORSE!"

And in spite of the darkness and confusion and the very real possibility that somebody here still had a round chambered, Elim moved with perfect grace: he took a step to the left, pulled back his fist, and delivered a ball-busting gelding punch to the rider's groin.

It finished beautifully as Molly Boone reared up – a great brown beauty pawing moonlight beside him – and dumped the hapless saddle-tramp straight off her back to hit the ground with a stunned *whump*.

Elim could have kissed her. He might still get a chance: Sil was getting up, and the strangers seemed to think they'd had enough for one night. One went riding off, another lit a shuck after his retreating horse, and the one Molly had helped to dismount only rolled over, just barely smart enough to avoid her down-coming hooves as he held himself in breathless pain.

Which left just enough room for a reunion.

"Miz Boone," Elim declared, "you are a brazen, shameless minx! Here I've gone to hell and back, and come to find you with another man ridin' up your garters. Ain't you shamed?"

Oh, most certainly. She was a one-horse hurricane of nickers and snorts and high-headed enthusiasm, whinnying and jostling at him until he had to walk her forward just to be sure her paramour there on the ground didn't take a hoof to the gut.

"You sure about that?" Elim scolded, his hands sternly interrogating her poll, smoothing back her forelock so he could look her dead in her sweet brown eye. "You swear you don't want no other man?"

She blew her promises down the front of his poncho, a wet grassy blast of fidelity and hairy-lipped assurances. Hell, she even still had her saddle. Who could ask for more than that?

Elim rubbed her cheek with a soul-cleansing sigh, luxuriating in her soft ears, her hot breath, her thick, horsey smell. He'd been so sure he'd never see her again. "You are a crass, wicked woman, Miz Boone. The things you do to me –"

He was interrupted by a strangled shriek from below. Elim and Molly both turned to look as the last remaining stranger caught an eyeful of something behind them, and then tore off as fast as his abused legs could go.

But it was just Sil standing there... albeit not the Sil that Elim had expected to see.

No, this was the one from that dire night a week ago: a sad, ghastly shadow of himself, a rotting shambles whose condition became clear with the next putrid shift of the wind. Elim couldn't make him out too well in the dark – and thank God for that – but there was no mistaking those pitiful yellowed eyes, that rancid misery in the air.

Elim swallowed, hard-pressed not to gag. "Sil, buddy – what happened to you?"

He might have expected that to get him a blistering reply... but maybe Sil had already taken out the worst of his frustrations on those road-agents. He turned his hands out in a fathomlessly weary shrug. "I wish I knew."

Elim found Molly's shoulder again, absently grounding himself in something warm and living and real. It was so hard to think past astonishment and exhaustion and instinctive, irrepressible disgust, and yet he couldn't let this chance go to waste. For the first time since Sil had fallen from the edge of the trail, the two of them were alone and *themselves* again, as sane and calm and safe as anyone was liable to get out here... even in spite of some gross bodily irregularities. This was an opportunity Elim couldn't waste.

So he wrung out all the brains he still had left, striving to find the right question. "Well... can you tell me what-all you do know?"

Sil looked out at the cool desert night all around them, and finally seemed to conclude that this was as good a time and place as any. He sat down with legs folded, ever the young gentleman, and answered with a moldering sigh.

"I know that I was hanged," he began, "and that I didn't survive it. I know that Día woke me up somehow, and she said that I had died, and of course I didn't believe it. I didn't think about it. I just pushed it all aside and concentrated on finding you. And when I couldn't ignore it any more..."

Molly had put her head down to investigate the scrub. Elim tied back her reins as he listened, freeing her to browse as he went and took a seat beside his partner... and just a little bit upwind.

"... Día said that I'd gotten stuck somehow. Weisei said that his crow-god could fix me. I believed it, but there was nothing I could do: by then I had fallen apart, and by the time anyone found me, it would be far too late for you or – you know, for anything else."

It was hard to see anything even with the moon, but Elim didn't miss Sil's sidelong glance.

"So I thought to myself about what I should have done differently, about how much I wanted another chance, and I wished... it sounds silly, but I wished for an advance, of sorts. I wished for a second life."

It took Elim a minute to untangle that – but when he did, the realization all but slapped him in the face. "You sold your soul."

Sil snorted. "Don't be daft."

That was rich, coming from a boy with a bullet-hole in his neck... but Elim wasn't about to rile him up again. "So what was the deal?"

"I don't know!" Sil said, with a burst of breath so foul that Elim had to leave off his own breathing for a minute. "I didn't – there was no agreement, no contract, no bloody signature on a dotted line. Nothing but my own stupid promises."

Elim stayed quiet for a bit, quelling nausea and his first deep misgivings. "So what did you promise?"

Sil rubbed his forehead – and just as quickly jerked his hand away, as if appalled by his own oozing flesh. "I'd – I don't remember," he said. "I asked for, for however much time I could still have, for whatever it – for whatever I was still worth."

And somehow that was the biggest surprise yet. Not that Sil had sold his soul – no, the only wonder there was that it had taken him this long to think of it. Not that someone, God or Sibyl, had even considered it worth buying. But that Great Master Halfwick, Mister Dollars-and-Cents-and-Interest-on-the-Loan himself, hadn't been shrewd enough to even guarantee what he was paying for.

None of which would make him feel any better now. "And this is what you got?" Elim said, as neutrally as he could.

Sil gave an anemic nod. "This at night. The – the other thing, in daytime." He looked just gutlessly frightened as he stared down at his knees, and his voice was as near to tears as Elim had ever heard it.

So Elim chose his next words with extra delicacy. "And is that why you been kicking the dickens out of me, you atrocious pissant?"

That was definitely the right thing to say. "I wouldn't have to if you could haul yourself out of a coma on your own initiative!" Sil retorted.

This time, Elim felt no shame in coughing at the rank foulness of the reply – or in giving Sil a hearty shove. "Try breathing on me next time, sugar-lips – if that don't do it, go ahead and bury me."

Sil rubbed his arm, and answered with a pallid, sickly grin. "Charming that you think I'd make the effort."

But he had. He'd gone to the ends of the earth to try and get Elim back in one piece – and somehow or other, he'd done it. Elim heaved a deeper, more wholesome breath. "Glad you're still here, Slim. I woulda had it way too easy without you."

Sil's smile faded; he nodded at the ground again. "Me too. For however long it is."

Elim didn't want to think about that. He didn't want to think about what kind of deal Sil might have done, or with whom – or when the bill was going to come due. Not because he didn't care, but because he couldn't do anything about any of it.

In fact, if he put his mind to it and gave it his all, he could probably just about scrape himself back up to walk again tomorrow – ride, he reminded himself, with a fresh spark of happiness at that handsome brown backside ambling over to the road.

"Right," he said at last, pushing himself up to a stand. "I'm gonna go unshuck my horse, and then I'm going back to sleep. Don't strike any more bargains, try not to fight any more road-agents, and... and you know, Sil, I don't think I ever got around to saying it, but I just... I wanted to tell you..."

Sil looked up. "What?"

Elim fixed him with a flat stare. "If I catch that foot in my face again tomorrow, I'm gonna break it clean off. *Comprende?*"

Sil rose to the challenge with a gleam in his jaundiced eye. "I guess we'll find out!" And then, much to Elim's surprise, he rose to his feet as well. "And in the meantime, I'll just chaperone you two, shall I?"

But as they went to go strip off Molly's tack, Elim felt wonderfully unbothered about the rest of it. They'd come this far, after all – and as soon as they made it back to Eaden, back to God's own country, all their strangeness would wash right off them. It had to. After all, Elim had his horse and his partner now, and everything after that was details.

IT WASN'T AS bad as all that, really. At least, not once the initial shock had worn off.

In fact, Sil's chief complaint wasn't even the time he spent moonlighting as a rancid shambling horror. It was that he still couldn't sleep. Not counting the oblivion he'd found at the end of the noose, he hadn't properly slept since... why, not since the night Elim had shot Dulei. What was that, two weeks ago now? Three?

Well, regardless: if he were going to go mad from insomnia, Sil expected he would have done it by now. For the most part, he'd stopped worrying about it. But without those nightly full-stops he'd once taken for granted, the world had become an endless run-on sentence – a flat, constant series of *and then*s. No, he shouldn't have been so awful to Elim... but besides the stark existential terror of watching his own body wax and wane with the daylight, Sil found it impossible not to sit there fermenting in the dark, burning with caustic, bilious envy as he watched the big man gorge himself on sleep.

Still, it did give him time to think. And by the time Sixes was in sight, Sil was well resolved.

"Elim, let's walk for a bit, can we?"

Elim glanced back at Sil, but raised no objections. He brought the horse to a halt, dismounted, and helped Sil down after him. Molly blew out through her nose.

You're welcome, Sil thought.

"So you reckon we ought to just up and announce ourselves?" Elim said.

It was a fresh, pleasant October morning: warm but not overly so, with a handsome view of the native farms and fields outside Sixes. Sil would have liked to say, *Yes, absolutely – let's just carry on this delightful little stroll, tip our hats to the locals on the way past, and head straight on home.*

"Well, almost," Sil said. He'd long since composed the words in his head, but it didn't make them easier to say. "Actually, I think you should go on in by yourself."

Elim halted on the spot. "Sil, what –"

"– and not because I don't care to come with you," Sil continued, forcing Elim to keep walking or be left behind, "but because I've thought about it, and I don't think I can do you any good. Just the opposite, actually. The people who – who dropped that rope over my head still think I'm dead. And as long as they believe that, they have no reason to bother you. But if I show up again, and they realize they left the job half-done" – and Sil all but shuddered to recall Faro's angelic, black-eyed smile – "they already know they can get to me through you. And you won't be safe anywhere inside those walls."

To his credit, Elim didn't reply straightaway. He led the horse along at a soft clopping walk, his gaze fixed on the blocky, irregular skyline of the town up ahead. "Yeah, but we're not... it's not like we're booking ourselves in for a long honeymoon. We just go in, get clear with the Azahi, and get out. That's it. That's all he asked for."

Sil didn't tell him that the Azahi was the one person besides Día who knew about his spontaneous resurrection, or mention the order he had issued to her afterwards: since Island Town had already recognized the death of Sil Halfwick, anyone found 'impersonating' him would be charged with some impressive-sounding list of offenses that Sil could no longer recall – identity theft, disgracing the dead, and so on. He had no idea how seriously the Azahi meant to follow up on that, but the implications were clear: within those walls, Sil was *persona non grata*.

He didn't say that. It would only give Elim ammunition to claim that Sil's secret was already out, and there was no point in hiding himself. And maybe that was true – but while there was any chance that a rumor hadn't spread, Sil had to err on the side of caution. "I know," he said, with more patience than he usually managed. "But think of what will happen if the Azahi's gone again, or if he keeps you there for any length of time. You know what I'll be like after sunset, and that's attention neither of us wants."

Elim considered that for a maddening long silence, the town looming closer all the while. Finally, just before Sil would have stopped, Calvert's mule found his next worry. "Yeah," he said at last. "But I can't – what'm I supposed to say?"

That was easy enough. "Well, what did you expect ME to say?"

Elim worried Molly's reins, comforting himself with the feel of supple, sweaty leather. "That, uh – that I did what I was supposed to do, and the a'Krah people let me go. And the Azahi promised me that if they did that, he'd do likewise, and that –"

Elim apparently reached the obvious conclusion then: if he could say it to Sil, he could just as easily say it to the Azahi. He stopped again, and this time refused to move. "Sil, I can't. I know what you're getting at, but I just – I don't have the grit for it. We don't need nothing from them anyway. Let's just go home."

Sil watched the worry furrowing his partner's long face, conflicted in spite of everything he'd already decided. Yes, he knew he could manipulate Elim into going in there – but no, he couldn't absolutely guarantee that he'd come back out again. Was it really worth the risk, however slight, when they were so close to being home free? The river was right there – the border was *right there* – and all they had to do was skirt around and swim over it.

But no, damn it, this was important. Not to satisfy some two-bit native mayor and his little proclamations, but for Elim himself. That monstrous huge thing he'd been before was still somewhere inside him, would be with him the rest of his life, and Boss Calvert and Lady Jane wouldn't always be around to keep him safe. If he were going to survive on either side of the border – if he were going to have any hope of making it on his own – he absolutely had to learn to answer for himself. Sil had no right to push him out of the nest like this, but at the end of the day, he couldn't count on anyone else to do it... and Elim might never get another chance.

So he swallowed, looked his partner in the eye, and laid down his trump card. "We can go home," Sil said. "Of course we can. It's just that... you know, she did ask us to tell Fours where she was."

It worked perfectly. Of course it did: Elim did for other people what he would never dare for himself. Sil could see it all in his expression: a bloom of shock, a terrible realization, and then an instant, switch-flipping shift from 'whether' to 'how'.

Elim looked back at the town, as if seeing it in a totally different light. "If I go in there, and they don't let me go..."

"I'll come for you," Sil pledged. "If you're not back by supper, I promise I'll come get you."

Elim gave him an interrogating look, an unspoken *You sure you won't leave me?*

Sil returned it with a steady, unblinking *When have I ever?*

And apparently that was good enough. Elim handed the sweaty reins over, as if he might lose his nerve by waiting. "You're gonna wait right here, right?"

Sil pointed over to the northeast. "There's liable to be traffic here – too many gossipy turnip farmers wandering about. I'll take Molly and skirt around to the river, about a mile north of town. We'll wait for you there."

Elim's jaw worked, as if he would extract one more promise, just to be on the safe side. Then he turned on his heel and went. No ceremony, no goodbyes: just a barefoot pilgrim in a borrowed poncho, armed with a pair of empty pockets and a half-baked plan.

Sil and Molly stood in the road and watched him until he was nothing more than a speck. When it was clear that Elim wouldn't lose his nerve and turn back, Sil clicked at the horse to turn her off the path –

– and would just about swear that the big mare was giving him the eye.

Maybe he was going sleep-mad after all. "Don't look at me like that," Sil said as they started off into the dry autumn grass. "He'll be fine."

After all, Fours was there, and – according to Día, at least – the Azahi was as honest a fellow as anyone could ask for. Elim had nothing but himself to worry about... and Sil intended to keep repeating that until he believed it.

THEY HAD LEFT Día.

They had *left* her.

Elim knew that. He'd been there when they'd done that. He had no excuse, no room for surprise.

But it was only just there, with Sil's almost casual mention of it, that the realization jolted through him like ice on a rotten tooth. As tired as he was, as numb as he'd been after all of that, it hadn't seemed real. It was only now, walking up to those warped wooden gates like a schoolboy on a dare, that the reality set in: he was going back to Sixes – to the place that had hung him up, burnt him, and flat-out tried to kill him – and if it got its claws into him again, there wasn't going to be any boot-blessing science-minded grave bride there to work them back out. Elim and Sil had... why, they'd let Atali'Krah do just the same thing to her – let it cut off her hair, hold her back in that blood-stained lair of theirs and do God-knew-what by now. Elim didn't really believe the a'Krah would kill her, but he had a horrible feeling they'd found other ways to even with her for Dulei.

And that was a boon, in a way – because otherwise Elim would never have had the guts to keep going. He would have withered under the stares of the field-workers he passed on his way up the wide, dry road. He would have frozen there on the creaky old bridge, staring helplessly up at those staked wooden walls, that moribund tilting church-steeple, that four-story adobe hive of humanity spreading out like a plaque over the southern end of town. He would have fled at his first sight of the stately black-iron manor at the opposite end of the road.

But someone somewhere in Sixes was missing Día, and on the other side of the border, two someones in Hell's Acre were missing him too, and now there was no way out but through. Elim held that thought just long enough to pass under the shadow of the gray wooden gates, crossing over the murky green river and beyond the point of no return, surrendering himself and his expectations as the infamous patchwork town loomed larger and nearer and then finally, silently swallowed him.

CHAPTER SEVENTEEN
SPECTACLES

AT LEAST IT didn't take long. Elim wandered into town on the main road, probably looking like a gunslinger spoiling for a fight. People stared at him. One ran away. It occurred to him, too late, that he didn't actually know where the Azahi lived, and by the time he allotted on looking for the jail, there was no point: the speckled mule – the lady-sheriff – was already coming for him.

Elim's gut clenched at the sight. She was as intimidating as she had been the first moment he caught sight of her boot-heels rapping down Fours' front steps: hard-faced and freckle-spattered, with coarse men's clothing and a wide-brimmed hat, and everything from her knife-cut hair to her skinned rabbit-fur vest to the pistol slung at her hip spoke of ruthless, unflinching resolve. She had dressed herself in violence, and her posture challenged anyone to question it.

Elim knew that wasn't all there was. He knew she could be soft, as she had been in the moments before Bootjack came to collect him – when it was just the two of them there in her dark, quiet jail-house, her hand clasping his through the bars. But the look in her eyes as she approached him now warned Elim to expect no such thing here in daylight, in public. As long as the rest of the world was watching, they were strangers, if not enemies.

He tried to assure her that he understood that. "*Luho*," Elim said, stopping a neighborly distance apart, tipping a hat he didn't have.

The sheriff stopped likewise, as if she might be contaminated by coming any closer, and looked to the gates behind him. When she failed to find anyone else in his company, she glanced back to where someone – a deputy? – was watching from the jail. "*Huitsak tráe*," she ordered.

The fellow ran off up the road.

The sheriff beckoned Elim to lift his hands, which he did, and then she walked all around him. When she found no weapons, she pointed to the right like a short, freckled weathervane. "*Marcha.*" She didn't need to imply the *or-else* at the end of that – that first flash of her wolfish white fangs said it all.

Elim went, letting himself be escorted in front of her: not north to the manor-house, thank God, but down south, towards the giant pueblo and... what, exactly?

"I want to see the Azahi," he said, which probably he ought to have mentioned up front. He couldn't tell how much of that was clear to her – he'd never heard her speak a word of Ardish – but if she understood the name, it made no difference to her calculations: she kept herding him on past houses and shops, in front of mistrustful mothers and wide-eyed children and men stooped with the weight of their labors, pushing Elim deeper into a world where he was nothing more than an irritating foreign speck in the collective eye – where he just absolutely did not matter at all.

And he was so unnerved by those stares, so fixed on walking the sheriff's invisible tightrope – eyes on feet, feet on line, no stray looks or extra steps anywhere – that when she finally grunted for him to stop, it took Elim a minute to recognize the place.

There were no animals in Fours' corral now, no yearlings for Elim to mind while Sil went in to do the talking. Now Sil was a million miles away outside, and it was the sheriff going up those porch-steps, and Elim following after her, uninvited and yet loathe to be left anywhere outside the circle of her authority. He wished he'd thought to ask Sil who had put that noose around his neck, or how to spot them.

The sheriff picked up the stick in the doorway and tapped at the front door. "*Quatros, akí estás?*"

And then, receiving no answer, again. "*Pendejo cabrón, abre!*"

So the pair of them waited there together, two mules from opposite sides of the border, apparently calling on a closeted fishman to translate between them. It was more than a little absurd.

The sheriff seemed to think so too. She threw the stick down, forced the door – Elim couldn't tell whether it had been shoddily locked or just stuck – and tromped inside. "*Quatros, dondeystás?*"

Elim had long since lost track of the days. He thought he couldn't have left more than two weeks ago. But as he stepped inside Fours' little shop, he might as well have been gone fifty years.

It had been eccentric enough before: a sunlit room full of too many treasures, every shelf and wall piled with warm, dusty clutter. Now it was a looted mausoleum. Half the old fellow's goods littered the floor, broken or stepped-on or simply left where they fell, and strewn among them were filthy clothes, festering food-fragments, and – as Elim took his first reluctant barefooted steps inside – peculiar damp spots in the warped wood floor. The whole place stank of mold and vinegar.

Something moved out of the corner of Elim's eye – like a giant rat scuttling behind the back shelves. The sheriff went wading into the mess after it, her scolding voice equal parts anger and anxiety as Elim edged back towards the door –

– and was accosted with a poncho-grabbing lunge.

"WHERE IS MY DAUGHTER?"

Elim jolted back, crashing up against a wall of old bottles as he stared in horror at the leprous gremlin clinging to his front.

That might have been Fours, once upon a time. Now it was a gaunt, hissing demon, sloughing great gray flakes and patches of dead skin as it bared its sharp teeth in a demented snarl. "I said WHERE IS SHE?"

"I don't know!" Elim cried as the sheriff made it over and hauled the horrible thing off him. It didn't put up a fight – it was far too thin to have any strength left, and couldn't weigh more than sixty pounds – but just the sight of it was a horror to rival Sil at his worst. Its clothes absolutely reeked of mildew.

"I don't – I didn't see anyone like that," he said, hurrying to forestall another outburst, hoping like the dickens that the daughter wasn't one of the dead fishmen he'd seen at the foot of the mountain. "I just, I just came to tell you – Día asked me to tell you that she's with the a'Krah."

The creature's expression melted, realization thawing the fury in its sunken black eyes, and then Elim saw

Fours again – albeit a parched, palsied, ruined Fours, with peeling parchment-skin and the gill-plumes dried out to cracked and bleeding tatters.

The old mereau all but collapsed back into the sheriff's arms, clutching her vest as he looked up at her with pleading desperation. "*Huitsak tráe! Akí lo tráe!*"

And as she began to reply, the penny finally dropped for Elim. Día WAS his daughter. Not by blood, of course, but if Fours was to her what the Calverts were to him... Elim glanced around the remains of the store, dreading to think what he would find at home.

"How?" Fours said at last, when he had found the strength to stand on his own. "Who took her? What happened?"

This was going to be so much harder than he imagined. Elim straightened likewise, suddenly aware of how little room he had to move. "Well, uh, we... we went to the crow city, like I was supposed to, and they did their deciding about me, and they let me go, but then they said – they wanted her to stay, and I tried not to let her, but then she said I was to go and leave her to do her job, so... so I did."

Well, it wasn't poetry, but that was about as plain as he could make it – at least, not without spilling the beans about Sil.

His efforts were not appreciated. "You LEFT her there?" Fours said with festering incredulity. "She wasn't even supposed to be there! She didn't – she had no business..."

His outraged sputtering died away with the rhythmic, sequential squeaking of the stairs outside. A huge shadow blotted out the light from the still-open doorway as its immense owner eased himself inside.

That was an a'Krah. No, not *an* a'Krah – *the* a'Krah. Their big boss, the one who had come with the sheriff and the Azahi and Día to decide about Elim after the night he'd spent in jail. Unlike Fours, he hadn't diminished a bit since the last time Elim saw him: still tall and fat and powerful, with his black hair hanging in plaited pigtails on either side of his fleshy face, he pulled off his blindfold and stood surveying the disgraceful interior, his eyes keen and his clothes just slightly rumpled from sleep.

Fours gave him no time to remark on it. "Huitsak, what is this?" he demanded. "Why is he telling me that Día is in Atali'Krah?"

The big man's brows lifted, their gaze lingering on Fours' shriveled figure. He tipped his head left and right in an unsettled shrug. "Let's find out. You," he said to Elim, with an inquisitive upward jerk of his chin. "Where are Vuchak and Weisei?"

Oh, this was not going to go well. Not at all. The a'Krah boss was standing there to Elim's right, still blocking the doorway, and Elim couldn't get to the side door up ahead without going through Fours and the sheriff and a whole pile of junk. He was trapped.

"I want to talk to the Azahi," he said, striving to keep his voice decent and level, like Sil would. "I'm only supposed to talk to the Azahi."

Fours and the a'Krah – Huitsak, if that was it – exchanged a glance. "He's not here," Huitsak said, a mistrustful gleam in his eye. "Stop wasting time and answer the question. Where are my men?"

This was bad. This was so bad. Why the hell had he listened to Sil? The churning in Elim's gut began to take on a life of its own, urging him to be anywhere but here.

"I, uh..." How to tell the truth without making it worse for himself? "They're still in Atali'Krah."

"Now there's a ripe lie," Huitsak snorted, folding his arms, somehow taking up even more space. "Even if Vuchak and Weisei were asked to stay, the Eldest would have still sent you back with Hakai. Where are they really?"

Fours was translating for the sheriff. Huitsak was standing there waiting for an answer. And Elim's spots were itching, his muscles aching to run. "They're still there," he promised, "all of them, all three of them are there –"

"Bullshit!" Huitsak thundered – both provoking and obscuring the conspicuous *pop* of Elim's knee. "What are you hiding?"

Elim could feel himself growing as the wild thing inside him came alive with mortal fear. He took a shuffling step, burying his left foot under a spilled heap of blankets, folding his arms to keep his right hand hidden under his poncho. "I'm – I'm telling you the truth; I don't –"

"Oh, spit it out!" Fours snapped – a sudden sidelong assault that split Elim's attention and his vision both. "Why should we believe you?"

"Because Bootjack's dead and Hawkeye's addled and Way-Say's probably killed himself by now!"

Elim heard it come out of his own mouth, but it was as foreign to him as the itch and shiver curling around his limbs. Still, it left enough of a silence for him to start trying to rein in the deathly panic lashing and pushing out from his insides. *Not now*, he told it. He couldn't afford to let it happen now.

Huitsak stared. The arrogance in his expression was gone. "... dead? How?"

And now that the cat was out of the bag, Elim felt no compunctions about siccing it on his keepers. "Because some crow woman with a knife came up behind him and cut his throat open like a stunned beef, and all the rest of them stood back and let her, and if you ever find out how come that was, you can write and tell me, cuz I said what I came to say and now I'm going."

Huitsak's expression didn't change – and yet he looked like he'd sprung a slow leak. He raised no objections, no anything at all.

Fours was another story. "You're not going anywhere," he snarled, and pushed away from the sheriff to put all of his five-foot-nothing straight up in Elim's face. "After everything she did for you, you left Día with those – those scavengers, and you're not leaving until I have her back!"

He was frightening in spite of his frailty, as mad and menacing as a shithouse rat, and Elim cringed as he felt the tingling ache in his limbs, the itching prickle of new-grown hair under his poncho, and his own burgeoning certainty that one wrong move would find him strung up between the posts again, tied out for Sil's mysterious killing-friends to find and finish with. Elim's reason clung fast to his fear as if it were a bucking horse, one back-popping snap away from being thrown off altogether. "No, I'm not," he said, closing his eyes to concentrate on getting the words out. "I'm a free man now, and you can't –"

"– you're a murderer and a cheat and a bastard twice over –" Fours snapped, but he wasn't so scary when Elim didn't have to look at him, and he wasn't about to take that.

"– and she's a free woman old enough to know her

own will –" Elim retorted, grabbing the reins for a hard pull.

"– and you didn't have the decency to save her!"

"I had the decency to LISTEN to her!" Elim roared, and by then he'd mustered the guts to stare down at the old fishman, even if his mismatched eyes made a clashing discordant mess of the view. "I didn't ask her to come for me, and I didn't tell her to stay, and I didn't force her to go with me after she refused – because she's free and grown and so am I, and it's probably about time you respected that."

Yes, that was it: he was *people*, dammit, and the frightened horsey thing inside him had been pushing him around too long, spooking and kicking and even actually killing that poor boy in the barn, and it wasn't going to gentle itself. He was going to have to make it.

And here for practice were three people whose power and authority outmatched any thoroughbred's. Elim squinted one eye closed for clarity, and tried to meet each of theirs in turn. "I'm sorry it didn't turn out like you wanted, with Bootjack and Día and the rest of them. I sorely am. But that ain't my fault, and I'm not your hostage. I went to clear my debt, and I came back to do you a courtesy. Now it's done, and I'm going home."

Elim put everything he had into each word, projecting every last ounce of the confidence it took to match wills with a thousand-pound animal and get it so clear on your intentions that it plain forgot its own – that it never even thought to ask how come it ought to listen to a hairless two-legged weakling it could ignore or maim or kill without a first thought, nevermind a second one.

These people didn't operate on horse-logic, of course.

Fours and Huitsak and the lady-sheriff had more smarts than Elim ever would. But regardless of what the rest of the world's people-creatures did, he would at least be the master of the one inside him. He couldn't afford not to.

"...Vuchak," the a'Krah boss said. "His name was Vuchak."

Elim swallowed, caught off guard. Had he been getting it wrong all this time? "I'm – I'm glad to know that," he said. "I was glad to know him, too."

Fours was saying something to the sheriff, who was staring at the left side of Elim's face with uncommon interest. He turned his head by old force of habit, though probably not to any useful purpose. The horse-eye was already giving him a headache.

And they stood there like that for a minute, four people just slightly too short on gumption to make the next move. Elim used the time to try and will away his strangeness, settling it back into its stall with assurances that the work was done, that they weren't in any danger, that nobody needed to get spooky or bolt, because Elim was the smart one, and he had taken a look at things and knew for a fact that they were fine.

... sort of.

"You did make your promise to the Azahi," Huitsak said at last. "I don't think anyone here feels qualified to let you go without him."

Elim took a big, calming breath while he worked on not hearing things that hadn't been said. "When's he getting back?"

"Today," Fours said, after another consultation with the sheriff. "This afternoon, we hope."

Elim was not too much in the mood for hoping... but

that would still get him back out of here before Sil came looking for him. What would Sil do here, anyway?

He would drive a bargain, that was what. Elim helped himself to another big breath, doing his best to get past that awful moldy smell and think about what he should ask for. No, better yet: what he should declare. "All right," he said at last. "I'll wait until sunset. If he's not back by then, I'm leaving. And I ain't going back in that jail, either," he added, just in case anybody had been thinking to stuff him back in a cage again.

This was relayed to the sheriff, whose face made it plain what she thought of Elim's presumption. Then she scratched viciously under her hat, and replied in a tone of voice that couldn't have been wrapped around anything but an order.

"She says you can wait here," Fours said, and nodded up at the ceiling. "I have a – a room you can use."

Elim did not care to spend another minute in this tragic garbage-heap... but one look at the sheriff's folded arms told him exactly how much further he wanted to push his luck.

"All right," he said. "All right, sure. But only until sunset. That's all."

"Fine by me," Fours said. "And you, Huitsak – I want to talk to you."

"Do it outside," the a'Krah boss said as he maneuvered himself back towards the door. "I'm not spending another second in this shit-pit."

Which left Elim, his strangeness diminishing right along with his bravery, picking his way through the mess and past the lingering gaze of the lady-sheriff as she watched him impose his weight on those rickety-creaky old stairs, one at a careful tentative time.

She must have noticed. She must have. But if she had, there was nothing Elim could do about it now. Nothing to do but keep his promise, and hope he had made the right one.

That got a little easier when he made it to the room upstairs.

It wasn't like the store. There was nothing nasty or awful about it. It was just garden-variety untidy, with papers stacked on the little desk, and clothes piled around the dresser and hung over the chair, and all manner of crafts and pagan artworks festooning the dusty walls and wash-deprived open windows.

And a bed.

An honest-to-God actual bed – the first one Elim had seen since... why, since he and Sil had left the fair.

It was old and ordinary and on the small side, with a flattish pillow and a sun-faded quilt spread neatly over the top. It was also the most beautiful thing he had ever seen.

Elim shouldn't. He definitely, definitely shouldn't. It was too small, for one thing, and he hadn't been invited, for another, and he needed to stay awake and alert no matter what. This was enemy territory, even in the daytime, and he couldn't let his guard down now.

And yet...

And yet he was drawn to it like a sunburned hog to fresh mud, helping himself to an ever-so-gentle sit at its foot – because where else was there to sit? – and then to a temporary lie-down – because the delicate little bed would take his weight better if he spread it out evenly – and before he knew it he was rolling himself in the quilt like a fairytale vagrant, luxuriating in a rest that was too small, too rude, too dangerous... and just right.

*   *   *

DISGRACEFUL. THE WHOLE thing was just disgraceful.

That was what Twoblood had called it. That was the word that kept echoing in Fours' mind after she and Huitsak had left.

The state of his house, yes. The state of his person, certainly. But the way that loutish brute up there could conjure the nerve to leave Día in the hands of the a'Krah, and then roll himself up *in her very bed* and fall asleep without a care in the world... by every god, it beggared belief.

Fours would get him back for that. Somehow he would. But for now, he had other things to do.

Día was alive – that was the principal thing. She was alive and had been taken hostage, and that meant he had no more time for suicidal wallowing. At any moment, the Azahi would return from his audience with Mother Opéra, and Fours had to be ready. He had to be listened to. He had to be believed. And nobody was going to believe anything from a dirty old madman.

So he salted some water and drank it, and then sugared some more and drank that too. And when he was sure he could hold on to it – that his pores would not renew their seeping, grieving, endlessly leaking despair – he went upstairs for a change of clothes, and pitched his mildewed ones right out the window.

A jar of pickled eggs from the dresser drawer, just so he would have something in his stomach. A swig from the flask beside it, to ease the tremor in his hands and dull the pounding in his head. A last baleful look at that overgrown parasite in the bed, because it felt so good to finally have someone besides himself to hate.

Then it was back downstairs, and to work.

But even as he cleared out the trash, stacked the spilled dishes and re-folded the linens, Fours was no closer to understanding than before. How had Día gone from sneaking that Halfwick boy out of town to being a prisoner of the a'Krah? And more to the point, what did they want with her? Huitsak hadn't been able to give him any satisfaction on that front – the shrewd master of the Island Town a'Krah had seemed uncharacteristically rattled since learning of that one fellow's death – and Fours couldn't begin to guess on his own.

So he was left with just the same thought that had been eating him alive for weeks now: Día had lied to him.

There was no way around it. Halfwick had sat up from his grave and demanded to see his partner, and Día had arranged for it to happen. She had come right here to this very house, right up there to that very room and asked him right to his very face: *Papá, how do you know the right thing to do?* And she had decided right there on the spot that she would lie to him – that she would behave as if nothing were out of the ordinary, that she would let Fours go on believing that she was leaving town just long enough to dispose of the body. He had only found out the truth from the Azahi when she didn't come back.

And who was to blame for that?

Her real father – that unyielding pious brick of a man?

That holy book of hers, stuffed with thou-shalt-nots?

Or her gutless, craven *papá* – the one who had spent his whole life lying to her. Lying to protect her, lying to safeguard her image of him, lying because he'd done it so long he couldn't even remember what the truth tasted like.

And now he'd tainted her. All her virtuous bloodline,

all those values her father had worked so hard to imprint on her – ruined as surely as if Fours had left a moldy handprint on a block of fresh cheese. What arrogance did he have to have ever thought he could parent a human child?

He stopped himself as he noticed the dampness sticking his shirt to his back and arms. *Nevermind*, he scolded his weeping flesh. There would be plenty of time for recriminations when he had her back. The Azahi had gone to Opéra, left Island Town and submitted himself to her in person to ask for her help in casting the widest possible freshwater net for his missing ambassador. And when he got back, Fours had to be able to look him in the eye and make him go wring the rest of the truth out of that two-colored man up there. More than that, some drought-tolerant earth-person was going to have to brave the trip to Atali'Krah to rescue Día, and Fours had to look like a man – like a father – who deserved to have his daughter back.

The doorknob rattled uselessly below the lock. "Hello?" a muffled Ardish voice called out.

Fours froze – and then groaned. "*Maugrebleu...*" Of course it would be a tourist.

But the scolding voice that followed was instantly, astonishingly familiar. "Fours, you lazy old cheat – what sort of hour do you call this? Quit flinching and shirking and open this door!"

She was dead. She was dead – Opéra had shot her and Faro had finished her and she was dead – and yet she was yelling at him.

The sound of her voice got Fours up from his janitorial crouch, his hands still full of chipped crockery. The next voice sent it clattering back to the floor.

"*Papá?* Are you there?"

Yes. Yes, he was there. He was surging past the shelves, and he was there. He was fumbling at the lock, and he was there. He was throwing the door open, blinking in the sunlight –

– and she was there.

And then there was nowhere to be but with her, around her, pressing her big warm-blooded body into his withered arms and biting her neck until it would bleed. "*Ma joie, ma claire, ma petite fifille* – oh, I thought I had lost you..."

But she'd lost herself. Fours drew back and stared at her, appalled past breathing as his trembling hands found her denuded head. "Día – Día, what have they done to you?"

Her face had long since crumpled; her welling eyes spilled wet tracks down her cheeks. "Nothing, *papá,*" she said, her voice hoarse and thick, her expression mirroring his as she stared at his grief-ravaged features. "I did it to myself."

The look in her eyes promised him that it was true, or at least that she believed it... which left Fours with either a daughter who could lie to him with impeccable guile, or else one who had willingly cut off her only inheritance from her own father – her real father – for who-knew-what despicable purpose.

Fours interrogated her gaze, feeling as if he would faint. "You're all right, *ma chère*?" he said weakly. "They haven't touched you, they haven't hurt you, they haven't despoiled you somehow?"

"No," she promised, her voice strong even through her tears. "No, *papá* – I'm fine, and I'm so sorry –"

Her apology ended in premature astonishment as Fours

reached up and grabbed her by the shoulders. "You stupid, wicked, wretched girl!" he cried, with a vigor he hadn't felt in years. "Do you have any idea what you've done? Do you know what could have happened to you? By heaven, Día, if you EVER do this to me again, I'll – I'll pitch you in the river and leave you for the fishmen!"

"Now, now," came the admonishing voice from behind her. "Let's not soak our petticoats over a little harmless mischief. She was overdue for a bit of impetuous youth, wouldn't you say?"

Shea was standing there in Día's shrinking shadow – dressed as an a'Krah, of all things. She had a hood drawn up over her baldness and a pair of moccasins excusing her foreshortened feet, and had darkened her skin to complement the costume – but there was no mistaking the twinkle in her eye, or her sardonic sharp-toothed smile.

Fours let go of his petrified daughter, too dumbstruck to decide whether they should still be estranged. "What are you doing here?"

Shea, of course, had elected to carry on as if nothing had happened, and threw her hand out at Día in manufactured incredulity. "Why, returning your truant child, since you can't seem to keep her in after curfew! Really, Fours, what is she going to learn from this appalling ingratitude of yours?"

And she came at him for an embrace, which Fours did not so much return as simply fail to avoid... but it was impossible not to answer the bite at his neck, or to keep from seeping just a little as his last earthbound sibling squeezed him like an old sponge.

"You shouldn't – you shouldn't be seen here," he stammered, belatedly aware of the interest their porchfront family reunion was garnering from across the street. "If he finds out you've returned..."

Shea drew back, a glimmer of wickedness in her eye. "Día, be a good girl and go fetch your *papá* a fresh shirt – you see what a mess he's made of this one."

Día glanced between her amphibious fosterers, the look behind her drying tears leaving Fours absolutely no room to wonder where she'd learned to deceive him: they were going to talk behind her back, and she knew it.

But that was the prerogative of parents, even the ones who weren't exiled spies hiding under the thumb of a legless tyrant and her smiling sociopath of an enforcer... and maybe Día knew that too. Regardless, she was the very picture of filial piety as she bowed her head and turned to go inside. "Yes, Miss. Yes, *papá*."

Fours thought about warning her about the mess, or at least about the man in her bed... but nevermind. She'd discover that soon enough. And as soon as the stairs announced her going, Shea was back to business, keeping the intimate distance between them as she finger-traced a design into the wet white fabric of his chest.

"Now then," she said. "I'm sure the two of you have eight thousand things to say to each other, but I should tell you this first: while Día and I were on our way here this morning, we met a perfectly pleasant little friend of hers about a mile upstream from here – a young Eadan gentleman of our mutual acquaintance. And we got to talking, and I got to thinking, and it occurs to me that we might just have an opportunity on our hands..."

She went on like that, her coy intimations becoming more explicit and outrageous by the moment, until even Fours' battered mind couldn't fail to grasp the conclusion: Día was home, safe and sound against all odds – and if Shea had her way, that would only be the beginning.

As THE OLD saying went, there was more than one way to skin a cat – and as it turned out, more than one way into Sixes.

By the time the grandfather clock chimed one, Sil had already proven one, and prepared to test the other.

It had been an unexpected boon to meet Día again. Better still to renew his acquaintance with her mereau governess, whom Sil had apparently met once before, in this very house. Apparently they'd left the Dog Lady to care for a wounded man, and elected to walk the last of the way to Island Town themselves, with the great lady and her charge to follow after dark.

Regardless, it was the easiest thing in the world for Sil to hand Molly off to the two ladies and avail himself of a little swim, a neat entry through the gap in the fence at the north end of the island, which Shea recommended with the authority of a veteran laundress. By the time she met him back there to confirm the plan, Sil was almost dry again.

He had found La Saciadería a pleasant, familiar place on that first fateful evening. And it was doubly so in the daytime, the plush furnishings and antique décor a positive oasis for a discerning traveler too long deprived of civilized comforts. Now, as Sil settled back into the great overstuffed chair in the parlor, he reveled in serenity and solitude and quiet, refined splendor. No, it wasn't quite home – but it was damned good.

And just when he thought the day couldn't get any

better, the immaculately-shined black dress-shoes descending the stairs conspired to prove otherwise.

"*Bien-día*, good afternoon," Faro began, winding a fine silver pocket-watch on his way in –

– and dropping it at his first full glimpse of Sil. It dangled from its waistcoat chain like a gaudy pendulum.

And then the world had no joy, no savor greater than the look on that blanching, stammering, pomaded pale face. "Why – why, Master Halfwick, how pleasant it is to see you again..."

Sil imagined that he must look a right galling sight: the very picture of glowing youth and health, dressed in bloodied, tattered rags, sitting with a noose coiled lightly in his lap.

So he reassured his visitor with a smile worthy of the dandy himself. "Faro – just the man I wanted to see! Smashing to be back again, really it is. I was wondering, old chap: could I trouble you for a favor?"

Faro looked as if he'd like to trouble Sil for a fainting-couch – but he'd played the game too long to buckle that easily. He returned a nervous copy of Sil's smile, and a stiff two-inches' tip of his head. "Why – of course. I'm ever at your service...!"

Sil remained comfortably seated, and laced his hands together across the arms of the chair. "Splendid! It's like this, you see: you remember how I'd won those pearls from you when we played at cards? Well, I'm red to my ears to realize that I've misplaced them somehow – really, I'm just sick at the thought. You haven't seen them here by chance, have you?"

You stole them. You dropped a noose around my neck and shoved me off a balcony and stole them, you conniving, murderous loon.

Sil caught a flicker of movement from the doorway behind Faro, but kept his eyes on the dandy and his smile guilelessly bright.

Faro swallowed. A tic tugged at his lip; his gaze flicked involuntarily to the rope in Sil's lap. "Why, I'm – I haven't, but I can... I'll just check your room, shall I?" He gestured back at the stairs, turned to go...

... and flinched back as two pairs of smoldering black eyes opened on either side of the doorway. Two camouflaged bodies stalked toward him: one a little taller, bolder in its stride, the other terribly thin, its concealment marred by dry gray patches. But they advanced on Faro with merciless purpose, as bloody single-minded as a pair of avenging fraternal twins.

"Brilliant," Sil said, rising smoothly to his feet. "Do let me know what you find – I'm positively at the end of my rope."

By then Faro was turning back towards Sil, his mouth already open to call for help.

But not a peep emerged as Sil tossed the noose over his head and yanked hard enough to bring the dandy crashing to the floor like a hooked trout, strangling to get a sound out.

Elim would be so proud.

The conspirators wasted no time after that: Sil handed the rope off to his new friends, pausing just long enough to liberate Faro's keys from his waistcoat before he cleared his partners to haul their kinsman away. His last view of the three mereaux was the sight of Faro's expensive heels drumming a frantic, muffled tattoo on the richly carpeted floor, his blue-white hands clawing at the rope around his neck as he was dragged down the hallway and out through the front door.

The manor-house returned to quiet after that, its peaceful afternoon stillness marked only by the ticking of the grandfather clock. When night fell, it would come alive again, filling with noise and people and every sort of merry debauchery. For now, the silence was broken only by the jingle of the keys as Sil set off in search of lost property.

IT HAD BEEN a shitty week. A shitty month, if Twoblood were speaking frankly.

First all the mess with Halfwick and that half-man of his, and everything with the a'Krah and Dulei, and that was before Twoblood had had to take a screaming chambermaid at her word, and go find Brant's headless body bleeding through his bedsheets. Then Día going missing, Fours falling apart, weeks of sending search parties out – all for the little cowbird to come waltzing back into town today, as casually as if she were stopping in for lunch. It had been a trial of a pain of a nightmare of a farce, and it wasn't even over yet. It wouldn't end until the Azahi had returned and booted those two good-for-nothing-foreigners back over the border.

But as Twoblood sat there in her house, awaiting the next inevitable shit-burst of an imposition, the view from her barred window treated her to a spectacular novelty.

Two naked fishmen were marching down the street in broad daylight, dragging the madam's clerk on a rope behind them. For a moment, Twoblood feared that he was dead, and that she would have to step in.

But no, actually: as his captors reached the promenade on the other side of the street and set about tying him between the posts, the clerk began to struggle – for all the good that did.

So as the fishmen tied him up and commenced tearing his fancy clothes off, Twoblood judiciously declined to intervene. Instead, she opted for a more conservative, supervisory approach: namely, propping her boots up on the table and leaning back to watch the spectacle.

It was going to be a good day after all.

THE AZAHI RETURNED without fanfare or forewarning. That was expected.

But after Island Town had received him again, there was just enough time for Fours to go upstairs and complete his costume – wig, ears, eyebrows, the works – before the inevitable summons arrived.

Well, almost enough time.

But there was no time to mourn the missing piece, nor even to compose himself while he tapped on the door – because the door was already open, and the Azahi was already waiting.

So Fours bowed there in the entryway, and made the best of a bad situation. "You wanted to speak with me, First?"

"Sit."

Fours admitted himself into the Azahi's lush, richly-decorated home, and seated himself on the opposite side of the little round floor-table as if he'd only been invited in for tea – as if he weren't in the deepest kind of blackwater trouble.

The man sitting across from him harbored no such illusions. His traveling-clothes were rumpled and dirty, the glittering marks of his office hanging heavy around his neck and forehead, and his uncommonly smooth middle-aged features were as hard as sandblasted stone. "Where are your glasses, Fours?"

Fours had been mentally preparing for this since he agreed to Shea's mad plan... but that didn't make it any easier to meet that molten golden-eyed stare. "I don't know, First. I had them yesterday."

And both those things were technically true.

The rainbow beads curtaining the Azahi's pinned hair clicked as he lifted his chin. "Well, then," he said, his voice perfectly measured, "what have you been doing today?"

Fours could not begin to match the intensity of the other man's gaze, but he had no energy left to flinch from it. "Oh, quite a lot," he said. "I woke up. Drank. Thought of killing myself, but couldn't find the laudanum. Then Día came back – has anyone told you that yet? – and we had lunch, tidied up a bit... oh, and my sister and I decided to hang Faro."

Well, that wasn't strictly true. "Actually, it was more of a pillorying," Fours added. He was walking a thin, dangerous line between honesty and insolence – a double rarity for anyone who knew him.

So perhaps the Azahi hadn't quite decided how to react: the soft, clean contours of his face remained a blank. "And why did you do that?"

As if that weren't obvious. They'd stripped him right there in the middle of the street, ripping his wig off and exposing his gill-plumes in full view of everyone. Opéra could rage and fume all she liked, but Faro was finished in Island Town: his cover had been blown.

Fours dipped his head. "It seemed like a good idea at the time."

If he were interviewing with Twoblood, this would have been the moment where she leapt across the table and throttled him.

Instead, the edge in the Azahi's voice reminded Fours to be grateful that he was not Twoblood. "And the fire? Did that seem like a good idea too?"

This was more dangerous territory – the point where their little coup had gone beyond mere humiliation. "I wouldn't know anything about that," Fours demurred.

A flick of the Azahi's wrist sent a pair of charred, twisted spectacles skittering across the table, their blackened hexagonal lenses staring up at Fours in wordless accusation.

"I may have dropped them in the confusion –"

The table jolted with the force of the Azahi's exasperated slap. "Damn it, Fours, we've been out there begging YOUR mother to help us find YOUR daughter, and this is how you thank us? By trying to kill her best man?"

It sounded awful when he put it that way, and Fours hastened to clarify. "No, sir. If I'd meant to kill him, I would have done it." And he hoped his expression conveyed just how easy it would have been – as simple as sprinkling a little rat poison on Faro's damp, thirsty flesh. He wouldn't have even needed to swallow.

But as tempting as it was to positively guarantee that Faro would never come back for vengeance, that would have made Fours a murderer... or at least, more of one than he already was. "Instead, I decided that I would just go and fetch my spectacles, and set them down just-so by the pile of clothes at his feet, and then I would leave him alone. Whatever happened after that, whatever transpired between the sun and the glass and the fabric – I left that for the gods to decide." Never overburdened with faith even in the best of times, Fours had thought this a beautiful, even inspiring solution.

The Azahi did not seem to agree. "And they decided to burn him alive."

"Why, not at all, sir," Fours hastily reassured him. "They saved his life. They saw fit to have Twoblood on watch just then, and she cut him down and promptly returned him to the water, where I have no doubt that he will heal... after a fashion." Fours absently pinched the cauterized, webless flesh between his fingers. "Of course, all that smoke will have ruined his lungs. I doubt he'll ever be able to live on land again. Certainly he won't be in any shape to threaten my Día."

Fours must have looked a little too serenely satisfied as he said that, because the Azahi's face was fast dissolving into a mask of horror. "You did this for HER? You... if you thought he was going to... you could have..." The beads clicked again as he shook his head, speechless with disgust. "You're despicable."

Fours tried for an apologetic shrug. "I'm a parent."

There was no other way to explain it. The past two weeks had been the worst of his life – and yet it had also been strangely liberating. Día was gone, Shea was gone, and Fours genuinely hadn't cared whether he lived or died – so there was nothing left to be afraid of. There was nothing Faro or anyone else could do to him. For the first time in his life, he had been free.

And now that Día was safely home again, the idea of going back to that caustic status quo – the thought of flinching and jumping and cringing at Faro's every whim, terrified that the least defiance would end in an invisible knife at his daughter's neck... God, who could ever bear it? Easy enough to go along with Shea's madcap scheming when literally any ending was preferable to that old, hideous continuation.

Fours didn't volunteer any of that, and the Azahi didn't ask. The First Man of Island Town only drew back from the table and jerked his head at the door. "Go. Get out. And send her here directly."

Fours rose to leave, wishing for enough sincerity to apologize with. "Yes, First. Though I should mention, just so you aren't surprised..."

The Azahi looked up at him with the dead-eyed certainty of a man who had lost his capacity for astonishment.

"... she knows about the slaves."

And as it turned out, the master of Island Town still knew how to blink. The mask cracked; he stared up at Fours with a slower, more intellectual fear – the look of a man who was just then realizing his ruin. "You told her?"

Fours shook his head, almost offended. "The a'Krah had none of their own messengers left to send back – so they decided to place their next order through Día."

The Azahi slumped forward, beads clicking as he cupped his forehead in stunned, hopeless passivity. "You're joking. Tell me you're joking."

Comedy had never been Fours' strong suit.

"What are we going to do? We might have all of three hours before the Dog Lady comes storming in here to reclaim her island, and you're telling me that my ambassador – that our ambassador has probably already filled the great lady's head with peerless tales of our depravity. What are we supposed to do?"

Fours had already been dismissed, of course. He

did not care to imagine how low he'd sunk in the Azahi's estimation. But it was a terrible thing to see the First Man of Island Town so afflicted – to hear 'me' breaking through the polished golden mirror of 'we'. No, Día wouldn't understand the kind of unfortunate compromises that went into running a city, or just how exhausting it was to lead a double life. But Fours was all too familiar.

So he sat back down, wishing he had some way to mark himself as a friend this time, and made an effort a consolation. "Fix a parade," he said.

The Azahi looked up. "What?"

Fours swept his hand out at the late afternoon sunlight streaming in through the window. "Welcome her, Hara! Rejoice, throw a party, be seen to celebrate. Island Town will host a living goddess – so take advantage of it! Yes, technically we're all squatting on her land, but it isn't as if she's bringing an Ara-Naure legion here to evict you with. Let her be your figurehead leader, if she wants to stay, or your patron deity, if she doesn't. Either way, it all serves you in the end: why should you have to keep bowing and scraping for Mother Opéra when you can have a great mother of your own?"

That was wisdom not lost on the First Man, and some of it he might have already considered. "Yes, but what reason does she have to tolerate us? We don't... wait. We do still have her son, don't we?"

Fours nodded, but not with conviction. "Yes, First. He's still asleep. And I wouldn't – before you think it, I wouldn't trot him out with a bow. He was terribly keen to leave this morning, and from what Día's told me, that's a family mess we'd do well not to step in."

Apparently that didn't help. "Then what shall we

say? And how? She doesn't – the earthly gods have no tongues, and we'll need someone who already knows her mind. Día was our perfect choice, our ambassador and apparently the Dog Lady's newest favorite, but now..." The Azahi shook his head, his gold-flecked skin pale in the light.

Fours felt bad for him. No-one could lead a city as fractious as Island Town without getting his hands dirty from time to time – and the Azahi had never hesitated to dirty or dishevel himself when Fours needed him. He had been a heroic constant in searching for Día over this last sleepless eternity – and while Fours couldn't restore her innocence or demand her goodwill, he might yet be able to conjure a suitable substitute.

"Ask Shea."

At the Azahi's first perplexed look, Fours elaborated. "She was your ambassador too, once upon a time. It was kind of you to take in the three of us remainders – and she won't have forgotten. Ask her back into service. She knows the Dog Lady better than anyone."

That, and after today's little stunt, Shea would do well to stay clear of Opéra's clutches.

The Azahi let out a slow breath, his attention resting on an indeterminate point between them. "And you?" he said at last. "What do I do with you?"

Fours looked down. "Whatever you want."

"What do you mean?" The concern in the Azahi's voice was flattering.

"Just what I said," Fours replied. "It doesn't matter anymore. Even if Opéra doesn't kill me, she won't trust me for anything, and Día..." Fours gave a rueful smile as he meditated on the charred glasses between them. "... you know, Hara, I think she doesn't need me anymore.

Not the way she used to. I'm sorry about that – I miss the days when she would come to me for everything – but she's grown so much since then, and more just in the time she's been away, and now... now I feel like I'm just marking time."

Yes, that was the heart of it. Fours could go on being her *papá*, and the Azahi's ambassador, and a peddler of secondhand goods, and maybe he was just being overly fatalistic here at the end of a soul-wrenching ordeal – but his wonderful newfound indifference had also bleached some of the color from the world, and it was hard to know whether that would ever come back.

The Azahi lifted his brows and sat back, somehow managing to look supremely unbothered about the world that had so recently consumed his attention. "Well, what would you want to do, if you had your choice?"

Now there was a savory hypothetical. Fours considered it for a long minute. If he somehow became the architect of his own life – if he could declare his own place in the world – what would he choose? "I think I'd like to be a doctor again," he said at last. "I enjoyed that." All those teas and poultices, the little remedies and clever divinations that robbed suffering and cheated pain... it had been an uncommonly satisfying work.

The Azahi smiled. "You'll get more business if you stop stringing people up in the streets."

Fours returned the humor. "I'll take that under advisement, First."

The Azahi glanced out the window again, his expression keenly aware of the sinking sun. "And in the meantime... how are you with parade-fixing?"

Fours was, of course, the last person anyone should

want to arrange their festivities. But the Dog Lady was partial to Día and Shea, and they in turn were partial to Fours, and that was as good a diplomatic connection as the Azahi was likely to get. It wasn't perfect – but for now, it would do.

"I'm sure I have a flag or two somewhere in stock. Let's see what we can find." And it was nothing short of a pleasure to rise and help the First Man of Island Town to his feet, one sullied hand in solidarity with another as the two of them set to it. After all, they'd reinvented the town before – what was one more new world order between friends?

It DID MAKE quite the spectacle. Even Día had to admit it. She watched from the loft of Fours' barn as night returned to Island Town – and so did the Dog Lady.

She came striding in through the western gate, already so immense that she had to duck to fit under, and trailing around and behind her was a parade of her own making: every dog within twenty miles had followed her into town, along with an assortment of sheep, goats, and one volubly enthusiastic donkey. She seemed to draw them to her like little furry needles to a holy lodestone: even as Día watched, the tame creatures of Island Town leapt fences and dug under pens, every bit as anxious as their human caretakers to celebrate the great lady's return.

And it was a celebration. Feast-fires blazed on the roofs of the Moon Quarter to the north and all over the great pueblo to the south, thickening the air with the aroma of mesquite-roasted squash and corn-cakes and the savory flesh of those creatures who had been selected to honor U'ru with their lives. The Azahi would not let her be seen choosing favorites, of course, but arranged for her to come and hold court in the great town square, near the crossroads in the center of town, where both the day and the night people converged on the festivities, competing to see who could bring the best gifts, drink the most wine, dance most outlandishly. And all the while, U'ru held Hakai as if he himself were the guest of honor, garlanding him, feeding him a bite at a time, letting him complete this peculiar new iconography: the return of the lost goddess, the blessing of the wounded native man in her arms, and the rejoicing of both the land and its people.

And U'ru loved it. Día could feel her own heart beating faster with the strength of someone else's delight, as if she herself were the patron-saint of that mad menagerie outside – as if she were the queen-reveler in all that fantastic chaos.

Puppy! came the raucous, inevitable thought. *Come and play!*

Día was nothing of the kind, of course. Her domains were books and study and the honoring of the dead. She wouldn't have the first idea how to behave at a party.

Still, there wouldn't be a better opportunity to learn. *I will*, she promised, with a reflection of U'ru's own enthusiasm. *In a little while.*

And as that ecstatic second-mind temporarily consented to leave hers, Día likewise turned away from the window, giving her attention and her company to the one person who would not be welcome at the feast.

"It sounds like a good time," Halfwick said. He was sitting at the opposite end of the loft, his knees drawn up, his back to the wall. In the deepening twilight, Día could look at his pale, drawn face and believe that he was still an ordinary, living person – that he was only somewhat ill.

He had already assured her otherwise.

"Yes," she said, and seated herself under the window. "I'm glad for that. It's been a long time since we had anything much to celebrate."

"You don't need to stay," he said – though of course she did. Halfwick would be gone tomorrow, at least if Elim had his way, and Día had far too many questions to leave unanswered.

"Neither did you," she said, "but it was kind of you to do it." Día had little memory of that night on the mountain – most of it was a painful blur – but she knew that he had done that much for her, and that soon it would be his turn to press on and leave her behind. "And I was hoping you could do me one more kindness, and – and tell me what He said to you."

Halfwick might have heard her invoking the holy pronoun, but he didn't return it. "What makes you think he said anything?"

"He must have!" Día cried, leaning forward to press her hands into the hay-strewn floor. "He did – I know he did. What did he tell you?"

There was a little too much silence from the other side of the loft. "That he loves you," Halfwick said at last. "That you've been good and faithful, and passed every test. That you glorify him by doing his work, and will be rewarded for it."

Día sat back. "You don't need to lie to me."

"Sorry," Halfwick said. She couldn't see much of his face, but he seemed sincere. "You sounded like you'd had too much of the truth already."

Día's eyes filled, unbidden, and she hurried to wipe them clear. She'd cried more in the past two weeks than she had in the past ten years, and was beginning to despair of the well ever running dry. "And what truth is that?"

"That none of us knows what we're doing," came the rough-edged reply. "That nobody has all the answers, and anybody who claims otherwise is deluded or selling you something. That we're all making it up as we go along, and the most you can hope for is a pocket of confidence big enough to hold some of your doubts, but not deep enough to stuff yourself in. And that if you're anything like me, and have spent your life running around with a – a bloody bag over your head, it's going to hurt when someone snatches it away."

Día couldn't argue with that. Winshin had made sure of it. "But you're His favorite," she said, her voice small in her own ears. "He loves you. He saved you."

Halfwick leaned forward, into the faint radiance of torchlight and stars beaming through the empty window. Even in the dim light, it was impossible to miss the red-purple rope bruise appearing around his neck, or the greenish rot slowly eating through his youthful features. "Do you really think so?"

"Well, what else am I to understand?" Día said, exasperated. "Think past what you look like and consider what you've done: He's obviously chosen you to be the worker of His miracles!"

Halfwick actually smiled at that, and leaned back into the shadows. "Funny," he said. "I was just thinking the same about you."

Día found nothing funny about it. "That's not remotely true. I didn't – nothing I did was any good.

God saved you, and the Dog Lady saved Elim. I could have stayed home." She sorely wished she had.

"True," said the clotting voice in the shadows. "Except that Elim wouldn't have been there if you hadn't kept him alive here in town – if you hadn't brought him help and water after I let him be strung up in the street. I wouldn't have gotten anywhere near him if you hadn't helped me get out of here. And I wouldn't be surprised to learn that you had something to do with that fire in the desert – the one Elim says kept the whole lot of them from being eaten alive."

There was a little tap-sound as Halfwick let his head rest back against the weathered wooden wall. "Think of it, Día. I might have instigated this whole mess, but you're the one who made something out of it. You cut me down when they hanged me. You woke me up before you buried me. And even though I don't pretend to understand what I might have been granted, I can promise you this: I never would have had the humility to ask for it if I hadn't been constantly eclipsed, humbled, just – in every way outshone by someone I considered completely beneath me."

It took Día a moment to realize that he was talking about her. It took a moment more to swallow the lump in her throat.

By then, Halfwick had carried on. "So... I'm sorry that I don't have any great revelations for you. But you should – I think you ought to go and enjoy the party out there, or at least credit yourself for it, because in a world without you – without every one of your efforts – I fail, and Elim dies, and none of this happens. God didn't need to choose you. You chose yourself."

For a man with no great revelations, he was doing a

lousy job. Dumbstruck, grasping at the edges of an idea whose full shape she couldn't begin to imagine, Día had no hope of framing a suitable reply. "Thank you," she said at last. "I don't... I've been struggling with that."

That earned her a moldering snort. "I know the feeling."

Her first thought was a disgusted *How could you possibly?*

Her second, more public expression was considerably kinder. "How so?"

There was a shifting in the darkness opposite, and her first whiff of what was fast becoming Halfwick's trademark smell. "I expected to die," he said. "I thought I would save Elim, make up for things by getting him pardoned, and then I would die. But I didn't, and I haven't: it was the Dog Lady or Marhuk or both that cleared the debt for him. And now... now I'm at a bit of a loose end." He might have shaken his head. "Scratch that – I AM a loose end. I haven't – this can't be a reward or a punishment, as I haven't done anything good or bad enough to deserve it. I haven't really done anything at all."

Día would have liked to help refute that. She would have liked to take that beautiful copy of the Verses that Winshin had given her, flip expertly open to the correct page, and read him something that would clear things right up – find a nice bit of prophecy to tie up everything.

But the book was still sitting back at her church, unopened... because although Día could have read whatever was written therein, she didn't trust herself to understand it. How could she, when she couldn't even make sense of what she'd seen with her own eyes? All those things she'd taken for signs, miracles: Halfwick's resurrection, the body she'd pulled from the oasis, the plum that had sprouted overnight, which she had buried somewhere in the desert. Día desperately needed an interpreter, a fellow human being to help make sense of it all... and Halfwick seemed to know even less than she did.

So she reached back to the last Penitent authority in her life, her hand curling around the fabric of her cassock where her dreadlocks used to be. What would he tell her? What had he known?

"Well," she said at last, "I don't think I've told you, but my father was the sexton here. He was only supposed to dig the graves, but sometimes when someone died in shame or sin – suicides, for example – and the priest didn't want to conduct a service, Father and I would have one in secret. He told me that we should always pray for that person's soul, no matter what they'd done. The priest said that the person went to their final reward as soon as they died, but Father said that because God exists outside time, the things we did for them after they died were just as important as the things *they* did when they were alive."

Día couldn't tell whether Halfwick's silence was reflective or simply confused. Was she making any sense at all?

"So we could... that is, their fate wasn't set in stone," she continued. "We offered prayers for the dead not to try to change God's mind about what to do with their soul, but to reach back *through* God, to touch the person they were back when they were still alive. We hoped – we believed that what we did in the present could change the past."

"Not bloody likely," Halfwick muttered.

"But if it were true, how would you know?" Día countered. A past life would change, and the present world would be changed in turn. It would happen instantly, imperceptibly.

"Anyway," she said. "What I mean to say is that... you know, maybe what you are now isn't about what you've already done. Maybe it's about what you WILL do. And regardless... whether or not you can find anything in your past that justifies your present, your present certainly is the root of your future. Perhaps it would be healthier to start thinking of what you mean to accomplish with what you've been given – you know, what you can do now that you couldn't before."

And on reflection, perhaps Día would do well to take some of her own advice. She'd been thinking of that over the past week, during the trip home. On the surface of it, she hadn't acquired much but an extra measure of courage and a pile of unanswered questions – but underneath that, a spark of envy was kindling. Seeing all those beautifully dark a'Krah – even being mistaken for one of them – and watching the way Fours and Miss du Chenne shared a siblings' embrace, and feeling how the Dog Lady cared for Elim... all of it had engendered an unbearable thirst for kinship, a wish to share in that priceless, effortless similarity. Día had little idea about the world east of the border, but she knew it included people like her – and she desperately wanted to meet them.

"Well," Halfwick said presently. "Perhaps I will. In the meantime, I can think of at least one thing you can accomplish on my behalf."

Día glanced up. "What's that?"

There was a little hint of whiteness back there in the shadows – perhaps a postmortem smile. "You could stop hanging about with rancid barn-dwelling vagrants and go enjoy yourself."

Honestly, Día didn't feel like it. Everyone out there would be noisy if not drunk, and she would be jostled and stepped on and endlessly pressed to drink.

But the return of a living goddess was far beyond a once-in-a-lifetime occasion... and if she were thinking with Halfwick's pragmatism, being seen in public as one of U'ru's favorite foster-puppies would almost certainly cut down on nervous looks and closed doors.

Día sighed, and tried to muster some enthusiasm. "I suppose I should. But I've enjoyed our time, and I'll look for you again before you leave."

Halfwick shifted again in the dark. "I'd like that."

Something had gone unsaid just there, but it might be impolite to linger and ask. So Día reluctantly climbed down from the loft and went out – to see and be seen, to present herself as a confident, contented young lady, and to hope that someday she would be one.

SIL SAT THERE long after Día had gone out. He watched the moon rise, the fires die down, and the festivities disperse. Eventually, he pulled out the little stone in his pocket – the flat one he'd started carving into a portable headstone during that long, strange walk through the desert. The pen-knife scratchings were too faint to make out in the dark, but his softening thumbnail had all but memorized them.

S.A. Halfwick.
1/4/47 – /9/64

He'd left the day blank, waiting for the moment when he finally collapsed from exposure and thirst. Now he considered filling in the last day of his old life – the one that had ended with a noose and a push and a moment of weightless surprise. Or perhaps he ought to just lob the silly thing straight out the window and have done.

In the end, Sil did neither. Instead, he sat back, thinking about what Día had said about having an eye towards future accomplishments – and what he had promised in a moment of mad, unthinking desperation.

Let me live, and I will profit you more than any man ever has.

CHAPTER EIGHTEEN
A DAY NOT PROMISED

IN THE END, it wasn't any bodily discomfort that drove Elim to wakefulness. Just the opposite: he was so comfortable, and the bed was so pleasant, that he thought he would open his eyes just long enough to see if there wasn't time for a little bit more of a lie-in before the chore-bell –

– and was amazed all over again to find himself in a stranger's room.

He wasn't at home. He was in Fours' upstairs bedroom. And the morning light promised that he'd been there awhile – that he'd survived one more night in Sixes, this time with no sunburn, no hangover, nothing at all to show for it...

... nothing except for a lone visitor, sitting and looking out the window.

"Hawkeye?" Elim sat bolt upright, hardly able to credit his eyes. The Sundowner fellow was clean and dressed, with no blindfold, no splint, not a scratch on him.

He turned at the sound of Elim's voice, his face pleasant even as his eyes drifted. "Sir?"

"Thank God, buddy – oh, thank God. I thought you were stove in. I thought you were done for. What happened to you?"

The translator shook his head. "I don't understand." The words came out faintly slurred, with ominous little gaps in between, as if Hawkeye were having to hand-pick each one of them.

Didn't he remember it? "The mountain, you know, when you were all so sick. You'd busted your leg, and I carried you, and you got them queer fits, and made the – and they made the rocks crumble up. You recall that?"

The translator's brow furrowed... the left side more so than the right. "Recall what?"

Elim's heart sank at the implications. He tried one more time, in his best Sunday Ardish. "Are you all right?"

The left side of Hawkeye's mouth ticked up in the suggestion of a smile. "I'm okk..." Then he hit a wall, groping for a word that wasn't there. "Okk..."

Was there anything of Hawkeye left? Did he even know who he was? Elim clutched at the bedspread, suddenly anxious not to be the only still-intact survivor of that whole funeral expedition – desperate to assure himself that he still had a fellow-veteran, a friend in arms. "Okay?" Elim suggested, willing the word to make itself true.

"Okay," Hawkeye dutifully repeated.

Elim exhaled, long and sorrowfully. He hadn't made it. He'd wanted so badly to get this one thing right: to save just one person, to beat the odds and keep Hawkeye alive, to prove to himself and the world that he was more than ignorance and a gun, and now...

Well, and now it might be time to put aside his own wants.

"You, uh... you want a smoke?" Elim ventured. "Your pipe?"

Hawkeye brightened at that. "Pipe."

Elim held his breath and watched as Hawkeye used his left hand to fish out a rusty tin from his left pocket, and a new pipe from his right. Then he reached for the cane beside him, tried and failed to clear the chair, and dropped back down into it.

Elim was on his feet in a hot second. "Do you need..."

But Hawkeye was already back at it – using every bit of his strength to haul himself up to standing, and then to move forward at a heavy, grinding drag: one step forward with his left foot, followed by one awkward pull of his right. He leaned heavily on the edge of Fours' overcrowded desk, feeling along the drawer-fronts as he went – until one apparently inspired him. He pulled it open and withdrew something, before helping himself laboriously back to a seat.

It was agonizingly tedious to watch. Elim could have fetched whatever that was in four seconds, if Hawkeye had told him where to look.

If Hawkeye could have told him where to look.

So he sat back down on the bed and watched as Hawkeye resettled himself, opened up his prize – a packet of matches – and set about fixing his pipe. It was a tricky business, trying to get the pipe filled, the match struck, and the contents lit with only one decent hand. He spilled some of the filling on his shirt-tail as he worked. It was almost impossible for Elim to avoid leaping up to intervene as he watched that first dangerous lick of flame spring to life.

But no, dammit: the man was blind and lame and addled to boot, and if he was going to make it, if he was going to have any decent life, he had to fix his own pipe. Elim needed that much. Hawkeye deserved that much.

And after the translator finally set the match aside and took his first drag, he breathed out a single smoking, profoundly satisfied word. "*Okupado.*"

Elim, who had neither the pipe nor the epiphany, took a minute to catch up.

Okupado. Occupied. Busy.

Elim exhaled – a huge, bottomless relief – and sat back.

Not 'okay'. *Okupado.* Busy with something – working on something. Even if he couldn't articulate it just then. Even if Elim didn't have the wit or worldliness to understand it just then.

That was all right. That would be enough. "It's good, ain't it?" Elim said.

"It's good," Hawkeye agreed.

So maybe he wasn't addled after all. Maybe he was still a little sorcerous – he sure had found those matches on the quick side – and maybe he still had more healing to do. Somebody had definitely been taking care of him.

Elim's empty stomach contracted as he realized who that somebody might be... and what it meant that she'd brought Hawkeye *here*.

And Sil – where was Sil? Had he come into town looking for Elim? Why wasn't he here?

"I gotta – I have to leave," Elim said. "Are you gonna be all right?"

"Right as rain." The sharper side of Hawkeye's face smiled, as if he'd made an especially clever remark. And he held out his hand, as if he needed help in standing.

But when Elim reached down to help him up, Hawkeye made no effort to rise. His fingers closed over

Elim's wrist, warm and sure, brown on brown – equally, perfectly human. "We survived, *emi*."

Elim didn't know about that last word, but he knew a handshake when he felt one. And he could not have been more pleased to return it. "We sure did, buddy. Thanks for making it through with me."

It was a poor, simple turn of phrase – one Hawkeye could have expressed better in three languages than Elim had ever managed in one. And it was going to have to do for a goodbye.

But after he'd gathered himself up to go, Elim paused at the stair, mentally fixing a last picture of his most improbable friend: an almost-ordinary middle-aged man, looking a little grayer but infinitely more satisfied as he rested there by the window, smoking and sitting and basking in the warmth of the new morning sun.

THE MAN, HAKAI, sat in silence thereafter. He finished his smoke, set down the pipe, and closed his eyes. The only movement in the room came from his breathing. He might have been asleep.

But his head did not drop. His shoulders did not slump. And cooling on the bureau was a sign, a pledge, a deadly-serious promise for anyone who cared enough to notice it. The match, burnt and cold on one end, had sprouted on the other.

ELIM FELT AS if he'd slept for a week. Maybe he had. Or maybe he'd actually gone backwards somehow – because when he ventured downstairs, it was like stepping back into an older, kinder world.

Fours' store was clean again, probably cleaner than it had been in awhile. Everything was put back in its place, overcrowded but stacked and sensibly arranged. Even Fours himself was back where he belonged: behind his little jury-rigged counter-top, doing a thinner but otherwise perfect impression of the white-haired grandfatherly proprietor he had been before. There was nothing left of the nightmare-world but a faintly sour smell, and even that was airing out in the cross-breeze that drifted through the two open doors.

He glanced up from his ledger at Elim's approach. "Your partner's just gone to visit with the Azahi, if you were looking for him."

Well, for a man missing his daughter, he seemed to have come to grips with it in blistering short order. "I was," Elim said. "Thanks. And, uh, I was wondering..." He nodded up at the ceiling. "Is he gonna be all right?"

There was a thaw in Fours' icy demeanor, then – his voice warmed with interest. "Well, it's early to say just yet, but certainly we can get him walking a little better. I'm going to get that cane cut down to fit him, first of all, and I think with enough practice he could even..."

Then he seemed to remember who he was speaking with, and the window behind his eyes closed right up again. "... well. I won't bore you with the details. Your horse is outside, as are your things, and I took the liberty of setting your boots out there as well. I don't recall who sold them to me, but they'll do more good on your feet than they will in my inventory."

All of which was a silver-dollar way of saying *Don't let the door hit you.*

Well, that was a shame. But then again, Fours' life had apparently been a bottomless shit-heap since the minute Elim decided to go splatter a man's brains all over his barn. He could hardly blame the old fishman for wanting to get quit of him... and hopefully Día would be back soon.

Now there was a can of worms that didn't need re-opening. Elim squelched the first set of words that came to mind, and went with the old standby. "Thanks. That's awfully kind of you."

Fours went back to his ledger. "No charge."

So that was about the size of it. Elim saw himself out to the porch and sat down to pull on his boots – and crusty socks aside, it was unutterably fine to finally, properly shoe himself again. Just having that half-inch of leather between him and the rest of the world was a priceless comfort: the kind of confidence that made a man walk a whole foot taller as he stepped out into the sun and strode around to see to his horse...

... and found that she had been out strumpeting again.

Elim stared at Molly from over the corral fence, struck absolutely dumb with astonishment. She was there waiting for him and breakfast, respectively, batting her big brown eyes as innocently as you pleased – and making no effort to excuse the blue-and-white finger-paints streaked in fanciful swirls down her sides, or the ribbons braided into her mane, or the turkey-feather in her forelock.

"Miz Boone," he said, "where HAVE you been?"

"It's not what it looks like," said a soft, measured voice behind him.

Elim turned, and had his last bit of surprise used up on the spot: Día was coming for him, carrying a folded cloth and looking perfectly serene, albeit a little tired around the edges. She smiled as she patted Molly's shoulder. "There was a bit of a get-together last night. We may have conducted ourselves with something less than perfect modesty."

Well, that was business as usual where the lady Boone was concerned – but Elim couldn't even pretend to keep up the joke. "You're back," he said, insightfully. "How... Are you all right?"

"I'm fine," Día said – and while Elim didn't believe that for a second, the look in her eyes suggested that whatever had happened to her had left a deep bruise, not an open wound. "It's good to be home again."

Well, that explained how Fours had suddenly found sense again – though of course it didn't make up for anything. "Día, I'm so sorry. I can't believe we just up and left you, and after you came all that way to get me –"

Her hand on his arm shut him up handily. Día looked up at him – and God, it was still so odd to see her without her hair – and he knew before she opened her mouth that he wasn't going to like what came out of it.

"I didn't," she said. "I'm sorry. I meant to tell you before. I didn't – I never meant to come after you. I never intended to leave Island Town at all. I was only going to lead Halfwick out far enough to find you on his own, and then he – and then I got lost, and... and the point is, you shouldn't thank me for anything."

Well, that was...

That was a pile of horse-apples, to put it politely. Even if she knocked that off the list, he still owed her for trying to warn him away from Sixes in the first place, and keeping him watered and chaperoned after he went and got all hung up in it anyway, and talking to the Azahi for him – which he hadn't had the brains to appreciate at the time – and more than that, too. Probably more than he even knew about.

Elim could have pointed that out. And then Día could have told him that she was just doing her job, probably with a whole bookish heap of words that all boiled down to a modest and ladylike *aw shucks*.

So he took a different tack, and nodded down at the garment in her hands. "Can I still thank you for bringing me my shirt?"

Día might have blushed at that. It was hard to tell. "Oh – er, yes, I suppose. I left it at the church by mistake, so I'm afraid it's been sitting dirty for awhile. The stain didn't quite come out, but it's better than it was."

If there were Ardish words to express how little that mattered right then, Elim didn't have them. He held it by the shoulders as the folds dropped open – and boy, was it a sight for sore eyes. There in his hands was his own soft gray work-shirt, clean and regular and so perfectly him-sized that it was only willpower and good Penitent shame that kept him from ripping that itchy wool poncho off right there in the middle of the street.

Barn. He would go to the barn, have a piss and a change and a drink from the pump, and then he would see about Sil.

... in a minute, of course. All in just a minute.

"It's just perfect," he said. "Thank you."

But that didn't seem like nearly enough. After everything she'd done for him, and all of the negative nothing he'd done for her – what was he going to do, flip a nickel at her and ride on out?

Not hardly. "And I, uh – hang on a sec. I got something for you too."

He didn't, actually. His own things were lost or

burned up, and he'd eaten most everything the a'Krah had given him. But that didn't stop Elim from rooting through his bag, hunting for an improvised prize.

Not his lone moccasin-shoe: it had been a present from Way-Say, and that was a sadness he didn't want to part with. Not the lock of hair he'd cut from poor Ax's mane – that was for Will. Not his bag of bullets, because what kind of present was that for a lady?

"Here," he said at last, and handed her up the last of the plums he'd picked on the way back. "It ain't much, but I reckoned you might like it."

It was a fair bet: they had been unusually big, especially for wild plums, and the three Elim had already eaten all tasted positively divine.

But maybe he'd chosen poorly somehow: Día stared and stared at the fruit in her hand, as if it had fallen straight out of the sky. "Where did you get this?"

Elim straightened and scratched his neck, hoping he hadn't put his foot in something. "We passed a big plum tree on our way here – maybe a day or so back. Nowhere special, not too far from the road. It was a heck of a thing, growing out there all by itself. I didn't know they could get that big."

Día cupped the fruit in both hands, as if it were a newborn bunny or hatchling chick. She stared at it for what felt like an age – and when she finally tore her gaze away, she leveled such a look at Elim that it was all he could do not to flinch from the intensity of it.

"Elim, take me with you."

He blinked, sure he'd gotten the wrong end of the conversational stick. "What?"

Día shook her head. "I'm serious. I mean it. If – if you really want to thank me... take me back with you."

Elim's breath was pressed out of him like air from punched-down dough. Everything else escaped likewise: the sunlit street, the fresh horse-fortified air, the distant sound of a woman's scolding – until he was left with nothing but a dark-eyed, wildly hopeful face, and the sad task of disappointing it. "I'm sorry," he said at last. "I can't do that."

"Yes you can!" she said, the second-loudest words he'd ever heard from her. "You're a free man. You said so yourself. And I'm a grown woman, and I don't – I don't belong here anymore."

The a'Krah must have wounded her even more deeply than he'd thought. Elim frowned. "Día, what's wrong? Ain't you glad to be home?"

"No, I'm not!" she cried. "I'm not anything! I don't – I can't fit anymore. I'm not the right shape anymore." And it was a disconcerting sight to see placid, bookish Día gesturing in frustration, furiously fumbling for words. "There has to be somewhere else, somewhere where I'm not... where I'm just... where I don't have to feel like this!"

Elim couldn't say what feeling that was. Maybe there was some of it waiting for him back at his home, too. He took a breath, inhaling patience. "Día, you don't know what it's like over there. You don't know what they'd do to you."

Her hands clenched; a wisp of smoke trailed up from between her toes. "You don't know what's already been done to me!"

Elim couldn't help it. He flinched, and shameful as it was, his first thought was not guilt or sympathy or compassion: it was raw, selfish fear. In that instant, he prayed that Fours wouldn't hear her strident carrying-on and get the wrong idea – that Elim wasn't about to be in a whole fresh pantload of trouble.

And wasn't that always the way? There in a nutshell was everything he wanted to spare her: going through life always anxious not to offend the gentle-folk, always afraid of what would happen if you caught the wrong eye at the wrong moment. Elim glanced at Día's bare head, and wished he had words to tell her how much more she still had to lose. Even if it didn't turn her into someone's property, the world east of the border would wear her down into two-legged prey animal: quiet and constrained, corseted and shod. Eaden would eat her alive.

"You're right," he finally said. "I don't. But I promise you that this won't fix it."

Día's face hardened. Her full lips narrowed, and her voice cooled. "You're telling me you won't do it." And she didn't need to say the words out loud for Elim to hear what came after: *After everything I've done for you.*

And even then, Elim couldn't bring himself to say *yes.* He couldn't give her a plain, point-blank refusal... because he did owe her, and because it was her life to decide about, and because any woman who could walk a hundred miles west through that desert and back again had already proven herself beyond all doubt: if she allotted on following him back to Hell's Acre, there wasn't a thing Elim could do about it.

And if he couldn't be chivalrous and convince her for her own sake, he would just have to be selfish and do it for his. "No," he said with leaden precision. "I'm asking you not to put that weight on me."

Maybe he should have said that more plainly. Maybe

he didn't need to. Maybe that crinkling of her brows meant that she understood how it was – how the boy he'd ended in that barn over there would hang on his soul for the rest of his life, and how the old man in that house beside it had already given Elim a terrible glimpse of how much heavier that burden could get.

Or maybe she just hated him.

"I see," Día said, her eyes already filling with clarity. "I won't trouble you further."

And just because Elim could have seen that coming didn't make it any more pleasant when it finally arrived. "Día, you know it ain't like that. Just cuz…"

But whatever she knew was already hurrying away with her, one hand clenching the plum, the other wiping at her eyes.

Dammit.

Which left Elim standing there by the corral, with nothing to console him but a pair of hairy lips at his neck.

He glanced over at Molly, her outlandish costume somehow even more inappropriate than before. "Made a pig's ear out of that, didn't we?"

We, because it would be unforgivably ungentlemanly to say *she*… and Elim was half a gentleman at least.

Not gentleman enough to think of what kind of weight *she* was carrying, he belatedly realized. Not smart enough to think of asking her what-all had lit that fire in her in the first place. God Almighty, if he had a nickel for every dumb-ass word…!

Well, he would try to find her again before they left. He would try for a better goodbye. And in the meantime, he would try not to step in anything else.

So he let himself back in to the barn, amazed at how

little it had changed from that first morning when he'd woken up there in the loft with a hangover and a hole in his memory. The battered stalls were all empty now – even the two mules were gone – but otherwise it was just the same.

Then, as now, he had wandered down the row, wondering just what kind of a mess he'd made. Then, as now, he had tried to get his mind right for leaving, for giving his companions a proper farewell and going on home without them. Then, as now, even a piss for the ages didn't make him feel much better.

So it seemed perfectly mirror-appropriate to hear the footsteps outside as he finished up – not knocking and pounding this time, because the door wasn't closed, but otherwise right on schedule.

"Hold on a minute, Sil," he said. "I'll get Molly tacked up and then we can go."

There was a little creak of somebody leaning up against the doorframe – but that cool, cruel voice wasn't Sil's.

"Well, slow down there, partner." The fishman, Champagne, flashed him a sharp-toothed smile. "What's your hurry?"

And standing there in sunlit silhouette was the other mother.

SHEA HAD TO admit that U'ru had been the very soul of patience. When sunrise had caught them a few miles short of Island Town, the great lady had let Día hurry on ahead – as long as Shea went along to mind her, of course. When night fell, U'ru had been perfectly delighted to put her family business on hold for the sake of a grand reunion with her beloved island home. Even this morning, with the festivities concluded and the Azahi satisfied and Hakai safely installed with Fours, the Dog Lady had lingered on the sight of Yashu-Diiwa overspilling the bed, and decided to let her tired puppy sleep.

Now he was awake, and it was her turn.

Which was news to the boy. He jumped, and then fumbled with whatever he was doing over there by the farther stalls – Shea couldn't see more than a flinching brown blur.

"Whoa, hey!" he snapped. "How 'bout y'all wait outside, huh?"

Honestly, had there ever been a more inconsiderate, ungrateful child? Shea scowled. "How about you try that again, you mannerless mongrel sheepf –"

What is he saying? U'ru wanted to know. *Why is he scared?* She didn't know him well enough to be able to read his thoughts, and any Ardish she'd learned was long since forgotten, but one didn't need to be an earthly god to hear stress in a human voice.

He doesn't understand, Shea answered. The story of his life.

By then the boy had composed himself, and even found the guts to come a little closer. "Fine – here it is again. Thank you very much for fixing my friend Hawkeye. Now I would please like you to stand aside so I can get on home."

U'ru said nothing, but Shea could hear the anxious whine in her throat. "Will you let her answer you?"

Even Yashu-Diiwa seemed to consider that that might be the least his selfish carcass owed her. Shea couldn't see much of his expression from here, but his arms folded under his poncho. "Sure – if she can do it without manhandling me or eating my brain."

Shea stepped forward. "Listen, you callow shit –"

Then U'ru grabbed her by the back of her ill-fitting hood. *Don't scare him!* she pleaded.

Right. Yes. Reconciliation. Kid gloves. Shea tried again. "Just... listen, all right? She's not going to bewitch you, she's not going to suck out what passes for your – look, Elim, do her one kindness in your life and hear her out, can't you?"

There was just enough silence to give Shea hope, and perhaps a firmer set to his jaw. "... all right. All right, sure."

Hopefully that actually meant something. "Right," Shea said. "Now pay attention with your mind, with your heart – she doesn't have anything for your ears."

Go ahead, Mother. He's ready to hear you.

U'ru took a nervous step forward, and Shea could feel her sprouting a single tiny blossom of hope.

My puppy. My baby. My Loves-Me.

She took a second step, and Shea sucked her teeth – but Yashu-Diiwa didn't flinch back.

I'm so sorry. I didn't mean to lose you. I would have done anything to keep you. And I see how you've grown without me, and I know you have another home, another mother who loves you and wants you and misses you. I know you must be a good boy, and not want to make her cry... but you must also know how much I love you too. U'ru began to take a third step, but then seemed to fear that that would be too much. She stood where she was, hands clasped tight over her soft furry stomach.

I hope that you will want to be with me too, at least

sometimes, and that you will let me start to know you again. I want to learn who you are now. I want to teach you who I am. Please, will you let us be a family again?

To his credit, the boy met her gaze all the while, paying her the strictest, most rapt attention...

... until his gaze drifted back over to Shea and dissolved into confusion. "Well?" he said. "Is she started yet?"

Shea's heart missed a beat, and briefly considered giving up altogether.

And in the deciding-space between, she heard Marhuk's voice again. *You were not a good mother to your children,* the old crow had said. *And so you will have no children.*

After all, the earthly gods had no tongues, and could be heard only by those who wished to listen... and as it turned out, a consenting mouth was no substitute for an open, willing heart.

I'm sorry, Mother, Shea said at last. *He can't hear you. He is deaf.*

MAYBE THAT WAS the wrong thing to say. The fishman didn't reply, but Elim could see the other mother's expression wilt like a paper flower dropped in a puddle.

And harden as she advanced.

And Elim's first thought was that it didn't matter how many women he sent away crying today: his only job was to get back home to the one woman who had been left weeping far too long already. He stood his ground, shoring himself up to stall or run or fight, if he had to – to find the violence in him one more time, to bite or kick or trample whoever got between him and that door...

But the look on his face was apparently a lethal weapon all its own. The other mother staggered to a stop, poisoned by whatever she saw in him. Her eyes filled with tears.

Elim ought to take advantage of that. He ought to leave now, for good and all this time.

But whether it was his boots or the barn or the lady Boone waiting for him outside, Elim felt safer in himself now than he had before – more anchored in his own skin. He was reliably different from the barefoot native woman in the furry brown robe, even in spite of the likeness in their faces. She had no power over him.

But he was indebted to her.

So it was easier to find the kindness that maybe he should have shown her earlier, and to try to stanch a little of her sadness. "Well, look," he said, his gaze switching between her and her fishman. "Maybe you could tell her something from me instead. Maybe you could tell her that I'm sorry for my meanness. I'm sorry that things happened like they did, and I'm sorry this didn't work out like it was supposed to."

What else was there? Elim dug down further, abashed in spite of everything. He'd just been so caught up with everything, so hounded with guilt and fear and brutal bone-wearing exhaustion, that he hadn't sat down and really thought about any of this. He didn't know half of what he should, and he couldn't afford to stay long enough to find out.

Still, if there was one thing he probably didn't need to be told, it was that a pagan goddess wasn't liable to be taken advantage of, or to wake up on the wrong side of someone else's bed. Which meant that for the first time in his life, Elim could entertain the idea that he was neither an accident nor a consequence – that he had been born wanted.

And that was a hell of a thing.

And the part of him that wasn't practically dragging him back across that border, that wasn't just mad with the thought that he was standing less than a thousand yards from Eadan territory, would have liked to find out more about that. About who his father was, and what he was made for and what went wrong, and what might still be put right.

But at the end of the day, there was nothing he could learn about the family he might have had that would justify his leaving the one he already belonged to, and every minute he spent dallying here was a cruelty to both.

"Anyway," he said, "I got people back home that I'm obliged to, and I can't leave them. Maybe someday that'll be different... but right now I'm all out of time and promises. I hope she – I hope you understand. I hope you can find some other happiness."

If the fishman was translating, Elim couldn't hear it – but then, the other mother had apparently spoken to him, and he couldn't hear that either.

But some of that must have gotten through, because she came at him with open arms and leaky eyes, and the wild, horsey, runaway thing in him took a hard rein as Elim made himself meet her halfway.

It was a good hug: warm and strong and soft, all wrapped in the smell of doggy fur and musk. He could believe she would have been a good mother. But the moment she touched him, she provoked his inheritance: in an instant, Elim felt himself growing height and hair and a dangerous pressure inside the swelling leather of his left boot... and strangeness was a luxury he could not afford. He pulled away.

And despite her wet face and trembly hot hands and stifled hiccup breaths, she didn't try to keep him.

"Lesson four," the fishman said from behind. "Ugly and ungrateful as you are, your mother still loves you more than you'll ever know."

One day, Elim decided, he would come back and learn how to understand the Dog Lady. Then they wouldn't need an arbitrator, and he could punch that fishman in its smarmy snaggle-toothed face.

That day was not today. Elim sighed. "Yeah, thanks, short-stack. I got that."

But he still hated to see that unbearable sadness on his – on the other mother's face. He couldn't stay... but that didn't mean he couldn't leave something behind. "Here," he said, after a moment's thought, and pulled off that poncho. "For you – if you want it."

He might as well have handed over a bouquet. She pressed the dirty wool to her face, inhaling sun-fermented weeks of Elim's skin and sweat, and one look at that expression of rapturous canine bliss promised that this new lovey was never, ever getting washed.

The fishman apparently considered that a good note to go out on. Elim watched it tug at her arm, coaxing her toward the door before she came down from that fleeting, smelly high. "Well, good luck and good riddance," it said over its shoulder – before digging in the pocket of its oversized native costume and chucking something shiny-bright straight at his face. "Do us a favor and try not to get yourself killed out there, can you?"

Elim's right hand snapped up and intercepted the thing

before his nose could do the honors. It was a beautiful sterling silver pocket-watch – which, knowing the giver, had probably been stolen off some unsuspecting dandy. But as it ticked quietly away, it melted his hoof-hard palm back into soft, brown, ordinary human flesh.

Elim stared and wondered at it for a moment, recalling all those tales of heroic soldiers loading their last silver bullet to fight the onrushing heathen hordes. Lead made them monstrous, the old-timers said. Silver turned them human.

Then he worked the watch between his hands like a bar of soap, massaging his palms with the soft circular contours until the metal was warm and just slightly slick – until his height and hair and the rest of his animal oddities had withdrawn back to his bones to hibernate.

It was hard to know what to think about that. Certainly he was glad to have such a handy souvenir – a little pocket-magic to help keep him on the right side of his heritage. And yet it was unnerving to realize that he might actually have a need for it – that this-all might not vanish like a bad dream once he was back home again. He already knew he'd lived too long here in this wild other-land: eaten its food, made friends and enemies of its people, left a trail of his blood and footprints from here to Atali'Krah. For better and worse, this place was in him now. More than that, though, meeting the other mother had broken open something inside him, maybe forever. Maybe he would spend the rest of his life as a mended shovel: still fit for work, but always liable to break along that same conspicuous fault.

That would have been worth putting up with the fishman to ask her about… but by the time Elim looked up to do it, the two of them were long gone.

Elim stood there for a minute, marshalling himself in the solitude of the hay-strewn sanctuary around him.

Yes, he could fill a book with everything he didn't know.

Yes, this-all almost certainly wasn't going to wash off in the river.

But at the end of the day, if you were going to be sick or sad or have bad dreams, there was nowhere better to do it than your own bed.

So Elim picked up his old homespun shirt and pulled it on over his head, infinitely relieved to feel the soft, thousand-times-washed cloth drop over him, and to find that it still fit. And when he had safely contained himself, he went back out again – homeward bound at last.

EVER THE OPTIMIST, Elim had naively assumed that he and Sil would be out by mid-morning, and eat breakfast in the saddle. But by the time Elim had finished offending all his callers and packed up Molly, it was well on towards noon.

And Sil still wasn't done.

So there wasn't much to do but balance the load – namely, by shifting a substantial portion of the food in the saddlebags to Elim's stomach – and then wait.

Elim used to like waiting. Waiting was admitting that yes, you had done everything in your humble power – ate, dressed, packed, fed, raked, tied, bridled, and saddled – and entrusting the rest to God.

That was harder to do now than it had been previously.

"'Bout time!" Elim said, when his truant partner finally deigned to appear. "What took you so long?"

Sil smiled as he approached the corral – and God Almighty, they were going to have to put that boy in new clothes somewhere between here and Hell's Acre – and nodded out towards the town square. "The Azahi wanted to send us off in style. You know, for posterity."

Well, that was probably better than having their posterities booted straight into the river. In fact, as Elim led Molly east through the square, among the charred spots and litter that were usually hallmarks of one hog-killing good time, he realized that they weren't going to have to swim or hire a boat or anything: their modest audience was waiting for them at the eastern gate, the one whose drawbridge could actually put them straight across onto Eadan soil.

Well, hot damn.

It wasn't much of a receiving line, which was just fine by Elim. He and Sil hadn't done much to endear themselves to the locals, and they all had work to do.

But it was good to see the Azahi again – so much better than seeing him through a set of cell bars! – and to meet his golden-eyed gaze on equal footing.

"Well, Elim Horseman," he said in his honey-soft voice. "This is a right thing that you have done. We are glad to see you returned."

And it was hard to know whether that last part was *glad you made it back* or *glad to be getting rid of you*. But there was no mistaking the rifle in his hand, or the ceremony with which he laid it flat across his palms and offered it back to its owner.

"Thank you kindly," Elim said, and took it with equal solemnity. The significance of the gesture wasn't lost on him. "Thank you for giving me the chance."

And Día was there too, thank goodness: a little red

around the eyes, but otherwise back to her old spirits – or at least some reasonably agreeable new ones. "Elim, I'm sorry about that just there," she said, her expression full of relief as she said it. "I shouldn't have asked. Please excuse me."

Well, at least she'd said *excuse* and not *forgive* – because as far as Elim was concerned, there was little enough for the one, and none at all for the other. "It's all right," he said, careful not to mention any particulars that she might not have already shared with the other folks within earshot. "I'm sorry it didn't work out. But I'm so much obliged to you, and I hope you feel better. Really, Día, you are God's living gift... and Him willing, I'll see you again."

That worked out better than the plum. She smiled – an uncommonly handsome sight – and dipped her head. "Thank you. I'd like that."

It didn't seem quite right to hug her – not when she was a woman of the cloth and he was a mule of questionable repute and Fours was probably watching from behind a twitching curtain somewhere. But Elim was glad to offer his hand, and gladder still when she took it at the forearm – as if to assure him that he was more than a job to her, and that she should be more than an acquaintance of his.

And then there was the lady sheriff, flanking the Azahi's opposite side. She had squared her feet and her shoulders, her hands clasped behind her back, and was watching Elim like a sergeant inspecting the troops. He wished he knew enough Marín to thank her properly and in private: there were no shortage of translators here among their present company, but she never seemed comfortable around him in public.

Well, he at least knew how to say 'thank you'. "*Grese,*" he said.

The lady-sheriff awarded him a professional nod – and from behind her back, she proffered Elim's own weather-beaten gray hat. God only knew where she'd gotten it.

"Hat."

It was the longest Ardish speech he'd heard from her – perfect eloquence paired with matchless brevity.

Under the circumstances, Elim felt perfectly gallant in putting it on and doffing it again. "Hat," he pledged.

And when they had run clean out of well-wishers – not that Sil had lifted a finger to acknowledge any of it – Elim turned to see his partner dickering with something in one of the saddlebags. "Is your lordship about ready?"

"Just about," His Grace breezily replied.

But as the two deputies at the end of the road set about lowering the bridge, and Elim and Sil drew up to a halt to wait for it, something ominous prickled the air between them.

"What?" Elim said.

"I didn't say anything," Sil protested.

But Elim knew that just-a-smidge-defensive look, and he knew he wasn't going to like whatever it portended. "You were going to. Spit it out."

"Well... actually, I had meant to tell you –"

Elim had already turned to face him, and at Sil's first automatic downward glance, Elim caught sight of the discomfort on his face – and the envelope in his hand.

"No," Elim said, ice trickling through his bowels. "Hell no. Don't you even think about it, Sil – don't even joke."

But when Will's little brother looked up at him, there was nothing but gravity in his cold blue eyes. "Do you see me laughing?"

"I see you trying to run out on me!" Elim cried, keenly aware of those still-watching eyes behind them – the ones Sil hadn't bothered to say goodbye to.

The ones he'd probably spent all that time arranging just for this moment. Just so Elim wouldn't make a scene.

Well, they were fixing to have front-row seats to a spectacular backfire.

"And it's all about you, isn't it?" Sil retorted, provoking an anxious toss of Molly's head as he squared up to Elim in front of her. "What you did. What you want. What your family wants. Well, think of mine for a minute, will you? What are Will and Nillie supposed to think when I lock myself in my room every day at sunset? God, that glorified broom-closet doesn't even HAVE a lock – and what do you think's going to happen when one of them walks in on me? How are they supposed to un-see that? What am I going to say?"

Elim was ashamed to admit that he hadn't actually thought about it. "They're – they won't think any less of you, Sil. They love you –"

"I KNOW that!" Sil snapped – and then seemed to remember himself. "I know they do," he amended. "That's why I'm not going to put them through that. Look, we both know I never fit in there anyhow. It was only a matter of time before I lit out on my own, and... you know, and there's no time like the present."

He offered the letter. Elim couldn't bring himself to take it. After all of that, losing Sil and finding him and losing and finding him again, and now to have to give him up here in the home stretch...

Elim put his hand on Molly's shoulder, grounding himself in the ordinary world. "Sil, buddy... are you sure about this? It's all just happened awfully fast, and if you just went and gave it a try, you might..."

Elim stopped of his own accord, finding no hesitation, not so much as a flicker of doubt in his partner's eyes.

But there was no more anger there either, and Sil's tone was as neighborly as it ever got as he nodded back towards Fours' barn. "You got to make your choice, Elim, and I never said a word to sway you. Let me have that too."

Elim let out a slow, defeated breath. It was one thing to know that somebody was going to be disappointed no matter what you did. A whole different animal to actually have to do the disappointing.

And the bridge was down, and the witnesses were waiting – Día and the Azahi and the lady-sheriff and the rest. Waiting to get on with their lives. Waiting to work Sil into their hodgepodge town, find a place for him somewhere among all this clashing patchwork of earth and life.

"... all right," Elim said at last. "All right, sure. But if they ask about you – if they make me come back after you..."

Sil gave him a half-smile, and the letter. "You know where to find me."

Elim hoped that was true. He thought he could just about stand it, if it were. For now, all they had left between them was a promise and a cold, hearty handshake.

"Take care of yourself, Slim," Elim said. "I expect I'll see you around."

And if that might not happen anytime soon, well... Sil might be around for a good long while yet.

Maybe he thought the same thing. He nodded back at the bridge, as easily as if they were only going to split up to cover more ground – as if this weren't the end of a partnership. "Go home, Elim. Your supper's getting cold."

And that was how they parted ways: Sil staying on to make something of himself in the new world, and Elim going back to try and fit himself back into the old one. It was an amiable parting. Probably the best either of them could have hoped for. But as every calm, wooden clop of Molly's hooves brought Elim that much closer to the end of the bridge, and the beginning of the dry autumn savannah on the other side, it seemed a shame that neither of them could afford to look back.

THERE WASN'T MUCH consoling U'ru after that – and Shea knew better than to try and abridge her sadness. Her last child had left her, taking her hopes for the future with him, and there was no prescribed mourning for a thing like that.

So she did what she could, copying U'ru's colors in amphibious sympathy, and letting herself be clutched and cried-on in mammalian grief.

Honestly, Shea felt a bit leaky herself. She had expected the boy to resist his mother's pleading, at least at first. She hadn't expected him not to hear it at all. And to watch U'ru's last thread of life ride off without her, realizing that he could be shot or lynched or killed falling off his horse – to know that he could die at literally any random moment, and let him go anyway…

Well, apparently that was what mothers did. But Shea wasn't his mother, and she didn't have to like it.

Still, as morning gave way to afternoon, and U'ru's sobbing yielded to a quieter reflection, Shea prevailed upon her to take a walk, and begin reacquainting herself with her holy land. For now, the Dog Lady was still here, still alive – and she had work to do. She had decades' worth of discoveries to catch up on, a woman of the Maia to find, and gods willing, a drought to end.

None of which interested her terribly much just then.

But he will come back, U'ru said, unquenchably thirsty for assurance on this point.

Of course, Shea answered, and even managed to believe it. *Don't fret, Mother. His mind is full of his other family right now, but they're only human. Their lives are already growing short, and his will be long indeed. Give him time, and when they're gone, he'll want to fill that hole in his heart again. He'll want to find you again, and to learn who he is.*

It was lovely to feel that flowering of hope in U'ru's mind – and to walk down Morning Snake Street savoring the sounds and smells of another cool October morning in Island Town. *Yes. Yes, of course he will. But will they take care of him? Do you think he'll choose a good wife? What if she doesn't...*

U'ru trailed off, her senses aroused – half a second before Shea almost slammed into someone coming up Yellow Road.

She squinted up at the newcomer like a dazzled mole, a sharp remark springing instantly to mind...

... and just as quickly squelched when she saw that kinky-haired, behatted human shape.

"Good afternoon, Second Man," Shea said with automatic courtesy. "A pleasure to find you here. Have you had the pleasure of our great lady U'ru's acquaintance?"

By the look on Twoblood's face, she had not. In fact, she looked as fearful as a deer caught foraging in someone's garden, her posture as wire-tight as if she would bolt on the spot.

But Shea had no such explanation for the Dog Lady's sudden surge of interest.

Puppy? U'ru ventured, her plump face alive with curiosity. *Do you know me?*

Shea took a step back to regard the two of them simultaneously, the Dog Lady's soft, maternal contours contrasting sharply with the Second Man's rough work-hardened edges.

And then Twoblood seemed to consider that the game was up. "*Ashishii, yema,*" she said, her eyes downcast and her voice subdued.

If Shea had had a perch, she would have fallen straight off it. That was Ara-Naure, and the meaning was plain as day: *Hello, Mother.*

Any restraint U'ru might have had vanished on the spot: she reached forward to cup Twoblood's face in her hands, nearly knocking off her hat before the freckled woman hurriedly clapped a hand over it, scouring anxiously for curious bystanders.

Who are you from? U'ru asked, transported with delight. *Where have you been?*

Twoblood perhaps didn't have enough Ara-Naure to answer that: she replied in Marín, her voice barely above a whisper. "My father was Lovoka – one of the Winter Wolves. He stole my mother from the Ara-Naure. They lived well together. He thought..." She scratched with wild abandon behind her ear, powdering her left shoulder with a fresh dusting of dandruff. "He spent many years believing that I was his."

Shea sucked her teeth at the implications. An Ara-Naure woman, taken just as she was kindling a white man's child... a baby born, perhaps a little on the light side, perhaps kept out of the sun... perhaps raised as both Lovoka and Ara-Naure. Father Wolf's apostates, and Grandfather Crow's proxies. The warriors of the North, and the peacemakers of the West. Could it be?

U'ru all but knocked Twoblood to the ground in her eagerness to find out. *Is she living? Are there more? Please, will you tell me?*

Twoblood ran her tongue over her fangs, and apparently decided that she was more reluctant to disappoint the Dog Lady than she was to feed the curiosity of her neighbors. "... yes, Mother. I would be pleased to walk with you."

Shea fell in step behind them, at a respectful remove. And as they continued on their way up the road, it occurred to her that U'ru's proclamation might yet come true. One way or another, the Ara-Naure had brought forth a child of two worlds – albeit perhaps not the two that the great lady had been thinking of – and Shea couldn't begin to imagine what their union might hold.

BUT IN SPITE of everything he'd said, Sil didn't rush into any new ventures. He waited a week, until he was absolutely sure that Elim would have made it home – until he was confident that that part of the bargain was truly complete.

And when Sil found himself still alive, or at least still endlessly, sleeplessly present, he set about assembling a new mode of living.

That was what found him there in the farthest back reaches of La Saciadería's ornate corridors, occupying the single undecorated chair at the end of the hallway. He'd fitted himself with new clothes, thanks to Fours' generous inventory – a little old, a little out of fashion, but it was a start.

Sil had no money of his own left: he hadn't been able to find the exact pearls that Faro had absconded with, but helped himself to an equivalent weight from the fop's private holdings, and left the rest for Shea's disposal. He had already outraged Mother Opéra by helping to depose her golden-curled favorite – he didn't need to make it worse by stealing from her too.

But during the long, quiet hours of night, Sil liked to imagine the look on Elim's face when he found the surprise in that saddlebag – when he returned Boss Calvert eleven exquisite freshwater pearls in payment for eleven yearling horses, and told the story of how Sil Halfwick had brokered the deal. Someday, Sil would go back and see what manner of reputation had grown up around his name in Hell's Acre. He would love to know what they said of him now.

"Master Halfwick?"

Sil looked up as one of the young ladies of the house emerged from the opening door – her pink evening finery swapped out for a plain, sensible house-dress here during the daylight hours. Inside, he could just glimpse a richly-appointed office, and smell a hint of herbal smoke.

"Miss Addie will see you now. What business do you have with her?"

Sil stood, hat in hand, to express his gratitude as she held the door for him. "Ah, thank you. I understand that she's recently found herself in need of a clerk…"

Yes, it was a bit brash, putting himself forward to fill a position whose last occupant Sil had conspired to have dragged kicking and strangling out the front door of this very house... but if Sil's own turn in the noose was any indication, the madam seemed to appreciate a good show of initiative.

Regardless, Sil had made an extravagant wish, one whose fulfillment promised to cost him dearly. He meant not to waste that – to take ownership of what he had bargained for, no matter how long it took, or how winding and humble the path.

For now, it was time to start making good on the debt.

IT WAS JUST a plum.

That much was obvious. It was over a week old now, and its firm red-orange flesh was beginning to soften.

Día lay on her side in her small, spare sacristy bed and watched the aging fruit, waiting less for a miracle than for enough willpower to do literally anything else.

The sacristy was never meant to be used for anyone's living quarters, of course. It was intended as nothing more than a holy supply closet. But she'd long ago filled the shelves with her books and crafts and instruments and collections, and discovered that if she made a roll-up mattress out of some old blankets, the floor was exactly large enough for her to comfortably lie down.

It still was. Despite those horribly silly things she'd said to Elim, Día did still fit here. In this little repurposed room, everything was as snug and orderly as ever. It was just the rest of it, the world outside that old scorched doorframe, that seemed to have lost all sense of proportion.

Día really ought to go out and rejoin it. It was nearly

noon – no time of day for any able-bodied person to be lying in bed.

But as soon as she stepped outside, she would have to be someone. She would have to *represent* someone. People would see her as the Azahi's ambassador, the Dog Lady's acolyte, a grave bride for the 'Starving' God ... and her behavior would reflect on them. Worse than that – *their* behavior would reflect on *her*. Their cruelties, their negligence, their cosmic injustices... by heaven, how could she have been so naïve?

And yet...

The plum stared at her, interrogating her with its baleful brown age spot.

And yet there were still things to believe in. Somewhere out in the desert, a tree was fruiting in open defiance of the season and the drought. Somewhere in a wounded man's mind was a living goddess, a chance to bring back the rains. And right here on this very island, an old dream was coming back to life.

Weisei had called the Dog Lady's plan an act of rebellion. Miss du Chenne had treated it as a calculated maneuver. But Día saw an endless, hopeful idealism in it now – one perhaps easier to recognize because it had so recently departed her own tender heart. To believe that the world could be mended with lust and joy and babies – to fling open the doors of a whole culture and welcome all comers – to smash every pedigree, hazard every happiness on the altar of hope and futurity and free hybrid vigor... whatever had happened afterwards, it was a dream born from love and audacity.

And now it had been rekindled in Island Town, flawed and ugly and imperfect as it was. Now Día could help it live again... if she wanted to.

She huddled down deeper under the thin wool blanket, acutely aware of her naked body, her barren head. She'd have to dress them eventually, make herself presentable. But she had nothing to wear but her cassock, and wrapping herself back in the trappings of her old life, her old self, would be perpetrating a monstrous fraud.

She thought of Winshin, all but exposing Día as a shameful pretender to her profession. She thought of Elim, and her badly-worded wish to go east into Eaden, find other Afriti, other Penitent scholars – someone to share kinship with, in body or mind or both. She thought of Weisei, whose kin had brought him the deepest grief.

Día hoped he'd read her letter. She desperately wanted to see him again.

In the end, her only certainty was the plum sitting there on the shelf. It was ripening and so was she, and neither of them would be any good if they were left lying in this little room to rot.

So Día got up and ate it as she dressed, every sweet, overripe bite a balm for a nervous appetite. Her shift needed washing, and her cassock needed mending, and the golden sun-wheel pendant she'd always worn around her neck had somehow found its way into her pocket instead, and none of them suited her quite as well as they had before.

Still, they would serve the purpose at least long enough for her to go out walking in the fresh autumn sunlight, and buy herself a dress.

EPILOGUE

THE TRIP HOME was a conspicuously quiet one. Not that Elim minded having a few peaceful days in the saddle to get his mind right about things. Still, it was strange to have no herd, no partner, no friends or fellow-travelers or posse of any kind.

Well, nobody except Molly, of course.

But she was good about listening to him as he tried to account for everything he'd seen and done and found out about, and to decide what he ought to say about it... or whether he ought to say anything at all.

He still hadn't settled that by the time she started picking up her pace. Elim didn't need to guide her along the back roads of Hell's Acre's dusty flats, but his heart quickened in tandem with hers as they passed every landmark in turn: the tidy little Clinkscale farm, the old abandoned Sugden place, the vast Hatpenny holdings, their furthest fields already gleaned and left lying fallow for next year, and then – Elim's stomach knotting at the sight of it – the weathered white walls of their own unmistakable home.

In the end, it was only that dreadful letter in Elim's

pocket that kept him from pressing Molly to a gallop, and the same thought that had haunted him all the way back from Sixes: he was carrying both the Calverts' happiness and the Halfwicks' pain, and there was no delivering one without the other.

But he slowed to a full stop at the first sight of that distant, solitary figure in his periphery. There in the west pasture, visible as a black silhouette against the sinking red sun, a man with hat and shovel paused in his work, and Elim felt the guilty lance in his heart. That was his work. Boss was having to pick up his slack.

And just as Elim went to call out to him, the figure pointed to the house, his long shadow spilling endlessly out over the fields. Elim needed no other instruction.

So he rode up to the porch, his heart spasming like a sleep-barking dog as he ground-tied Molly outside, took the steps up two at a time, and pulled open the whitewashed door, simultaneously elated and terrified to discover what had happened in his absence – to discover which one of his ten thousand what-ifs would be made real as soon as he stepped inside.

She was lying slumped over the kitchen table in her usual seat. She had her head pillowed in the sleeve of her worn blue calico dress, her silver-threaded auburn hair pulled a little loose from its pins. Her hands were still dusted with flour, as if she'd been working the biscuit there by the sink and only stopped to rest – as if she'd gone on without him as long as she possibly could, and had just that very moment given up waiting.

Elim held his breath. She stirred at his first tentative footsteps and looked up blearily, squinting, blinking, her face opening like a weathered flower in the dust-gleaming light. "... Elim?"

"Lady Jane." Elim pulled off his hat and closed the door on the world outside. "Mom."

THE END

Glossary

A – Ardish, the primary language of Eadan settlers

F – Fraichais, a language spoken by freshwater mereaux

M – Marín, a trade language, the international standard for business

K – ei'Krah, the language of the a'Krah people

a'Pue (K) – literally 'people of no star'; children born during the last days of the a'Krah calendar year. Since they were not born under the auspices of any constellation, they are considered highly unlucky.

ashet (K) – a gesture of deep respect, performed by lowering the gaze and extending the arms, wrists upturned.

atleya (K) – the natural, well-functioning order of things. Sometimes translated as 'right living', 'correct placement', or 'harmonious equilibrium'.

atodak (K) – a holy protector or 'knight' whose life's purpose is to guard a child of Marhuk (see 'marka'). An atodak may not marry, parent children, or outlive his or her charge. Plural 'atodaxa'; feminine 'atodaka'.

cohort (F) – a group of mereau siblings hatched from the same roe (clutch of eggs). Each cohort represents one generation of a given house. Traditionally, one from each cohort is selected to undergo metamorphosis and become a prince, or mature male. See 'Many' and 'Few'.

earth-person – among mereaux, the polite term for human beings. 'Earthling' is a less-respectful alternative.

emi – a Maia word for 'big brother'.

gallery (A) – a long, horizontal corridor dug into a mine

grave bride (A) – in the Penitent faith, a celibate woman of the church. Her duties include tending and burying the newly deceased.

half – a common term for people of mixed race; see also 'mule'.

ihi'ghiva (K) – a special kind of slave who wears the ritual blindfold (see 'yuye') and has received years of exacting training as a scribe, go-between, and sometimes assassin. He is considered incorruptible, and may not be bought or sold.

marka (K) – title of a son, daughter, or son of a daughter of Marhuk (feminine 'markaya'). They are gifted with exceptional divine powers, and expected to devote their lives to the service of all a'Krah.

marrouak – a monstrous, infected creature, no longer human.

même (F) – short for 'moi-même', or 'myself'. A term of affection used by siblings of the same cohort.

mereau – plural 'mereaux'. The amphibious people colloquially called 'fishmen'.

mule (A) – a slang term for a person of mixed race; others include 'half', 'mestizo', and 'two-blood'.

oyami – a Maia word for 'little brother'.

Penitence – the majority religion of the Eaden Federacy. It has many denominations, but all are based on belief in one true God. Its adherents are called Penitents.

Pue'Va (K) – the five 'monthless' days of the a'Krah calendar. They are considered highly unlucky: no business is conducted, visiting is discouraged, and children born during this time are highly suspect (see a'Pue).

serape (M) – a blanket-like outerwear garment. Also called a poncho.

sexton (A) – in most Penitent churches, the gravedigger and keeper of the church yard.

stope (A) – a hollow dome-like excavation in a mine

stove in (A) – a slang term meaning 'wrecked' or 'broken'. Literally 'smashed inward'.

tarré (F) – an aromatic spice used in some mereau dishes. For human beings, it is a ruinously addictive drug.

Verses, the – holy poems of the Penitent faith, originally passed down through recitation.

voice (F) – one of the Many, who acts as a herald, envoy, and/or translator for one of the Few. Both male and female mereaux select a voice upon reaching maturity, usually from among their own cohort; those in positions of greater authority may have more than one voice.

winze (A) – a small hole connecting two levels of a mine

yuye (K) – a thin black mesh cloth, which lessens the light absorbed by the human eye without blinding the wearer. The yuye may be worn ritually (as by an ihi'ghiva), or by a'Krah who work during daylight hours.

People & Places

a'Krah – children of Marhuk and one of the four Great Nations. They are known for dark skin, exceptional night vision, and a sensitivity to sunlight.

Actor – Will Halfwick's horse, borrowed by Sil – 'Ax' for short. Elim shot him after he became infected.

Addie – the fearsome madam of La Saciadería, sometimes called its queen.

Afriti – a race of dark-skinned humans, originally imported for use as slaves. Their innate talent for fire-starting has been considered dangerous.

Ah Che – a Maia boy, left blind and epileptic by a brain infection in childhood.

Ah Set – Ah Che's younger brother, killed by the epidemic that devastated their village.

All-Year River – the cold, fast-flowing mountain river that forms the eastern border of the Eiya'Krah.

Amateur – 'the lover,' a mereau god of greed and untimely death.

Ara-Naure – a dispersed native tribe; children of U'ru, the Dog Lady.

Ardish – the primary language of the Eaden Federacy,

still spoken by a minority of Island Town residents.

Artisan – a mereau creator-goddess: the crafter of the world and all its creatures.

Aso'ta Marhuk – one of the a'Krah Eldest. He oversees the education of slaves.

Atali'Krah – the ancestral capital of the a'Krah, where the god Marhuk roosts. Sits near the peak of the Mother of Mountains.

Azahi – a native people whose kingdom in the south has risen to considerable power. Sut Hara, the First Man of Island Town, is popularly called 'the Azahi.'

Bombé – one of the Many in Prince Jeté's cohort, left crippled by one of Vuchak's arrows.

Born-Awake – short for 'She Who Was Born Awake': Vuchak's niece, Yeh'ne and Suitak's first child, who lived for less than a day.

Boss Calvert – a small-time horse rancher in Hell's Acre, and the axis of Elim's world.

Brant – the deceptively charming evening host of La Saciadería. Executed on a technicality.

Burnt Quarter – the northwest quarter of Island Town, so called because it burnt to the ground on the night the town was retaken. Deserted except for Día's church.

Champagne – Shea's original given name.

Corn Woman – see 'Ten-Maia'.

Día – an Afriti woman, a grave bride, and ambassador to the Azahi.

Dog Lady – U'ru, holy mother of the Ara-Naure.

Du Chenne, Miss – the name Shea used when she served as Sixes' schoolmistress

Dulei – a slain prince of the a'Krah, shot by Elim in a fatal misunderstanding. His *atodak* is Echep. Son of Winshin, nephew of Weisei. By the a'Krah kinship system, he is also considered a son of Marhuk.

Eadan – of or from Eaden.

Eaden – short for Eaden Federacy; the nation of settlers founded by descendants of the Northmen.

Eaten – a pejorative term for an Eadan.

Echep – Dulei's missing *atodak*, and Vuchak's friend. He was sent from Island Town to Atali'Krah on an errand, and disappeared.

ei'Krah – the native language of the a'Krah people. These days, most swearing is done in Marín.

Eiya'Krah, the – the ancestral lands of the a'Krah people, whose eastern border is the All-Year River.

Mostly mountainous, high desert terrain.

Eldest – the most reverend elders of the a'Krah.

Elim – full name Appaloosa Elim: a marbled mule who belongs to the Calvert family, and apparently the Dog Lady's son.

Emboucheaux – 'mouth-of-the-river people'; a nation of freshwater mereaux.

Eula Lightly – a local girl in Hell's Acre. Her dalliance with Elim nearly cost him his life.

Elver Lightly – a farmer in Hell's Acre; Eula's father and Boss Calvert's neighbor.

Etascado River – the river in which Island Town sits; currently the border between Eaden and native territory. Its water is drinkable, but tastes unpleasantly of salt.

Faro – the dandily-dressed clerk at La Saciadería, and Opéra's right-hand (fish)man.

Few, the – fertile 'royal' mereaux, referred to as princes and princesses. The Few are large, mostly water-bound, and have some abilities not shared by the Many.

First Man of Island Town – the title of Island Town's governor. Currently held by Sut Hara, often called 'the Azahi'.

Flamant-Rose – one of the Many in Prince Jeté's cohort;

a small, shy geologist. Killed by one of Vuchak's arrows.

Fours – an unhappy man, currently running a livery and secondhand-goods store in Island Town. One of the Azahi's two remaining ambassadors, and Día's foster-father.

Fraichais – first language of the Emboucheaux; the spoken alternative to freshwater sign language.

Fuseau – one of the Many in Prince Jeté's cohort, who serves as the prince's voice.

Giving Hands – a pair of giant carved stone hands in Atali'Krah, where the bodies of exceptional a'Krah are laid to rest.

Grandfather Crow – another name for Marhuk, god of the a'Krah.

Hakai – one of the two ihi'ghiva who serves Huitsak, temporarily on loan to Vuchak and Weisei. He serves as a translator, and seems to have a talent for earth magic.

Harak – Penten Marhuk's atodak, aged but loyal.

Hell's Acre – Elim's hometown, and Sil's long-term residence.

Henry Bon – a mixed-race bounty hunter from the eastern bayous; Shea's temporary paramour.

Huitsak – the master of the Island Town a'Krah,

sometimes called the 'king' of La Saciadería. In size, strength, and intellect, he is overwhelming.

Irabei – a young a'Krah girl; she lives in Atali'Krah with her family.

Island Town – the modern name for Sixes.

Ismat – Winshin Marhuk's *atodaka*: a fierce older woman.

Jeté – a newly-matured prince of the House of Losange, and leader of his cohort.

La Saciadería – the great hotel at the northern end of Island Town. Sells enjoyments of every kind.

'Lady' Jane Calvert – Boss Calvert's wife, an older woman of considerable education.

Last Word, the – Marhuk's oldest living daughter, who serves as his human voice.

Losange, House of – one of the houses of the Emboucheaux; represented by Prince Jeté and his cohort.

Lovoka – one of the four Great Nations; sometimes called the People of the Wolf. See also 'Winter Wolves'

Maia – children of Ten-Maia, the Corn Woman. They were renowned for their earthworks, and were dispersed soon after her death.

Many, the – collective term for ordinary or asexual mereaux. With some painful alterations, they can pass for human. See also 'Few'.

Marhuk – also called Grandfather Crow, holy father of the a'Krah.

Marhuka – the collective name for the children of Marhuk: his sons, his daughters, and the sons of his daughters.

Marín – a trade language, and the international standard for business.

Melisant – one of the Few, and Mother to the house that bears her name. Former mother to Fours and Shea, before they were gifted to the House of Opéra.

Merin-Ka – the fallen canyon city of the Ohoti people. Its last surviving residents turned to cannibalism at the end of a brutal siege, and became marrouak.

Mille-Feuille – one of Fours and Shea's siblings, who was likewise gifted to the House of Opéra and sent to live in Sixes as a human spy.

Molly Boone – Elim's horse, a bay mare of considerable size and questionable modesty.

Mother of Mountains, the – a sacred mountain situated near the eastern border of the Eiya'Krah. Atali'Krah, the ancestral capital of the a'Krah people, sits near its peak.

Nillie Halfwick – Sil's sister, and Will's twin. She has an exceptional talent for ice-making.

Northman – the common name for a 'pedigreed' white person from Eaden. Some retain a talent for freezing or chilling objects.

Opéra – one of the Few, and Mother of the house that bears her name. The Etascado River, and by extension Island Town, is part of her domain.

Ondine – a young princess of the House of Losange, and Jeté's younger sister. Killed by the Dog Lady.

Osho-Dacha – an Ara-Naure boy, young enough to still be called by his baby-name. Killed by the Winter Wolves.

Oyachen – the a'Krah proprietor of a popular eatery in the Moon Quarter of Island Town.

Penten Marhuk – the youngest of the Eldest; a daughter of Marhuk who was born male. She is considered a wise and compassionate negotiator.

Pipat – an older widow of the a'Krah and a night citizen of Island Town; formerly Vuchak's girlfriend.

Pirouet – one of the Many in Prince Jeté's cohort. Killed by one of Vuchak's arrows.

Porté – one of the Many in Prince Jeté's cohort; a stevedore grieving for their slain siblings. Their name means 'carried'.

Red Brothers, the – a pair of hills flanking the beginning of the Mother of Mountains' southern trail.

Shea – a mereau spy with more identities than manners. Fours' sister, U'ru's herald, and Día's nemesis. See also 'Champagne' and 'Miss du Chenne'.

Sibyl, the – in the Penitent faith, the originator of evil, and mother of demons.

Sil Halfwick – Elim's partner; a sickly young Northman who found himself on the wrong end of a hangman's noose. Has been looking a bit green around the edges.

Sixes – the former (Eadan) name for Island Town.

Spirit Towers – five raised wooden platforms in Atali'Krah, where the dead are laid to rest.

Starving God – a pejorative term for the god of the Penitent faith.

Suitak – Vuchak's brother-in-law, Yeh'ne's husband, and Born-Awake's father.

Sundowner – an Eadan term for a native person of any nation.

Tadai – a young man of the a'Krah, in Huitsak's employ at la Saciadería.

Ten-Maia – the Corn Woman, youngest of the Three Sisters, holy mother of the Kaia and Maia. She was killed under mysterious circumstances over twenty years ago.

To'taka Marhuk – one of the a'Krah Eldest. He is responsible for pairing the children of Marhuk with their life-guardians, and overseeing their education. See 'marka' and 'atodak'.

Twoblood – the curiously-titled Second Man of Island Town. Remarkable for her fangs, freckles, and unshakable dedication to her job. In Eadan parlance, she would be called a 'speckled' mule.

U'ru – the Dog Lady, freshly-resurrected holy mother of the Ara-Naure. Desperate to find Yashu-Diiwa at any cost.

Vuchak – Weisei's atodak and Echep's friend, as loyal as he is frustrated. See 'atodak' and 'a'Pue'.

Wally Hen – short for 'Wall-Eyed Henry'; a half-white, half-Maia boy who rescued Ah Che.

Washchaw – children of O-San, the Silver Bear. They are recognizable by their considerable height and build.

Weisei – a cheerful, kind-hearted son of Marhuk; Winshin's brother, and Dulei's uncle. His refusal to live as an adult has caused Vuchak no end of heartache.

Will Halfwick – Sil's brother, and Nillie's twin.

Winshin Marhuk – Dulei's mother and Weisei's sister:

a fearsome force of nature, whose service to the a'Krah has cost her dearly.

Winter Wolves – a heretical faction of the Lovoka who broke with holy law and attacked the Ara-Naure.

Yaga Chini – a vital oasis in the desert, recently despoiled with the bodies of seven mysterious murder victims.

Yashu-Diiwa – the baby-name of the Dog Lady's last surviving child, kidnapped in infancy and now believed to be Elim. It means 'He Loves Me'.

Yeh'ne – Vuchak's younger sister; Born-Awake's mother.

ACKNOWLEDGMENTS

That right there is the line where your name goes. You can write it in right now.

It's a bit crass, leaving you to fill it in yourself – but I want to thank you first, before anything. Because if you're reading this right now – if you've gone to the mountain with me and come back again – then you are the rarest kind of person. You are a reader I should never have had.

There were a million reasons why this wasn't supposed to work. I heard quite a lot of them firsthand. And it's still a little surreal to me to be writing this right now – to be putting the capstone on a story I started back in 1999, with a knight in shining armor named Elim and a jackass called Champagne. Finishing it has left me a little bit at loose ends. For the first time in my life, I don't know what to write next.

But I do know what you should read next.

Because here's the thing. Acknowledgments are generally written for the people who are going to read them – for people who might otherwise never see their names in print. And I do need to tell you about those people. You deserve to hear about Chris Weiler-Allen, a Blackfoot among Hopi, without whom the Dog Lady would have no meaningful redemption. You ought to know Dr. Sheri Wells-Jensen, who was born into a body that could not see light, without whom Ah Che's story would have no savor. And you absolutely must meet my friend Kerri Linn, the Korean-born adopted daughter of white Midwestern parents, and ever-generous queen of creature comforts – my friend Jonathan Rafferty, whose inconvenient bigness is surpassed only by his unrelenting goodness – my friend Merlin Wilson, the soul of gentle, stoic, git-r-done perseverence – without all of whom neither Elim nor I would be even half worthy of your esteem.

But I've neglected to thank the people who won't see this, who don't know me – the ones from whom I took without asking. Here is the truth: any affection you have for Vuchak and Weisei comes straight from Sherman Alexie – from *Smoke Signals'* Victor Joseph and Thomas Builds-the-Fire. Just so, if you enjoyed Elim and Sil, you owe it to yourself to meet Faulkner's Cash and Jewel Bundren. To hear Fours, go listen to Tish Hinojosa's "Carlos Dominguez". And there are so many more of these people – these inspired voices, these thoroughly American artists whose work is a truer, more essential story of this nation than anything you will read in a textbook. Most of them are not household names. Most of them have not received even a tenth of the acclaim they deserve.

And that's what I would like your help in correcting. That is what you should read next. If you want another story built over racial divides, read Piri Thomas' *Down These Mean Streets*. For an exercise in injustice and forgiveness, read John Edgar Wideman's *Brothers and Keepers*. For fantasy of the Americas, read Nalo Hopkinson, Liliana Bodoc, Silvia Moreno-Garcia, Aliette de Bodard, Daniel José Older, Junot Díaz, Rudy Ch. García, Daniel Heath Justice, Owl Goingback – or better yet, make it your mission to find another new voice and shine a spotlight on their work. At the end of the day, I have been a tourist in their lives – and if you've enjoyed my little mosaic of pictures and souvenirs, you owe it to yourself to see the real thing. There are more stories to tell in the World That Is, but don't wait on me. Treat yourself to a broader telling of the story that is our world.